W9-DDR-028

The December Rose

By Robert J. Grant

Island's End Publishing

Published by Island's End Publishing
P. O. Box 452
Carmel, Indiana 46032-0452

ISBN 0-9645498-0-8

Printed in the United States of America, on recycled paper.
February 1995
First Edition

To Scott and Jeffrey,
May they live their dreams.

ACKNOWLEDGMENT

One of the surprises in writing this book was how many people came to play a role in what, for the most part, is a work of fiction. I am especially grateful for the perspectives on baseball provided by Jim Brosnam, the late Gordy Coleman, Bill Hands, Joe Nuxhall and Woody Woodward. Moreover, I am equally thankful to those ballplayers from the 1950s and '60s, whose names are too numerous to mention, yet whose inspiration to the writing of this novel is too significant to forget.

Then there are the medical professionals who supplemented my study of the complexities of modern science. The patience they displayed in explaining things to me rivals that demonstrated by the story's character, Dr. Dornhoffer; any mistakes in interpretation are purely mine. They include the following individuals: Kathy Anderson, Ph.D.; David Gorenstein, Ph.D.; Carlos Lopez, Ph.D.; Dr. Kenneth Ryder; Ron Mahler, DVM; and my wonderful family physician, Dr. James Vandivier.

I also am indebted to several Food and Drug Administration professionals who provided perspectives on regulatory matters. In particular, there was Dr. Robert Temple, the FDA's director of drug evaluation, who showed me that there are indeed enlightened individuals within the federal agencies.

From the newspaper world, thanks to Dan Carpenter and Dave Garlick, who were as helpful as character Stan Moore is biased. Then there was Bob Coverdale who helped me gain a greater appreciation for the joys of farming.

And thanks to my adviser, Leon Gottfried, Ph.D. and editor, Lisa Coffey. Last and not least, a special thanks to Sara and Lou Monari for their wisdom and support throughout the long process to produce this labor of love.

God gave us memories so that we might have roses in December.

—James M. Barrie

1
Down on the Farm

A January wind cut a stinging path across the Southern Ohio landscape. The farmer maneuvered his '74 tractor into place and lowered its forklift, dropping the final round-bale to the frozen earth. He was thankful this was the last feeding stop before his own lunch. Hopping off the cracked leather seat, he raised the feeding rims and swung them around the compressed bundles of alfalfa and orchard grass.

From there, he moved to the feeding trough, head tucked in against a gale, and emptied a bag of supplements. Forty-some Angus heifers, clods of dirt climbing their legs, stirred to the sound of pellets dancing on steel. Little did the animals appreciate that in their midst stood one of baseball's all-time greats. Yet, Luke Elliot Hanlon conducted himself with such aplomb that had he been one of them, the herd surely would have followed his lead.

Using his jersey gloves, he slapped away several strands of hay from his faded parka. The only similarity between this Midwest farmer and a nine-time All-Star was the baseball-style cap atop his receding hairline. Even there the resemblance was coincidental; an embroidered emblem read "John Deere."

Luke had been away from the game for a quarter century. "Away" was a fitting word, for he rarely went to see games, let alone attend an old timers' contest. He had found other interests. Yet, on this winter day, baseball again tugged at his mind.

Luke ratcheted the stick shift into gear for the half-mile ride home. The tractor's age reflected his modest finances. It chugged across the bumpy terrain, past a windshield of pin oaks and past two prized black Angus bulls, sequestered by a three-slatted, pitted white fence. It didn't much matter to him that the grasslands were three shades of yellow from their summertime splendor, nor that the adjacent cornfields were a flattened mixture of blackened earth and chopped stalks. Instead, he relished the serenity provided by the open spaces of his 350-acre cattle ranch.

Luke had demonstrated a desire to separate careers years before when he named the ranch, choosing simply "The Homestead". He rejected his eldest son David's suggestions of "Field of Play" and "Off The Basepaths."

Bouncing along, Luke drew a deep breath. The air frosted his nasal passages. He didn't mind. It reinforced his connection with nature. Connection was what he loved about baseball. Yes, you could talk about baseball as an art. The fluidity. The poetry. But for him, it was about connection. Connection with dirt and grass, with the rain and New Jersey mud used to rub up the ball, with the sun and wind. At least it was supposed to be, which was why he detested astroturf and domed stadiums.

Then too, there was the connection with his fellow man through the spirit of competition. Pitcher against batter, fielder against hitter, runner against catcher, manager against manager.

Luke's connection to the game started back in '35 when his father christened him with the name of the .300-hitting, All-Star Chicago White Sox shortstop Luke Appling. Oh, it wasn't an exact match, but then, what self-respecting Irishman would have adopted the name Lucius?

That year also marked the retirement of Babe Ruth; the launch of Cincinnati radio broadcasts with a youngster named Red Barber at the mike; the nadir of attendance for the St. Louis Browns—just 80,922 for the entire *season*; and the start of night baseball. Yes, it was a year of transition, much like the time when Luke hung up his spikes thirty-seven years later.

Luke's eyes wandered to the valley on his left. Three hillsides rolled together, forming a seam where an angled creek lay frozen. A gnarled locust, several limbs dead, its trunk twisting skyward, stood out among the scribbling of branches from the maples, ashes and oaks. All so imperfect, and yet, he reflected, it was all so perfect. Perfectly natural. Baseball represented a similar paradox: No two hits were ever the same and no two pitchers ever threw with the same motion, but for Luke, it was as close to perfection as one got.

Thoughts of the game crept into his mind, like his grandchild playing peek-a-boo behind an armchair—thoughts triggered by yesterday's phone call from former teammate Mike Corrigan. Luke replayed the scene in his mind. "Luke Hanlon! Why, I thought you'd retreated into some cornfield with Shoeless Joe Jackson."

"What d'you say, Mike?" Luke greeted. "Are the Reds that desperate for a manager, or is Vandermark trying to be charitable?"

"Eat my ass," Corrigan countered with a smile in his voice. "If you think you can do a better job, you can have it."

"Thanks, but no. Baseball's behind me." Long ago Luke had decided to make room for the new generation of athletes.

"Don't sell yourself short. I was going over the roster and got to thinking that I could sure use a player with your power." Some called it the gift of gab, others pure salesmanship. Luke realized Mike had it. "I was kind of hoping I could interest you and Kate in a six-week paid vacation."

"Doesn't sound like you have a vacation in mind to me."

"Okay, so I'd like you to be my hitting instructor—just for spring training. You wouldn't even have to ride the buses to the away games."

"I'd like to help, Mike, but there's a lot to do here, what with spring coming."

"C'mon. You've got Derrick."

"Only part time." Luke paused and thought about his ranchhand. "Anyway, Bret will be pitching for the university. I want to see some of his games."

"You'd be back by the beginning of April."

True, Bret still would be playing well into May. And he realized Mike needed all the help he could get. Luke knew the Reds to be a ragtag team at best. "It's been a long time, Mike. I'm sure you can find someone who's more up to date on hitting than me."

"Does a coonhound ever forget to hunt? Besides, I'd have to pay the younger guys more than I can get you for." There was a needle in Mike's voice, and he knew how to use it.

Luke once found it easy to turn down such requests. Family activities provided a menu of excuses: David's baseball games; Megan's dance and 4-H activities; and Bret's multitude of athletic pursuits. But this was different. The kids were on their own now.

Then there was Mike. Mike was a good friend and godfather to Bret. Luke knew how hard he had fought to get where he was—twenty years of bumming around the minors, first a coach, then manager. Finally, he had a chance to give the majors a try.

"Don't worry," Mike added. "I'll take care of you."

"I'm afraid of that. Besides, I'm not so sure what my better half would think."

"Kate? You'll have no problem with her. Matter of fact, if you can't make it, send her down. She can keep Laura company while I get the team ready for the season."

Thoughts of yesterday's phone call faded as Luke caught sight of his barn. "Hey there, Rusty," Luke shouted above the tractor's cough. The Brittany spaniel sprinted along the dirt road, his mouth open in greeting. The eight-year-old dog was aptly named. A multitude of reddish spots splattered his white coat. Those closest to Luke claimed the dog was likely named after scout Rusty Robbins. Rusty had signed Luke to play for Cincinnati fresh out of high school in the early '50s.

Inside the weather-soaked barn, the dog stuck its snout through the slats where Diamond Boy, Luke's steed, stood in silence. Luke parked the vehicle, while Rusty sniffed at the horse. "Sorry Rusty. No riding today," Luke explained, while handing a fistful of hay to his horse.

The paunchy-figured man who pulled the barn door closed bore only a faded resemblance to the naive youngster Mr. Robbins had signed. Age had etched crevices in the once downy-cheeked smile of the Reds center fielder. His blue eyes were now framed by wire-rimmed glasses. Still, facial bones as solid as his determination maintained the underpinnings of his rugged good looks.

"Let's go." Luke broke into a plodding trot, shapeless clouds of vapor leading the way. Rusty raced ahead, along the trail that curved around an iced-over pond. As the two neared the house, several sparrows sprang from a row of ilex bushes, sending Rusty in pursuit.

Luke climbed the porch of the white, two-story house. Like its owner, the home was built for functionality. It sat on an elevated plot of Southern Ohio land. The roof peaked at sharp angles to keep snow from accumulating. Two blue spruces climbed the western side of the structure, while a well-crowned silver oak provided the clapboards with protection from winter's wind and cooling in the summer.

He pulled his Red Wings off inside the back door and found Kate on the kitchen phone. "Sounds like you won't be seeing much of Mike while you're down there....Well, I'd like to keep you company, too." Kate cradled the receiver in her neck, while stirring a pot on the electric stove—one of the few modern appliances in their faxless, computerless home.

"Listen, Luke just came in....Uh huh." She winked a hello. "I'm sure he'll call Mike before the week's out....You too. Bye."

"Sounds like you and Laura have already decided about Florida."

"Are you kidding? I learned long ago not to make decisions for Luke Hanlon." Luke looked askance at Kate before she added, "I can engage in wishful thinking, can't I? Want a taste?" She held up a steaming ladle of homemade vegetable soup which Luke promptly slurped down.

"I'll buy the whole pot."

While Kate dished out a bowl, Luke's eyes were drawn to the corral where he once played ball with the boys. Kate had enticed his appetite, but Mike's call had captured his mind.

After lunch, Luke retreated to the attic. There, he searched out a lap-sized box. Parting the flaps, he unwound the twist-tie bag protecting his glove. He removed a scuffed ball from the webbing and slipped the oil-darkened leather onto his hand with all the reverence of a bishop donning his miter.

You made a lot of catches for me my friend, he thought. Seven years worth of lining, fading, bad hop and diving baseballs. Only the stitching had been replaced. He could've had his pick of gloves near the end of his career—for free. But why change? For change's sake?

Luke punched the well-formed pocket; the suppleness surprised him. Again he looked inside the box. A pair of spikes, toes curled, begging for shoetrees. The glove, the spikes—tools of a trade he had loved ever since his dad first rolled him a ball across the floor at age two, more than sixty years before.

Somewhere buried in the terraces of boxes, lay pictures of a rugged-looking Irishman, hardened as the steel he crafted. Good old Harry Hanlon. There had not been enough years in his dad's life for Luke to thank him for instilling his love of the game.

Buried in Luke's mind were snapshots of his father pitching ball on a summer's eve, hiding his aches from a day spent in a Youngstown steel mill. In an attic of silent memories, Luke could hear dad's firm voice, "Come on, Luke. Keep your eye on it this time. Concentrate." Harry Hanlon barked as often as he smoked—he maintained a two-pack-a-day habit until his end when Luke was just twenty-four.

A strict disciplinarian, Dad never let Luke think of himself as better than anyone else. It wasn't until his teens that Luke realized he could speak up. And then he did so with his bat.

Sure, Dad was short-tempered, Luke reflected, but he had reason to be. After all, he spent his days sweating inside the mill. For most of his years, Dad labored as a "teemer." It had nothing to do with play-ing on a ball team— although that was what his father would have loved to do. Rather, he tended ladles of molten steel in an open-hearth furnace, opening and closing the hole that allowed the 1,000-degree liquid to flow, or teem, into ingot molds. Luke realized that he, too, would have ended up working within sight of the "fire of God" except for a certain knack at hitting a baseball half the mill's length.

Luke reaped the benefits of being born into a lineage of laborers. Fortunately, he also inherited the softer features and temperament of his mother, Maureen. Another snapshot drifted into Luke's mind, this one of a lady with a creamy white complexion framed by coffee-black hair. He still could hear Mom's voice, as understanding as Dad's was demanding, "Don't be discouraged, Luke. You keep working at it, and the arithmetic will come."

"Luke," a woman's voice called. This one belonged to the living. "Luke." It grew louder.

He stood, straddling a package near the roughened railing that boxed off the opening. "Up here, Kate. I'm in the attic."

"I'm going down to Northgate. Need anything?"

"Nah." Luke held all he needed on his left hand. That and a pair of plane tickets would do.

2

The Competitor

"I'd like to get this thing settled, Walt, but it's out of my hands right now. They're the ones not treating *me* fair."

"Are you prepared to sit out the spring?" the sports reporter probed.

"If I have to. But hey, I'm being optimistic. Hopefully, they'll realize we're serious and come around."

"And if they don't?"

"I'll have no choice but to stay home." Cincinnati ballplayer Ty Hartmann, found himself cornered beneath a romanesque archway. There was no hiding place on this January night. It was the annual Competitors in Sports dinner at New York's *Waldorf-Astoria*, and the invitees packed the cocktail party.

Only weeks before, the same century-old hotel had hosted New Year's Eve revelers who flocked there to turn out the old and herald in the new, and supposedly better, opportunities. Yet, most had welcomed in the New Year with tears to the tune of "Auld Lang Syne".

"You're saying you'll lay your $6.5 million on the line if the Reds don't renegotiate?"

"If they aren't willing to pay me what I'm worth, then yeah. I'm sure there're teams out there happy to pay me a whole lot more." The Reds twenty-six-year-old center fielder tilted his head back and planted a foot against the wall. He took a drink from his double shot of Absolut.

"How 'bout arbitration?"

"I don't need some fast-talking lawyer telling me what's rightfully mine." At 6'3", the tanned athlete was as handsome as recognizable—a strong chin, protruding like a loosened brick, and hair that rose and fell in uneven, murky waves, forming a shoreline on his collar. Ty's shoulders stretched a yard wide under his white dinner coat. A matching red cummerbund and bow tie completed the *savoir-faire* look. Only the diamond loop in his left ear looked out of place.

"Hey Ty, how's it going?" a fellow ballplayer interrupted, one of countless athletes parading the two-story room.

Ty used the interruption to survey what he regarded as the finer things standing amidst the forest of tuxedos: a collection of spouses and short-term lovers, braless and draped with the latest in *haute couture*.

Ty liked the excitement of the Big Apple. He liked the change of seasons. But he had distanced himself from both. His summers were spent playing ball in Ohio, while the off season took him to Phoenix. And even tonight, while physically close to his New Jersey roots, he felt far removed from that life. Thank goodness. And good riddance to the fifty-year-old, fourth-floor tenement too small for a youngster to find space to think, where residents joked that they didn't have many insects because "even the cockroaches and spiders don't like it here."

"You realize, of course, Vandermark has a policy against renegotiating."

"There's an exception to everything, right?" Ty paused while the reporter took notes in his spiral pad. "I mean, the facts speak for themselves. The Reds said I'd be their top-paid player. It says so right in my contract. Now they've gone and given Worley half a mill more."

Ty wanted to be the highest-paid Reds player. He figured the team owed him as much. After all, he had acted in good faith following the players strike and settled for less than what his agent estimated to be his national market value. Instead, he had accepted the Reds' argument about Cincinnati's relatively small television market.

Ty was prepared to fight for what belonged to him. But then fighting was nothing new to him. He had spent his entire life fighting the odds: born in a slum neighborhood; the youngest of three children raised by his Italian mother who worked all day as a seamstress in an off-the-books sweatshop; ignored by an alcoholic father who separated from Mom after spending more time at Curly's pub than at home.

Ty continued, "Just look at what entertainers make." That was how he saw himself, as a uniquely qualified entertainer.

"You have a figure in mind?"

"I don't believe in negotiating in the press."

Walt suppressed a smile. "Okay, we'll put that aside for now. What d'you think of Corrigan?"

"From all I hear, he sounds like a pretty fair guy. But then I never had a problem with Axelrod," he replied, alluding to his former, fired manager. "I guess those who didn't get the playing time were unhappy, and he tended to play the veterans." *But if there's an age gap,* Ty thought, *why bring in a guy approaching sixty? And one who's never managed in the majors to boot. Who cares; I probably won't be with the team anyway.*

Ty shoved his glass at a passing waiter. "Absolut straight up."

The columnist waived off a drink. "He did lead Indianapolis to the Triple A championship last year."

"Come on, Walt, we're not talking about the minors now."

"Money aside, how do you feel about the trade for Kyle Worley?"

"I'm glad I won't have to face him anymore." Ty chuckled, thinking of the Phillie reliever, Worley, now property of the Reds.

"Would you consider him the stopper you've been missing?"

"He is with a club that hits. You know our pitchers aren't as bad as we made 'em look last year. We just didn't score enough runs. I'd rather they go sign someone who can get on base. Someone I can knock in." Ty pushed off the archway and straightened up. "Listen I gotta find my date."

"Okay. Thanks. See you in spring training." The reporter flipped his pad closed.

"If you don't, you'll know why," Ty said. He weaved his way through the crowd to the scarlet-carpeted foyer. There, two autograph hounds seized upon the three-time All-Star. They lifted their programs and pens up close enough till he barely could see their faces. "Sign this, please," they harmonized.

Ty scratched out his prized signature and bolted through the silver-trimmed doors before another "hound" could complete his race up the staircase. Hartmann's .293 average, 107 RBI's and 37 home runs made him a popular figure in New York, even if he didn't play for the struggling Mets or George's almighty Yankees.

Halfway down the marbled corridor, Ty spotted his ladyfriend conversing with a group of women. The dimple-cheeked redhead with the royal blue gown and elbow-length gloves feigned indignation between chomps on chewing gum. "I was beginning to wonder if you gave up on me!" The voice betrayed her Queensborough roots.

"Sorry, Andrea, I got talkin' to someone important and couldn't get away."

"I'll forgive ya."

Ty escorted her into the Grand Ballroom. There he scanned the rapidly filling chamber for his table number. The magnificence of the room impressed even him. There were nearly a hundred matching tables, each with a centerpiece of seasonal evergreens set off with miniature white lights and scarlet bows. Stuck in the middle of each was one of several tiny plastic sports balls. Overhead, garland-draped balcony bays housed additional settings. Ty linked the images with those from his past. Of evergreens picked up late on Christmas Eve from among leftover trees. And of Dad helping to decorate one tree by slipping his empty beer bottles on the ends of its branches.

"Can I help you, sir?" A waiter with a Spanish accent interrupted

Ty's thoughts. The black-tie attendant was one of the dozens who subjugated their hot tempers for an evening's wages.

"Yeah, looking for No. 24," Ty said, handing over his invitation. "Follow me."

Once all had been seated, the waiters introduced a well-orchestrated dinner. Clinking silverware and porcelain dishes that landed as quietly as marbles on glass provided the background music. No sooner had cheesecake been set out to silence the tongues than the lights dimmed. Master of Ceremonies, Hugh McCluskey, stepped to the microphone. Hugh tugged at his bow tie and brushed his closely cropped white hair. "Honored athletes, owners and managers, writers and photographers, spouses and significant others, good evening. Tonight we gather to recognize those athletes who best exemplify the essence of sporting competition.

"When an individual places his or her foot on a field of play—whether it be a six-year-old in peewee football or a sixty-year-old on the senior golf tour—the spirit of competition takes hold. In most cases, they provide an exhibition far more entertaining than a movie director, with all of the special effects at his disposal, could ever hope to achieve.

"I can think of nothing more symbolic of that spirit than this statue of the young hero who challenged the mighty Goliath." A spotlight illuminated a life-size, gold-plated rendering of the biblical hero on stage right. "Just as shroud-clad men and women in ancient times stood and chanted their support for young David while he slew the much feared foe, the fans have selected tonight's award recipients."

One of Ty's tablemates, Pittsburgh Pirates' GM, Nick DiCenso, leaned toward a racing car owner seated next to him, "I wonder what they'd have to pay David to slay the guy today?"

The wheelman smiled. "If he based it on what the guys are asking now, old Goliath might be viewed as the good guy."

Ty caught DiCenso looking his way and forced a close-mouthed smile. He chugged his Absolut.

McCluskey began by reading the names of stars from the American Professional Soccer League. It was well past 10:00 p.m. by the time he ran down the final "David" award nominees, those from the world of baseball. It seemed appropriate that the sport wait for its award. Once dominant among a handful of national sports, it now competed with the plethora of athletic pursuits represented on the evening's program.

For the twenty-eighth time that evening, Hugh read a list of nominees: "Ben Seabright of the Pittsburgh Pirates...." Ty Hartmann leaned forward and rested his chin on his folded hands.

"Steve Sipperel of the Baltimore Orioles, Ty Hartmann of the Cincinnati Reds...." Andrea hugged Ty's arm. She might have been a fly alighting on his tux for all the notice he gave. "And Drew Householder of the Los Angeles Dodgers."

"And the winner is...the gutsy pitcher who won 21 games, Steve Sipperel of the Baltimore Orioles!"

Soon after the announcement, Ty rose. "I have an early flight back to Phoenix, so if you'll excuse me."

Inside the elevator, Andrea consoled her date, "You're still the best competitor I know."

"It doesn't matter. It's only a trophy. Besides, Sipperel had a great year for a shitty team." Ty's voice betrayed his true feelings.

Andrea ran her finger beneath the elevator's control panel. A continuous blue message read: "22 DEGREES F...PLEASE ENJOY YOUR STAY AT THE WALDORF-ASTORIA...BREAKFAST WILL BE SERVED AT 6:00 A.M. IN PEACOCK ALLEY..."

"Twenty-two degrees outside. I wonder if we can help raise the temperature?" Andrea enticed, stripping off her gloves.

Ty gazed into her eyes, which sparkled beneath frosted shadowing. She pressed her hips against his and slipped her hands around his neck. Their mouths met, and Ty rubbed her breast through the satiny dress. A bell signalled it was time to depart. Ty held the kiss while the door opened to an empty hallway. "Maybe we should have left sooner," Ty said thinking of more reasons than sex.

The couple's amorous intentions were stalled while Ty darted about in search of his room number. "No, it's not that way; that's just for the odd-number rooms," he called to Andrea.

Once inside, Ty collapsed on the brass-framed bed. Andrea threw herself alongside him and cradled her baby face in her palm. "How about showing me what a competitor you really are?"

Ty rolled halfway atop his ladyfriend and grabbed her outstretched wrists, pinning her to the bed, "And who you gonna compare me to?"

"That big guy. Uh, what's his name...oh yeah, Goliath," she smiled.

He drew close and kissed her for what seemed like several innings. Coming up for air, Ty whispered, "They said I'm not David, but I think I can make you forget about Goliath."

That night, Ty dreamed not about awards that might have been, but about the financial rewards that were to be.

3

Rites of Spring

Luke Hanlon sauntered into the Reds clubhouse clad in jeans and cowboy boots. No one seemed to recognize the baseball recluse. Then, midway into the room, someone called out his name. He spun to see the balding, wrinkled-face equipment manager, Gus Stoltz, approaching. Luke wrapped his free arm around Gus' shoulders. They hugged for several seconds. Backing up, Luke noticed his friend reach under his glasses and wipe his eye. Had he looked inside the teardrop, he might have seen a youthful rendering of himself from some forty years before, when his athletic feats captured the hearts of those around the Reds locker room, including Gus. Gus represented one of the few constants for Luke, having served as a bat boy when he first arrived in camp in '55.

"You better watch what you eat while you're down here. I don't do alterations," Gus smiled.

"I don't eat as much, Gus, but damn, it seems to get tougher and tougher keeping the weight off. Say, you're looking in good shape," Luke said, tossing his duffel bag into the open plastic locker.

"The guys keep me running around pretty good."

Luke conjured up images of players from a bygone era, arriving at camp stuffed into last year's pants, with T-shirts seemingly shrunken over the winter. A sharp contrast with the lean and mean bodies that stood before him—decorated not with fat, but with an assortment of gold amulets and charms dangling from their necks. He touched his softened mid-section and felt a bit embarrassed, even if he was just a coach. Then again, these ballplayers earned enough that they could afford to devote the off-season to keeping in shape.

Years before, Luke recalled working full time during the winter. It wasn't until the championship season of '61 that he settled down to simple winter chores around the farm he made a down payment on with his winner's share.

Gus held aloft a uniform, a throwback to the outfits Luke had worn throughout most of his career. It was sleeveless and trimmed in red with a large bent "C" on the chest, matching one on the pin-striped hat on the locker shelf. "Recognize it?" Gus asked, twirling it around. "Look, we've even got you your old number."

Luke smiled at the sight of "27" on the buttoned and belted garment. "You're still taking good care of me." For him, there was nothing quite like the feel of a baseball uniform, a costume that transformed men into boys, dreams into reality, clouds into sun. "Thank goodness they got rid of those body stockings," Luke continued, referring to the polyester garb introduced in his final season. "Not sure I could fit into one right now."

"Actually, this here's made of something called "Biokryl." Gus enunciated his words as if revealing some secret.

"Sounds like some sort of wonder drug."

"It does contain an *anti-bacterial* chemical—prevents fungus and such. But its mostly cotton."

"So long as it doesn't prevent breathing," Luke smiled. His off-balanced grin brought out a curl in his right cheek, as if a twist of lemon once had been lodged there.

Luke's eyes fell upon the adjacent locker, crammed with uniforms and windbreakers. He recalled the days when each player had to share their spring training locker at Al Lopez field. And they were half the size of these to boot.

A hat pricked with a pailful of fishing lures sat on the top shelf of his neighbor's stall. Down below there were baseballs and shoes, and more shoes. He looked at his own locker. It, too, contained several multi-colored boxes of footwear. "Hey Gus, d'you order me all these?"

"No. I just gave your size to the sales reps. They send them over."

"For free?" Luke asked while he counted five, six, seven in all. There were as many high-tech features as shoes—pumps, airfoils, thrusters and bearing-balanced.

"D'you think they'd ask players to pay for them?" Gus asked. "You're a coach, or you'd have more. Most of the guys get at least a dozen."

Luke thought how he used to buy his own footwear and bats— although at $6.00 a pop for shoes and $2.50 lumber it wasn't so bad.

"How's Kate and the children?" Gus asked, wide-eyed.

"They're all fine. Only the kids are no longer that. All grown up now. You'll probably see her at the park."

"Good. I'll bring her some of my turtle soup."

"She'll love it, I'm sure," Luke said, straightening his glasses.

"If you need anything, Luke, anything at all, you give me a call." Gus instructed before exiting.

Luke sat on a three-legged stool and yanked off his boots. He felt out of place. *Perhaps it's the unfamiliarity of it all,* he thought. It had been more than a decade since he had last donned a uniform for an Old Timers' game. Then there were the players. Stolen glances told him they were pretty much an unknown group. And while this homogenized stadium offered much more in the way of conveniences, that in itself was unsettling. He was struck by a player wandering by carrying a pair of free weights and wearing a frayed tank top cut off above the navel. In the background someone switched over to rap music. He knew he had a ways to go to readjust to the katzenjammer of the contemporary locker room.

Slipping on the sleeveless uniform shirt, Luke was reminded of Ted Kluszewski. *Big Klu. There was a guy who could make you feel at home.* Then a nine-year veteran, Kluszewski had taken Luke under his wing during his rookie spring at a time when youngsters were apt to be intimidated by clubhouse veterans.

Then everybody loved Big Klu—so much so that the team had changed its uniform because of him, Luke recalled. Kluszewski had rather large shoulders, so one day he cut off the sleeves for more freedom. League officials jumped in and said it wasn't allowed; no player could have a different uniform. Rather than making Klu go back to a sleeved shirt, the rest of the team cut theirs to match! *I wonder how many teams could get all the players to agree to a change like that today?*

Just then, a crew-cut player spoke. "Hello, Luke. I'm Rich Kurkowski. Part-time fisherman, full-time catcher."

"Morning, Rich." Luke nodded a greeting to the player whose locker was situated cater-corner to his. Rich was a backstop physically and functionally. He wore shorts and white hose that stretched halfway up his beefy, bowed legs. His brown hair matched the shading on the mole that adorned his left cheek.

"It's a pleasure to meet you. I used to watch you on the Saturday game of the week...back when I was in peewees."

Luke curled his toes in the carpeting. A player carrying a stack of blue, black and red gloves echoed his thoughts. "Nice, Ducky. You really know how to pay a guy compliments."

"I didn't mean...." Ducky whined.

"Forget it, son," Luke chuckled. "I'm glad to hear someone re-members us 'Old Timers.'"

Ducky thumbed across the room to where the other player now stood. "The wise guy's Clint Twiddy. He's the team cutup."

"Welcome, Luke," Clint saluted before reaching inside his pants to adjust his supporter. "By the way, we all call him Ducky."

Luke noted Ducky's crescent-shaped eyebrows, which came to-gether just above his beaked nose, giving him a bird-like appearance. He figured that was where the nickname came from, although "pigeon" seemed more appropriate.

"Call me Ducky if you like, everyone else does—just so long as you don't ask me about the name."

"He won't have to. He'll just watch you run." Clint shared a hearty laugh with several players.

The catcher threw a pack of Ring-Dings toward Clint.

The banter continued with others joining in. It gave Luke an opportunity to complete his change of clothes. Dropping his pants to the floor, he felt a cool draft on his legs. *Air conditioning. Carpeting instead of cement. These guys have it pretty good.*

Luke descended the runway leading to the field and heard the forgotten sound of spikes click-clacking against concrete. It helped renew his connection with the game he once dominated. Emerging from the dugout shadow, he flipped his shades and searched for his manager. A bright morning sun radiated off the players. Clusters of threes and fours highstepped it near the clay warmup track. A handful of men, bespectacled with reflective sunglasses, conversed near the pitchers mound. Others lay on the grass, stretching their legs in the air, a corps of automated Swiss army knives. Two players, their caps turned backwards, signed autographs alongside the chainlink fence.

Luke caught up with his friend near first. The two had been teammates for three years, until Mike's untimely stint in Vietnam. By the time he had returned, his career opportunity had passed him by.

Luke threw his head in the direction of the gathering crowd and gave a hearty greeting, "All these folks come here 'cause of you?"

"More like you, Luke." Corrigan spoke with an air of confidence. His hair was thinning and white, his bushy eyebrows grey. The skipper's smile revealed caps and bridgework, a sign that his spirit once was more combative than conciliatory. Luke knew that his 5'7" frame belied his physical strength.

Out of nowhere, Mike tossed him a ball. Luke snared it. "You're not as rusty as I thought," Mike teased. "Actually, this is nothing. Just wait till the games start. We'll draw seven or eight thousand."

That would've made a good afternoon crowd at old Crosley, Luke reflected, thinking about the park where he'd spent all but two seasons. Even in '72, his final year, spring training could be looked upon as a safe haven from fans and the press; 1,500 was regarded as a great draw. This morning he estimated there was already that number lining the fences for the February workout.

The erstwhile teammates continued on, discussing everything from Mike's godchild to the rookies' salaries, which at a minimum $265,000 was more than double Luke's final season income. They ended on Luke's role with the team. Luke liked what Mike had to say, "Don't feel you have to force yourself on the players. Just stand back and observe. First, one or two will seek you out. Then others will see what you're doing and I'm quite sure you'll have more than you can handle."

◆　　◆　　◆　　◆

Upstairs in an office with a field-eye wall of windows, Reds President Peter Vandermark engaged agent Jack Austin in contract discussions for missing player, Ty Hartmann.

"Jack, if we jumped every time a ballplayer asked to renegotiate, we'd be out of business. As it is, we lost over $3 million last year."

"Yeah, and if it wasn't for Ty, you'd have lost six." Jack leaned to the side and snuffed his cigarette in an ashtray. "If it were my club, I'd raise ticket prices before losing a star."

"We're not going to raise prices in order to satisfy one player's demands," Peter bellowed. Besides, he thought, he couldn't if he wanted to. After price hikes that saw tickets quintuple from a couple of dollars in the mid-1970s he and his fellow owners finally had discovered elasticity in baseball's demand curve. The bitter strike of '94-95 had made sure of that.

"Well, perhaps you should trade him to a club that can afford to pay what he's worth." The mustached agent widened his steely eyes for emphasis. His voice was sonorous, his figure portly. He cloaked his size beneath a $1,000-navy, sport coat and an open-collar silk shirt.

"I'd call $6.5 million more than fair." Peter punched keys on his computer. Columns of numbers appeared: salaries by Reds players projected out three years. He paged down to an exhibit titled "Ranking Of Major League Ballplayer Salaries: Outfielders" and swung the screen around.

"Look here. Ty is the eighth highest offensive player in all of baseball," Peter ran his finger across the screen, "earning $2.3 million more than the average starting outfielder." The owner knew figures. He owed his success in business to it. He also felt confident in his ability to negotiate deals. After all, he had built his fortune in real estate. However, he never had closed a deal with a superstar athlete.

Up until three years before, Peter had run Cincinnati's largest commercial real estate concern. That's when the pepper-haired executive reached out for a new challenge and led a group in buying America's oldest baseball franchise from Marge Schott. Peter found himself installed as president. He also found himself enjoined with twenty-seven other owners embroiled in a battle against shrinking attendance and TV revenue. Financial considerations drove Peter to take on the double duties of owner and general manager.

It was at times like this that Peter thought of Mrs. Schott, now happily raising Saint Bernards at her Indian Hills estate. Articles reported she found it a lot less taxing than running a ballclub. Writers were less apt to criticize her if a pup didn't turn out to measure up to championship caliber. And there was the satisfaction of knowing that none of her dogs bit the hand that fed them.

It pained Peter to listen to Austin. Patience was never his long suit. But as an experienced negotiator, he allowed Jack to explain his side. "I'll grant you, Ty earns a good income, but that could be gone in two years. Look at the players who've had to drop out in the past year for one reason or another—injuries, age, budget cutting. Now we both know, Peter, Ty's contract stipulates that he be the highest paid player on your club. With the signing of Worley, that's no longer true." Austin shared an exhibit of his own.

Yearly Salary Comparison-Cincinnati Reds

	Hartmann	Worley
	$6.1	——
	$6.3	——
Current Year:	$6.5	$6.3
	$6.7	$6.5
		$7.2
		$7.6
	------	------
Average Salary:	$6.4	$6.9
	------	------
Total Compensation:	$25.6	$27.6

"You can see where Kyle's contract provides half a million more per year, and two million more in total than Ty's."

Peter slammed his palm on the desk and howled, "Look at it yourself, Jack! For the next two years, he'll still be our highest paid player."

The agent blew a column of smoke toward the ceiling. "Just because you've back-loaded Worley's salary, you can't hide the fact that...."

"I'm hiding nothing. That just covers inflation! If Ty continues to perform, he'll see growth in his salary, too." Peter paused and ran his hand through his hair. He had a long, thin face and he felt it growing longer that spring. "Let me make it real simple: Ty has a contract for the next two years, and we expect him to honor it."

"Don't be penny-wise, Peter. You're not dealing with some construction company. There's a man's livelihood at stake here."

"Bullshit!" Peter cried. "Talk to me about construction *workers*, not *companies* and I'll show you people who really depend on their jobs for income. Not some ballplayer making millions."

Jack pulled a quick drag and spoke through a cloud, "Sorry, Peter, I shouldn't have said that. Listen, I'm willing to be flexible, and so is Ty. Let's see if we can come up with terms acceptable to all of us."

"I *do not* renegotiate contracts."

"There's another way. Now I haven't bounced this off Ty, but I think I can get him to go for it. If the Reds would come up with some incentives that made up the difference...." Austin slipped another exhibit in front of the GM. "I took the liberty of drafting some clauses you might consider."

Peter tossed the paper at the agent and stood. "You don't seem to get the message. We are not prepared to change the contract and that includes bonuses. Now all players are due in camp on the fifth—most of them are here now." The owner motioned toward the field.

"I'm sorry you wish to end things here, Peter." Austin shuffled his papers and buttoned them inside his leather satchel. "If you have any new thoughts, you can reach me through my New York office."

"Don't hold your breath." *Or perhaps I should encourage you to do so,* Vandermark thought.

Walking to the door, Jack turned, clutching his paisley suspender and spoke. "It's your call, Peter, but you have to ask yourself, is this the situation you want to hand over to your new manager?"

4
Negotiations

Ring-ring...ring-ring. Ty Hartmann rolled over and groped for the phone. Ring-ring...ring. He rubbed his forehead and spoke. "Hello."

"'Morning ,Ty. How ya doing?"

Through his grogginess Ty recognized Jack Austin's husky voice. "What the hell you calling me at this hour for?"

The female figure, lying nearby in a loose fetal position, stirred. A crimson silk sheet partially covered her naked, bronze back. Her hand flopped over onto Ty's chest.

"Sorry, Ty, but it's 9:30 here in Fort Meyers, and I, ah, wanted to be sure to get you before you went out."

"Yeah? It's only 7:30 out here, and I don't go anywhere this early in the morning when it's the off-season. And unless you have some great news, it's still the off-season for me."

"That's what I wanted to talk about," Jack reassured him. "I've had a series of conversations with Vandermark. I sense his impatience at not having you in camp."

Ty rose and walked to the window with the remote handset. "I'm not exactly celebrating myself. It's been over two weeks, in case you forgot."

"I appreciate that, Ty. But you need to keep in mind the Reds have a new manager. He needs you down there. They didn't look good in their first two exhibition games."

A spirit of friendship returned to Ty's voice. His head began to clear. "Yeah, they got smacked around pretty good yesterday." *ESPN* had detailed their 10-2 defeat.

"Right. Here's where we stand. I think I have Vandermark ready to make a trade. Interested?"

"Sure. It'd be nice to play for the Giants. I could drive across town and be in camp this afternoon."

"Well, that's what I called about. I need a list. You know, teams you'd be willing to be traded to."

"I can tell you right now. The Giants, Dodgers, California, uh, the Yankees and Mets."

"Okay, so you want to pretty much stick with the coastal teams. I can understand that. What about the Marlins or Texas? They're both in the sunshine. You know there's that satellite TV issue. I'm not sure how many of those you named are going to be willing to deal with the Reds."

"I'll leave that for you to worry about. But if I'm gonna go somewhere, I want it to be with a team that's got a shot at winning." Ty smelled the stale air, laced with last night's reefers, the remains of which sat in a bedside ashtray. He slid the glass door open and inhaled. The morning Phoenix air tasted as clean as the cloudless sky.

"I'll give the list to Vandermark this morning. Just keep yourself in shape."

"Don't worry about me. I've been working out—playing a lot of basketball. And this morning I'm hitting the batting cage."

"Excellent." Ty paid little attention to the words that followed, inserting a "yeah" every now and then. He fixed his eyes on the landscape and savored the beauty. The bedroom terrace afforded an uninterrupted view of the desert rambling across to the sandstone hills of Pinnacle Peak. In between, stately saguaros stood at attention against a backdrop of brick-red and grey earthtones.

Ty had been drawn to Phoenix by offers of an athletic scholarship from Arizona State. From his very first visit, he had taken a liking to the area. He relished Phoenix's open spaces, clean air and natural setting—unblemished by tenements, abandoned cars and homeless people sleeping in storefronts.

After being drafted by Cincinnati, Ty held onto his apartment in Phoenix. And when he signed the now disputed contract, he purchased his current 4,300 square foot hacienda in suburban Paradise Valley.

"...hang in there. There's nothing to worry about."

"Easy for you to say. You're still actively employed."

"Look at it as an extra vacation."

"Maybe you'd like me to put you on a vacation."

"I hear you. Listen, have I ever let you down?" Jack asked.

"Not yet."

"I'll give you a call by the end of the week."

"Sooner if you hear something." Ty moved inside and smiled at his ladyfriend, who by now was wide awake.

"Listen, Shannon, I'm going to have to get a move on."

"Shawwwnna," she exclaimed, slinging a pillow his way.

"Sorry, Shawwwnna," Ty mimicked, resetting the pillow.

Shawna knelt up in bed, naked save a pair of white lace panties. Her bony shoulders narrowed to a tiny waist in a perfect 'V.' Grabbing his arm, she implored, "Awww, what's the rush?"

Her teardrop breasts invited him to stay, but baseball was his other mistress, and he was anxious to pay her a visit at the Arizona campus. "I'd love to, but I've gotta work on keeping this ol' bod in shape."

"Oh, there's plenty of time for that," she cajoled, running her hot pink fingernails through his chest hair.

Ty's voice was firm, "Feel free to freshen up while I make some coffee. There's plenty of towels in the closet—the door next to the shower." Ty grabbed her arms, kissed her breast and gave her a pinch on her hip.

He treated his lover of the day to a cup of coffee, then parted company. Before he left home, he opened a pantry cabinet, which revealed a wall calendar with names and numbers handwritten on several of the dates. He wrote "Shawna," on that day's date. *Let's see, I'd give her an 8*, Ty thought, before recording the rating next to her name.

Ty's cherry-red Maserati made quick work of the winding, thirty-five-mile trip to his alma mater. There he entered the University Athletic Center (UAC).

"Hi there, fellow," a raspy, high-pitched voice greeted.

Ty turned to see a black man with a bumpy, bald head and with shoulders weighted down by a full stomach. He wore a grey T-shirt with the university name in block letters.

"Hi. Ty Hartmann. Class of...I played for State back in the late '80s."

"I remember you, Ty. My name's Willy."

"Pleased to meet you, Willy."

"My pleasure," the attendant greeted. "I was working here when you were knocking balls out of the park."

In his three years at State, Ty never had entered the UAC locker room, always joining the privileged set over at Packard. "I was hoping to get a locker."

"Sure, right this way."

Willy led Ty to an empty locker, and handed him a bleached towel and bar of soap. He was glad Willy didn't ask him why he wasn't in camp himself. Then again, he probably knew.

"Here you go." Ty held out a five-dollar bill.

"Oh no, no need for that," Willy laughed. "It's my job. You need anything else, you just holler."

Ty slid the bill in his jeans and watched Willy shuffle off. Removing his shirt, Ty watched the old man pick up a broom and begin to sweep. The athlete found himself swept up in a contemplative mood. The smile. The attitude. Willy reminded him of an old friend from high school days, "Slim" Sam Wilkins. He, too, had helped Ty, but in a much larger way.

Slim, who by the time Ty met him no longer deserved the moniker, had played for the Newark Eagles of the Negro League. That is, until he was called up for active duty in World War II. Slim had befriended Ty during his sophomore year at Plainfield High. The older man worked there on the maintenance crew.

While Ty grew up in a racially mixed neighborhood, he and his friends never really mixed with the blacks and Hispanics—not even on the high school sports teams. Slim was the first minority with whom he grew close. Slim had helped him understand that color didn't figure in the computing of baseball stats.

It was Slim who also helped the freshman third sacker realize he had the potential to be a major league ballplayer—if he worked at it. Slim entertained Ty in off hours, painting images of famous ballplayers from the Negro League.

"Yeah, they was a talented group. As talented as ballplayers go. We had the best infield I ever did see. You could take all those great ones of the Yankees and Dodgers—Hodges, Reese, Coleman and Rizzuto—and still not match the talent we had. There was Mule Suttles at first, Clarence 'half pint' Israel at second, Willie 'devil' Wells at short and perhaps the greatest glove man ever to play third, wishbone Ray Dandridge—called him that 'cause he had the darnedest bowed legs. But that was all you could say was wrong with Ray."

Such tales mesmerized the youngster. And while the laborer held no lofty position, his kindness offered Ty something lacking at home. He was someone he could count on not to cause him embarrassment or hurt. Slim became a genuine hero to Ty.

"You remind me of Ray, son, and not because of his legs. He hit for average—lifetime over .300. They say no pitch was ever too high or wide for him. And boy could he field. Sometimes I never saw him pick up the ball; he was that quick!"

But it was "Mule," the Eagle's 6'6" 230-pound slugger, that Ty enjoyed hearing about most of all. "How far could he hit it?"

"Further than Babe Ruth. Towering shots. Down in Cuba they say he hit a ball over 600 feet—into the wind."

"Did you see it?" Ty asked, fascinated by the thought of hitting a baseball farther than any human.

"No, but they got a plaque there to prove it." Sam himself was a fair athlete until a gunshot shattered his leg during the Battle of the Bulge. It ended his dreams of ever playing in the white man's league. "That's too bad," Ty consoled.

"I'll say. It wasn't too long after the war that Jackie Robinson created the opening for us."

"You think many of the guys you played with could have made it in the majors?"

"Think?" Slim feigned indignation. "I know. I attended games in both leagues. God didn't just start making great black players when Jackie came along."

But it was Sam's words of support that Ty liked most. "Listen, son, you can be a great one, too. Just remember, though, no matter how good you may think you are, you're only as good as your effort."

With Slim's words rekindled in his mind, Ty ran up the stairs into the rising temperatures. He jogged past the tennis courts and onto the track adjacent to the ballfield. He warmed up with a couple of laps, then entered the stadium. Crossing the outfield grass, he thought back to when he raced across that same field in pursuit of a ball. The chase. That was what ultimately convinced him to make the switch from third to center. For despite his sure hands and lateral movement, despite Slim's comparison of him to Ray Dandridge, he grew to love the outfield best of all. He thrived on tracking balls down and uncorking missiles from the warning track. During high school practices, Ty loved nothing better than to stand behind second and have someone hit him flies. He'd give chase while fellow students watched in awe. He drew upon the sense of power it gave him as if it were an antidote for some disease.

Ty scanned the familiar surroundings of Packard Field, starting with the stars on the outfield wall that honored fourteen former Sun Devils, including himself, who had appeared in major league All-Star games. It seemed like only yesterday he ran carefree out there, unencumbered by the press, management and his agent. But no, he wouldn't trade things for a moment, except maybe to have this damn contract issue settled.

What the hell, Ty thought, the dispute was just a blip on an otherwise great life. True, his father had been shot dead in a bar fight just after Ty's freshman year at Plainfield, but since then everything had fallen into place. All-American high school athlete. State championship baseball team. Plenty of girls, plenty of friends. Full scholarship to a nationally ranked college. Starting outfielder in his freshman year. Easy access to money and more girls. Number five draft choice overall and number one for the Cincinnati Reds. And a $1 million dollar contract in his second year.

Yet there always seemed to be something nagging at him. Like now. He entered the locker room and looked about for one of the coaches to unlock the batting cage. Once again he felt the pangs of guilt that had followed him throughout the spring. He was a man playing hooky, while the rest of his teammates were in "school." He realized then how much he wanted this situation to end.

◆　　◆　　◆　　◆

Three days later, Peter Vandermark checked on his manager. "Morning there, Michael."

"Hi, Peter."

"How's Worley's arm?"

"Doc says it's just a bit of tendinitis." Mike clasped his hands behind his head and updated the Reds owner on the reliever. "With treatment he should be ready in time for opening day."

"Let's make sure of that. We need him." The owner thought about his team's early struggles.

"Any word on Ty?" Mike shot back.

Peter pulled a newspaper from under his arm and tossed it on Mike's desk. "Here, you can read as well as I can." Mike read the facing article by Cincinnati *Star-Gazette* columnist, Stan Moore, while Peter flipped through a magazine.

Moore on Sports—March 15

Tempe, Ariz.—Beneath the crystal clear Arizona skies there's a storm brewing. Caught in the middle are the Cincinnati Reds, their new manager, Mike Corrigan, and star center fielder, Ty Hartmann. Hurricane force winds blowing out of Cincinnati threaten to split Hartmann from the team.

At the eye of the storm is Hartmann's contract dispute. He maintains that the Reds violated his contract with the recent signing of the 6'5" fireballer, Kyle Worley. Ty has it in writing that he is to be the highest paid Cincinnati ball player. The Reds maintain that Ty is still paid the most money on an annual basis. He'll make $6.5 million (if he reports) this year to Worley's $6.3 million.

This reporter caught up with Ty at Arizona State where he is working out. Ty says that he has given the Reds a list of five teams to whom he is willing to accept a trade. They are the Yankees, Mets, Dodgers, Giants and Angels. My sources tell me the Reds are reluctant to deal Hartmann in their own league. That doesn't leave much room for a trade. Most teams on Ty's list are at odds with the Reds over Cincinnati's participation in the Satellite TV network.

Still, I'd look for a multi-player deal if a solution isn't found in the next week. The team is not hitting, having scored an average of only two runs a game in compiling a 3-8 grapefruit record to date. They miss Hartmann, not to mention Lenhardt and Jennings whom Vandermark traded away in the deal that brought Worley and his controversial contract to the team. So far Worley has not distinguished himself, giving up 10 runs in his first three outings. Currently, he's warming the bench with a sore arm.

Not even the presence of former great Luke Hanlon can inspire the team. Of course, one has to wonder if Luke is there to inspire the team or motivate the fans to buy tickets. But if Vandermark really wants to please the public, he'll work to get the contract dispute settled with his All Star outfielder. Ty has been the Reds' one steady influence since he came into the league, compiling a .313 lifetime average in four years.

Mike grinned, "Gee, I like this writer. He gave all of us equal space."

"But not equal treatment," Peter shot back.

"Any truth about a trade?"

"The idea's coming from his agent. But if we could get equal value in return, what would you think?" Peter asked, hopeful for a positive response. He had about all he could stand of his holdout.

"I don't know." Mike stared at the ceiling. "It would be hard to replace someone like Hartmann. You can see we need his bat."

"Don't worry, I'm not about to give him away." Peter turned toward the door, then paused. "By the way, have you had the conversation we talked about with Hanlon?"

"Not yet."

"Don't wait too long. I'm convinced he can help us. Kitchell's swinging real well, and Taylor's never looked better." Besides, Peter thought, Stan Moore was right about one thing. Luke probably would put a few extra fannies in the seats.

5
Hijackers of the Diamonds

Peter Vandermark drove his rented luxury car across the Ringling Causeway to the barrier island of Longboat Key. His destination was the springtime home of the Pirate's deal maker, Nick DiCenso. The island resort was in easy driving distance of Pittsburgh's training complex in nearby Bradenton. Peter had accepted Nick's invitation to talk over breakfast about his interest in trading Ty Hartmann.

The Reds' acting GM rationalized his actions that morning. *If Ty is asking to renegotiate his contract now, when he's still the highest paid player, what's he going to be like in another year when his contract is up for renewal?* The message of discontent Ty sent was not the message Peter wanted the rest of the team to hear.

It didn't matter to Peter that the Pirates weren't tops on Hartmann's list. If he wasn't willing to play for the Reds, he'd have to live with what they could work out in a deal. Besides, most of the teams on Ty's list were on the coasts. Such teams were at odds with Peter and several small market owners ever since ten of them had formed their own satellite TV package in which they agreed to share revenues from air-ing their games throughout the country. The other teams viewed the satellite as cutting into the ratings and income of the *ABC-NBC* baseball package. Peter couldn't understand why it was fine for one team, such as the Braves or Cubs, to have an exclusive superstation contract, but wrong for a collection of teams to do so.

Peter turned onto Palm Meadow Lane and passed a series of sprawling Spanish-style, single-family homes. The surroundings told him he was in the right neighborhood for the flashy Pirates owner.

A housekeeper greeted Peter and led him around back to the slate patio. There he found the Pirate GM reading the paper, attired in a black polo shirt and white linen slacks. Nick jumped to his feet. "If it isn't the Cincinnati kid! Morning, Peter. Come, come have a seat." After Peter returned the greeting, Nick continued. "I was about to send in an order for breakfast. What would you like? Eggs, pancakes, waffles? We can get you just about anything."

"Just coffee. I ate before I left." Peter unfolded a napkin as a housekeeper wasted no time in pouring him juice and coffee. "Nice place you have here."

"Thanks. Sometimes I ask myself why I don't just give it all up and retire," Nick remarked, his head turning from the imposing ranch home to the flag-stick on the nearby golf green. A sawgrass-edged pond was all that separated the course from his backyard.

"Think you could be happy doing nothing?" Peter asked, stretching to watch a long plumed egret parading near the water's edge. He sensed Nick might be attempting to relax him into complacency. Instead, it put him on guard. He knew Nick's reputation as a salesman, how he once bragged he could sell rolls of sandpaper to a hemorrhoid sufferer.

"I'd find something to do. But you're right. Whatever it was, it probably wouldn't be enough," DiCenso replied, rubbing his freshly shaven chin. Neat comb tracks were preserved in his gel-ladened hair.

"It doesn't look like life's treated you too badly," Peter said.

"True, true, we really have the best of both worlds."

Peter saw a smile form in the creases around his competitor's shrunken lips. "How's your golf game?"

"Golf? Who's got time for golf?" Nick shouted, waving his hands. "I'm trying to figure out how to make some money."

"You do all right on the course." Peter recalled losing a hundred dollar Nassau to him at the owners' meeting.

"Some days I get lucky. It's the same with baseball. Sometimes we get lucky with the players. Now in your case, it sounds like your luck has about run out with Hartmann."

"Let's say he isn't being real cooperative."

"Think it's Austin's doing?" Nick asked, as his housekeeper set down his omelet. "You sure you don't want anything?"

Peter shook his head. He was filled with thoughts of Ty's agent. "Not sure. This is my first real dealing with Jack."

"I've had a few go-rounds with him. He's what I'd call a 'hijacker of the diamonds.'" Nick said, before shoveling in a forkful of egg, anchored to his plate by a string of mozzarella.

"A what?" Peter laughed.

"Hijacker of the diamonds. You know, the ball diamond. They're the guys who use whatever leverage they have with the players to get whatever they can. They use the ballplayers as their hostages. But that's okay. I can handle him. Of course, any trade would have to be contingent on Hartmann first agreeing to terms with our club."

"You mentioned you'd be willing to trade Eberly. What about throwing in Greevey or Wiley?" Peter asked, seeking the proven short-stop. Just then Peter caught sight of a streaked blond strutting across the patio toward the pool, which was situated pitching distance from where he sat.

"Hey, honey, come on over here. I've got someone I'd like you to meet," Nick cried out. The answer to Peter's counterproposal would have to wait.

As Mrs. DiCenso approached, a Gulf breeze spread her suncoat open at the slit. Peter glanced at her tightly tuned leg, tanned all the way up to her floral bikini.

"My wife, Phoebe Ann. Phoebe, this here's Peter Vandermark.

Peter owns the Cincinnati Reds."

"Pleased to meet you." Peter estimated her to be around thirty.

"Oh, please sit. Don't let your food get cold," Phoebe motioned, fanning her fingers weighted with an assortment of gold and diamond rings. She spoke with a slow southern drawl; Peter figured Georgia or Tennessee. "Cincinnati's a neat town. Reminds me in many ways of Pittsburgh. You know with the river. And the view from that arch is breathtaking...."

"That was St. Louis, dear." Nick's smile indicated her comment came as no surprise.

"Oh, you're right. How could I get them mixed up?" Phoebe replied before retreating to a poolside lounge chair.

The owners resumed their trade discussions. They were in agreement on the primary players, Hartmann and star rookie outfielder Dale Eberly. But they were stuck on who else the Pirates might throw in the deal. DiCenso stood firm on third baseman Earl Stansfield.

"He's too old for my liking," Peter replied.

"Hey, he's one hell of a ballplayer. And a young thirty-three; remember Concepcion played until he was thirty-eight," Nick murmured, referring to the Reds' great shortstop. As he talked, his pupils danced around like two bees trapped inside a glass jar: from himself, to his wife, to a foursome parading down the fairway to his left. "You even said you've got defensive problems at short."

Peter said nothing for what seemed liked several minutes. He had checked the numbers on the Pirate players the night before. Stansfield made in the vicinity of $3.5 million a year—guaranteed—despite a .228 batting average. For all teams it was no longer sufficient to think in terms of getting equal talent in trade. One had to think about equating salaries. And Peter figured that was the thinking behind Nick's wanting to include him in the deal.

The talks resumed without further progress. Finally, Nick suggested they take time and think about it. Easy for him, Peter thought. He didn't have a disgruntled player staging a holdout. *Hijackers of the Diamonds.* The term fit Ty and his agent well.

"You know where to reach me. I want to help you if I can. Remember, I'd be risking a lot with Hartmann."

"There's not much at risk. He's a proven player," Peter shot back.

Driving back to Plant City, Peter ran down the trade options. Oakland and Philadelphia could use Ty's bat, but they had no big hitters to offer in return. Montreal and Kansas City expressed interest, but they offered overpriced aging superstars. Then there were the Yankees. In the post-free agency days, they rarely had let a player's ego stand in the way of a contract. But they, along with Oakland and Philadelphia, were among the teams boycotting the Reds over the Satellite network issue.

Peter was fast coming to the conclusion that like so many troubled marriages, reconciliation was preferable to divorce.

6

The Financier

The sounds of popping gloves signaled another morning work-out for the Reds players. They were to break camp in just a little more than a week. And still no sign of Ty Hartmann.

Luke tossed the ball with third baseman Dean Taylor. Spring training agreed with Luke. He felt more at ease than he ever had expected. There was not the pressure to perform that he had sensed in his two other post-retirement camps. He even questioned whether perhaps he had missed out by not coming down in years past. Then again, it was his absence from the game that had worn the shine off him in the media's eye.

Despite his prolonged absence, Luke demonstrated that he still possessed the natural athletic motions. An errant ball, launched three feet above his head, was caught with grace. He returned each throw with an effortless movement, his arm flexing at the elbow, the ball seemingly jumping off his fingertips. Until finally, a sign of age. Bending to field one at his shoe tops, the ball eluded him like some dustball in the wind.

Dean's next throw was a hummer. It stung Luke through his glove and callouses. He fired a pea in return. *Ouch!* There it was again. A piercing pain in his right shoulder. An ache that called to mind his limitations. The team doctor had diagnosed it as bursitis and muscle strain. He had told Luke to take it easy. *Take it easy.* Three words Luke found hard to think or say.

He hung with it for three more throws, but the pain kept poking at him. He flipped the ball to utility man Cecil Gomez approaching from the dugout. "Gotta go," Luke yelled, waving his glove to Dean.

Luke retreated to the locker room where he saw second baseman Logan Wells catching up on the day's *Wall Street Journal.* Logan wore a pair of round wire-rim reading glasses, one side taped at the temple. His face, wrinkled with concentration, narrowed to a pointed chin.

"How are the oat futures?" Luke quipped. "Think I should stock up?"

Logan rustled the pages closed. "Better to get into health services. The industry's up 6.7 percent on the year, with plenty of growth left."

"I'll file it for now. Got a feeling I'll be paying plenty into those things without havin' to buy stock." Luke liked Wells. He respected the way the third-year player applied himself to the game with all the energy he might employ to analyze a high flier.

Luke had heard players teasing Logan about being obsessed with making money. It didn't help that he drove a nine-year-old Ford Escort, nor that he took food home from the after-game buffets so he could "have it for breakfast."

"How many papers you read a day?" Luke asked, twisting the top off a water bottle.

"Usually three. Oh, there are a couple of weeklies too—*Barrons* and *Value Line.*" Logan went on to explain, "My dad used to read six or seven."

Logan's father was an investor relations manager for a Fortune 500 corporation, essentially a PR link with Wall Street's security analysts. Copies of *Investor's Choice,* the *Nikkei Weekly* and assorted newsletters littered the family's end tables. The literature had attracted the youth's interest and analytical mind. He'd invested almost every penny he earned since he was a child. Before he signed his first major league contract, he already was worth six figures.

Later that afternoon, in the game against the New York Mets, Luke watched Logan gather up a ball in the dirt. "You got a good one there," he said to Corrigan.

"You mean our financier?"

Luke sniffed a laugh and nodded.

"D'he ever tell you what he plans to do with all his money?"

"Uh uh."

"Says he wants to buy a ballclub someday."

"The way he's going—not to mention the way the value of clubs are going—it wouldn't surprise me if he did."

Three more innings went by, and the Reds built a 2-0 lead behind Reynold's homer and Taylor's double. Kevin the "K-man" Sweeney held the New Yorkers in check, striking out better than one an inning.

As he had for most of the spring, Luke assumed an observant perch in the dugout, one foot planted on the middle step, his arms crossed and resting on his knee. He studied each player, watching for signs of weakness: an early opening of the pitcher's shoulder, a problem in an infielder's setup, a hitch in a player's swing. Manager Corrigan stood close by.

The two watched outfielder Bailey march to the plate. He tugged at his batters gloves, pulling them toward his sweatbands. "Where's his elbow pads?" Luke needled.

Miles went down swinging, but Kurkowski shot one in the gap for a double. Luke figured even *he* could have legged it into a triple. But he knew the book on the Duckster—great glove and decent stick, just no speed. Mike had confided that he could live with his slow pace, so long as he kept his weight down. And the best way to accomplish that was to keep him happy. For the twenty-four-year-old was a worrier; the more he worried, the more he ate. The more he ate, the less effective he was at bat and setting up for throws. "Sounds simple,"

Luke said at the time. "Just keep him worry-free."

Kitchell, one of Luke's hitting disciples, lined a single driving in Kurkowski.

"By the way, thanks for helping the hitters—I can see an impact already."

"Not sure I did that much. Just made a few suggestions here and there."

Mike extended a welcoming handshake to Ducky. "I've got those brats and red sauce on order, Ducky," he said, referring to the Milwaukee native's favorite hometown dish.

"And don't forget the sour cream," Ducky added.

Luke shook his head and made a face as if presented with a fresh cow pie.

Reynolds' single brought Mike back to the game. "You know, I saw these guys play near the end of last season. They weren't hitting squat. Reynolds, in particular, is finally getting his big body into the ball. Why those dingers he rapped out yesterday and today, they exploded out of here."

"Sometimes he'd start with too much weight on his front foot. I've been working on getting him to keep it back. That way he can get a better shift. The better the shift, the more power...." Mike had switched Luke onto a subject he loved.

The Reds went down without further scoring, bringing up the Mets in the sixth. "Shit," Mike cried, as a ball bounced through "Boots" Barnett's legs at short. A runner scored from second. Mike slung some pebbles, which danced in the dirt. "I can't figure out what to do with the guy. Zender's been working with him, yet he still pulls plays like that."

"Some dogs you just can't teach to hunt," Luke said.

"You may be right."

"Looks like it happens with slow runners at the plate."

Mike turned to his adviser. "And?"

"Maybe he doesn't bear down enough. Thinks he's got plenty of time."

"Pretty fair insight for someone who doesn't think he has much to contribute."

"Never said I couldn't contribute. Just that coaching isn't enough for me."

Mike continued to shift his sights, from the field to his hitting coach. "I could sure use the help. Managing in the bigs is more work than even *I* thought. What d'you say?"

"How'd I know this week wouldn't go by without that coming up'. Forget it. I've gotta farm to run."

"You have to or *want to*?" Mike clarified.

"Both. It's not fair leavin' it to Derrick."

"Peter would pay y'enough to hire a bunch of Derricks."

Luke stared ahead. His mind was made up. Sweeney threw a third strike, which ended the inning and the discussion.

"Let's get the run back, guys," Mike cried to his troops upon their return from the battlefield. One out later, he strolled along the bench to utility infielder Cecil Gomez. "Cece, loosen up. You're playing short next inning."

Cecil ran down the line while Mike visited with Barnett. "Take a rest. And next time keep your head down." Boots slapped his glove on the hardwood and took off, presumably for the fishing docks.

The Reds went down in order. With the players retaking the field, Luke asked, "How far you going with Sweeney?"

"I'd like him to get ninety pitches. He's thrown seventy-eight so far...." His voice trailed off as he watched the flight of a ball launched off the bat of Mets slugger Durk Ferraro.

"Catch it," Mike mumbled.

Reynolds, playing center in Hartmann's absence, raced in pursuit, back, back, back toward the eight-foot advertising billboard. The one-time college basketball standout reached the warning track a step behind the ball and leaped, extending his 6'5" inch body. *Smack!* The ball came to rest in the webbing an instant before Treat fell into the wall.

"Way to go!" Mike cheered.

"That makes seventy-nine," Luke smiled, updating the pitch count. The grapefruit crowd awarded Reynolds a standing ovation. "Does he make you forget Hartmann?"

"No, we need Ty's bat every bit as much as his glove."

"This guy reminds me of the 'Big Bopper.'" Luke offered, comparing Treat to one-time Red's first baseman Lee May.

"Yeah, in a way. I'd love it if he could hit thirty homers," Mike said, thinking of Lee's yearly highs. "By the way, I finally got through to Hartmann last night."

"And?"

"I did most of the talking. Told him we really wanted him, but the team had certain policies and were going to abide by them—that included renegotiation." Mike interrupted himself to shout some instructions to Ducky Kurkowski. "I told him if he joined us before the start of the season, there would be no added fines, other than his spring salary. Said he could have his job in center soon as he's ready."

"Any response?"

"I think he took it as a concession. You know something...."

Luke raised his eyebrows.

"I'm convinced he's dying to be here. He'd just like a way to save face."

The Mets rallied in the ninth for a 4-3 win. The big blow came off the catalyst in the Hartmann dispute, Kyle Worley. Luke hoped he was wrong, but his gut told him the team faced an uphill struggle in the coming season. Without a hitter of Ty's stature to anchor the line-up, they were looking at a sheer cliff.

Afterwards, inside the trainer's room, Reynolds sat on the surgical table, getting ice on the shoulder he had banged into the wall. Trainer Will Evans worked from an ace bandage feeder roll and mummified the center fielder's chest with the speed of a weaver at his loom. Snipping the cloth, he tucked the end inside the wrap near the bump where the ice pack lay hidden, "That should do you."

Reynolds greeted an entering Hanlon. "Hey coach, how's it goin'?"

"Just dandy. And how's your fender bender?"

"Okay. This is just a little precautionary ice."

"I liked the way you let out the shaft in the fourth."

"Thanks. The new setup really helps."

Luke struck a hitter's pose and mimed a swing with an exaggerated weight shift. He said nothing, but Treat nodded, signaling he understood the sign language.

Treat left the room and bumped into Miles Bailey in the hall. "Nice shot there, man," Miles congratulated. "You're really smoking the ball."

"I've got me a good coach," the black ballplayer announced, loud enough for Luke to hear.

"The old man's helped you, huh?" Miles whispered as they continued walking.

"I'd swear by him," Treat said.

"He's as quiet as bird doo."

Treat laughed and shook his head. "What he says counts. He's not one of those instructors who tells you what you did wrong after every swing."

Miles spit some tobacco juice at the wastebasket; most ended up running down the outside. "If he's that good a talker, maybe he should speak with our tight-assed owner about getting it settled with Ty."

"I hear you," Treat nodded.

7
The Arrival

Six days later at Tampa International Airport, at least a hundred travelers flooded the lounge at Gateway 41. Ty Hartmann was among the first to deplane. He wore a gold-embossed sweatsuit and hid behind wraparound sunglasses and an "ASU" baseball cap. His right hand clung to a suede sports bag.

Ty stepped aboard the tram to the landside terminal. He passed up an open seat and grabbed the pole nearest the door. He couldn't wait to get back on solid land, having left Phoenix near sunrise.

Ty stole a peek at the passengers. His eyes were met by a fortyish woman standing across the cabin. She was garnished with make-up and jewels, her shoulder sloped by a strap anchoring a carry-on bag. He zeroed in on an attractive blond, two-thirds legs, dressed in high-cut, navy shorts. A silver-haired grandmother occupied the seat in front of him. His eyes returned to the legs.

The doors to the transporter opened on the side opposite Ty, catching him by surprise. He fought his way through the exiting throng and past the anxious well-wishers. Beyond the security checkpoint, several drivers waited with handheld signs: *Harrington Driver, CoachWorks Limousine, Allstar Limousine.* Ty did a double take at the last one, thinking perhaps it could be a code name for his driver, but, alas, a greeting from a mustached gentleman drew his attention. There, measuring in at barely 5'6" with lifts, was the portly figure of Jack Austin.

Jack took one last drag on his Winston, dropped it to the floor and ground it flat. He exhaled smoke and spoke, "Welcome to Florida, Ty. So good to see you."

Ty shook Jack's extended hand. "Good to see you, man. Let's get out of this place." His tone was subdued, but confident.

Austin draped his arm around the ballplayer's shoulder and guided him toward the escalator. "Real good. Real good. You look like you're in great shape." The flattery came off as intentional, but somehow Ty found he managed to get away with it.

"Yeah, but I'm beat right now. Too much traveling."

"Got us a car downstairs. I'll get someone to grab your luggage, just give me your claim tickets." Jack loosened his tie and announced with a wink, "I made sure the bar was well stocked for the ride to Plant City."

Down the escalator and past the baggage carousels, Ty caught sight of the blond he had seen on the tram. This time he identified her by her legs and blouse as she and her male companion were nested together like two pieces of a block puzzle.

Ty exited the terminal and ducked into a waiting white limo. He watched Jack take care of the skycap who wheeled the luggage cart. Moments later, the car weaved away from the curb through the maze of taxis, buses and cars. It sped onto Highway 4 to Plant City, home of the Reds' training complex.

Jack stroked his jacket which he neatly had folded across his knees. After a few remarks that Ty construed as ice breakers, Austin shifted to business. "You'll probably get a few questions from reporters when we get to the hotel."

"What?" Ty exclaimed, not at all amused.

"I, ah, made a few phone calls." Jack held up his hand. "Now listen, it's not a full-blown press conference or anything. It's better that you meet them tonight, rather than face them at the ballpark in front of your teammates. Besides, they'll ask fewer and better questions if you give them time to think."

"And what exactly did you tell them?" Ty felt this was the last thing he needed on this long day. He lifted one of two bottles of Absolut from the bar.

"Just that you'd be getting into town tonight. And that you'd be arriving at the hotel around 6:00. I figured I'd let you do the talking."

"Thanks," he replied sarcastically, before splashing vodka into his glass.

Jack pulled a pack of Winstons from his jacket. "You mind?"

"Matter of fact, I do." Ty took satisfaction in turning Jack down. What he really wanted was to tell him where to go, but he was in no mood for a fight.

"Hand me one of those, would you?" Jack pulled out his pocket watch from his vest and checked the time before grabbing his drink. Ty had filled it high, and it slopped over the rim, some falling on Jack's pant leg. He used a napkin to wipe the glass before leaning forward to sip. "Simply point out that you're ready to play ball; you can tell them you're turning the contract matter over to your attorney. And you're confident the arbitrator will give a fair ruling."

"What else?" Ty didn't feel much like thinking, so he figured he'd make Jack do it for him.

"I'm sure they'll want to know what your plans are if there's a ruling in your favor."

"I can handle that."

Out at the Holiday Inn, nearly two dozen reporters milled around the hotel's Citrus Room, ready to provide a reception for the star ballplayer. Ty, still wearing his sweatsuit, followed Jack into the room. "Hey, Ty!" a reporter called, while still photographers snapped away at the twenty-eight-day holdout. Half a dozen others shouted questions simultaneously.

Austin stepped in front of his valued *employer* and held his hands high in the air. "Easy, gentlemen, Mr. Hartmann will try and address each of your questions. But let's have them one at a time." He stood back and cradled a match in his hands, lighting his cigarette.

Ty stood tall with his chin up in a confident pose. Two cameramen clicked away.

"Ty did Vandermark agree to renegotiate your contract?"

"No." Ty glanced over to Jack, who took a deep draw on his smoke. Exhaling, the agent gave a thumbs up.

A male reporter with his hair in a ponytail spoke next. "What made you finally decide to report?"

"I thought about how much you guys must miss me." Laughter filled the room. Ty suddenly felt invigorated. He was in his element. Back with baseball, back at the center of attention. "Actually, Mr. Corrigan called, and we had a good conversation. He said he was willing to let me play while we let the courts decide what happens next."

"Could you please elaborate?" The reporter asked.

Austin nodded for Ty to handle the question.

"My attorney will file a petition seeking to have my contract voided." Ty figured that mention of his appeal to baseball's arbitrator would make interesting reading for Peter Vandermark in the morning.

A television reporter asked a question into his mike, then thrust it forward, "What do you think of the team's chances this year?"

"A lot better now that I'm here."

The press fired questions for better than three-quarters of an hour before Austin stepped forward. "Gentlemen, Mr. Hartmann has had a very long day. I'm sure you'll find plenty of opportunity to talk with him in the days ahead. Right now we ask for your indulgence so Ty can get some rest." The announcement was greeted with a few groans while Jack escorted Ty out of the room.

◆　　◆　　◆　　◆

The Reds players, complete with Hartmann, winged their way to Cincinnati the following Saturday. Stepping amidst overstuffed suitcases, trunks and garment bags, Luke exchanged good-byes with his teammates. Corrigan told him to come visit any chance he had.

Luke did find it harder to leave than he had thought it would be. He had underestimated the sense of camaraderie and the excitement of the coming season. But he told himself that his place was back at the farm.

Most local pundits displayed little optimism for the one-time Big Red Machine, despite Ty's presence. Luke read one columnist's viewpoint that weekend.

Cincinnati—Reds Outlook

Mike Corrigan predicts a three-team race in the National League Central. Too bad his team looks no better than a fourth-place ballclub. St. Louis, Chicago and Houston all figure to finish ahead of Cincinnati.

The Reds' talent is sporadic. Even with the return of the narcissistic center fielder, Ty Hartmann, the Reds remain a below-average hitting squad. And one has to question Ty's commitment to the team. If nothing else, his petition to have his contract voided has to be giving Peter Vandermark sleepless nights.

Scanning the line-up, the Reds have Treat Reynolds who showed flashes of brilliance this spring in putting up a .320 average. But is he just teasing us once again? It is time the 25-year-old starts to deliver. Randy Kitchell looked promising, hitting .292 and knocking out six round trippers, but he's a career .250 hitter. Beyond those two, the team combined for an unimpressive .208 grapefruit average.

The left side of the Reds defense has been weakened by the trade of third baseman Chris Jennings. Third-year player Dean Taylor needs to step out of the shadows, but this reporter guesses he'll have a tough time filling Chris' shoes. Dean has a gun for an arm but lacks the range, especially important considering that Richie "Boots" Barnett is playing next to him at short.

The Reds' strong suit is their outfield, with Reynolds in left, Bailey in right and assuming Ty remains in center. Behind the plate there's Ducky Kurkowski, a reliable, if overweight, backstop.

As for Cincinnati's pitching, it fluctuates more often than Mayor Barnsworth's ratings in the polls. Sweeney and Brouse are rock solid *if* they get run support. Clint Twiddy provides the team a lot of innings and the opposition a lot of runs. Chad Lattimore and Mark Shaw, whom Corrigan brought up with him from Triple A, look promising, but you can't count on two rookies to anchor a rotation.

In the bullpen there's newly acquired Kyle Worley, a definite improvement seeing how the Reds didn't have a bullpen last year. Here's hoping he's fully recovered from the arm problems that nagged him during the spring.

Then there's the new skipper, Mike Corrigan. It will be interesting to see how successful Corrigan is at getting the most out of last year's mediocre club. Can he work the same magic he did in Triple A, or is he just a journeyman minor leaguer manager?

If Mike gets lucky with the pitching, the team just might make a run at third. My guess is that the combination of weak hitting and lack of pitching will find the Reds finishing no better than fourth.

8
College Reunion

A week into the baseball season, a sparse forty-five fans nestled inside an enclosed wooden grandstand. It was a ballpark where players only fantasized about million-dollar salaries. In the fifth and final row from the field, Luke watched intently. He advertised his allegiances with a University of Cincinnati cap.

Wife Kate rubbed her arms for warmth. Her turtleneck and cardigan weren't enough for the day's 60-degree temperatures.

Whoosh! The sound of a batter's weapon flailing at a baseball made sweet music to a pitcher at any level. Bret Hanlon signaled his satisfaction by snapping his glove closed on the return throw. He stared in for the sign and with a high leg kick, the twenty-year-old fired another gasball plateward.

"Sssssstrike three!" The home plate ump dramatized the call. Only the third inning, and Bret already had recorded five K's against Northwestern's Wildcats.

Luke watched his son throw the next batter four balls, allowing the visitors their first runner. He listened to infield chatter. "Let's get two...C'mon Bret...humm, baby." Situated less than forty feet from home, Luke enjoyed the cozy confines of the college stadium. It was pure baseball. No exploding scoreboards, no dancing chickens and no artificial turf.

Smack! The ball ascended quickly toward the university spires. "He sure hung that one," Luke commented to no one in particular. Inside, his stomach churned. He knew Bret possessed a wicked heater, but the youngster needed work on the curve. Occasionally, his "hook" hung like a bee hovering over a sunflower. It reminded Luke of Jim Maloney's *slop slider,* as his former teammate's curve derisively was referred to early on. It took Maloney four seasons to master the curve, and master it he did. Perhaps there was hope for Bret.

Luke's youngest maintained his composure and retired the next two batters to end the inning. The clang of the wrought iron gate signaled another fan's arrival at Meyers field.

"I've always said one finds the loveliest ladies at the ballpark," the distinguished-looking gentleman with the slim build announced.

"Dr. Dornhoffer, so good to see you," Kate squealed, jumping to her feet. She squeezed the university scientist as he held his smoldering Peterson pipe away from her.

"You certainly know how to make one feel welcomed. I may just go out and come in again," Dr. Adrian Dornhoffer replied. He had discarded his lab coat for a lightweight, navy windbreaker. The smell of Old English tobacco curled from his pipe. It appeared to form a wreath above his head; fitting, Luke thought, in recognition of his scientific work.

With Kate's arm still wrapped around his waist, Doc reached across and shook hands with the retired ballplayer. "Excuse me, Kate. Hello there, Luke, how are you."

"Real good, Doc. And yourself?"

"Wonderful. Just wonderful."

"Have a seat," Luke invited, moving into the row to make room for his friend.

Shorter than Luke, Doc had a full head of independent white

hair and a ruddy complexion. The professor's thin, blue eyes seemed to sparkle, his right one narrower than the left from fighting off years of smoke. Positive thinking was etched in the lines around his mouth, which curled up in a permanent smile. But his most expressive features were his eyebrows. They fluttered like shutters on a navyman's signal box, flashing messages and questions about as often as he spoke.

"I've been watching Eric. You've got a fine-looking boy out there," Luke complimented, referring to UC's shortstop.

Two sweatshirt-clad ladies seated near the fence turned and smiled at the trio.

"Oh, do you think so?" Doc inquired, as if verifying a bit of scientific evidence.

"Great range. And he's got real good hands. Just like his dad," Luke winked.

"Thank you. But I'm afraid he doesn't intimidate the pitchers very much."

"He got a single in the first," Kate chimed in with wide-eyed encouragement. "Anyway, great shortstops don't need to hit for average."

There was more to Kate's fondness for Doc than his engaging personality. Ask her, and she'd say he saved her life. Six years before, she lay in a hospital bed with a 106-degree fever, her body pricked and pictured by one specialist after another. Yet, none could diagnose her puzzling illness.

"High fever and inflamed lymph nodes—most likely mononucleosis....No, blood tests were negative; we've ordered a spinal tap. We want to rule out encephalitis....They're doing some additional tests, Mr. Hanlon." The doctors suspected lymphoma—Hodgkin's disease—but kept their thoughts to themselves to avoid alarming Luke. There would be time enough for that if the lab results turned out positive.

"Dr. Clemmons, I'm afraid we've detected an enlargement of her heart," a specialist advised the Hanlons' family doctor. It was Clemmons who recommended bringing in Dr. Dornhoffer. "Luke, he's a physician and microbiologist by training. Nowadays he's pretty much focused on biotechnology; runs the University's Caulfield Science Center. He has a remarkable understanding of infectious diseases."

After an hour reviewing medical tests and examining the patient, Dr. Dornhoffer conferred with the team of physicians. "Any of the fluid left from the spinal tap?...Yes, good, let's have that, and I'll also need a biopsy of the lymph nodes. Right...and a fluorescent examination of the antibodies in her blood."

"But Doctor, we did that five days ago."

"Yes, yes. I saw that in the lab reports. But in cases like this, initial testing often turns out negative."

By day's end, Dr. Dornhoffer called Luke into his temporary hospital quarters. "Have a seat Mr. Hanlon. Do you have any cats on your farm?"

"Why, er, yes." The question struck Luke as odd, so far afield from the matter at hand.

"I don't have conclusive results just yet—and won't for another week—but all signs point to an infectious disease called tox-o-plas-mosis," he explained, pulling at his ear while enunciating each syllable. "I suspected it when I detected some lesions on the posteria of her eye. She tested positive for the antibodies. With your permission I'd like to begin treating her for it immediately."

Luke felt his head spinning. Toxo-what? He wanted to believe this was the answer, but was it? Or was it just another misdiagnosis? Then it came to him. There was something in the doctor's demeanor—measured, definite, composed. It gave him a sense this individual knew what he was talking about.

"What exactly is it?"

"It's a parasitic disease infecting the central nervous system. Actually, it's very rare in these parts, less than 0.2 percent incidence. Oh, we've seen a marked increase in people suffering from the HIV-virus. But in the general population, it's often transmitted by cats—the microbes live in their feces and can be picked up from their litter boxes.

In most cases we can treat it successfully, assuming we catch it early enough."

"Have we?"

"You just say your prayers and leave the rest up to me."

Doc wasted no time in putting his course of treatment into action. "Dr. Clemmons, I recommend we start Mrs. Hanlon on loading doses of 50 mg of sufamethazine and pyrimethamine for the next two days. Cut back to half that amount for sustaining therapy. And monitor her platelet count to watch for toxicity."

Doc spoke next to Luke. "You'll need to bring in your cats. We'll check them for the parasites."

Within two days Kate had responded to the treatment. Doc explained the situation to her, "I should point out that while we will kill all the living parasites, some cysts will likely remain. Now it's nothing to be alarmed about. But we want to keep a watch out for a possible flare-up. Now that we know what we're looking for, it can be readily treated if it ever surfaces again."

Eight years had passed, and the disease never had returned. But Dr. Dornhoffer had. Luke and Kate welcomed him and his wife, Pat, to their home on several occasions. Luke found Doc's unassuming personality a good match for his. And Adrian Dornhoffer would be the first to admit the opportunity to be around one of the game's immortals was as exciting as his drug discovery work. It was a case of mutual admiration for what each had accomplished in their chosen fields.

"Luke, I read where you went down to spring training this year," Doc commented between puffs of his pipe.

"He went on vacation to Florida with an old drinking buddy is what he did," Kate interjected with cockeyed charm.

She stroked her blond hair, which still bore highlights of the Florida sun.

"Is that true, Luke?"

"Kate here's the one who had all the fun." Luke grabbed her Levi-clad knee and rocked it. "She hung around the beaches while I worked with the players."

"Wooowww!" the young girls seated up front in the Chi Omega shirts cried out. Kate and Doc jerked back in reaction to a foul ball that hit the netting ten feet in front. Luke just smiled.

"And how'd it feel to get out on the field again?" Doc asked.

"I didn't have to do too much, just gave some hitting instruction. Kate's probably right, lifting the beer mug was about as strenuous as it got. Oh, I threw the ball around a bit."

"Until he threw out his shoulder," Kate added, rubbing the injured area.

"Is that so?" Doc showed concern. "How is it now?"

"It'll be awright, I just need to give it some rest."

"I think he likes my nightly rubdowns," Kate said.

The crowd erupted as a UC player legged out a triple. It brought Eric Dornhoffer to the plate with the score tied in the sixth. The professor relit his pipe and puffed rapidly. His son took a ball, then fouled one back.

"He had a good cut on that curve," Luke observed.

Eric stepped out of the box, slid the bat between his pant legs and wiped his hand on his jersey sleeve. Doc continued puffing. Down the first base line, the Bearcats' bowlegged manager paced around the coaching box, his hat sitting high on his head. He held his hands straight out, clapping them more as a symbol of encouragement than for sound.

The pitcher stretched, checked the runner and delivered. Eric connected, sending a fly ball into medium center. "Get back there," Doc urged through his teeth, clenched tightly on the pipe.

Luke smiled, recognizing it was the most emotion the scientist was apt to express. The wind, blowing out, forced the center fielder back on the play. He caught the ball and fired toward home. It came in a bit right of the plate and a step behind the go ahead runner, who slid across, cutting a ten-foot swath in the dirt.

"Clutch hitting by Eric," Luke congratulated, while Kate and Doc clapped.

"It's a wonderful game, isn't it?" Doc bubbled, finally removing his pipe. "Just a simple play like that and such excitement!"

Northwestern retired the next two UC players, but the Bearcats had the lead, 3-2. The teams changed sides, and Doc turned to Luke. "By the way, have you had your shoulder examined?"

"Yeah, they did one of those MRI things."

"And?"

"Said it's just a strain of the rotator, no tear. That and some bursitis, which I've had before."

"The reason I ask, we're about to begin testing a new drug. It's proven quite effective in treating chronic muscular-related injuries, with none of the side effects of traditional anti-inflamatory medications. If you're interested, give me a call before the end of the month."

"Save your treatment for the younger folks. This just has to do with something called old age." Luke rotated his shoulder. All the talk of it had heightened his sensitivity to the tightness.

"Actually we're looking for a diverse patient population," Doc said.

"How's that?" Luke shot Doc a quizzical expression.

"You know: young-old, men-women, short-tall. By the way, Kate, when was the last time you stopped in for a checkup?" While Doc limited his practice to supervising clinical studies, he had arranged for Kate's blood testing as a favor.

"Oh, let's see," Kate dragged out her words, feigning forgetfulness. She pulled her sweater closed. "I guess it's been two years. But I feel great."

"Hmm. It's probably a good idea for you to schedule an appointment. The visit's free. And it will give me another chance to see you," Doc replied, winking and leaning against her shoulder.

"Oh, if that's it, we can have you and Pat over for dinner. Matter of fact, have her give me a call."

"I'll do that." Doc tapped his pipe against the sole of his shoe and pulled out a metal tamper that he used to remove the remaining ashes. "But I'd like to see you at the clinic. Perhaps we can interest your partner there in coming along. You know, Luke, sixty is no longer old. When you get to be a hundred, *then* you can say you're old."

Luke shot back an understanding smile. He focused on his son who came to bat in the seventh. The father wished sixty weren't really old, but to a professional athlete, even forty seemed ancient.

After taking two balls, Bret smashed a double. "Ah— like father, like son," Doc observed, blowing out the words with a cloud of smoke. "If he keeps hitting like that, they'll have to find him another position. You know, get his bat in the line-up every day."

"Nah, Bret actually prefers pitching to hitting," Luke replied. *And it's just as well,* he thought. *The family isn't big enough for two sluggers.*

Luke was thrilled to watch his youngest son play collegiate ball. He never had the opportunity with his first born, David. And Megan was into dance, not sports.

Luke had devoted a good bit of time to David and Megan growing up. He involved them in farm chores and took them to old Crosley Field on countless occasions. But even in the days when the team drew barely half a million fans, crowds besieged him wherever he went. While he sought to please people with autographs, his children found it tough to watch him receive such adulation without feeling in awe and inadequate. Luke didn't know it then, but he knew it now.

David, in particular, found the pressure of playing in the footsteps of a major league star a heavy burden. He had dropped out of the game after high school—not that the colleges weren't interested in the powerfully built youngster. Several invited him to try out, but none would commit to a scholarship. Too many strikeouts. Too many fielding miscues. There wasn't anything the coaches or Luke could do to help him. No one was able to find the right drills to overcome his real handicap, which lay between his ears.

Luke vividly remembered the day David received the last of his college acceptance letters, void of any scholarship offer. The boy took it as a final assessment of his playing ability. Luke found him around eight o'clock that evening, up on the farm's high point, feeling at his low point. David couldn't hide his red, puffy eyes. Luke consoled him with few words. He pointed out how much joy and satisfaction he got from raising cattle. The message was simple—it had taken Luke a long time to figure it out, but there's a lot more to life than baseball.

Bret, the Hanlons' youngest child, never actually witnessed his dad's heroics. By the time this so-called "late season" surprise came along, Luke was finishing up coaching. Word was, Luke passed up a shot at managing because of Bret.

What his siblings lacked in confidence, Bret exuded. He had it all—athletic prowess, his father's handsome smile and a sharp mind. Kate bragged that Bret could reach a sound conclusion as quickly as he could throw a fastball.

With one out in the top of the eighth, Bret found himself in need of a sinking fastball. The Bearcats still clung to their 3-2 lead, but the bases were loaded with Wildcats. Luke said a prayer. His son stared in for the sign, then backed off the mound and blew on his hand. Returning to the rubber, Bret stretched, checked the runners and hurled the ball plateward. The batter turned on the ball, lining it sharply in the hole between short and third. Eric dove and snared it in mid-air, as it was about to escape into the outfield. He drew himself into a kneeling position and threw toward third, just ahead of the sliding runner who had ventured too far off the bag.

"Double play!" Kate cried out, spanking Doc on the back.

A male student let out a shrill whistle. The collegiates stood and cheered the team as it ran off the field. "Way to go, Eric!" It seemed fitting to Luke that Eric and Bret had helped one another out. Long before the boys joined ranks at UC, they had become good friends through their parents' connection.

Bret tied a neat bow on the game, striking out the last two batters for an even dozen. Doc shook hands with Luke and Kate. Standing, he sucked in the crisp air and announced, "Ah, nothing quite like victory."

"I'd have to agree with you on that," Luke answered. He knew Doc loved the game of baseball. He had listened to him explain the parallels between the game and his scientific research. Doc viewed himself a solid .300 hitter, often stymied, but in the end he could count on three hits for every seven outs. And once in a while, his lab would deliver a home run shot.

Doc squinted and motioned toward Bret emerging from a throng of teammates. "Reminds me of that other hard-throwing Bearcat pitcher. The one with the unusual name...oh yes, Koufax."

"He's got a ways to go to be like Sandy," Luke grinned.

"Good-bye, my lady." Doc kissed Kate's cheek.

"Remember to have Pat give me a call," Kate said.

"I'll do that. Remember to schedule yourself for a checkup," Doc countered as they exited the grandstands. "And bring your young friend here along."

9

The Enabler

After brewing a cup of tea, Dr. Dornhoffer made his morning rounds inside the Caulfield Science Center. He enjoyed meeting with scientists far more than reading lab reports. Face to face contact told him so much more.

He passed half a dozen darkened labs before noticing the light on in room D-14. He knocked on the open doorframe. Dr. Emily Einhardt gave no response. Her head was tucked inside the four-foot-wide laminar-flow hood, its continuous whir ringing in her ears. Doc knocked again, this time using his unlit pipe.

Emily's body jerked upwards. "Oh, I didn't hear you come in," she greeted with a startled laugh.

"Sorry if I frightened you, Emily." Doc used her first name as he did with everyone. "And how's our distinguished scientist this morning?"

"Fine," replied Emily.

"And the cloning?"

"Excellent. I'll be ready to go into mass production as soon as we hear from our friends in Washington."

Mass production. Transferring the cloned cells of a gene known as "the enabler," together with a growth medium, to large roller flasks. There they'd multiply by the tens of thousands, the quantity needed for her upcoming, six-month study—if it were approved.

Emily's work, her challenge, lay in understanding how genes function, genes such as the one she was working with this day. How they are regulated, what turns them on, what turns them off and, most important, how they affect cellular processes. Normally produced inside the membranes of individual cells, these genes were synthesized inside the four-story building, home to advanced biological research at the University of Cincinnati.

For Emily, the morning's work was akin to an accountant running numbers; it allowed for no experimentation. Yet, Doc knew it was an important step along the path to clinical testing of the genetic treatment she had spent five years developing. Each petri dish contained multiple copies of the *Enabler*—or *ena-1* as it was known to the scientists. Emily had identified it as holding the key to enabling the body to accelerate the repair of damaged—even torn—muscle, tendon and ligament tissue.

Doc appreciated her dedication to the study of *ena-1*. He recognized she had sacrificed her personal life for the project. To his knowledge, the thirty-two-year-old, raven-haired scientist had few dates. She certainly had pleasant enough features, albeit a bit disguised behind coke-bottle glasses, hair that looked as if it never met a curling iron and barely a brush of make-up. No, her dedication to science left little time for such things.

Doc also knew that Emily's willingness to be a "jack of all trades" was part of the price a researcher paid for working in his genetics lab. He employed a lean staff, the result of his decision to forgo corporate funding as a way of remaining independent. But it guaranteed freedom from sponsors who might want to take control over the direction of his research.

Shortly after he was hired to set up the lab—a tribute to his leadership and scientific acumen inasmuch as he was a physician rather than molecular biologist—Adrian had fought with the University over his desire to remain independent. "Adrian's folly," they had called it. But no one laughed when the self-funding lab produced a breakthrough drug for leukemia and entered into a licensing agreement for $7 million up front and a 3 percent royalty.

Since then, the Caulfield Center's work grew in stature along with grants from the National Institute of Health (NIH). Over the latest five-year period, the grants had totalled $21 million at a time when cutbacks were more the norm.

Emily snapped off her rubber gloves and wrung her reddened hands to remove the slimy feel built up during her labors. "I'm beginning to think our submission got mixed up with the folders being sent to the FDA's archives."

"Now Emily, think positive!" Doc counseled.

"You know as well as I that some of their helpers aren't qualified to read the newspaper, let alone a research report."

"Let's be kind. My guess is they're in the process of getting everyone signed on." Doc fought to remain upbeat. He realized there was truth in what Emily said; the delay was rather long. The two had met in Washington with Dr. Milton Lashkey three months earlier, requesting approval for the six- month study. Dr. Lashkey was a chief medical officer for CBER, the FDA's Center for Biological Drug Evaluation and Research, the division overseeing testing of genetic drugs.

In some cases studies were approved within ten days of a hearing. But Lashkey wanted to see more data. This required going back to the six-month animal studies. The FDAer had questioned an increase in the metabolic rate noted in people during the four-week Phase II study.

Adrian crossed his arms and rubbed his ear. His voice took on a philosophical tone. "I remember when I was a boy— and believe me that was a long time ago—I was waiting to get a free baseball in the mail. Every day I checked the mailbox, and nothing. Then, I don't know why, one day I just forgot about it. And you know if it didn't come within a day or two after that."

"I get the message," Emily sighed. "I just hope I see this drug on the market before I retire."

"Patience, my young friend. Look at it this way: How many scientists have the opportunity to lay claim to such a significant discovery at your age?"

"Hey, most great scientists make their discoveries by the time they're twenty-eight. Look at Einstein...."

"I know, I know." Doc knew that Einstein was a mere twenty-six when he published his theory of relativity. Yet, Emily was only twenty-seven when she discovered the *enabler*. "Einstein didn't have to conduct five years of clinicals."

Emily's testing protocol was mapped out in a document known as the *Notice of Claimed Investigational Exemption for a New Drug Application*. Clinicians liked to shorten it to IND. That was about all that Emily could shorten. Three binders worth of information were compiled. In them was everything from in vitro data—laboratory studies inside test tubes—to the pre-clinical trials in rats and guinea pigs.

Indeed, Doc thought, *it would have been interesting to see how Einstein or Edison would have dealt with an FDA protocol.* It had taken the government eight months to okay the first phase of clinicals with *ena-1*. Single injection treatments were all that was allowed—surely not sufficient time to measure any effect. And even if it were, Phase I clinicals meant testing in only young, healthy patients. College students fit her bill.

Phase II clinicals were where the learning really began, where truth met up with hypotheses. It took her a year to prepare, field and evaluate two consecutive four-week studies. They gave Emily her first real look at the effectiveness of *ena-1* in humans. The results were outstanding. Ninety-four percent of patients from four clinical sites reported improvement from assorted muscular injuries. The nearly universal, positive results made it especially hard for Emily to accept the FDA's protracted handling of the six-month Phase III clinical application.

"I'll try to be patient," Emily replied, hopping back in her seat. "But if I don't hear anything by month's end, I may just fly to Washington and shake loose an answer."

"I'm sure that won't be necessary." Doc's tone was as optimistic as his message.

◆　　◆　　◆　　◆

Thirty-some miles away, in Millville, Ohio, medical science was being practiced on a more rudimentary level. Evidence came from the pungent smell of wintergreen, which wafted through the Hanlon master bedroom. Wife Kate encountered the odor as she ascended the mahogany staircase. It was a sorry comparison to the smell of homemade stew coming from her kitchen.

She peered into the bathroom mirror and watched Luke, naked from the waist up, rub liniment into his shoulder. "Smells like a locker room in here!" She teased. "It isn't getting any better, is it?"

"Oh, it'll be fine with some rest. I just worked it too hard."

"I saw you carrying a cow into the barn."

"A calf."

"Okay, a calf. Was it really necessary?"

"Sure. It wasn't nursin'." Luke had carried the hundred pound calf to the feeding pen. He spun the bar of soap under the running water in an effort to clean off the ointment. He wished he could rinse away the signs of old age with it. "Actually, what did it was helping Derrick load the feedbags." Luke knew a truckload of 50-pound bags was more than the doctor would have prescribed.

Kate slid her hands around his waist and leaned against his hip, avoiding his treated shoulder. "Listen, guy, I expect to have you around here another sixty years, so take it easy."

"Alright Kitten. Guess it's time I go see that orthopedic fellow."

"How about the medication Doc mentioned last week?"

"What do you think I am, a guinea pig?" Luke believed "old-fashioned" remedies were as good—if not better—than most new treatments. Besides, at this point in his life he didn't care much about participating in a group experiment. He dried his hands and returned to the bedroom.

"C'mon. You know Adrian wouldn't put you on anything if he wasn't absolutely convinced it was safe."

"I guess," Luke said, donning a clean shirt. Kate watched from the corner of the four poster-bed, her legs crossed, her arms wrapped around the lathed column. Luke recognized that she indeed had taken good care of herself. It was hard to imagine that she had seen fifty-eight winters.

"Well, if you change your mind, I have an appointment at UC next week."

"I'll think about it," Luke replied. While his instincts told him no, he had learned to listen to his wife.

Kate's advice had proven valuable more often than not. Like the time she suggested they purchase the land where they now lived. It came at a bargain price, since it was unsuitable for widespread growing of row crops. The terrain had been crafted by the leading edge of a continental glacier some 2.5 million years before. As the ice mass plowed down from Canada, it skimmed the cream of the soil and deposited mounds of the rock-embedded earth throughout the region. The land they called home had proven great for grazing a hundred head of cattle, which fulfilled Kate's dream and launched a second career for Luke. Yes, Luke knew to listen to one Kate Hanlon.

"Then again he might not want you in the study after all." She shot him a taunting smile and hopped off the bed. "He might have decided you're beyond hope!"

Rusty peeked through the doorway. He raised his snout and moved it ever so slowly back and forth, sniffing the air.

"Aw, look, even Rusty's wondering what smells in here."

"I think he actually likes it," Luke said. "Say, Rusty, you like it better than Kate's cooking?"

"Watch it, bud. He might end up with your supper tonight." She left the room with their dog following close behind, the point of his tail raised in a signal of contentment. Rusty appeared to know better things awaited him downstairs.

10
News in the Making

Stan Moore leaned back in his swivel chair and scanned the *Sporting News,* absorbing facts, quotes and viewpoints from the world of baseball. His left foot rested on an opened file drawer; the other floated inches off the carpeting. Stan's hair resembled a slightly used Brillo pad. His face had the color and texture of a conch.

Stan munched on a crumbling Danish. His half-finished cup of coffee emitted a stale smell. Stacks of newspapers, magazines and a wire in-box of computer printouts, teletype pages and assorted notes covered his desktop. The *Cincinnati Star-Gazette's* lead baseball columnist much preferred organizing thoughts in his mind to documents on his desk.

His "space" was situated amidst a parlor-sized room of eight empty green desks. Only the sports editor and Stan's nemesis, the city editor, rated offices.

Normally, the beer-bellied reporter was out chasing down stories, conducting an interview on the road or just catching up on sleep he missed while covering some ballgame. Today was one of the rare occasions one could find him at his desk. Typically, stories were typed away from the office on his laptop computer and transmitted electronically back to the editors.

Copy boy Chip Pettigrew peered in through a glass panel. He swung open the door and raced to hand Stan an AP wire message. "They just declared Hartmann a free agent!"

Stan catapulted from his chair and grabbed the sheet. He sat on an adjoining desk and stroked his mustache as he studied each word. The further he read, the more his dark eyes widened, while his leg vibrated like a jackhammer.

April 30. New York City—Major league baseball's arbitrator, David Rausch, announced his decision today in the case involving Reds outfielder Ty Hartmann. Rausch stated that the Reds had failed to live up to the terms of their contract with the All-Star center fielder. As such, Rausch declared the contract void, which leaves Hartmann free to negotiate his services with any major league team.

In announcing the decision, the arbitrator cited the clause which guaranteed that Hartmann would be the Reds' highest paid player. In his view, it was used as an incentive to get the ballplayer to agree to a salary level three years before, which was below the then prevailing market.

Mr. Rausch ruled that the way one spaces out payments in a contract can be arbitrary, and that by signing Kyle Worley to a contract with a higher average annual salary, the team had in effect established a "new high" for the Reds' salaries. In so doing, the Reds had violated the intent of the aforementioned clause in Ty's contract. The arbitrator went on to state that since the new season already had begun, the Reds had violated the terms of the agreement and Mr. Hartmann has the right to rescind the contract. Agent Jack Austin stated that it was the ballplayer's intent to do just that.

Peter Vandermark, president and GM of the Reds, declined comment. The team issued a terse two-line statement: "The Reds are naturally disappointed in Mr. Rausch's ruling. Team officials will meet with their attorneys to determine appropriate next steps."

"Welcome to major league baseball, Mr. Vandermark," Stan announced to no one in particular. He felt a degree of satisfaction. In his column he had predicted that Hartmann had better than even odds of winning his case.

Stan turned to reporter Matt Phillipe, who had joined Chip in looking over his shoulder. "Who'd we have covering this story?"

"Andy's on it in New York," Matt answered.

Stan glanced at his watch, then to the pudgy youth tottering back and forth. "The Reds are playing tonight so the players won't be arriving until at least 4:00."

"That gives us, ah, about two hours," Chip said.

"You'll never make it here thinking like that, son." There was an edge to Stan's voice, as sharp as his pen. "You can't wait on a story like this. If you want to be helpful, go find us a photographer. We're going to Riverfront. I want to be the first to hear what Corrigan has to say."

Stan barely could contain his excitement. Here was an opportunity to immerse himself in the type of story he loved best. News in the making. People reacting, caught by surprise. Not just on the scene, but behind it. And to think that his dad had said a writer's craft was passive.

"Writers are spectators on the world stage," Stan recalled his attorney-father saying. "You ought to get yourself into something that contributes to people's lives." *Yeah, like defending criminals so they don't end up in jail.*

Growing up, Stan had gravitated toward sports rather than academics. But at a scrawny 5'6', he realized he was not cut out for most athletics, so he shifted to writing about them. He grew to believe that it took more talent to provide insight into the athlete's mind than to be an athlete. *After all, anyone with enough God-given ability can learn to play sports,* he figured.

Stan was a college junior when the massacre at Kent State brought the uproar over the Vietnam War to a climax. He joined the peace sit-ins and turned his pen to covering political issues; it stimulated his thirst for investigative journalism. And with his father's ability to pursue leads and ask the tough, penetrating questions, he became a success.

The graduate bounced around a series of "alternative newspapers" covering such mundane stories as county road construction scandals and neighborhood tenant fights. Eventually, he landed a job with a Dayton daily where he received notoriety for a series on a prostitution ring involving several Cincinnati athletes. He seasoned the story with such details as how one player liked to dress up in women's lingerie, while another demanded that his hooker wear football pads and a helmet to bed.

Stan was rewarded with a job offer from the Cincinnati *Star-Gazette*. The paper and Stan seemed made for one another. What shock radio was to the airwaves, the *Star-Gazette* was to the news media. Stan thrived in that environment and quickly ascended to columnist. Often controversial but never dull, Stan created a loyal following. Readers either loved him or hated him. There was no middle ground. Many of the players lined up on the negative side, saying he was "always digging for a headline."

The *Star's* editor, William "Fuzzy" Armstrong, loved Stan. He loved controversy; it sold papers. And in a city barely big enough for one major daily, he had to compete with both the Cincinnati *Enquirer* and *Post*.

Stan stood, ready to pounce on the latest bad news about the one-time Big Red Machine. Writer Phillipe shook his head in disappointment. "It's going to be another long season for the Reds." He was a reporter first, but that didn't stop him from rooting.

"That doesn't mean the news has to be dull," Stan smiled.

"No sympathy for the downtrodden, huh?" Phillipe asked.

"The only place for sympathy in a reporter's repertoire, Matt, is between the words 'shit' and 'syphilis' in the dictionary." Matt and Chip exchanged glances, as Stan grabbed his windbreaker and took off through the gridwork of desks in the main pressroom. At every third row, he dodged the narrow white support posts that grew from the floor like pencils on end. As he raced along, he sucked documents off several of the paper towers.

Stan stopped long enough to duck his head into an editor's office. "Tell Fuzzy to hold the front page. I'm working on a breaking story about Ty Hartmann. It's big time!" Stan was in too much of a hurry to tell the editor himself.

11
The Approval

Dr. Einhardt marched down the sterile-looking hallway of the Caulfield Science Center. Waist-high window panels rose to the ceiling, offering a view of the streets below, but she cast her eyes straight ahead. A sense of anticipation filled each step. She clutched the folded message asking her to stop by Dr. Dornhoffer's second-floor office. *Could it be he's heard from the FDA?* There was nothing specific in the message. Yet she had a feeling.

Emily gave a barely audible "hi" to a passing white coat and descended the corner staircase, her shoes clicking rapidly on the tiled steps. Moments later she stood outside Dr. Dornhoffer's folder-laden office.

"Come in, come in." Doc rose, pipe in hand, and backhanded the metal door closed with a secure thud.

What the office lacked in tidiness it made up for in hominess. Three bookshelves overlooked a crowded desk. A half-full pipe rack sat on the bottom shelf above a circular ashtray that retained the scent of Londonderry tobacco. A trio of diplomas hung from the lone solid wall, as if Dr. Dornhoffer needed to show his credentials. And on the credenza was an inscribed wooden plaque that, in Emily's eyes, said more about the man than all his diplomas:

> *If a man does not keep pace with his compan-*
> *ions, perhaps it is because he hears a different drum-*
> *mer. Let him step to the music which he hears, how-*
> *ever measured or far away.*
>
> Henry David Thoreau

"Coffee, tea?"

"No thanks, but go right ahead."

Doc lifted a Pyrex pot off a hotplate and poured a cloud of steam. Emily picked at one of her fingernails. "Are you going to keep me in suspense?"

"No, no, I'll be happy to tell you the good news."

"You've got the FDA letter!" Emily shrieked.

"You read minds, too?"

"What's it say?" Emily wiggled in her seat.

"Essentially, they've okayed the study. But here, see for yourself." Doc smiled and handed her the letter. He tugged on his ear, a nervous habit he had developed when not cradling his lit pipe—department rules prevented him from smoking it anywhere but in his enclosed office.

Scanning, Emily read sections out loud: " 'We refer to the additional information contained in your April 2 submission...answers to our satisfaction the questions raised in our letter dated March 15...have reviewed the data showing the metabolic changes in the longitudinal animal studies. Taken together with the results of the Phase I and Phase II human studies, we are satisfied that further testing would not pose an unreasonable risk to humans...conditionally approve your protocol for a six-month study...." Emily emphasized the words "approve your protocol." "Yessss! This means we can begin before summer."

Doc smiled and nodded.

Emily read on: "'We acknowledge that results to date are quite promising. Nonetheless...please advise your clinical Review Board if any untoward effects develop.' This is fantastic!"

"Right. And for Lashkey to admit the data is 'quite promising' is like finding a whore in church," Doc said. Emily rolled her eyes. He shifted back to serious conversation. "I believe you said you have enough serum made?"

"Three cases on ice," Emily replied, referring to the scientific refrigeration unit where genetic materials were stored for lengthy periods at -70 degrees C. "I'll fax a copy of this to the four other investigators. And I need to check with the Clinical Review Board...." Emily ran down a checklist of activities, tapping her thumb against each fingertip as she did.

◆　　◆　　◆　　◆

Three weeks later, Luke steered his 1963 split-window Corvette toward the college town of Clifton, Ohio. The fixed-roof coupe hugged the curves of Martin Luther King Drive, while the sun transformed the 'vette's silver pearl finish to a glistening white. Its engine growled like a dog guarding a bone. Kate gazed out the passenger window and surveyed the smooth cement structures on the University of Cincinnati campus. To the left, lavender and white flowers blossomed on the trees and shrubs of Burnett Woods.

Up a hill, then down again, Luke turned into a side street parking garage across from the Caulfield Science Center. The couple entered the door marked "Clinical Testing—Patients Only." Inside, four potted plants and a perimeter of blush-colored chairs awaited them.

Kate signed in while Luke grabbed a magazine. "I have an appointment with Dr. Dornhoffer, and my husband...he's taking part in a clinical study."

"That must be Dr. Einhardt's clinical trial. Thank you," the receptionist answered, retrieving the clipboard and raising her head to check the names through her Ben Franklin glasses. "Please have a seat, Mrs. Hanlon, the doctor should be right out. Mr. Hanlon, you'll need to fill out this registration sheet."

The fortyish brunette glanced surreptitiously at Luke as he approached her window. She gushed a smile like some teenybopper gazing at a rock and roll star. "It's so nice to meet you."

"Nice to meet you, too, Miss, er, Kennsington." Luke said, seeing her name on a lapel badge.

"Oh, please, you can call me Margaret," she announced in a loud voice. "I remember watching you play out at Crosley Field."

"That was quite a while ago."

"Oh, I'm older than I look," Margaret blushed. "Listen, I have a son who would be thrilled if I brought him your autograph."

"Sure, what's his name?"

"Garth. Here." She handed him a slip of paper to sign.

Luke signed his best wishes and checked the "yes" and "no" answers on the medical history form. A buzzer rang on the intercom, and a fuzzy-sounding voice announced, "Margaret, you can send Mr. Hanlon back to see Nurse Metzger now."

Luke followed the directions from his admiring fan, which led him past several offices to a patient treatment room. "Hello, I'm Nancy Metzger. Actually, I'm a registered nurse, and I'll be taking care of you on your visits." The collegiate-looking lady with curly black hair extended her hand in greeting.

"Hello, nurse."

"You can call me Nancy—most everyone here goes by their first name." She paused to read from Luke's chart. "It says here you've been suffering some shoulder discomfort. Tell me about it."

Luke explained the problems he'd been having, while Nancy took copious notes. The discussion brought to mind spring training and the Cincinnati ballclub. He thought how he owed Mike Corrigan a call, if for nothing more than to lend a sympathetic ear. He had heard about the Reds losing Hartmann and their being mired in last place.

The nurse handed Luke a couple of instruction pages. "Look these over, and you'll need to sign this waiver."

Luke noted how she was much more matter-of-fact than Dr. Dornhoffer. No idle chatter. But then there was probably only room there for one such dynamo. Luke glanced up between paragraphs to see the nurse checking supplies and unwrapping a medical vial. He set aside the completed papers and announced, "Did they tell you I tend to faint at the sight of a needle?"

"No, but that's why we have 'Nurse Ratched' here." She tipped her head in the direction of a wired box.

"Nurse Ratched?" Luke recalled the character from the movie "One Flew Over the Cuckoo's Nest," but missed the connection. He eyed the plastic device, which resembled a Trimlite telephone receiver, linked by cable to a pale blue control box. "Are you going to phone the drug into me?"

"Not quite. Actually, it's an electronic syringe. IV-5000 was designed to take the guesswork out of giving injections. It's also designed to be more comfortable for the patient."

"That part sounds good."

She pointed to tiny circles on the underside of the hand-held device. "See these little sensors?"

"Uh huh."

"They emit a very mild electronic stimulation so you hardly feel anything when the needle is inserted. Other electrodes pinpoint the location and depth of your veins, then feed it back to a computer chip inside the handle. In a fraction of a second, the unit calibrates where to aim the needle and how far it should penetrate."

"Sorta like a stud finder."

"Exactly," she smiled.

"Go ahead when you're ready." Luke watched Nancy insert a disposable needle. He picked up the discarded wrapper; the label read "Glide Thru Needle." *Let's see if it glides as well as she claims,* he thought, as he watched a drop of fluid bubble up on the needle point. Not that Luke was afraid of pain. He had withstood his share before the advent of laser and athroscopic surgery. The worst involved the carving of his right knee to repair damage that led to his current arthritic condition. He still could recall the excruciating pain caused when his spikes caught while sliding into second base. To fix it thirty-some years before, doctors had slashed a six-inch opening in his leg and dug around with their instruments. Afterwards, it felt as if the surgeons had left a dozen hot tacks inside; every time he bent the knee during rehabilitation, he could almost feel the hot tacks.

The cool sensation of alcohol on his biceps brought Luke's mind back to the present. A trickle ran down his arm as the nurse put the unit in place. He stared across the room at the four glass canisters of medical paraphernalia and waited for the prick. Yet, all he felt was Nancy rolling the vein-finder around his arm.

The green diode lit up. He felt no pain, just a mild vibration as she had promised. For the next fifteen seconds the unit delivered the intitial dose of the *enabler* into his bloodstream.

"All done." Nancy said, releasing the needle into a medical waste container. "Now, how was that?"

"When are you going to begin?" Luke jested. "I didn't feel much of anything,"

"Amazing, isn't it?"

"I could sure use one of them on the farm. It'd help with all the inoculating we do," he said, walking over to retrieve his shirt. "Did Dr. Dornhoffer come up with that?"

"No. Actually, it was developed by two engineering students right here at UC. They've applied for a patent and are seeking to sell it to some company. Doc agreed to try it here at the Center."

This study's gonna be rather simple, Luke figured.

12
In First Place

The elevator doors closed on the executive level at Yankee Stadium, and the elevator began its descent. Inside, Ty Hartmann thought about questions he was about to face. He rotated his neck with a loud crack. The noise triggered a smile from that season's Yankee general manager, part of the entourage that included the team's vice president of public relations, field manager and two security guards.

The doors parted inside the upper level of the Stadium Club Restaurant. Ty followed the general manager toward the blue carpeted stairs. He heard a shout "Here they are!" and glanced over the railing but was blinded by a rapid fire of flashes and television strobe lights. He gripped the banister and focused on the scuffed shoes walking in front of him. A cacophony of greetings cried out, "Welcome, Ty," "Hey, Ty, look this way," "How's it feel to be a Yankee, Ty?".

The PR executive raised his arms to signal quiet, and the GM took center stage. Ty tucked himself behind a mahogany pillar and slid a hand inside his uniform pants to smooth his shirt. This was his moment. He peeked from behind the pillar. There, eyes riveted on the speaker, was a sea of reporters, several with faces disguised as black lens snouts. It was the twenty-seven-year-old's first experience with a New York style press conference.

"Thump, thump, thump...." The Yankee GM tapped on the main mike's wire mesh. Ty counted the voice recorders—*four...seven...ten...fourteen...eighteen.* They sprouted from the rostrum like bunches of Tootsie Roll Pops©. Yet, Ty knew that they provided little in the way of oral gratification. On the contrary, if he were not careful in speaking into them, he would end up with a bitter taste in his mouth.

Before his contract dispute, Ty had faced but four or five journalists at a time, unless it was an All-Star Game where he was accompanied by several other players. Nothing like this. The New York press made Cincinnati look like a desert outpost for news reporters during a Mideast truce.

Yes, Ty Francis Hartmann clearly stood alone. Without teammates, and for that matter, without peers in salary. Five years for a cool $52.5 million. Better than $10 million a year. The highest annual salary in baseball. But what the hell, the Yankees could cover it five times over with their yearly cable TV deal.

The details of his contract would be "leaked" to the press and reported in the morning papers—all part of the "code of honor" among agents. After all, the disclosee and agents stood to benefit long-term—other players they represented could use it as leverage in their salary disputes or at arbitration time.

Ty thought briefly about the money, about what it meant to be the highest paid player, then shifted to thoughts of the reporters. Suddenly, he felt a tic in his eyelid. A slight flicker, like the annoying flutter of a fluorescent light gone bad. He rubbed his eye and tried to make it go away. In the background he heard the GM speak.

"Ladies and gentlemen, thank you all for coming. Over the years the New York Yankees have built a tradition of introducing you to a number of outstanding ballplayers whom it has purchased the rights to, beginning with the Babe. Yes, for those who may have forgotten,

Babe Ruth was our first high-priced signing back on January 3, 1920—it took a whopping $125,000 to pry him from the Red Sox." A rumble of laughter swept through the crowd. The GM turned and scrunched up his face in an "only kidding" wink at Ty.

"More recently, there's been Catfish Hunter, Reggie Jackson, Jesse Barfield and Danny Tartabull...."

Ty found it hard to concentrate on the speaker. His eyes drifted to the two-story stained glass window with the revered Yankee insignia, a top hat and bat, affixed against a red trimmed baseball. Growing up across the Hudson River, Ty had fantasized about playing for the pinstripers, but he never really expected it to happen. If anything, he figured he'd end up with the Mets. They were more his style: blue collar, battlers. Above the emblem, lights filtered through a scene of a Yankee player dropping a bat, seemingly after hitting a home run. He wanted to be that player. He would be that player.

"Well, I'm very pleased to introduce you to the ballclub's latest acquisition, an individual we're confident will earn a spot right up there with the likes of those I just mentioned—four-time All-Star, Ty Hartmann!"

The Yankee manager ushered the former Cincinnati Reds player to the podium to the whirl of TV cams and the click of cameras. Lights exploded in blinding fashion. Shirtsleeved photographers with unkempt hair jockeyed for position. More than ninety members of the media and support staff overflowed the leather armchairs assembled for the press conference. In a town where stage appeal counted for a lot, Ty Hartmann fit like a marquee on Broadway.

Ty stepped to the podium dressed in the pinstripes of baseball's most successful franchise. He shifted side to side, nearly bumping into the GM and manager before finally stepping forward. Once again he felt the tic near his eye. *Hopefully*, he thought, *it won't show up in the films.*

Ty Hartmann was where he wanted to be, alone at the top. He felt on cloud nine, but it brought a feeling of pressure like he never had known before. And it was all just beginning.

13
Summer Chores

The mood at the Homestead contrasted sharply with events at Yankee Stadium. A certain serenity permeated the family happenings. The workplace tempo was busy all right—a flurry of activity accompanied the birth of forty-eight calves in April and an additional twelve in May. But for Luke and part-time ranch hand Derrick Wosniak, it was a labor of love.

Calving brought castrations and inoculations, visits to the farm co-op and the prepping of acreage for the homegrown feed crop—a mix of hay and oat grains. Derrick helped Luke spot patch the grasslands, trim trees, and clear twisted limbs and branches hurled about by storms that had visited while he was in Florida.

Derrick had come with the farm when Luke purchased it some thirty years before. Luke struck up an immediate friendship with the Polishman. He reminded him of the many hard-working Slavic neighbors he had grown up with in the ethnically rich communities around Youngstown. In the early years, the ranch hand's duties were far more extensive, as Luke gave his full attention to the game. After retirement, Luke found he could ill afford to hire a stable of ranch hands. That was fine with him; he relished the outdoors, whether it be a ball diamond or a cow pasture. Luke had found both a refreshing change from the smoke-charred air and land-starved row houses of his birthplace.

Between that summer's farm activities, Luke squeezed in his biweekly trips to the clinic at UC. He grew to appreciate his participation in the study; true to Doc's promise, the pain in his shoulder disappeared, seemingly overnight.

And the benefits extended beyond his shoulder. Luke began to sense a rejuvenation throughout his entire body. Energy flowed within him like sap inside a sprouting shrub. His tissues blossomed with renewed flexibility and vitality. Mysteriously, his appetite grew, but his weight didn't; the effort he exerted absorbed calories like a shop vac sucking up water. He even took up jogging as he experienced dramatic improvement in his long-standing fight with arthritic knees.

The announcement of Ty Hartmann's free agency and subsequent signing to play with the Yankees created the only blemish on Luke's spring. True, Luke had witnessed a certain constancy in the game that he loved while in Florida. But that failed to disguise what he saw as a sickness within represented by Ty's situation.

Luke summed up his reaction to Derrick during a lunchtime pause inside the splintering barn office. "I'll never understand it," he said, shaking his head and clenching his teeth.

"If he's worth ten million, you'd probably be worth twenty," Derrick offered. The sixty-two-year-old ranch hand tossed his hat aside and reached into his chipped, black metal lunch-pail for a foil-wrapped sandwich. Long days outdoors over many years had left their mark. His squared-off face looked as if he had run smack into a spider's web.

Luke broke from his pensive pose. "It's not the figure so much as how he acts like they're giving him hog slop. You'd think a guy earning what he does would be happy."

"Yeah, but don't you figure it's payback time for the owners? I mean they took advantage of you, right?"

"Hey, I thought I was well paid for something I loved doing," Luke laughed. He recalled having argued for raises, only to end up fighting off pay cuts. "Sure, there were times I wish I had gotten more. But I wouldn't trade places with these guys for all their millions. "

Luke had thought about players' salaries on more than one occasion—it was hard not to when reading the sports pages. He wasn't opposed to the players standing on equal footing with the owners. Lord knows he wished he had had such an opportunity. But now that the players had the advantage, he thought it wrong for them to abuse, especially the way Ty was doing it, negotiating in the press and courts. To him there was a clear difference between getting what one deserves and holding out for whatever one could get.

Then, too, he realized, the free-spending owners were equally to blame. How a group of businessmen could fork over salaries that bore little connection to the laws of supply and demand, he'd never understand. *Why, they use less care in throwing money around than we do in applying fertilizer. I guess they think it's made out of the same substance.*

But what really bothered him was what he saw it doing to the game and the fans who supported it. Perhaps therein lay the answer. As simple as it sounded, Luke thought, if everyone would sit down and agree to put the game and fans first—and not just pay them lip service—answers would emerge. Instead, each side usually put itself first. As a result, the owners and players unwittingly were shifting the focus from the competition on the field to the exchange of money off it. "I guess I wouldn't be concerned so long as it didn't affect their play. But that's a hard thing for many of them. Sooner or later the edge seems to wear off."

"Intensity?" Derrick asked between sips of beer.

"Yeah, intensity's a good word. I mean, a ballplayer can't wait until he gets to the stadium to think about the game—the great ones know that. Those who don't, well, they find that it's a long-assed half step between safe and out."

"I guess baseball's become like everything else nowadays; it's just a big business. Sorta like farming," Derrick explained.

"Sad but true, my friend," Luke sighed. There was that nasty word, "business." Agents, arbitration, contract disputes, renegotiation, lockouts, walkouts, and strikes—Luke saw them as lethal knives cutting into the sport's hide. Players change teams. Teams change owners. Owners change cities. Loyalty lasted only as long as the next contract, and sometimes not even that long. Luke had kept such thoughts to himself during spring training. He realized many players might think he was as out of touch. But in his mind, he saw the game from his rural acreage as America saw it.

Derrick stopped chewing. His hard roll bulged inside his cheek, replacing the usual chaw of tobacco. "Well, what would you ask for if you were playin'?"

"That's a good question." Luke balled up his sandwich foil and tossed it toward the trash pail. *Swish.* "But then, it's one I don't have to worry about."

Most assuredly, financial remuneration was not at the root of Luke's goals in life—or else why would he have chosen cattle ranching? The "fat cattle" as the Black Angus were called might yield $1,000 or $1,200 apiece at next year's auction—the bulls a $100 more. Out of those gross receipts Luke subtracted the cost of maintaining the herd and upkeeping the land for grazing. Then there was the servicing of the buildings, fencing and equipment. Yes, he and Kate had decided to trade wealth for their love of the farming life. That, not money, gave them happiness.

Luke's earnings off the ranch were modest, and his pension was all that he had to show for playing ball. Oh, he had saved money, but an ill-timed investment with a financial adviser who suckered in more than a dozen athletes left the Hanlons near bankruptcy in the mid-'70s.

"I've noticed you haven't been wearing your glasses. You get contacts?" Derrick asked.

"No, I just don't need 'em as much." Luke found it strange but his eyesight seemed to be improving. He had begun to think that it might have something to do with Doc's medicine.

More than Luke's vision changed. A week later, after a morning round of feedings, he encountered Kate peeling carrots at the kitchen sink. He wrapped his arms around her waist, bringing a halt to her harmonizing with the radio. "Morning. All done with the feedings?"

"For the morning, yes." Luke nestled against her head and inhaled the scent of her shampoo. "Say, you smell good."

"You're easy to please. I'm not wearing anything," Kate said, laying her head aside his while continuing to peel. "Just think what I can save on perfume."

"I need to find me something else to do. Any ideas?"

"Why don't you just take it easy? You've been keeping a pretty good pace most of the summer."

"So?"

"All work and no play eventually catches up with you."

Play, Luke thought. *Okay, I'll play.* He kissed the nape of her neck and slid his hands down the front of her peasant dress, coming to rest on her lower abdomen.

"Hey, what are you up to?" she exclaimed, slightly amused. She glanced at the digital display on the microwave. "Your body clock is all off. It's only 10:20. This is morning, remember."

"I don't need a clock to tell me when to hold the woman I love." He moved his hands down the cotton dress and rubbed the insides of her thighs.

Kate jerked forward, nearly doubling over. "Listen, you...." She grabbed the dish towel lying near the sink, wiped her hands and spun around. Luke trapped her between himself and the cabinet. He pressed his body against her and smiled.

Kate wrapped the towel around his neck and returned the embrace. They kissed, then parted. "You smell like you've been hanging out with the cows again."

"I was. That's when I decided you'd make better company."

Kate threw her head back and laughed heartily.

He knew she didn't really mind the earthy "aroma." She had often said how she found the scent a pleasant one. He kissed her again, this time longer.

Breaking apart, Kate rubbed herself against him and whispered, "How 'bout containing yourself 'till later on? You know, I'm going to have to call Adrian and tell him what he's really created is an aphrodisiac."

As quickly as throwing on a saddle, Luke reached down and pulled up her skirt, baring her stockingless legs up to her full thighs. "What's wrong with right here, Kitten?"

Kate knocked his hands away and brushed her dress down in quick, repetitive strokes. "Yeah, with Derrick or Bret liable to walk in at any moment."

"Ah, they're both gone. But if you insist, guess we could move to the living room."

"All right. Hold this." Kate gave him the bowl of carrots as she tossed aside the dish towel. It was enough of a distraction to get away. The race ensued into the living room, around the landing and up the staircase. Luke followed close behind, giving his better half enough of a lead to trap herself in the bedroom. He entered and shut the door. Kate stared back with a resigned look from her seat on the bed.

Luke had his prey where he wanted her. But in this case, he figured the hunted welcomed being caught.

14
Clear Evidence

Luke engaged Bret in a game of pitch and hit, just as he and his dad had done half a century before. Only instead of hiking down to a park near the polluted Mahoning River, these generations got together in a three-acre horse corral. While it was unusually large for four horses, Luke had sunk the fenceposts years before with thoughts of playing ball, first with David and now with his youngest who was on summer vacation.

The worn spots marking the pitcher's mound and bases were all but grown over. Just enough remained for today's two players to situate themselves. And out in center on the top slat, one barely could make out the hand-lettered, black numbers "375."

Once more it was Hanlon against Hanlon, father against son. The pitch flew plateward. It had good velocity, but the batter still connected and sent it far, far away, well beyond the faded distance marker in center.

"Nice shot. That was one of my better sinking fastballs," Bret shouted.

Yes, it was Luke who was being served the pitches. For a fleeting moment, the retired ballplayer saw himself standing at home on a dirt field in Northern Ohio. There he took cuts at his father's pitches of recycled baseballs made whole again by his mother while she sat listening to her Crosley radio. To save her fingers, Mom alternated between fashioning fabrics into family garments and restitching the rawhide on the balls Luke pummeled.

"Give me one of your high, hard ones," Luke shouted to Bret.

His son rotated the ball behind his back and stared in at the truck tire affixed to a wooden backstop rescued from obscurity in the barn. He fired. *Thud.* The ball collided with the plywood and fell harmlessly into the hollow tire. Somehow it had managed to elude Luke's vicious cut. Bret percolated a wide grin.

Grabbing a handful of dirt, Luke scuffed his feet several times and stared at the pitcher. Bret was no longer his son; he was the opposition.

The young man took a full wind-up and released another one plateward. Luke studied the rotation—plenty of topspin. Taken together with the cross body motion, he read it as a curve. Sure enough, the ball tailed down and away. He strode into the dancing ball. *Smack.* He nailed it high and far, over the opposite field fence in right, where it banged against the barn's roof. It was Luke's turn to smile, but he didn't say a word. Instead, Bret spoke. "That probably would've made it out of old Crosley."

Probably not, Luke thought. *Three hundred sixty-six feet to right, and up another thirty-some rows of grandstands. Then again, there was no roof on that ballpark to stop it.* Didn't matter. What mattered, was that after more than twenty-five years away from the game, Luke Hanlon once again was having fun hitting a baseball. More like ecstasy. The thrill of connecting off a pitcher's best stuff. Add to it the thrill of being able to throw with velocity and without pain.

Luke realized he had Doc to thank for his miraculous turnaround. His shoulder ache was long gone. The treatments allowed him to do things no longer thought possible. He knew little about how the drug worked. Yet, he could not deny its role in helping him to get around on a pitch.

Luke laced another curveball on a line to the left side of the simulated diamond. It died quickly beneath tufts of clover.

"Let's see that hummer again." Luke twirled the bat with renewed confidence. He wanted another chance at his son's 85 mile an hour heater. In it came and out it went, the ball smashing into the top fence board in left with such force that it sent wood chips flying. "Uh oh, looks like some more repair work," Luke whispered to himself, smiling.

Bret took a slow walk over to the water bucket that sat by the fence. He removed his hat and wiped his brow. "The way you're hitting, Pop, you ought to get back in the bigs. Just think of the salary you could land."

"You mean I could hold some team hostage?"

Bret took a gulp from the ladle and exhaled his words. "I don't think you'd have to demand anything. They'd throw money at you."

"That's the problem. When I played, the owners counted every penny. Today, they act like dollars were pennies."

"For the big names, that's true. But what about the guys who struggle to get to majors and barely stay for a cup of coffee?"

Luke knew there was some truth in what Bret said. He had read where 15 percent of ballplayers ate up half the salary pot. "If they go into the game for the right reason, they'll get their reward."

"Tell me you don't wish you had earned a couple of million."

"And what would I do with it all?"

"Give it to your children," Bret grinned.

"Now that would be a dumb thing," Luke said, walking back to the oversized beanbag that served as home plate. "C'mon, get out there and throw."

Bret smoothed the dirt and adjusted his cap. He choked the ball in the palm of his hand, gripping it across the wide seams—a change-up. Compared to the previous pitches, this one seemed to take an eternity to reach the plate.

Luke recognized the pitch. Patience and timing were the key. He kept his weight on his back foot until the ball seemingly had arrived at the plate. Then, within a fraction of a second, he set his swing in motion. *Crunch.* The sound of spanked rawhide signaled that Bret once again had failed to get it by his father. If Luke had a blind spot, it certainly wasn't at the plate.

Inside the family clubhouse, the Hanlon clan gathered for a late summer cookout. Time was running out for such seasonal get-togethers. In a week Bret would be leaving for his junior year at UC.

Kate slid a black raspberry pie—Bret's favorite—into the lower oven rack. Nearby, Megan shredded carrots over side salads.

"Hey, guys, this isn't some ballfield!" Kate reprimanded. "Back outside and leave the shoes at the door, please."

"Sorry, Kitten," Luke said. He hung on the door frame and removed his sneakers. He was in a jovial mood. "I always thought people ought to have stayed with dirt floors."

"You're hopeless, Luke Hanlon." Kate shook her head then continued. "How's Bret's pitching coming along?"

"His curve's lookin' much better," Luke replied, digging into the relish tray and crunching a celery stick. He caught a knowing look from his son and returned a wink.

"Well, that's good news," Kate cheered.

"Dad's being kind. Judging by the way he handled 'em, I've got some work to do," Bret said, leaning his Chippendale frame against the counter. Luke grabbed the newspaper and headed for the solitude of the family room.

Megan stopped peeling radish curls and looked up. "What's this, Dad was hitting against you?"

"He hit about everything I had to throw."

"Mom's been telling me about that medicine he's been taking." Megan looked to her mom. "She said he's been acting like he's twenty. But I never thought...."

"I saw proof of that today," Bret was quick to add.

"I'll tell you, if they ever market that product, I'll buy some,"

Kate said. "I'd welcome a few years taken off."

"Hey, you're in pretty good shape, Mom," Bret countered, wrapping his arm around her shoulders.

"That's sweet of you. No, I didn't mean appearances. It's just, well, sometimes your father makes me feel like my get up and go got up and went," she said, laughing at her own line. "Maybe I just need to stop trying to keep up with him." Kate placed a potholder and casserole dish on the cottage table. "Dinner's served!"

As they took their seats, Megan called to mind the missing family member. "What d'you hear from David?"

"When was it he called, last Saturday?" Kate asked.

"Yeah. They're all doing real well. Tracy starts third grade next week." Luke was glad to hear the conversation shift to something besides his medicine. The talk of it was starting to become a pain. "And guess who's pregnant?"

"Sheila!" Megan cheered, dropping her fork and wiping her mouth.

"Luke," Kate chastised. "I thought we were going to let them surprise everyone over Labor Day."

"Oh, we'll act surprised when they announce it," Megan said.

"Please do," Kate sighed. "Although it looks like just Sheila and Tracy are coming."

Luke registered concern. "How come?" It hurt that David didn't come down more often.

"He doesn't think he'll be able to get away. You know how it is with his fall season," Kate answered, referring to their son's business.

Luke's disappointment was softened by David's success. His oldest had taken a few years to get his life in order, but he now seemed on the right path. Luke figured he owed most of it to Sheila.

After David had dropped out of college, Luke tried helping out, opening doors for him to become an illustrator with a Chicago ad agency—he had majored in art for two years at Ohio State. Luke realized later he should have forgotten the favor. David lasted one friction-filled year before it was mutually agreed that it would be best if he left. He'd only be satisfied with being top dog.

A series of construction jobs provided David some income over the next several years. During that time he met and married Sheila. It was she, Luke realized, who injected David with the confidence to start his own business. David's new calling utilized both his tradesman skills and his creative talents. It involved designing and building customized closets. With people's ever increasing need for storage space, David's company thrived.

"Speaking of babies," Bret interjected, reaching for the butter. "D'you see where Ty Hartmann was hit with a paternity suit?"

"He shouldn't have much trouble paying for it with $10 million a year," Megan declared.

Luke shook his head. "The Yankees really got the short end of the stick with him." Luke was alluding to the fact that even before the latest news, Ty already had missed two months of the season with a torn hamstring.

"I was talking with one of my fraterity brothers out East. He says the word around New York is that Ty's been hitting the bottle a bit much," Bret explained.

"Dealing with the press out there could do that to you." Luke hated to see the sensationalizing of a player's life— even Ty's—taking up more space than what he did on the field. "Pass the corn, please."

"They're nice and fresh. Megan picked them this afternoon."

"It's been great all season," Luke bragged. Food was tasting better in general these days. Again, he wondered whether it had anything to do with what Doc was feeding him. He had a number of questions to ask during his checkup that Friday.

15
The Results

Nurse Metzger was missing when Luke entered the treatment room at the Caulfield Science Center for his next appointment. Instead, Dr. Dornhoffer, wearing his white lab coat, greeted him.

Normally not one to worry about health matters, Luke sensed something was up. Clearly, he had undergone enough tests during his visits that the doctors were capable of finding a single cold germ were it hiding somewhere in his body. His checkups included the usual external readings and blood tests. But of late there had been an increased number of invasive procedures.

Luke figured if there were a medical test, he had had it. Still, he would not fret over bad news. He always had played the cards life dealt him. He just wanted to know what the cards were. "Okay, Doc, what'd you find out?"

"Relax. You're fine, Luke. A remarkably healthy specimen." Doc slid his hand from his coat pocket and played with his earlobe. "No, it's the study that I wanted to talk with you about. We've had to suspend it. And since I was the one who coaxed you into it, I thought I ought to be the one to explain what happened."

"Something wrong with the drug?"

"Not quite. If anything, it works too well—far better than we ever imagined," Doc chuckled. "We need to take time to understand its true capabilities."

Luke nodded. He reflected on what the drug had done for him—for his shoulder, his knees, his reflexes, his strength and his overall energy level. Then too, there was the thrill he had playing ball with Bret. "As I mentioned when you and Pat were at the house, it's done more for me than I ever expected."

"And you're not the only one." Doc put on his Franklin glasses and picked up a stuffed folder. He flipped through the clipped pages and stopped at a yellow *Post-It©* note. "To give you an idea of what we're seeing...." Doc read from the medical file:

> A 47-year-old female. Claimed total relief from pain related to damage around the third lumbar disc. The disc itself had been removed four years before. CAT scan showed it to be completely restored!

Doc looked over his glasses, then thumbed through several more pages. He stopped at the next yellow slip.

> A 35-year-old male subject. Regained complete feeling and mobility in right hand. Sensation had been partially lost as a result of nerves being severed in a circular saw accident. Transmission of nerve impulses confirmed with electromyogram.

Doc flipped through the sheets without looking up and read from another case history.

> A 58-year-old female, suffering from osteoporosis with accompanying back pain and curvature of the spine. Regained nearly 2 inches in height through improved posture and apparent bone growth. Pre-post densonometer readings clearly established increased calcium density levels in bone structure.

"And this next one really amazed me,"

> A 39-year-old female with previously diagnosed
> heart murmur in lower left ventricle valve resulting from
> rheumatic fever during childhood. Detected a marked
> decrease in murmur throughout the course of treat-
> ment. Ultrasonogram at week 10 displayed no
> discernable damage to subject valve.

The reports held Luke spellbound. If he hadn't experienced the drug himself, he would have found such accounts hard to believe. But he, too, had experienced dramatic changes.

"Oh, and you'll enjoy this last one," Doc announced with enthusiasm, looking at Luke.

> A 53-year-old marathon runner claimed a signifi-
> cant increase in stamina. Won 10-K race, improving
> time by 14 minutes over 10-year best. Reported finish-
> ing ahead of three previous winners, the oldest of whom
> was 28!

Doc popped the file closed and smiled at Luke, who said, "Well, you can add my story to those."

"Oh, you're in here, all right. We've received similar reports from each of the five clinics. Many of the findings are less dramatic, but nonetheless remarkable—individuals needing new eyeglasses because their prescriptions were suddenly too *strong*. Others with documented hearing improvement. I must say, it's amazed even me!"

"And here I thought you knew everything there was to know about medicine," Luke quipped, standing up.

"For everything scientists know, Luke, there are probably a thousand things we don't—and I'm no different. But thanks for the compliment."

"Have any idea how one drug was able to do all that?"

"Yes and no. We have some pretty good data on what's going on inside the cells—you need to understand there are over 250 different tissue types inside your body. Each one has a corresponding gene that suppresses cell mitosis or reproduction. Yet, it seems that this one particular gene we've been using neutralizes most, if not all, of the different suppressor genes."

"So instead of just helping my muscles, it's been making all my body parts grow?"

"To some degree." Doc raised his hand. "The gene doesn't order cells to reproduce—no, that's controlled by other genes. Rather, it allows the orders to be carried out when the body senses a need for specific tissue cells to reproduce."

Luke noted that Doc emphasized certain words: *doesn't order, allows for.* "Well if the—gene, you say?" Doc nodded to Luke, who continued. "If this gene works in the same way for all cells, what's the problem?"

"Well, there is always the risk of the unknown. We've established that it has broader implications than we originally thought. What we don't know are its limits." Doc pulled a pen from his shirt pocket and twirled it end to end. "For example, it's understandable that it would act on the regenerative cells, say muscle tissue. But there are a number of tissues we call non-regenerative—the heart, nerves and even certain types of muscle. These normally stop reproducing early on in our lives. Yet, we've seen where this drug affects even those cells."

Luke nodded. While his scientific knowledge was limited, his own experience helped him digest what Doc had to say.

"Oh, and by the way, we ask that you say nothing about this to anyone—other than Kate."

"Gotcha."

"We must keep this very quiet. The youth-elixir claims are ripe for fraud. We'd have the charlatans and peddlers flocking here faster than flies on your cow chips."

"I can imagine," Luke said, smiling. He enjoyed Doc's earthy analogies. "It's a shame you've got to stop the study, though."

"It's for everyone's protection."

"How long d'you figure before you might start it up again?"

"Oh, I imagine it'll be quite a while, at least insofar as human clinicals. The FDA is going to want to see a lot more testing." Doc widened his bushy white eyebrows and changed his tone. "I've been doing most of the talking. Did you have any questions?"

Luke shrugged. "Oh, just about what I can expect. You know, now that I'm going off the drug?"

"The improvement you've seen in injured tissues should remain. As for your general body changes—increased strength, lung capacity and so forth—you're likely to see them return to a pre-clinical condition."

"So my shoulder shouldn't start acting up again?"

"Not unless you re-injure it."

Luke resigned himself to the study's end. Never one to believe in quick fixes, he had figured it was too good to last. Life would go on. It always had. He was prepared to accept whatever it held in store for him and Kate; growing old together, he didn't mind that at all.

"If you can find something to do for half an hour, I'll buy you lunch."

"Thanks. But I gotta be getting on—I have some chores to take care of before I go back to being an old man."

"You'll never be old, Luke." Doc squinted and pointed to his temple. "It's all in the mind."

16
The Season Ends

"Tomorrow will be better, Mr. Hartmann." Yankee clubhouse man Hector Morales spoke in broken English.

Ty nodded and slipped on his team windbreaker, while Hector went back to collecting the dirty towels, socks and jocks that hadn't quite made it into the laundry hampers. The ballplayer slouched out of the locker room, the last to leave the "House that Ruth built" after another frustrating loss. A mirror hanging by the last locker flashed him a look. He examined a cut on his cheek, then stared at his right eye. There it was again—the tiny flicker. He saw it, then he didn't. It seemed to dog him as much as the strikeouts. He thought about the end of the season. Time off. Time to get away and rest.

Tonight, Ty was graceful in defeat. Resigned was a more apt description. He realized he had only so much fight in him before his spirit wore down. Deep down there came a point where fleeing was the more painful route. *What stories will they write if I'm not there? They'll probably just speculate that the paternity suit has me running away. Ty Hartmann doesn't run away from anything or anybody.*

Ty found something refreshing about facing up to his shortcomings. It was his crucifixion and redemption. Whatever, he had hung around answering reporters' questions for the better part of half an hour. Questions focused on his stranding five runners, including three who filled the bases in the bottom of the ninth, when a single would have sent the game into extra innings. It wasn't such an unreasonable question to ask of the $10-million-dollar man.

As the clock wound down on this September Sunday, thirteen regular season games remained. The Bronx Bombers had just dropped four games behind Boston. Every day meant one less opportunity to make up ground on the high-flying Red Sox. Every day put the boys from Beantown one step closer to the Division championship. And the Central Division's Milwaukee club had a leg up on the Yanks for the lone Wild Card playoff spot.

Ty made the lonely walk through the stadium's catacombs. Up above were the box seats where just ninety minutes before fickle fans set their beers on the ground and implored the walking sports-bank to get a hit. Instead, he had struck out.

Shuffling up the two short flights of steps, his eyes cast downward, his confidence submerged in an eddy of missed opportunities, Ty found consolation in the twenty-plus years of spit and gum embedded in the cement. The percentages said that many who had walked that way also had hung their heads in defeat.

He bid goodnight to the security guard standing beneath the "Yankee Offices" sign. The officer pushed open the glass doors, and Ty entered the twilight. A timely exit. For he had been living in the twilight zone for much of the year, rather than the zone great hitters usually talk about.

The air was filled with the smell of roasted peanuts, pretzels and exhaust fumes. A handful of fans begged Ty for his autograph. He scratched his name on a pair of hats, a yearbook and a baseball card before turning to a white-haired, black gentleman hidden in the shadows. Ty stared blankly at the hunched figure. "You got something you'd like me to sign?"

The senior citizen stood his ground, his mouth half opened. Ty waited and waited, but all he received was a stare. In the background, the constant "whoosh" from cars flashing by on the Major Deegan expressway went unnoticed.

After a minute, Ty shook his head and stepped off the stoop. The man spoke. "Nah, I don't want no autographs, Ty. But a nice hello would do."

Ty halted in mid-step and turned around. From that angle the lamplight hit the stranger square in the face. The voice was a bit frail, almost hoarse, but the features came into focus. "Sam?"

"Hey, you remembered your old friend." Sam Wilkins grinned. After eight years and some rather unkind treatment by Father Time, Ty remembered.

Sam embraced his grown-up protege and patted his back as a tear dripped onto Ty's navy jacket.

"Say, man, you're looking great," Ty said, backing up.

"Remember, son, I taught you always to tell the truth," Sam laughed. "You sure look good."

"Thanks. Physically, I'm feelin' pretty good."

"How's the hamstring?"

"Oh, that doesn't bother me so much now. They tape it real tight before each game."

"You turned out to be one heck of a ballplayer, Ty. But then I told you y'would, didn't I?"

"You did at that."

It had been a long time since the one-time Negro League ballplayer, war hero and school janitor had seen Ty close up—too long. Ty had exchanged a few letters and Christmas cards, but all that ended four years before, when Ty moved into his Arizona hacienda. He had seen fit to notify only his immediate family of his whereabouts at the time.

Ty wrapped an arm around Sam. "You got a car?"

Sam shook his head. "You forget, I stopped drivin' a long time ago. I haven't owned a vehicle since that green Rambler gave out."

"C'mon, I'll give you a lift. We can grab a bite and catch up on old times." The thought lifted Ty's spirits. He was pleased to renew acquaintances. But there was more. Sam would serve as a diversion, an antidote for the afternoon's disappointments. He led his friend across the brick promenade to the lot used by Yankee players and officials. A two-story cyclone fence separated the Porsches, Jags, Lexuses and Ty's Lamborghini Countach from those who contributed toward their lease payments.

"Okay. Something simple would do me fine."

Ty thought how he probably threw out better food than Sam ate on most good days. He pressed the accelerator on his sports car—one of four he owned—and pointed it in the direction of his apartment in Cliffside Park, New Jersey. The low profile roadster shifted lanes, dodging the approaching brake lights until the Sunday traffic choked his passage at the George Washington Bridge exit.

As the car inched along, Ty coaxed Sam into updating him on his life. Sam told him how his funds were indeed low and how he had fallen short of the years needed to qualify for a pension from the school system. He survived on Social Security and meager benefits from the Veterans Administration. Still, the tone of Sam's voice rose and fell, signaling his happiness. "When you get to be my age, you don't need too much. And you don't do too much. I just thank the good Lord for letting me get up in the morning."

"You still living in Newark?"

"Yeah, but I got me a new place. Had to."

"How's that?"

"Guess you could say I was evicted by one of those big-time developers." Sam explained how they had torn down his three-story apartment building and erected a skyscraper in its place. "They say you can see New York City from the top floors."

With a penthouse of his own, Ty could relate to that. He kept the focus on Sam. "You got some friends in your new place?"

"Picked me up a stray dog. He's old like me. Him an' me, we get along fine." Sam paused while Ty shifted into high gear and outran a yellow light. "How d'you like being back home? You know, now that you're a Yankee?"

"Good. But then, it has its disadvantages. Everyone expects so much more around here." Ty drove underneath the blue pagoda canopy that sheltered the Palisadium Restaurant.

"You live in one of those?" Sam motioned toward a high-rise out his window.

"No, that one up there." Ty pointed to the newer, grandiose structure towering beyond the tennis courts and overlooking the river.

Two valets sprang to greet the arriving passengers. Sam strained to pull himself through the gull wing door. He looked at the marble steps leading to the silver trimmed entrance. "D'we need a coat in here?"

"Not to worry," Ty reassured. He led Sam through the elegant hallway with its oriental carpeting and artworks.

"Good evening, Mr. Hartmann." A tuxedo-clad maitre d' greeted.

"Hey there, Julio."

"Will it just be the two of you tonight?"

"Right."

The mustached host feigned indifference at Sam's appearance. Yet, his eyes made several passes at Sam's wrinkled khaki slacks and cotton sweater with its grease stain near the collar. Ty figured Julio knew better than to question one of his best customers about the company he kept. Hell, the tip he threw his way at Christmas was more than most residents spent on a month of dinners.

Julio escorted them into the casual dining area, a brass-trimmed atrium set on the Palisades, overlooking the marshlands 500 feet below. Their window seats afforded a panoramic view of New York's West Side. On this particular evening, the curtain of haze had been lifted, and one could observe the tapered-top towers of midtown Manhattan, highlighted by the yellow glow of the Chrysler steeple and the Empire State Building's red, white and blue lights. Try as he might, Ty could not help but think about Yankee Stadium situated over there. He fought to block it from his mind just as the Bronx apartments shielded it from view.

"You didn't have to pick such a fancy place on account of me," Sam explained in a hoarse whisper.

"I owe you more than this."

"Owe me? For what?"

"For all the help you gave me back in high school."

"You'd have been a great ballplayer without me, Ty."

"Hey, you kept up my interest in the game when I could have been getting into things I shouldn't have. Anyway, this is one place where I know we can have some privacy."

An Oriental girl in her early twenties approached the table and waited for a break in their conversation. "Can I get you gentlemen something from the bar?"

"What would you like there, Sam?"

"A cola b'fine."

Ty flashed his best photo-shot smile at the hostess. He saw innocence in her almond eyes. "Make mine a double of *Absolut* straight up. And see if you can get us a couple of menus. My friend and I are real hungry."

"I'll be right back."

"Thanks, babe." Ty bridged his fingertips and watched the girl's movement as she retreated to the bar. He turned back to Sam. "So, what keeps you busy these days?"

"I get together with some friends at the senior citizen club. Play some cards. Watch some ballgames on TV—I've seen you play quite a bit."

Ty forced a grin, "I hope you've seen me more than this year."

Sam's face tightened, and Ty saw the Sam from years before, the one who counseled him in the empty gymnasium. Sam locked his eyes on him "What happened, Ty?"

Ty pressed his shoulders back in the chair and spoke matter-of-factly, out of the side of his mouth. "I never really had a chance to get it in gear this season. You probably read where I started spring late. Then I had the layoff while I waited to sign. Not being in condition, well, my hamstring just popped. As you once said, it's hard to get it going when you don't play regularly." He closed with a deep, nervous laugh.

The waitress returned, saving Ty from further explanations. He stroked her arm as she set out the drinks. "You have such incredibly smooth skin." She murmered a polite "thank you" and placed a menu in his hands.

After a toast, Ty offered a prediction. "Just wait till next year, Sam. Things are gonna be a lot different."

"I read about the paternity suit."

Sam's words shattered Ty's crystal ball. The ballplayer nodded as he took a drink and exhaled an answer. "Okay... okay, I admit I've had my troubles. But hey, everyone can have a string of bad luck."

The words trailed off, but Sam continued to stare back. Ty shifted in his seat. What he had thought was going to be an enjoyable re-union was turning into an unsettling experience. He looked out the window and wished that he was somewhere else, lost in the Big Apple or aboard the pleasure boat he saw cruising up the Hudson. Anywhere but here, facing Sam's grilling. He played with the corner of his napkin. "I didn't go seeking out problems, Sam."

"Sometimes if we let them, problems seek us out."

"What are you saying? That I should have stayed with the Reds?"

"You're the one who had to make that call, Ty. But keep in mind it's our fortunes, not fortune, that count." After a pause Sam broke into a chuckle, "Maybe it's me in my old age, but I'd sure find it hard to keep my mind on the game while keepin' track of all the lady-friends, contract issues...."

Ty didn't let him finish. "Things are different." Ty thought how much Sam was out of touch with the modern world, his world. Life was far more complex. The old rules didn't always apply. There were a lot more distractions, for one thing. There was far more exposure from all the modern media, and with that came friends, followers, money and girls. What was he to do? Hole up in his apartment and go out for ballgames and family gatherings? Hell, he had put up with a lot in earning his money, so why couldn't he enjoy it? He had put up with a lot in life, period. It was time to reap the rewards and forget about the past. "Life isn't so simple anymore, Sam."

"Even if it was—and I don't deny that it isn't—should the approach to the game be any different? After all, what's most important?"

"I hear you, Sam." Ty returned to his bravado voice. Again, there was the "devil-may-care" laughter Ty used so effectively so often. He thought how he wasn't in high school anymore. It was Sam's turn to listen. "I'm already thinking ahead to next year. I'm going to show up early for camp. I plan to have an MVP season, you watch."

"You can if you stay focused. Remember that when I'm not around."

"Hey, don't talk like that, Sam."

Sam erupted into laughter. "I didn't mean it quite that way. But now that you mention it, I am living on borrowed time. Aren't too many of the guys I hung around with left. Don't misunderstand, I'm not throwing in the towel, not yet."

"How'd you like to come live with me?"

"I snore a lot."

"I didn't mean in my place! There are a couple of empty units up there. I was thinking of picking one up as an investment. Pay me whatever you're paying for your place in Newark. I'll still make money when I sell it."

Sam laughed. "I'd be afraid to walk there without taking my shoes off. Besides, there're some folks who depend on me where I live. No thanks, I'm fine where I am."

The waitress returned. She made it a point to stand out of Ty's reach. "Have you gentlemen decided?"

"Give us another minute," Ty replied. He retrieved his menu, although he wasn't as hungry as when they arrived.

17
Time For Healing

Luke laid aside his newspaper and looked across the living room at Kate. "You all right?"

"I'm just a little dizzy," sighed Kate. She leaned forward in her armchair and rested her head in her palm.

It was the second time that day she had complained of dizziness. Luke made dinner, but Kate touched little, saying she felt nauseous. She fixed herself a cup of tea. That was an hour and a half ago. Since then she seemed fine as she occupied herself with cross-stitching.

Luke listened to the droning sound of a passing car; weeknight traffic was rare on their country road. He glanced again at Kate. She returned a smile, which Luke thought a bit forced but he decided not to press the issue. Instead, he opened the sports pages and scanned the headlines.

ST. LOUIS TAKES OVER 1ST WITH EIGHTH IN ROW.

He realized it mattered little at this point. The Reds were mired in fourth place, eighteen games out with just a week left in the season. Turning the page, his eye was attracted to another banner.

LANGLEY TO LEAD LIST OF FREE AGENTS.

Ah, getting to be that time of year. Stories of pennant races and World Series predictions now shared space with articles on the upcoming player auction. Of course, that was appropriate, Luke thought, seeing how the auction sales dwarfed Series revenue.

"Uuhh." Kate's utterance raised Luke's concern; she rarely expressed pain. She let her cross-stitching slide off her lap. It plopped on the hardwood and stirred Rusty, lying near the window on a braided oval rug. Bloodshot rings came slowly into view around the dog's chestnut eyes as he fluffed out his ears. He followed Luke to the couch.

Except for her hospitalization with the rare infection, Kate had been a picture of health. Luke knelt and took her free hand between his. "What's wrong?"

She squeezed her eyes closed. "I've got this shooting pain that radiates up the back of my neck and...oohhhh...."

He laid his hand on her forehead. *Good. At least there's no fever.* "Let me take you to the couch." She murmured an "okay." Reaching under her knees and back, he felt her full weight; she seemed much heavier than in those times when he swept her in his arms. Laying her down ever so softly, Luke propped a throw pillow under her head. He listened to her labored breathing and brushed back her hair.

Kate raised her hand and motioned as if to grab her neck. "Oohhhhh...my heaaa...Luu." The halting delivery frightened him. And the tone, so much deeper than the soft, airy voice he knew. Luke leaned in closer in search of answers that weren't there. Her head jerked side to side. "Easy, Kate. I'll call Doc Clemmons."

His voice seemed to bring her around. Her eyes became tiny slits, and she tightened her grip on his hand. "I lo—ve you, Luke."

Luke planted a kiss on her forehead. "I love you too, honey. Rest now." Luke stayed there another minute until she faded off into unconsciousness. He grabbed the phone and pressed a programmed number, not for Dr. Clemmons, but for the hospital.

"Yes, this is the Hanlon residence in Millville. My wife's taken ill....Yes, it's an emergency....She's unconscious now....We need an ambulance out here right away...." Luke thought back on his own words, words that had come automatically. "It's an emergency...." He twisted the phone wire, inserting his fingers between the loops, before stopping to rub Rusty's back.

Relax, he told himself. *No paralysis...maybe just another flare-up of Toxomosis or whatever it's called...although she was just checked by Doc Dornhoffer last month.* This was different: the sudden onset, the shooting pain. He stared at Kate's restless body and half listened to the dispatcher's measured voice.

Luke gave directions for the ambulance, then dashed up the stairs and grabbed two blankets from the closet. He hurdled the last few steps on the way down. Kneeling alongside Kate, he unbuttoned her corduroy skirt to ease her breathing, then covered her. "Kate?" No response. He felt her pulse and waited for the sweep second hand to complete the quarter of a minute. *24 beats. 96 a minute.*

Usually patient, Luke found the wait for the ambulance intolerable. For one of the few times in his life, he felt utterly helpless. He only could watch as every so often Kate's body jerked, or she emitted some unrecognizable sound. He shifted between holding her hand and pacing by the window. Her state of unconsciousness concerned him most. The last time, he had driven her to the hospital *before* she had lost consciousness.

When the vehicle arrived, the pace quickened. Luke stood by, answering several questions, while two white-coat clad paramedics wheeled in a stretcher, lowered its height by the couch and slid Kate onto it. The bearded driver spoke to Luke. "D'you want to follow us over in your car?"

"Huh?" Luke answered, preoccupied by the sight of Kate being strapped to the gurney. "No, if it's not a problem, I'd just as soon ride with my wife." He wanted to be by her side.

"That's fine. Okay, guys, ready to roll?"

Kate's body settled down on the ride to the hospital. The head spasms eased, while the oxygen mask suppressed any sounds. Luke sat in silence, but his insides were churning. He continued to hold her hand, occasionally rubbing the back of it with his thumb. The only time he let go was while the orderly hooked her up to a monitor and inserted an IV. Tubes, wires, mask and needles all served to underscore the seriousness of the situation.

Luke listened to the muffled sound of the siren and shifted his gaze from Kate to the rainbow of colors flashing on the passing trees. Thoughts of his fading energy—he'd been off treatment for six weeks— seemed so insignificant now. Just having Kate feel healthy was so much more important. He consoled himself with the thought that she now was receiving medical care. *Hopefully, the doctors will diagnose her condition quicker than last time.*

One of the attendants radioed ahead with her condition. Luke hung on each word. "Yes, we have a patient here in a comatose state. Her blood pressure is 160 over 90. Her heartbeat is irregular, with a pulse of 98. Temperature is 99.3."

The pace quickened upon arrival at McCullough-Hyde hospital in Oxford. The white coats sprang from the ambulance, removed the stretcher and wheeled it through swinging doors to an examination room. Luke followed close on their heels. He stood in the background as the medical team went to work, removing Kate's top garments, hooking her up to monitors and transferring her oxygen supply. A grey-haired physician who seemed in charge whispered to a nurse. The woman nodded and approached Luke, advising him he would have to leave the room. "We'll keep you posted as soon as there's any news," she explained, leading him to the front desk where he filled out some papers and a surgery consent form.

Five minutes later, Dr. Clemmons, the family doctor, arrived. He spoke briefly with Luke, then headed back to join the attending physicians.

For the next thirty minutes, Luke flipped through magazines. He found it impossible to concentrate long enough to read a story. At one point, Dr. Clemmons came out to advise him on her course of therapy. "They suspect an aneurysm. They've given her some medication to slow her pulse." Luke asked a few questions to which Dr. Clemmons apologized for not having the answers. "They'll be taking her upstairs for a CAT scan. She's in good hands, Luke. Fortunately, Dr. Weingart is on duty. He's an excellent neurologist."

Aneurysm. The word shook Luke. *Oh God, take care of Kate.* He spent another twenty minutes in prayer before the nurse approached again and led him back to a consultation room, saying only that the doctor wanted to see him. *Will they want my permission to operate? Brain surgery. Serious stuff. Here's hoping they take her to one of the university hospitals in Clifton.* Luke entered the box-like room, and the nurse closed the door behind him. Dr. Clemmons, seated on the corner of a plain white table, stood. "Luke, they took her upstairs and...." He paused as his eyes fell to the floor. "They didn't get a chance.... I'm sorry, we've lost her." Luke buried his head in the physician's shoulder. Dr. Clemmons cried along with Luke.

Funerals by nature are sad affairs. This one was no exception. Why a women as lovely as Kate was struck down at her age was beyond Luke's capacity to understand. *Why not me?*

More than over 250 friends, relatives and acquaintances overflowed the pews inside Queen of Peace Catholic Church. The house of worship seemed a fitting place for Kate to be laid to rest. She often had commented how serene she found it, situated as it was on a hillside overlooking the grasslands and cross streets that formed the tiny town of Millville. All three of her children had received their sacraments there.

Attendees included Dr. and Mrs. Dornhoffer, Derrick Wosniak, the Corrigans, the Vandermarks, several former ballplayers and the National League President, as well as many whose lives Kate had touched through her volunteer work with the 4-H organization. The club itself pledged to honor Mrs. Hanlon with a scholarship in her name.

The weather took some sting out of the service. Sunshine radiated on the simple, tan brick church. By burial time the temperature would climb to 78 degrees, rather mild for late September. "I bet your mom had something to do with arranging this weather," Luke comforted Megan—Kate's passing had hit her the hardest. "You know how much she enjoyed working outdoors."

The Hanlon men were by nature strong, but not one got through the mass with a dry eye, including Luke. Ordinarily one to shun public speaking, he delivered the eulogy. "I've enjoyed a degree of success in my life, and a lot of people helped along the way, but no one did so more than Kate." His voice broke. He wiped his eyes with his crumpled handkerchief, its creases sealed with moisture. "It was Kate who taught me the joy of a 6:00 a.m. livestock feeding...the pleasure of listening to the wind blow across a field of grain....It was Kate who gave me the courage to do the things I never thought possible, things much harder for me than hitting a baseball, like speaking here today."

Luke turned to the coffin at the conclusion of his talk. "Goodbye for now, my love." His words so moved Laura Corrigan that she dashed out a side door into the parking lot, sobbing uncontrollably.

Following Luke, four young 4-H'ers brought forward ribbons they had won under Kate's guidance and laid them atop her coffin. As they did, they recited a point of the pledge: "My head to clearer thinking...my heart to greater loyalty...my hands to larger service...my health to better living."

The mention of health brought to Luke's mind Dr. Clemmons' final assessment regarding Kate. "It was a congenital defect in the muscle and elastic components of her cerebral artery...a time bomb waiting to go off. It could have happened at any age. Be thankful for the years you had together."

It is said that those who lose a loved one go through a period of denial, followed by anger, then sadness. In the days following the funeral, Luke went straight to sadness. He thought about what she would miss and how she would be missed—David's child was on the way, and there was the likelihood of marriages for Megan and Bret.

The burden of her passing was aggravated by Luke's dwindling energy. He now found himself weakened physically and emotionally.

With each passing day a new sign of his chronological age crept back into his joints. For the most part, he ignored the minor aches that, until a few weeks before, were all but a distant memory. Ignoring the emotional loss was not as easy.

Luke also found sleep difficult. Eleven days after he thought he had said good-bye to Kate for good, he awoke to see a figure standing in the doorway of his bedroom. He sat up with a start. The figure moved slowly in the dark, just beyond the foot of the bed. "Kate?" A shiver cascaded through his shoulders and down his back. "What are you doing here?"

"They released me from the hospital," she said, climbing under the covers. His heart jumped for joy! He wrapped his arms around her and squeezed her soft body. He thought he would crush her. Suddenly, he awoke to find his arms clutching her pillow.

Luke did see Kate's death bringing the immediate family members closer together. And from that he drew some solace. David made a rare trip down with Sheila for a weekend visit. Before leaving, they extended Luke an invitation to spend the Thanksgiving weekend with them.

But it was Megan who drew closest to her dad. She took a two-week leave of absence from teaching to stay with him and lose herself in farm chores. Afterwards, she visited him on weekends and occasionally after school—rising early the next morning to make the hour commute to the elementary school near Dayton where she taught. It was a toss-up as to who needed the other more.

Kate's presence permeated the ranch where she'd been a fixture for more than thirty years. Luke found thoughts of her springing forth like the tiny thorns that poked at him whenever he ventured into the bramble bushes. Just when he extricated himself from one branch, another would stick him from behind.

But Luke didn't help matters. He showed little inclination toward touching anything belonging to his late wife. Every morning, as he left the master bedroom, he passed by a collage of unwitting reminders. There, above her dresser, edges sandwiched between the cherrywood frame and the glass mirror, was a collection of unframed family photographs of varying shapes and sizes. Each had had special meaning for her. He knew they were there. He knew they called her to mind, but he liked the remembrances. Besides, he always had thought it impolite to touch Kate's personal belongings.

The second photo down stood out. It recorded Kate at her radiant best, holding their only granddaughter decked out in a holy communion gown. Atop the photo was a piece of flattened ribbon Sheila had sent along that Tracy wore in her hair on the joyous occasion.

Several weeks later, on a late October afternoon, Luke stopped on his way back to the house and picked up a tree branch lying on the brick walkway. He tossed the twisted stick high in the darkening sky for the sport of Rusty, who had been trailing along. It came to rest where Kate once tended the family's garden.

Luke leaned against the corral fence and pulled at a tuft of horse hair lodged beneath a splinter. Waiting for Rusty, he reflected on Kate laboring in the garden, her knees anchored in the soil between rows of fruits and vegetables, pulling pesky weeds from between footlong cucumbers and yellow squash; peeling back cornhusks in search of the ripe, white ears so sweet and tender that Luke often enjoyed them raw; dusting away the aphids and spittle bugs from the tomatoes and strawberries with the white powder that made Bret sneeze. Yes, Kate's presence was alive everywhere. But for now, memories of her were more painful than pleasant.

18
The Slide Show

Lights darkened inside the auditorium. Luke sat alongside Dr. Dornhoffer and played with his armrest. It wasn't some sporting event, although Luke would have preferred to be at a game, name the sport. Instead, he found himself surrounded by scientists and lab workers, most from the Caulfield Science Center. He had accepted Doc's offer to attend the closed scientific review of Dr. Emily Einhardt's experimental drug, ena-1, with which he himself had been treated for better than three months.

Oh, he recognized Doc's invitation for what it was, a ploy to get him back into circulation on this early November afternoon. And, being one never to believe in self-pity, he had decided it made sense to get out of the house and Kate's passing off his mind.

He leaned on his left elbow, then his right, legs crossing at the knees, then apart. The drapes parted on a grey translucent screen and, *click* a slide came into view. There, magnified 12,000 times, was a black and white photograph of a human cell. Luke listened as Emily leaned toward the podium mike and spoke.

"The cell. The foundation of life. The most amazing factory ever created. One of several trillion contained within our bodies. A complex structure, yet it consists mostly of water—in excess of 70 percent by volume. Encased within its double membrane is the master program, the place where orders are drawn up. A central computer wired with strands of DNA. Encoded within the DNA are genes. One such gene, which we've labeled *ena-1,* is the subject of my presentation. It is this gene that we believe plays a critical role in the reproduction of most, if not all, human cells."

Doc laid his hand on Luke's arm and whispered, "This is what's known in showbiz as the warm-up."

Luke nodded and thought how he had been wrong to think sports was the only field showbiz had invaded.

"We've known for some time now that after cells stop replicating, they retain the genetic blueprint to order the creation of new cells. What we haven't understood is exactly how the process gets turned on and off. Today, I will attempt to shed light on this mystery of nature. In so doing, I will share with you what we believe is a breakthrough in unlocking senescence, the aging process." A rumble of hushed voices signaled great interest in what Emily had to say.

Click. A new slide flashed on the screen: "Hypothesis: *Ena-1* works to neutralize cellular senescence."

Dr. Einhardt stepped from the podium and stood to the side, with her arm still clutching the stand. A trio of potted plants hid her feet. "Many were skeptical when Dr. Thomas Johnson of the University of California first reported that he had doubled the earthworm's life span by mutating a single gene. Yet we are about to present evidence that *ena-1,* or the *enabler,* has the capacity to alter the life span of human cells through the production of a unique, controlling nuclear protein*, Ena-1.*

"We've known for some time how protein transcription factors regulate, either positively or negatively, the expression of genes required for cell replication. What we haven't understood is what causes this process to die out over time. Why it is that cells are able to reproduce only a certain number of times?"

Click. A photograph of Nobel Prize-winning French scientists

Jacques Lucien Monod and Francois Jacob flashed on the screen.

"My research supports Monod and Jacob's hypothesis that there exists a repressor genetic protein that slows down and eventually turns off cell mitosis. We first identified this suppressor enzyme in muscle tissue and labeled it *Sup-7*, since our research shows that it is produced by a gene on the seventh chromosome."

Dr. Einhardt poured herself a glass of water and sipped before continuing. "Our experiments lead us to believe that cells control reproduction by limiting the capacity of the enabler gene to order the production of the *Ena-1* protein. As we age, the enabler slows down, to the point where it eventually becomes turned off throughout most cells. Yet, the elements necessary for cell mitosis are still present in the DNA.

"For you see, by introducing new, functional copies of this particular gene into aging tissue cells, we've demonstrated the ability to temporarily turn off the suppressor gene."

Click. The screen flow-charted the interrelationship between proteins and genes in regulating cell activity.

Emily telescoped her pointer and traced the process. Doc whispered a translation to Luke. "Think of when your tractor has a lot of gunk in the engine that keeps it from turning over. That's the suppressor. The engine's still good. All it needs is a little carburetor cleaner. That's the *enabler*; it dissolves the gunk. The more cleaner you use, the faster it'll do the job."

Luke winked his understanding. He turned and followed Emily's pointer. "...In those cells where the *enabler* gene is active, it gives the orders to produce the *Ena-1* protein. That in turn neutralizes the suppressor enzyme activity. It actually turns it into a harmless phosphoric compound. Naturally, this has a cascading effect on cell growth."

Once more Doc leaned over and spoke. "That's the fascinating part to me, Luke—how life regulates itself. It is indeed a complicated system, with these genes turning one another on and off as they perform certain tasks. It's going on right as we sit here."

"Easy for you to say," Luke smiled. But it did give him a greater appreciation for the complexities of Doc's world. And having been part of the study, it helped him follow what Dr. Einhardt had to say. For he knew from personal experience that something had transformed him from a semi-retired grandfather into a very active individual.

He observed Emily playing with the slide control as she surveyed her captivated audience and continued. "Amazingly, this process even seems to work in the non-regenerative tissue where cell mitosis normally stops at an early age."

Non-regenerative cells. Now there's a term I recognize. Luke recalled Doc explaining how hastening the reproduction of bones, skin and blood cells in mature individuals was astonishing enough, but getting those tissues that lacked the capacity to reproduce, such as nerves and certain muscle tissue, to do so was quite another matter.

Click. A photo of muscle tissue appeared on the screen.

"I first identified the *Ena-1* protein while studying the MyoD transcription factor, which, you may recall, is responsible for turning new cells into muscle tissue. It intrigued me when I determined that the protein was an enzyme protein." Emily paused to drink water and continued. "The patient had a torn quadricep. It was not the first time that we had observed the enzyme, but we had always dismissed it as one of the myriad of inactive proteins in the nucleoplasm. That is, until we noted elevated levels of it in the cells surrounding the damaged tissue. We thought perhaps it might be some type of growth factor."

Luke listened as Emily traced through a series of slides presenting her clinical research, from rats to humans. He detected an increased sense of ease as she turned from the unfamiliar faces in the audience to the subject matter on the screen with which she was well familiar. She told how they ruled the enabler protein out as a growth factor. "It only enhanced muscle cell growth. It did not stimulate it."

Emily admitted her error in assuming that the enabler gene was unique to muscle tissue. "It became a self-fulfilling prophecy when I focused on evaluating the protein molecule in just those cells. I had seen where there were different suppressor enzymes produced for dif-

ferent tissues. Little did I realize that one gene would block all different types of suppressors; that this one gene would, in essence, control
the human aging process for so many, if not all, tissue types."

She went on to explain how the nature of the treatment made it
difficult to see the broader indications in the Phase I human clinicals.
"Looking back, that was understandable. We were dealing with healthy
populations and college-age subjects in whom the *enabler* genes normally would be active in muscle tissue."

Click. Phase II clinicals: documented evidence of *ena-1's* effect in
thirty-three tissue types.

"It was only when we undertook the longer term clinicals using a
general patient population that we began getting anecdotal data on its
impact on a wide variety of tissue types."

As Dr. Einhardt reviewed the reports from the clinical investigators, Luke's restlessness grew. He wasn't used to sitting that long, and
the discussion went far deeper into the scientific matter than he needed.
"How much longer is this?"

"She's almost done with the slides," Doc whispered. "Then she'll
take questions. You can leave when you want, although I thought we'd
have lunch."

"I promised that, didn't I? Okay." Luke looked forward to a meal
with Doc. He found his cheerful attitude contagious, something he
could use as much as food.

Doc elbowed Luke. "Watch these next couple of slides. You'll see
evidence of yourself in here."

Click. A bar chart summarized patient hematology tests demonstrating bone growth.

"As we read the reports indicating a possible broader impact for
ena-1, we took a closer look at the blood tests. They supported what
the individuals had been reporting.

"Here you can see evidence of bone growth in the elevated levels
of the alkaline phosphatase enzyme in subjects over the age of forty."
Dr. Einhardt pointed to the average readings of the International units/
liter for the test group compared to the medical norms.

BONE GROWTH AS MEASURED BY PRESENCE OF ALKALINE PHOSPHATASE

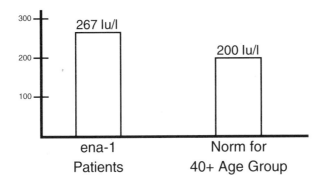

"Two patient readings even approached the 300 Iu/l level seen in children during their growth years," Emily added.

Click. Another bar chart showed enzyme levels demonstrating muscle growth.

"Because of the different levels of creatine kinase normally seen in males and females, we separated the results by sex. In both cases, the averages exceeded the norms."

MUSCLE GROWTH AS MEASURED BY LEVELS OF CREATINE KINASE

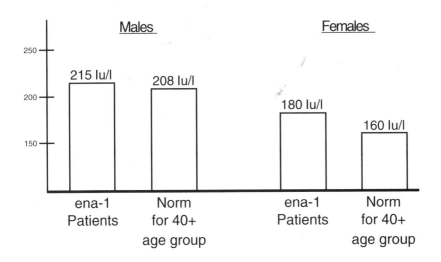

The final patient reports presented results from a series of nerve conduction studies. Luke recognized he was walking proof of the improved sensitivity and response rate seen in the older, treated subjects, whom Emily described as "normally having a reduced number of nerve axons."

Click. "*ena-1* Introduced Using Gene Transfer Technique With Retrovirus."

Emily concluded by describing the procedure Dr. Metzger had been using to ferry the *enabler* gene into Luke's body. She explained one important limitation of the gene transfer technique. "The retroviruses, having been disabled, are unable to permanently insert the enabler gene into the genetic material. Therefore, we had to inject subjects on a bi-weekly basis to maintain the desired activity level."

Dr. Einhardt skimmed through a summary slide, then pushed the button atop the podium, raising the full set of overhead lights. Stepping to the front, she slipped her hands into her lab coat pockets. "At this point I'd be happy to entertain any questions."

An Oriental man with neatly combed, slicked back hair was the first to speak. "First, my compliments for the work you have done in uncovering this breakthrough. Excellent, just excellent."

Doc whispered to Luke, "That's one of our special invited guests, Dr. Miyamoto from the University of California. He's a Nobel Prize winner."

The research fellow continued. "Have you or the other clinicians observed any evidence that this enabler protein contributes to irregular cell growth?"

"No. We've been following up with a number of the patients since the study was terminated, some eleven weeks ago, and no problems have emerged to date." Luke nodded, realizing now why he had been asked to take part in post-clinical monitoring.

Another questioner rose. "How do you envision this drug being used? And have you given thought to the indications you plan to seek approval for?"

"Those are good questions. The answer to the second is not yet.

As to what I could see as its use, well, it has unlimited potential as a means of slowing down the aging process. Of course, initially we will probably have to go for a much narrower indication. I foresee its use in rejuvenating non-renewable tissues—individuals who, because of injuries or disease, have suffered losses to their irreparable tissues. Say, victims of stroke or heart attack."

Dr. Einhardt entertained questions for the next fifteen minutes before closing the lively discussion. "Okay, let's take one more."

A young lab worker stood. "How long do you anticipate it taking to start up new human clinicals?"

"That really depends upon our friends at the FDA. Currently, the drug has been placed on Clinical Hold. Dr. Dornhoffer and I have had some preliminary discussions with Dr. Lashkey, but I'm not too optimistic about fast action. As he explained to us, the drug doesn't treat any serious diseases, so there isn't a sense of urgency to rush it along." Emily brushed her hair to the side. "Besides, they are concerned with the broad impact the enabler appears to have. You know, on all cell types. He's requested a series of long-term animal studies— three to five years, to be exact. They've even asked us to figure out a way to determine its impact on all cell types." She paused with an exasperated smile. "Of course, that could keep us busy well into the next century. As Dr. Dornhoffer has said, we'd go broke in the process!"

Too bad, Luke thought, not only for people in need, but for Doc and this lady's sake. But his real disappointment, the thought that lingered in his mind, was that this medical breakthrough had not been available to save Kate.

19
Buying, Selling and Trading

A fortnight after the scientific presentation, Luke's alarm rousted him from another restless sleep. It was only 4:30 a.m., but Derrick was due shortly with a rented livestock trailer. They were to load up yearlings destined for that morning's cattle auction in Indianapolis—the plight of the Ohio cattle business was reflected in the Cincinnati market's closing during the '70s.

Luke dressed quickly and cooked up a pot of coffee, enough to fill a large thermos for their trip. They'd need it after working outside in the 18-degree temperature. December was barely under way, but already Luke had experienced a number of subfreezing days—a sign of a hard winter ahead. That was fine with him. It meant more work and anything that kept him busy was good medicine for his mind.

"That makes fourteen," Derrick counted off the last of the livestock and spit a stream of tobacco juice. His double-collared parka was open at the neck, curls of grey stiff in the cold. "Let's get rolling."

Luke closed the livestock gate and climbed in alongside his ranch hand. His mood dictated silence. For most of the two-hour ride, he fell in and out of sleep. He knew he wasn't great company, but Derrick was as understanding as they come.

As the sun splashed a pink wash on the clouds over Indiana, Luke offered his driver a second cup of coffee.

"Yeah, I think I will," Derrick replied. "Say, how was your Thanksgiving?"

Thanksgiving. A weekend visit with David, his pregnant wife and their daughter. Luke had enjoyed them all, especially Tracy, with her words of love for Grandpa. "Really nice. David's got himself a great family there." With such pleasant memories, he should have felt better, but he didn't. Kate's absence from the festive occasion colored his disposition. He now knew what post-holiday blues were all about.

"How's his business?"

"As he says, 'It's busting out of the closet,'" Luke said, forcing a smile.

Derrick gave a throaty laugh. "Hey, that's a good one."

"He took me downtown to see it. From the size of the shop, I'd say he's doing quite well. Must have a dozen carpenters working for him."

"D' offer you a job?"

"He knows better. Big cities and small closets would do me in."

Just then, downtown Indianapolis came into view. Derrick looked out his mirror as he sought to cross over toward southbound I-65. A tractor trailer blocked his path. He slowed, yet another eighteen wheeler tagged behind the first. Luke saw the tension build in Derrick's face. "It looks clear after this one."

"Right," Derrick gritted. He pressed the accelerator. The lane dissolved into a cement barrier just as their trailer swung across the white line.

"See what I mean about cities?" Luke jested.

"Hey, this is nothing compared to Chicago." Derrick sighed. "By the way, how's that young' un?"

"Tracy? She's a real kicker. She kept me running pretty good. Just wanted Grandpa to throw the baseball to her."

"In this cold?"

"Down in the basement."

"You must have enjoyed that."

Luke nodded. And he did.

Derrick pulled into the cratered dirt lot that surrounded the live-stock market. He backed his vehicle toward the beam that edged along the cement loading dock.

Inside the registry, Luke allowed Derrick to lead the way—a change for one who was inclined to take charge. They signed over the Angus and headed up the catwalk to the auction house, situated in the middle of the stockyards. Beneath the steel bridge, half-empty metal pens reflected the seasonal lull. Warm breath from the cattle condensed into a steam cloud that rose through their path. The livestock's mournful baying gave the impression that they knew they were headed for slaughter that afternoon. Derrick swung open the auction door, and two pigeons flapped overhead among the rusted rafters.

"Hey, if it isn't Woznie," a cattleman in a blue-jean jacket called to Derrick. Luke took a seat.

"Hi there, Gib. You buyin' today?" Derrick asked.

"Yeah, what you got, some big ones?" He said it as one word, "biguns."

"A herd of Angus." Derrick hitched his pants and adjusted his leather cowboy hat. The hat served to disguise his fireplug-like figure as much as keep his head warm. "I doubt you can afford it. We've brought only the best today."

"Crossbred?"

"Hell no. Nothin' mixed in these ladies."

A second rancher, seated up front, swung around, wrinkling his neck as if it were a dishtowel. His smile revealed two silver capped teeth. "Forget it, Gib. I'm gonna plow you under," he said, referring to the bidding.

The farmer named Gib smiled and waved the other man off.

Luke, slouched in his chair with his hat down low, listened in on the conversation.

The slam of the auctioneer's gavel signaled things were ready to begin. Derrick squeezed into the row and sat next to his boss as the auction began. In all there were a dozen ranchers, five of whom lined the rails up front. The rest were scattered in the half dozen rows of baseball-like box seats.

"Okay, fat cattle are next. Thank y'buyers for comin'. We'll try to get you in and out just as fast as we can. First up, we have ourselves ten ladies," the auctioneer announced. The mechanical doors sprang open, and the heifers scurried inside the dirt covered pen. *Snap, snap*—the livestock manager cracked his whip in mid-air. *Snap, snap*—he cracked it repeatedly to keep the cattle moving—twirling, running, spinning— from one end of the thirty-foot pen to the other. Up above, the auc- tioneer sang the bidding like some square dance caller, while pointing his finger frantically from side to side. *Snap.* "Sixty, by five, five and a half, five and a half, got a half. Sixty by six—*snap, snap*—give me a quarter, six and a quarter, and a quarter by six. *Slam.* Sold for sixty- six, twenty-five." *Snap, snap.* The manager ushered the heifers out the other end.

Other days, in other years, Luke had felt electrified by the auctioner's call, as if watching a favorite thoroughbred pound toward the finish line—the thrill of the sale, the pride of seeing his cattle bring in top dollar. But this morning that feeling was lost.

Three more transactions and the doors flung open, *snap, snap.* In rushed Luke's fourteen yearlings. When it was over the electronic tote board registered another successful sale for the Homestead. The buyer was a gentleman seated in the front row, with a cellular tele- phone cradled next to his ear.

INDIANA LIVESTOCK EXCHANGE	
HEAD	14
AVERAGE WT.	1,457
WEIGHT	20,398
PRICE/100	$85.50

"Over seventeen grand. Not bad for a morning's work," Derrick announced during the return ride.

Luke nodded. He knew what his foreman had omitted from the gross figure—eighteen months of feed and work put into raising the heifers.

Crossing into Ohio, they were welcomed by a splattering of snowflakes on the windshield. Nearly an inch lay on the driveway when they arrived at the farm. Luke cautioned Derrick, "You better get straight home. Looks like we're gonna get dumped on pretty good."

"Nah, don't worry. It's only four miles. I'll give you a hand with the feeding, then get on the road. If I get stuck, I figure you'll put me up." The cowhand nudged Luke's arm. Such dedication by Derrick had earned his boss' admiration. Luke felt that much worse for having been so unsociable throughout the morning. He understood that he needed to focus more of his attention on the present. Sure, Kate was gone, but she would be the first to chew him out for dwelling on her, especially at Derrick's expense.

They fed the cattle and moved inside the barn, where they spread a fresh bed of hay for the horses. Luke tended to Diamond Boy, while Derrick talked his way into taking care of Kate's mare, Clover—Luke figured Derrick was as good a psychologist as those who had spent years in school.

Having finished, Luke leaned against the doorjamb and stared out at a dozen or so cattle. He sensed a supporting hand touch his shoulder. Without losing focus on the elements, he spoke. "How long does the hurt last?"

Derrick spat a chaw of tobacco outside the doorway. It seared its way through the snow like a heartbreak through life. He had lost his own wife six years earlier. "It gets better each day. Just seems sometimes the days don't go by fast enough to get us far enough away from the hurt."

Luke nodded, his eyes transfixed ahead.

Derrick continued, his guttural voice softening. "I sort of found that getting myself involved in something I like doin' helped get my mind off it."

"What'd you find?"

"Being out here with the animals. Helpin' them just sort of helped me. That and being around farmers I enjoy— even moody ones like you."

The comment brought a knowing smile from Luke. Derrick was right. If he could occupy his mind, it would take care of his moodiness. He needed to do both.

Days later, an offer of lunch drew Luke to Mike Corrigan's office. Never one to indulge in self-pity, Luke heeded Derrick's advice to get out and about. His coterie of friends amounted to a mere dozen. And most, like Mike, Derrick and Doc, still worked. The rest were part-time farmers whom he met with at the Millville Tavern, but that held little interest for him now.

Luke turned the corner of the lifeless locker room and peered into the manager's office. In an age of multi-million-dollar salaries and palatial players' homes, it would have been reasonable to envision an office befitting a Fortune 100 executive. However, Mike's windowless room barely rivaled that of a high school coach. A personal computer, together with a nine-inch television seated atop a dusty VCR, constituted the luxuries. The desk was metal, the chairs worn. A torn box held pictures Mike had collected over the years but had yet to hang.

"Dang, if it isn't our hitting coach," bellowed the Reds' skipper, jumping to his feet and clearing papers from a side chair.

"Hi, Mike."

"You look in great shape, friend," Mike said. He dumped the papers on the floor. "How d'you feel?"

"Hanging in there."

Mike leaned back in his chair and folded his arms. "Laura said to be sure to tell you, you're invited for Christmas."

"Thanks, but I'll be going back to Chicago with the children."

"Sounds like a better opportunity. How 'bout when you get back?

I could use someone to watch the bowl games with."

"I'll have to see. Not sure what day I'll be returning." Luke shied away from commitments now more than ever. He went by how he felt at the moment. And then there was Laura; he found it hard to look her straight in the eye for fear he might see Kate. "Still looking for a couple of ballplayers?"

"Yeah, there's a few holes I'd like to fill. Another pitcher...a utility infielder and a power hitter—we've yet to find a replacement for Hartmann."

"What about this guy Estabe?" Luke spoke of the twenty-four-year-old infielder from the Dominican Republic, Raphael Estabe, acquired from the Texas Rangers in exchange for Boots Barnett and a promising minor league pitcher.

"I'm excited about him. Reminds me a lot of Chico."

Luke recalled the fine shortstop of the '60s, Leo Cardenas, with whom both Luke and Mike had played. "Great range and he can peg it to first with the best of 'em. Plus he's a speedster."

"How's his stick?"

"Better than his .218 average."

"I read somewhere that he's had problems handling the ball." Luke was being kind. The article had said something like, "The Reds made a kitchen trade today, exchanging one strainer at short for another."

"Yeah, made something like thirty-eight miscues. But twenty-eight of them were on balls to his right. Word is he allowed himself to get intimidated by their third sacker. They got a crusty veteran who thinks that's his turf—I'm told at one point he threatened to break Estabe's arm if he cut in front of him again. With Taylor, that won't be a problem. I'll tell him to go after anything he can get. The only thing Taylor is liable to break with him is bread."

Luke laughed at the remark about the Reds' third baseman, Dean "the preacher" Taylor. Dean was a born-again Christian who hailed from Georgia.

"Keep it under your hat, but Vandermark's close to getting us that power hitter we've been after."

"Who?" Luke asked.

"Sean Wheatly of Kansas City. Plays outfield."

"Sure, I've heard of him. Now he's got some pop in his bat."

Mike wrung his hands with delight. "Exactly. Rapped out 27 last year, although admittedly he's no diamond cutter when it comes to fielding."

Luke motioned toward the computer behind the manager's back. "You really like those things, don't you?"

"Oh, this?" Mike patted the monitor crammed full of green and blue numbers. "Actually, it's gotten so I can't live without it."

"You said the same thing about me. Does that mean we're of equal value?" Luke grinned for the first time since he had arrived.

"You have no equals, Luke," Mike rejoined. "But we've got ourselves at least two dozen new faces coming to camp. This gives me all their stats. And I can use it to look at any prospect, on any team. If I find someone I like, I just print out a sheet and give it to Vandermark— makes it real easy to make my case."

Mike rummaged through several pages of computer printout and held one out for Luke to examine. "Take a look. It records nearly every swing, every footstep a player makes from the instructional leagues on up to the majors; I can even retrieve information on guys playing in Japan."

"Does it tell you how fast a guy's heart beats when he steps to bat with the game on the line?"

"No, that's my job," Mike winked.

Luke enjoyed Mike's upbeat attitude. Then, too, his optimistic outlook may have explained why Mike saw the game's changes from a different perspective.

The two left for lunch, passing by the batting cage along the way. There they found Randy Kitchell getting in some off-season practice against Iron Mike. Luke watched Randy swing in machine-like fashion at pitches fired automatically every four seconds. The batter's work habits had impressed Luke during spring training. The fact that he was here in Cincinnati during December rather than with his siblings in Florida gave added evidence of the young man's commitment to the game.

Luke knew Randy possessed the raw skills. And his openness to Luke's suggestions had paid dividends. He had raised his average from .247 to .292 in the just completed season. But Luke wouldn't take credit for the improvement. In many ways Randy reminded Luke of himself: talented, introspective and willing to make whatever sacrifice necessary to hone his skills.

"Hey, Kitch, I brought someone to see you," Mike announced.

Sweatpants rose up tight on Randy's twisting legs and deep semi-circles darkened his armpits, while a clump of hair waved from below his helmet. He took one final power cut, smashing the ball into the mesh webbing draped overhead. He turned toward his visitors. "Hi, Luke. Wanna swing?"

"No thanks." Deep down, Luke thought how he'd like nothing better. It was a love taken from him years before, albeit in that case it came with some warning.

Randy rested the bat handle on the astroturf and looked through the chain linkfence. *Ping.* Another ball rapped against the cage in the background.

Luke eyed the concave top end of Randy's bat. Such hollowed-out weapons had come into vogue late in Luke's career, but he never saw fit to use them. "Hey, Randy, somebody take a bite out of your bat?"

"You told me to use whatever leverage I can get," Randy answered. He raised the fat end for a closer look. "I pick up more bat speed this way."

"Okay. But don't go telling anyone that I suggested you use such a bastardized piece of wood."

"Luke's a purist, in case you haven't guessed," Mike explained.

"You're kidding," Randy deadpanned.

"Say, Luke, bet you ten bucks you can't connect with two in a row," Mike offered.

"I wouldn't want to take your money. Anyway, I don't have my spikes." It was Luke's turn to smile as he lifted up a workboot. He'd like to take a cut; the sight of batted balls inspired him. Perhaps if it were the summer, when he was receiving treatments. But not now that his reflexes once again had dimmed. Still, Luke felt what he had fought to block out since the day he retired—his longing for the game. The sport of it. The competition. Then, too, he sensed the irony of how easy it was to remember the good times and screen out the bad— the road trips, the times away from home, all of the missed opportunities at the plate and the occasional miscues that even he made. He had enough horse sense to know the tricks the mind played, especially at times like this when thoughts of the present hurt so much.

Making their way toward the elevator, Mike wrapped his arm around Luke. "I hope you're gonna join me again in Florida."

"And if I say no, I'll have to put up with you pestering me, right?"

Mike nodded.

"Let's say I'm thinking about it."

20
A Christmas Wish

A column of snowflakes swept Luke up the steps of the Dornhoffer's Greek-revival old home, just blocks from the UC campus. He brought with him a bottle of wine and a determined mindset. While he knew more tough days lay ahead—Christmas without Kate would be especially trying—he sought to focus on the positives. That evening's gathering with the Dornhoffers provided such an opportunity.

Moments later, Doc graciously accepted the wine, freeing Luke to receive an embrace and peck from his matronly-looking wife. "Merry Christmas, Luke. S'nice to see you."

"Thanks, Pat. Good to see you, too."

The resemblance to Mrs. Claus was uncanny. Pat's full figure was clothed in a red blazer, her cheeks were rosy, and her rounded face flowed uninterrupted into her neck. She wore her white hair in a soft perm, combed upwards, giving the impression that she was taller than Doc. But Luke knew from past meetings who stood taller in her eyes.

The holiday imagery carried beyond Mrs. Dornhoffer. An evergreen rope entwined the heavy wooden banister, leading up the three-story, central hall. Mistletoe, tied to a single red velvet ball, dangled from the mahogany entranceway to a parlor on the left. And a Kris Kringle dwarf with hairline cracks spreading throughout its ceramic face hid in the corner atop an accent table.

Doc helped Luke off with his coat, balancing a handmade Danish pipe which filled the air with a berry scent.

"I feel fine," Luke replied when asked, and he truly did. His mind no longer was wandering aimlessly between the land of the living and the dead. There were still moments, days even, when the loneliness seemed overwhelming. And he reckoned he'd never be quite the same, but he had set his mind on overcoming the grief. He again had a goal in life, a goal his host was going to help him achieve.

"That's wonderful to hear!" Pat said, clasping her hands together. "I've been praying for you and your family every day."

"Thanks," Luke said, wiping away the wet remnants of snow-flakes from his head.

"How would everyone like something to drink?" Doc asked.

"Sure," Luke replied, appreciative of the shift in topics.

Doc fixed Luke an Old Fashioned before Pat treated Luke to a favorite of his, sauerbraten with potato pancakes and seasonal touches of red cabbage and Brussels sprouts. Afterwards, the men retired, coffee cups in hand, to the warmth of the twelve-foot high parlor. While neither had room for dessert, Luke looked forward to their conversation to top off his meal. He stopped to inspect decades of ornaments on the seven-foot Christmas tree, while Doc stoked the fire. He couldn't help but notice a picture, framed by an angel. It showed Doc and Pat cuddled together, both with dark hair. Turning around, Luke saw his host stooped over, grappling with tongs in an attempt to place another log atop the dying embers. "Can I give you a hand?"

"That shouldn't be necessary. I just about have this in therrrrre." The log dropped with a thud, and Doc closed the chainlink screen. "That should keep us warm for a while."

"I meant to ask, where's Eric?"

"Out on some date."

"I should have guessed. He and Bret seem to have no shortage of girls."

"If I'm any judge, being an athlete is more popular with the ladies than being a scientist. He certainly fares a lot better than his father did."

"I don't know about that. Seems you did all right."

"Yes, yes." Doc sank into his chair until he and it were one. "Pat and I have had thirty-four wonderful years together."

"Will your two oldest be here for the holidays?" Luke referred to Doc's married daughter, Alicia, herself a professor in Pittsburgh, and Russell, an investment banker with Goldman Sachs in New York.

"Alicia and Dan are coming with our first grandchild. But Russ is very busy with work. I doubt he'll have time to open up gifts!" A glint of pride appeared in Doc's smile. "Pat and I have tickets to fly out to see him after New Year's. And when do you leave for Chicago?"

"It depends on when Megan can get here after teaching. We'll either leave Thursday night or early Friday." *Pittsburgh, Cincinnati, New York, Chicago. Years ago,* Luke thought, *those cities constituted half the National League; today they represented mailing addresses for family members.*

"Anything new with Dr. Einhardt's drug?" Luke inquired.

Doc relit his pipe and shook his head. "No. We're still working on a strategy for going back to the FDA. I'm hoping we can satisfy their needs with an additional year of animal testing instead of the three to five they've asked for."

"What about testing in humans?"

"Unfortunately, as you heard Dr. Einhardt say, we don't anticipate resuming those clinicals for a couple of years."

"How about testing on just one?" Luke fingered the afghan, draped over the Queen Anne couch.

Doc took a long draw on his pipe and held his breath for a thoughtful pause. He exhaled as he spoke. "Not sure what you mean."

"What if one person wanted to sign up for the treatment?"

"Sign up?" Doc laughed. "It doesn't quite work that way. I mean, it's not an approved drug."

"Couldn't a doctor make an exception?"

"Not even for testing. You see, the FDA has placed it on Clinical Hold. Oh, there have been instances where the government has allowed unapproved drugs to be used, but only in life-threatening situations—certain types of cancer, AIDS—not in a case such as this, where it's purely an elective treatment."

Luke didn't want to hear about the FDA. He was big enough to take care of himself. So he filled his voice with the tenacity he felt for what he wanted to do. "Well, I'd like to be one of those exceptions. I mean, hell, I've already been on the treatment, so what's the harm?"

"What for? Do you have some sort of injury? I mean, there are other treatments...."

"No. Nothing like that," Luke interrupted. "I just have my reasons."

"I see." Doc's foot moved back and forth, its movement not some nervous jiggle, but calm and rhythmic, like the patient thoughts inside his head. He reminded Luke they had terminated the study for his own protection.

"I understand. Then again, Doc, there are no certainties in life. If I didn't realize that before, I, ah, know it now." Luke dropped his head and rubbed his palms together.

"I understand."

"I guess what I'm saying is, I'm willing to live with the unknowns. You see, I want to try and play ball again."

"Baseball? I thought they dissolved the senior league."

"I'm talking about the majors."

Luke's words landed like a plate of hot chestnuts in Doc's lap. "The majors! Luke, you're over *sixty!*"

"And with the treatment, I felt like I was twenty. I know it sounds crazy, but I'd like to give it a shot."

Doc shook his head and gnawed on his pipe. "Listen, there are other things in your life to live for—like your children. Think of them."

"That doesn't mean I can't pursue something important to me."

"I'm not saying that you can't. But I have to protect you as a friend as well my patient," Doc explained. "Why, if you went back on the treatment, it might eventually alter the makeup of your cells—metastasize. Cancer, Luke! No, no, for your own safety, I wouldn't."

"But you're a risk taker."

"I take prudent risks." Doc wore a pained expression which displayed his torn feelings.

Luke reminded Doc about Dr. Einhardt's comments, about how they had seen no real side effects with patients in earlier clinicals, even going back to the animal studies.

"Luke, I understand Kate's loss has created a void in your life—"

"It's more than Kate, Doc." Luke had cut in for the second time, something he rarely did once. He rose with nervous energy and walked to the window. If anything, the discussion had brought forth a spark that had been missing since Kate's death. He slid his hands in his pockets and gazed into the night. Thoughts whirled in his mind like the snow flakes outside. "Other than my family, I've never found anything that gives me more pleasure than playing ball. This summer, when I started feeling stronger, I began tossing the ball around with Bret. And you know, havin' a taste of hitting the rawhide, of running to shag flies—and I mean, being able to do it well, not just going through the motions—well, it brought back a feeling inside that's hard to describe." Luke whirled and looked straight at Doc. "If there was the slightest possibility that I might be able to get on the field and play, I'd do it in a heartbeat. I'd trade it for any risks down the road."

Doc bent and rubbed his ear. The roaring fire crackled in the background, breaking the silence and drawing his gaze. He recalled for Luke his early days as a GP, seeing twenty, thirty patients a day, then going to the lab to work on some experiment and, in between, raising a family. "It seemed impossible at times, yet all so exciting. Then again, memories are often deceiving. The more time passes, the more we tend to block out the negatives. It's how we humans adapt and carry on."

"I wasn't being deceived when I was out there with Bret."

"I'm not questioning whether or not you had these feelings. It's just that you need to think about all that goes with it—the traveling, the age differences."

"The game itself hasn't changed, by and large. And that's what I'd be going back for."

Doc nodded. "But Luke, you had a marvelous career. You won home run titles. You were a most valuable player. For Christ's sake, you're in the Hall of Fame!"

Luke stopped in front of a crowded bookshelf alongside the fireplace. His eyes were drawn to several volumes of scientific literature. "If you won the Nobel Prize for medicine, would you retire?"

The question broke the tension and elicited laughter from Doc. "I wouldn't know, I'm still looking for my first one. But I understand. The point's well taken."

"What d'ya say, then?"

"I wish it were that simple Luke. Believe me I do." Doc furrowed his brow and stared at the fire. He puffed repeatedly on his pipe as if trying to light it.

Sitting there, waiting for Doc to speak again, Luke realized that he had underestimated the complexity of the matter for his friend. His tone became apologetic. "Here I am, getting all fired up about this and forgetting what it means for you."

Squinting his eyes, Doc held his thoughtful pose.

After what seemed like an eternity, Luke spoke again. "You can level, Doc. If it's not doable, tell me."

"I haven't said that, have I?"

"No, but you've got that look." Luke spoke in all seriousness.

"When was the last time you were in for a checkup?"

"Monday."

"I'll look at your lab tests tomorrow. Perhaps if things still look promising, we can give it a try." Doc looked toward the ceiling and thought out loud. "We could try to control the risks with more frequent monitoring."

Luke nodded and watched Dr. Dornhoffer's every movement. Finally, Doc returned the look and shook his pipe at him as he spoke. "Now, I make no promises. And you'd first have to understand the full scope of the risk you'd be incurring— and it's no small risk at that."

"I hear you," Luke said, rubbing his palms together.

Just then Pat peeked around the corner. Her timing couldn't have been better as far as Luke was concerned. He didn't want to push Doc any further that night. Time would tell if he got his wish.

"My, you two look like a serious bunch. Are you ready for that dessert?"

"I guess you could twist my arm. What do you say Luke, or are you already in training?" Doc said, with a considerably lighter tone than moments before. Pat shot him an inquisitive look.

◆　　◆　　◆　　◆

Three days before Christmas, Ty Hartmann stopped at the foot of his driveway in Hidden Hills, Arizona, and retrieved his mail. His morning was spent playing basketball at a local playground.

Once inside, Ty tossed several flyers into the trash without so much as a glance, then thumbed through a stack of letters and holiday cards. There he saw it. Sandwiched between an envelope from *Rossmore, Edgecomb, and Moretti* and a fund-raising solicitation, he spotted another Christmas card. Only the handwriting was his and the addressee Mr. Sam Wilkins. He stared at the red postal ink under the heading "Return to Sender." A checkmark had been made next to the box "deceased."

Ty dropped the mail on the counter, not even opening an envelope from his sister. For one of the few times in his life Ty broke into tears. The last occasion was his dad's funeral, more than a decade before. Now Sam was gone—the best friend he ever had. He thought about the wide-eyed, warm-hearted grin and grabbed a tissue.

The jagged jaws of guilt bit Ty, not over anything he had done, but for what he hadn't—the years he had allowed to pass without calling Sam. He sought excuses for his lapse since making it to the bigs. He found none. Hell, he thought, the only time they had together after he turned pro was one meal.

That evening Ty stayed home and doused his sorrows with a half-filled fifth of vodka. When he awoke the next afternoon, a thought weaved its way through the cotton balls clogging his head. It was as if Sam himself had put it there; he would dedicate himself and his season to the memory of No. 22, Sam Wilkins. But first, there was a business matter to rectify. Ty placed a call to his attorney, Vincent Moretti. He brushed aside the holiday pleasantries. "What's the latest Andrea is asking for?"

"You can do it two ways."

Nothing was ever easy when it came to lawyers, Ty thought.

"You can give her so much a month or pay her off up front—which will cost you a lot more. But I...."

"I want to clear it up in one lump sum," Ty barked before bending to do a crossover toe touch with his free hand.

"She's looking for a million-five, Ty. I certainly wouldn't recommend paying it. I mean they don't have definitive evidence that the kid's yours, anyway."

"No, but I've got every reason to think that it is." Ty switched hands with the phone and reached for his other foot.

"If I were you, I'd at least have the DNA testing."

"I've heard those things don't always work." Ty regarded such medical tests with as much respect as he had for pitchers. "Anyway, I want to clear it up before the season starts. Understand?"

"Sure, although that's no reason to give her a small fortune. It's your money, but I'm here to protect your best interests."

"Fuck that. It's in my best interest to have this thing taken care of—now," Ty roared.

"Easy, Ty, I know it's the holiday season, but don't do something you'll regret later." The attorney paused, waiting for a response that wasn't coming. Ty let his point sink in. Moretti continued. "Okay, give me a week. I'll let you know what they're willing to take. If you want we can have this thing settled before the groundhog sees his shadow."

Ty hung up and moved to the Nautilus equipment in an adjoining room. *Yes, this season will be different,* Ty thought. *No more distractions, Sam. No more distractions.*

◆　　◆　　◆　　◆

During his Christmas in Chicago, Luke remained silent about his request to Dr. Dornhoffer. Upon his return home, he placed a call to Doc which resulted in another meeting, this time at the Caulfield Center. There, Doc provided a detailed review of the pros and cons of resuming treatments. Luke was unswayed from his decision. He was prepared to accept whatever risks were involved.

"I see I'm not going to talk you out of it," Doc said.

"We'll start with treatments tomorrow—I first need to get some supplies out of the refrigeration unit."

"Did you figure I'd change my mind?" Luke smiled.

"No. But if I'm going to be your physician, I have to take an objective view of things."

Driving home, Luke felt himself coming out of his depression. Oh, he knew it would take a long time to get over the loss of his wife, and in some ways he never wanted to, certainly not if it meant losing the feelings he had for Kate—but at least now he had hope.

That afternoon, Luke confided in Bret about his treatment. It seemed only fair seeing how he planned to have Bret join him at UC's fieldhouse to serve as his batting practice pitcher. In Luke's mind there was no time to waste; spring training began in just seven short weeks.

21
A Great New Spring

Knook. The retort of a baseball being struck resounded from the batting cage at Plant City Stadium. Mike Corrigan, hands hidden inside his hip pockets, strolled into the soft morning sunshine. With a soccer kick, he dislodged a dew soaked ball from its grass nest near firstbase.

Springtime, and a man's fancy turns to love. For Mike, that love was baseball. And he had fresh hope for the coming season. His team had yet to lose a game, forget that they had yet to play one. Everyone started with the same record, if not the same opportunities. Mike was determined to make the most of his and the team's. He had learned so much during his first season. He would be tougher, more demanding; the need to get to know everyone had been satisfied.

Mike eyed several pitchers loosening up along the foul line. In the distance a trio of athletes ran windsprints near the padded red fence. *Knook.* Mike followed a missile which sailed out towards left and bounded in front of the runners. They wisely cut back their stride.

Knook. He squinted at the pitcher hiding behind the chain link protector, and followed his delivery. What he saw surprised him—none other than Luke Hanlon stinging the ball.

The Cincinnati Stinger, the term still fits. Mike recalled Luke's nickname. The often told story was that he had earned it as a child for homering after being stung by a trio of bees.

Mike watched his friend lace-looping pitches to all corners of the field. He approached the cage and shouted, "You looking for a spot on the team?"

"I just might be," Luke grimaced as he ripped another.

Five times over the next week, Luke took on Ben "Jock" Sparmarti's pitches. Of course, with Jock it was really no contest. Players teased the fifty-year-old bullpen catcher about his "wicked" 65 mile an hour fastball. But Luke loved it. It was just the speed he needed to tune his swing.

Luke didn't have much competition for Jock's services. The hitters weren't due to report until February 25, and for those who wanted to test the system, the official start of training camp was a week after that. By the time the players arrived, Luke was in good form, even challenging pitcher Scott Brouse, who went easy on the "old timer."

Mike had not expected Luke in camp until the regulars. But there he was, tossing the ball with the rookies and taking his cuts. It pleased him to see Luke enjoying himself. He perceived his friend to be seeking refuge from the pain up north. He was well aware of how much Kate had meant to him. Ever since 1958, baseball had been Luke's second love.

Near the end of the week, Mike noticed Luke having his palms taped. He spoke in private with trainer Will Evans. "What's with Hanlon?"

"Just a case of blisters," Evans murmured.

"Looks to me like he's overdoing it."

"Now that you mention it, I haven't seen a case that bad in a long time. Couple of his fingers even were bleeding. Surprising, seeing how he works on a farm."

"Yeah, but have you seen him out there? Every time I look, he's swatting balls."

"What for?"

"Said something about if he's going to be a hitting coach, he ought to be able to swing the bat. I think it's really more like therapy." Mike pointed to his temple. "Don't say anything, but he lost his wife over the winter."

"Thanks for telling me," Evans replied, placing rolls of tape inside a draw and sliding it shut. "I wouldn't worry about the blisters. Never had a patient die from them."

Mike smiled, "Knowing Luke, it'll take a lot more to do him in."

Luke waited four days before saying anything to Mike, but with the games set to begin soon, it was time to act. He grabbed Mike's arm after the morning coaches meeting. "Got a minute, Mike?"

"Sure." The manager retreated to the corner of his desk and anchored his hands on his thighs. "What's up?"

"I, uh, wanna be more than just a spring training coach." He expected the discussion to be difficult, and it was. How does one talk about the seemingly impossible? Far younger and better conditioned ex-players had tried their hands at returning, only to fall far short. Hell, Jim Palmer failed at age 42, and everyone knew from his underwear ads what a fine specimen he was. But what he didn't have was *ena-1*.

"Hey, say the word, and you've got a permanent job." Mike alluded to his desire for Luke to join the team for the regular season.

"That's part of it." Luke swallowed hard. "But I want to make it as a player."

"You want to play?" Mike cried in a hoarse whisper.

"I know it sounds crazy, but...."

"You're damn right it sounds crazy!" Mike interrupted.

Luke gave him a look that said more than any words he could think of.

"But Luke, no one has ever played the game in their fifties, let alone sixties. Except maybe Satchell."

"This old body is a lot younger than my age, Mike." He patted his slimmed down gut, then thought about his pledge of secrecy to Doc Dornhoffer. "Listen, I've been really working at getting in shape— even before I came down—and I know I can do it. All I want is a chance."

"I've no doubt you're special, Luke, but there comes a time when even the best of us can't hold back the ravages of time. Hey, I've even given up doing windsprints with the guys."

"It's different for me, Mike. I'd like to tell you more, but I can't. Look, you've seen me hitting the ball this week. And I can even out-run Kurkowski." Luke smiled.

"My eighty-year-old mom can do that," Mike countered.

"Give me a try, say for the next two weeks. If I'm not cutting it, I'll step aside." Luke's newly softened cheeks formed an off-balanced smile.

"Two weeks huh?"

"That's all."

"I'll give you ten days."

"Two weeks or I go to the Dodgers."

"Oh, all right. I'd suggest you shorten up the tree you're using," Mike commented, referring to Luke's 36-ounce bat that measured the same in inches.

"If I don't make it, it won't be because of the bat." Luke had been using the same model ever since 1958, when teammate Jerry Lynch reached into the carton he guarded inside his locker. "Here Luke, with your power you should be using a real club. Try one of mine."

Luke knew he was lucky that Mike was his friend. Any other manager would have laughed him out of the office. Mike probably felt the same way, but he cared too much about people, especially him.

Luke's play gave Mike little reason to think he could keep up with the "kids," some less than a third his age. He came to bat in the seventh inning of the third game looking for his first hit, having been hung with the proverbial collar up to that point. He had played flaw-less defense, but he figured it didn't take miracle drugs to catch fly balls.

With runners dancing off second and third, Luke listened to the umpire shout "Stttriiike one!" The call brought with it a ping of doubt. Perhaps Doc was right; as much as the new drug could restore one's strength, there was no guarantee it could restore one's athletic ability.

The pitcher stepped off the mound and rubbed up the ball. Luke felt the intensity of the heat and the trickle of sweat it formed on the back of his neck. Grabbing a button, he pulled his shirt away from the moisture that sucked it to his body. Suddenly it didn't feel so comfortable being out there; even his contoured baseball shoes felt tight compared to his Redwings.

Luke heard the fans' chants—something he used to readily block out. "Let's go, Luke....Hit one for us old folks." Old folks. What was he doing out here anyway? Who was he trying to kid? He heard the voice of his father, "Always try your best, son, but never hang around doing what you can't do well." Then he thought of his successes against Bret and the way he had stung the ball in the batting cage a week before. He told himself to be patient. True, neither of those pitchers was Sad Sam Jones, but neither was this guy on the mound. He turned on the next pitch, lining it foul into the stands.

He took one outside, then watched a letter high fast ball barrel its way plateward. He attacked it. Up, up it went, high into the afternoon sky, so high that he reached first before the ball began its downward descent. The second baseman backpeddled onto the grass and snapped his glove shut for the out while the runners held. Luke found consolation in the fact that such a "can of corn" is often a sign that one has just missed a homer. But at this point, "just missed" was a question more than a conclusion.

Luke returned to the dugout, his head hung low. No slamming of helmets. No kicking the water cooler. He had yet to prove himself worthy of such actions.

At the inning's end, Corrigan sent Quinn Pearson in to play left. "Luke, I wanna get a look at Quinn." Luke said nothing. He held no animosity toward his manager. Luke believed only he, himself, controlled his destiny.

Luke passed somberly behind Mike. The skipper swung his head around and delivered a side comment: "Just remember you've got two weeks to show me what you can do." The message wasn't lost on Luke. Three games did not a trial make. He appreciated the pledge renewal.

Early the next morning, Peter Vandermark shoved open the door to Corrigan's office. The determined Dutchman's face displayed the tension with which he gripped the *Cincinnati Star-Gazette's* sports pages. He tossed it on the desk. "You see this?" He allowed Mike to scan the article.

Reds Desperate for Hitting— Suit up Hanlon.

Tampa, Fla.—Peter Vandermark may be accused of lacking baseball acumen, but never a penchant for creativity in promoting his team. One might have thought his "best backside at the ballpark" contest would have tapped his promotional boundaries. But that would have been selling Peter short. He has now sold Luke Hanlon on returning to the baseball diamond. Lest we forget, Luke is in his seventh decade on earth.

While Peter may have pulled the wool over the one-time "Cincinnati Stinger's" eyes, it is suspect whether he can trick many ticket buyers into believing Hanlon's going to make the trip north as anything but a coach.

As for Luke, I'm a bit surprised (shocked?) that this classiest of ballplayers would partake in such a publicity stunt. Then again, maybe he thinks the Reds are so bad that even at his age he can raise their level of play.

"What's the hell's going on here?" Peter snapped.

Mike creaked back in his chair, bracing his foot against the desktop, and replied matter-of-factly, "He asked for a shot with the team. So I told him I'd give him one."

"C'mon Mike. We've got some serious things to figure out down here. I understand Hanlon's been through a lot, but this isn't some charity we're running. And I don't need publicity like this."

"Not to worry, Peter. I told him he could have two weeks. Then we'll, ah, have him back on the coaching lines."

"Make it a week."

"Sorry. Gave my word."

It wasn't the first time Mike had knocked heads with the impulsive owner, and it wouldn't be the last. He simply smiled whenever Peter called him his "pigheaded Irishman."

Peter shook his head with disgust. "Make sure the team's ready to play opening day."

With Vandermark's words fresh in his mind, Mike took to the field. There, he surveyed his coaches putting the players through their drills. Beyond first, a group of Reds danced in sequence along the foul line—clearly a collection of rejects from the Rockettes. He should have felt better, but he kept thinking about his good friend, Luke. He knew he didn't have a chance of making the team. Still, all he could do was let Luke find out for himself.

Game four and five passed, and Luke continued to struggle, collecting a scratch single and three more strikeouts. Mike decided to give him a day off. Ordered him. He said it wouldn't count against his trial period. If anything, Mike figured Luke needed to rest his old body. He suggested he go to the beach with Laura or do anything he wanted, just so long as he stayed away from the ballpark. Luke offered no argument and accepted an invitation to play golf with former teammate Johnny Bench. Mike quietly had asked the Hall of Famer to help get Luke's mind off the sport.

Refreshed, Luke returned for game seven and immediately sliced a clean single in the first, which brought a smile from him and his manager. Standing on the bag, Luke noticed the sun beaming overhead. True, it had been sunny most days he had been in camp, but this was the first time he felt the rays.

In the fourth, Luke came to bat with a runner on second. Nearing the plate, he stopped and took a couple of practice cuts. He could feel the nervous adhesions breaking apart. He cocked his bat back, rippled his fingers on and off the handle and glared out at his mound opponent. Sliding his jaw back and forth, he watched a pitch barrel plateward as big as a harvest moon. He jumped on it. *Smash.* It sailed toward the light stanchion in left, well beyond the fence. The fans erupted with their biggest outburst of the spring.

Whether it was the day off, Mike's supportive comments or the inevitability of straightening himself out, Luke ended the day three for four with five ribbies. He continued on a tear during the next five games. Even his outs were hammered with authority.

Luke's turnaround spun the turnstiles. Every home game became a sellout. Fans of all ages sandwiched themselves into the park hoping to witness Luke's resurrection.

Mike, showing concern for Luke's age, gave him another day off. Luke hadn't even been taking advantage of the "half days" he was allowed—throughout spring training, most players would leave after putting in their five or six innings to go fish, play golf or hang-out poolside to catch some rays or babes.

"Hey Mike, I thought I had a full two weeks," Luke grumbled, noting his name missing from the line-up.

"The deal still stands. But even non-mortals need a rest," Mike smiled.

"Save it. I'd prefer to keep my timing sharp."

"Don't worry. We've got a big game against the Cards tomorrow, and I want you raring to go." Mike recognized there had been a change in Luke that went beyond his hitting streak. Yes, there was a spring in his step not seen in decades. A rhythm. A buoyancy reminiscent of a man on the moon, playfully bouncing along as if years of gravity had no effect. And his expression went with it, like some teen walking home from a date christened with his first real kiss from a girl who previously only had moistened his dreams.

The game against the defending Division champions was billed as a preview of the seasonal race. Luke got the Reds going in the second, drawing a walk and racing to third on Taylor's single. He scored just ahead of a throw on a fly to medium right—even he had to be impressed with his speed. The Stinger then homered in the fourth and came to bat for what was to be his final appearance in the seventh. With Kitchell and Estabe on base and the game knotted 5-5, Luke ripped one down the line. The third sacker dove but the ball dodged his outstretched glove and both runners scored, providing the margin of victory.

Afterwards, Chad Lattimore shouted across the locker room to the winner, Kevin Sweeney. "Hey K-man, d'you know what the Stinger eats for breakfast?"

"No, but I hear he reads Superman comic books at night," Sweeney replied between chomps on a triple-decker hero.

Luke, took the thinly disguised tribute in stride. He felt a swat of a folded towel from the second oldest player, thirty-six-year-old Steve "Boomer" Cannon. "Nice game, old man." For most, the term would have been viewed in a less than endearing way. But to Luke it was just another sign that in a dozen short days, he had been initiated into the Reds' present-day fraternity.

Newly acquired Sean Wheatly, parading the room, beer in hand, joined in the banter. Wheatly, christened "the Officer" for his square face and short-cropped hair, spoke with a heavy Boston accent. "Maybe I ought to get a subscription to that magazine. D'ya think it could help me?"

"It's bound to help more than that *Playboy* you take to bed each night," Chad quipped.

"Hey, wise-ass, y'never know what you'll find in there. Why I even saw a photo of your mom!" Sean rejoined.

That evening, Luke heard a knock at his hotel door. His letter to Megan would have to wait. He hopped off the bed and moved to the peephole, where he eyed a familiar face. Twisting the deadbolt, Luke ushered Dr. Dornhoffer inside.

"Is this the celebrity I've been reading so much about?" Doc's polo shirt and spring golf jacket showed that he had made the transition from Midwest scientist to Florida tourist.

Mindful of hallway traffic, Luke shut the door before speaking. "I really appreciate you coming down here."

"My pleasure, Luke, my pleasure. I'm more than happy to help out my most famous patient, especially when the treatment seems to be having such positive results."

"Did Pat come along?"

"No, she's seeing our granddaughter in Pittsburgh. She's not much for baking in the sun."

Luke pulled the curtain closed on the pool and patio. "Did you make it to the game?"

"No, I had some things to take care of." Doc explained how he had to wait for the experimental treatment, which was Fed-Exed in dry ice. Luke knew him as someone who never took chances with logistical details. "But I do plan to get over tomorrow. Will you be playing?"

"Should be. They've given me two weeks to show 'em what I can do."

"From the little I glean from the box scores, you seem to be having a darn good start." Doc grabbed a clean bath towel and spread it on the vanity.

"So far so good." Luke eyed Doc unwrapping a syringe. "That medicine sure has done wonders for my play."

"Now Luke, I will not allow you to credit the treatment for what you yourself are doing. It doesn't time the pitches, or run the bases or, or—what d'you say—make those shoestring catches. All it can do is make sure your body parts are functioning properly."

"That's all, huh?" Luke's expression indicated what the drug had meant to him.

"I can't remember the last time I made a house call. Must be thirty-years," Doc thought out loud.

"Bet you never traveled so far for one."

"For sure."

"By the way, are you licensed down here?" Luke made light of the matter as he rolled up his sleeve and stretched out his arm.

"If I'm not, do you want me to stop now?" Doc smiled, rubbing alcohol onto the target area. "Actually, I picked up a seven-day license to practice in Florida. It's quite common."

For Luke, the antiseptic smell brought thoughts of hospitals and the unpleasant memories of his final trip with Kate. Watching Doc plunge the syringe into the membrane-topped vial, he felt a sinking feeling flush over him, as in those rare times when he thought everything to be in order, only to realize something important—or someone in this case—was missing.

"This should only take a second," Doc said as *ena-1* flowed into Luke's bloodstream. While Adrian hadn't brought "Nurse Ratched" along, Luke was oblivious to any pain.

The two-week trial period came and went. The question of Luke's tenure had been made academic by his .367 batting average and four home runs during the final eight games. Returning from his morning workout, Luke entered the dugout to the shouts of fans begging for autographs. He looked for more encouragement down the steps where he searched for his name on the line-up card. Sure enough, he found No. 27 penciled in. Turning around, Luke eyed Mike emerging from the tunnel. The skipper wore a stern expression as he said, "And if you're not there ready to play at game time, I'll fine your ass."

Walking back, Luke threw Mike an elbow. "Thanks a lot, Skip." The first milestone had passed. Luke now set his sights on making the opening day roster.

22
The Decision

Across town, Yankee players were getting in shape at their new Tampa complex. Veteran pinstripers oozed the pride of their team's illustrious heritage, while wide-eyed rookies dreamed of adding to it. Ty Hartmann was somewhere in the middle—a veteran needing to prove himself. With the paternity suit behind him and his pocket a bit lighter, he also felt renewed.

Chants of "Please, Ty!" and "Here, do mine!" rang out as he signed autographs along the foul line in spanking new Billy Martin Stadium. After two minutes of scribbling his name, Ty donned his hat, placed his glove under his arm and skipped out toward the field.

"What d'ya say, Ty?"

"Hey man, great day, huh?" Ty returned the greeting of third sacker Mantu Roddae. Gametime was an hour away. He hardly could wait, even if it was an exhibition; this one meant something.

"That was an awesome shot you had yesterday," the South African native praised.

Ty bent and grabbed his ankles just above the handwritten, white number "22" on the back of his shoes, in memory of a certain friend. *Awesome*—he liked the sound of the descriptor. Well deserved, not for its prodigious length—yes, it had that—but it also won the game in the ninth against the cross-town rivals, the "Metsies." Ty was leading the Yankees in about every offensive category. And his leadership led to winning; the team's 16-4 record looked "awesome" as well, spring training or not.

"We'll see how good the Red Sox really are today," Mantu said with a British accent.

"Forget it, Mantu. We're gonna kick their butts this year. You just watch." Ty's bravado had returned along with his offensive stats. He stepped toward the outfield, where dozens of palms hung high atop the bleachers.

"Hey, Ty. Got a few minutes?" The voice of a *New York News* reporter, Walt Fisher, halted him in mid-step.

"Just a couple. I wanna get in some fielding." In previous years, Ty never missed a chance to voice his opinions. That all changed during last year's forgettable season. He recalled writers making up stories about his having a drinking problem, when, after all, the only thing physically wrong was his leg. Okay, maybe he went on a bender or two, but that was while he was on the disabled list.

Ty grouped Walt with the few reporters who hadn't kicked him while he struggled. He flipped his darkened glasses to shield away the sun beaming over the writer's shoulder.

"I'm doing a story on the Eastern Division, and I'd like to get your thoughts."

Ty clasped his hands behind his head and pulled his arms apart. "Sure. Go ahead."

"Some are billing today's game against Boston as a tune-up for the Division race. What d'you think?"

"Hey, I don't worry about any one team. There are at least three, maybe four, that could win this thing." *No, he's not going to trap me into inciting the other division teams by saying it's a two-horse race.* "Some think that Boston's the team to beat—and they did win it last year—

but as far as I'm concerned, we all start out even."

"What about the Yankees?"

"We got ourselves a great team. Ended up only five out at the end of last season, and that was with more than our share of injuries. So, if we avoid that...."

"Not the least of which was yours."

"Yeah. A lot of people forget I played less than half a season." *And I didn't have a spring training, thanks to a certain Cincinnati general manager's stubbornness.* A shrill whistle from the stands drew a smile from Ty.

While Ty answered several more questions, he could hear the fans' cries in the background: "Ty, hit one for us today."..."You bum. Why didn't you hit like this last year when it counted?"..."Hey Ty, how about a loan?"

"Do you see yourself as a leader on this team?" Walt asked.

"We've got twenty-five leaders. But there comes a time when someone's got to step forward, and when that happens, I'm prepared to do it."

"Have you set any goals for yourself this year?"

"To bring home a World's championship. That and win the MVP award would be all right." He smiled. *Yes, that would be a nice comeback.*

"By the way, any thoughts on your old team's chances these days?"

"I don't know. I still have friends on the Reds, and I wish them well. But they look like they're short a player or two." He thought how they had yet to replace him. Sure, they picked up Sean Wheatly. The guy could hit, but he'd cost them in the field. And, as for Hanlon, Ty was among those who figured that the whole thing was a prank. He had seen the "old man" come up empty when the Yanks played the Reds in the fourth spring training contest.

"Listen, we'll talk more during the season," Ty said, starting a slow backpedal.

"Sure. Good luck."

Ty whirled and trotted across the infield. Ten steps onto the grass, he caught sight of a fly and accelerated after it. He tracked the ball sailing high overhead, as smooth and fast as a seagull, until finally, it descended deep in left-center. He reached out and snared it, as it was ready to hit the ground. Ty did a quick body roll and bounced up to the crowd's raucous cheers. He caught sight of several fans swirling their shirts above their heads and tipped his hat before rifling a throw to the cutoff man.

Returning to center, Ty read the right fielder's amazed expression. He smiled broadly. He was back at Plainfield High.

◆　　　◆　　　◆　　　◆

The days dwindled toward the March 29th deadline for extending contracts to major league ballplayers. Peter Vandermark realized he had to offer Luke one or give him his outright release. Assigning him to a minor league team was not an alternative in any case.

Peter straightened a paper clip as he studied a stat sheet at his desk. Instead of showing what a player had accomplished on the field, this one listed salaries and incentive programs. *What, do you offer a player in his mid-sixties, regardless of his spring training stats?* As much as he was amazed by what Luke had accomplished—8 homers and a .341 average—he was certain that there were only weeks, maybe days, before it all came to an end. Either this recycled ballplayer's energy would give out, or he would suffer some season-ending injury.

But Peter found it hard to argue with statistics: Luke's, the team's and, most of all, regular season ticket sales, which Noah Hall had reported to be up significantly. *This season might be a good one after all.*

"ZZZAP!" sounded the buzzer on the owner's speaker phone. He pressed the intercom. "Mr. Hanlon's here to see you."

"Send him in, Julie. Thanks."

Vandermark greeted the Hall of Famer and led him to a leather couch. He tossed the contract folder onto the circular glass table and took a seat in a matching armchair.

"You've had yourself quite a spring." It was an odd way for a GM to begin contract negotiations, but then Luke wasn't just any ballplayer. Vandermark was as impressed as anyone with this senior citizen.

"It's a good start." Luke hunched forward and folded his hands on the table. He spoke with the voice of a farmer hedging bets on what his field might yield. "They're some things I'm still a little rusty with, but I'll work 'em out."

"Some people wonder whether you ever get worn out?" He studied Luke's reaction.

If there was bait lying there, Luke wasn't biting. "Oh, I get tired like everyone else."

"It certainly hasn't affected your play."

"I know when to rest," Luke smiled.

"As you might have guessed, I've been impressed with your performance—as has Mike—and I, er, would like to make you an offer." The owner flicked the corner of his folder, while Luke held his position. Peter thought Luke might be nervous, but what he saw and what he felt indicated that it was he who felt uneasy. "I understand from Mike that you don't have an agent."

"No, I've never used one, and I don't see why I should get one now." Luke fell back into the cushion and laid his arm up over the couch. He thought about the financial adviser who had cost him thousands and nearly the farm.

"Did you have a particular figure in mind, you know, what you might be looking to earn?" Peter's negotiating strategy called for first finding out where the other party stood.

Luke shook his head. He wasn't playing for money. The things he wanted out of life were priceless. "Why don't you tell me what you think is fair? You know more about salaries than me."

Peter retrieved a pot of coffee and, after motioning it toward Luke, who waived it off, poured himself a cup. The owner found the quiet ones toughest to deal with. He opened his folder and slid out a blank contract. "The minimum salary for a player with ten or more years is $420,000." That was a starting point.

Twenty minutes later, the parties had worked out a deal. Luke satisfied Peter's uneasiness over how much he might play by agreeing to a flat rate of $20,000 per game. It would kick in once the minimum was satisfied.

What a bargain, Peter thought. At most, Luke might last thirty, or forty games, a mere $800,000, pennies by modern baseball standards. And any season tickets sales generated by Luke's early season presence would be guaranteed income for the entire year. His liking for Luke made the signing even sweeter.

As part of the negotiations, Luke insisted that there be no press conference regarding the signing. Peter was torn between Luke's request for privacy and his own desire to notify potential ticket buyers. They settled on a press release listing the official opening day roster. Luke's name was conspicuous by its presence.

More good news came Luke's way the following morning, when a sunrise call put him in touch with David. "Hey, Pop, 'got someone you might like to throw the ball around with...if you're not too busy playing with the Reds."

"Who's that?" Luke glanced at the clock and rubbed the sleep from his eyes.

"They can't talk on the phone just yet."

"Hey, did Sheila have her baby? What is it? I mean a boy, girl?"

"A boy. Sean Patrick."

A boy, Luke thought, someone to carry on the family name. And perhaps another ballplayer, if that was what he wanted to do. "Fantastic! Who's he look like?"

"You."

"C'mon."

"No, really. Even Sheila said so. And he's a big guy. Ten pounds, two ounces."

"Sounds like Bret. I think he was around ten."

The contract and now a grandson. Things indeed were looking up. True, Kate was gone, but life would continued. He could see that from the vantage point of a proud grandfather. Not that he didn't miss his wife—there wasn't a day gone by that he hadn't thought of Kate once, twice, sometimes for hours at a time. Yet, in a strange twist of fate, she actually had helped bring him closer to David. Kate still was helping out the family from her new life.

"Say, Pop, I hear you're doing really well down there."

Luke hadn't talked to his son in nearly three weeks. "Yeah, they offered me a contract yesterday."

"Unbelievable. Bret mentioned how you're taking some special medication."

"Well, we're not talking about that. No one's supposed to know."

"Right, he mentioned that, too."

Grandpa Hanlon found sleep an impossibility, so he left early for the ballpark with a rabbit hopping in his heart. He ran into Gus Stoltz in the hallway. Gus jerked his head and motioned to something inside the room. Around the corner, Luke could see what Gus wasn't saying. There, in the vicinity of his locker, a pack of reporters milled about.

He recalled his dad's advice from long ago: "Be careful of the three W's, son: women, wine and writers."

Luke stepped toward his locker. He figured he might as well get their questions over with before his mates arrived. Besides, nothing could dampen his spirits today, not even a grilling by the media.

The reporters engulfed Luke like a rising tide's sudsy waters submerging a sandcastle. A baldheaded reporter in a safari jacket threw out the first question. "Were you surprised at all making the ballclub?"

He smiled and thought what really surprised him was how quickly they had found out. "If I didn't think I had a good chance of making the team, I wouldn't have come here in the first place." His words came out slow and confident. His foot rested atop a stool.

Luke motioned to a columnist he had seen in the past, although he couldn't recall his name. "What made you decide to try a comeback?"

It was an oft-asked question. His answer varied little. Everything he said was true. He just left out certain details. "Oh, after I hit sixty, I decided I needed to work harder at keeping myself in shape. Then I got to playing ball with my son and, well, found that my limitations were more in my mind than on the field."

Stan Moore next won out among a rabble of voices. "Did the loss of your wife have anything to do with your decision to play ball again?"

"No." Luke's tone left no room for doubt.

Stan persisted. "Would you have tried to play if she were still alive?"

The blood rushed to Luke's neck. He cast the columnist a cold stare and unfastened his shirt buttons. So much for being able to grieve in private. He never considered his personal life fair game for reporters, and he wasn't about to change today or this season. He figured that wouldn't be so hard, being one who drank little and never ran around.

Across the room a woman seized the momentary pause. "People have been wondering how you're able to play when many your age have a tough time just getting out of bed. Any thoughts?"

Luke glanced at the freckled-blotched head of columnist Guy Lester. Guy had been a staff writer when Luke broke in the game. "Why don't you ask Guy here how he's still able to lift his pen?" The comment was delivered with warmth, rather than sarcasm.

The crowd roared. Several reporters fired barbs toward their colleague. "Yeah, why don't you retire Guy and let someone else move up?" The banter lasted for nearly a minute, time enough for Luke to dodge the issue. As much as he didn't want to divulge his secret, he very much wanted to avoid telling a lie.

Another asked, "Can you tell us anything about the details of your contract?"

"Only that it's more than I used to play for and probably less than many players make today. But I'm real happy with it." Luke spotted his manager passing the mob scene. They made eye contact. He flashed the look of a caged puppy. Mike smiled and waved as he left the room.

"How's it you didn't hire yourself an agent?"

"Didn't see it as any big deal. I guess if I was going for a multiyear deal, then I might have wanted help." What he'd like to do was let his bat do the talking, although he recalled a time when that wasn't enough—great years might mean you wouldn't have to take a pay cut. "Then, too, I might be at an advantage. If more guys had cut their teeth negotiating with the likes of Gabe Paul and Bill DeWitt, perhaps there wouldn't be as many agents." Luke thought back to the steely-eyed Dewitt, general manager and owner of the Reds. With slicked-back hair and wire-rim glasses, he bore a closer resemblance to an accountant than the lawyer he was. A teammate once cautioned Luke, "Place a dime in DeWitt's hands, and he'll squeeze out a dozen pennies!"

By now Luke had his shirt off. He started to unhook his belt when his eyes picked out the lady reporter on his right.

She smiled. He tightened his lips and closed the buckle.

A question came from the back, and with it a boom mike mounted on a long pole closed in on him. "What does your family think about you playing?"

Luke hesitated but saw no real harm in the question. Besides, he much preferred to give an answer than have the press track down his children. "They're real happy for me. And, seeing how none of them live at home anymore, they don't mind me traveling...."

His answer was cut short by a shout from beyond the reporters. "Is this some form of age discrimination? Aren't any of you interested in us younger guys?" The voice belonged to Chad Lattimore. The lanky pitcher waved to Luke before heading off.

A reporter up front spoke. "Do you expect any problem trying to compete with today's athletes?"

From his vantage point, Luke saw the comment as slighting the players of days gone by. He rubbed the back of his head. The last thing he wanted was to offend the modern players, those he would play with and against. "There's no doubt today's players are bigger and stronger, but that doesn't guarantee they're any better. Seems I don't recall too many .220 hitters or starting pitchers with five plus ERA's around when I played. So, from that respect I'd say I might have an advantage."

Luke noticed his ears ringing. A middle-aged reporter in a sweater branded with a polo pony spoke. "How long do you expect to play?"

"About as long as you can think up questions." The response drew more chuckles. Luke found himself more relaxed with the media than in his earlier playing days. It was as if he had found his rhythm answering their questions. Of course, the issues were mild and the news only good. He was glad for that. As he grew tired of the questions, his answers grew shorter. They asked why he thought the team was so much better than last year's ("the addition of Estabe and Wheatly, coupled with having Reynolds healthy again"); who would be the Reds' biggest competition in the division ("St. Louis, Chicago and even Houston"); and what he found the toughest part of playing now versus years before ("deciding which brand of shoes to wear; that and having twice the number of reporters to deal with").

"How 'bout one more, fellows—and ladies."

Guy Lester lifted his index finger. "I'd like to know your secret for staying young."

"Guess it has to do with my genes." Luke smiled and stepped from the stool. "Okay, I'll see you all after the game." He moved toward the rest room. A few members of the contingent trailed along, firing questions, but Luke ignored them. He chose instead to talk with Treat Reynolds, who wrapped his arm around him.

"I guess I can officially welcome you to the team, big guy."

The team. The season. Luke hardly could wait.

23

Let the Games Begin

Opening day. A new season and for Luke so much was new. Riding along I-75, he journeyed past Liberty Street and the memory of a ballfield he called home for most of his career. His means of transport was his '73 sunflower yellow Corvette, the one given him by Sparky Anderson and his teammates upon retirement.

Winding toward downtown, recollections filled his head. Gone were the electric-powered buses, with their anemic arms raised high, clinging to the network of wires running along the streets. Gone too were the peanut vendors with their stovepipe hats and wilted tuxedos, replaced by bag-hawking salesmen clad in T-shirts. Gone for the most part were the sport coats and dress slacks, remnants of a bygone man's world. And with them, the top hats in boring shades of grey, replaced by brightly colored caps and visors.

Turning into Riverfront Stadium's parking garage, Luke thought about another remembrance that meant more than all the others: the cozy confines of Crosley Field. It was a field of memories, of catches and homers, wins and losses, teammates and friends. He had left so much behind there. Crosley, home to natural grass and bricks, with its potpourri of ads, frozen in stop action. A shortage of seats had done it in as much as age. Luke found it hard to separate his love for the game from his love for the park. As if preserving the memory of a loved one, he even refused to call the new stadiums "ballparks."

There would be no comebacks for old Crosley. A wrecking ball had seen to that in '72. He remembered stopping by after a game to gaze at the gnarled girders and broken bricks.

Luke entered the clubhouse and thought how he'd just have to create new memories within the symmetrical confines of Riverfront. He noted there were positive changes: the lush carpeting, for one, a welcomed departure from the splinter-filled, wooden slats that covered the second-floor locker room at Crosley.

He exchanged greetings with players and reporters, put on his uniform and game face, and left for the dugout. From there he watched a procession of local dignitaries, many who came to recognize the Reds as much as be recognized: Mayor David Barnsworth, city council members, TV talk show hosts, newspaper editors and members of the Rosey Reds' Fan club.

Many bestowed some small memento—plaques, trophies, certificates—to the home team. Then there was the one from the Cincinnati Zoo. Vandermark had arranged for his favorite charity to send over an elephant to throw out the first pitch. Luke watched as Peter presented it with an oversized Reds hat. It would not be worn again, Luke thought. Too large, even for some of the swelled heads now playing ball.

As the pachyderm stomped toward the mound, Kurkowski elbowed Luke, pointing to a spot near first. "Watch where you step. I doubt any of the officials are going to pick up that gift."

Luke appreciated the comment, anything to break the tension. He thought about some humorous rejoinder, but at this juncture he found talking difficult.

Twenty minutes later, Treat led the team's charge onto the field. As a female member of the Cincinnati police sang the National Anthem, Luke felt himself overcome with emotion: the exhilaration of playing the game he loved; the thrill of standing before a packed house; and the sense that somewhere out there Kate was watching.

Luke flexed his knees and touched the ground. He tossed the ball with Reynolds in center. Thanks to Dr. Einhardt's miraculous discovery, he felt in great shape. His enabling genes were functioning quite well. In the background he listened to a plea from the PA announcer: "Will the media please leave the field so we can begin today's game." *Have we come to the point where the press can hold up the start of a season?* Luke thought ruefully.

The moment of the first pitch, in the first inning of his first game in more than twenty years, approached agonizingly slowly. Since leaving home he had come to feel trapped in one of those troublesome dreams, in which one starts out with a place in mind, and then spends the rest of the night tossing and turning, getting sidetracked and sideswiped, never arriving at one's destination before the alarm clock buzzer sounds, signaling the start of a new day.

From his position in left, Luke felt the focus of 50,000 pairs of eyes. He spat on the turf. *Good thing I changed to gum after retirement. Tobacco juice would stain this rug.*

On the few occasions when Luke had attended games at Riverfront, he had thought how this was no longer the same sport Abner Doubleday developed—a game played on a dirt field with patches of natural grass, by adult men doing it for the love of it, rather than the riches. The impressions flashing before him during those visits painted a picture of a stage show, a production. It was theater in the round, complete with electronically reproduced music blasting through 1,000-watt speakers, with theater-sized TV screens, broadcasting what he appreciated best live. A drama played out on a carpeted platform with painted stripes showing the performers where to stand. Actors decked out in designer costumes that accentuated their physiques. Leading men nattily attired with "dinner gloves" as they came to bat, taking bows as they exited the stage after a dramatized rendition of "My Old Home Run" trot.

Such thoughts now vaporized into the night air. Yes, so much had changed. A visit to the park no longer represented a respite from the sights and sounds of the outside world. The modern world and the game had blended together as one. Yet, it was still very much a game loved by the kid in him. He held hope that it would survive its metamorphosis, just as an ingenue retains her charm on Oscar night, despite being duped into donning some outrageous designer dress concealing her natural persona.

The top of the first came and went. A solitary walk was the only blemish to ace Kevin Sweeney's opening. Corrigan cheered the players on their return to the dugout. "Awright, Raphee, build a run."

Luke watched the Dominican native draw a walk and quickly swipe second, while Wells struck out. That brought No. 27 to the plate and the fans to their feet.

"Batting third...." A tremendous roar blocked out the announcer's bass vocals and prickled Luke's body with goosebumps as he swirled two bats overhead. He felt pins and needles along his bat handle. His knees wanted to fold as he dug his feet into the clay, and a gossamer of thoughts made it difficult for him to focus on the pitcher. More years had passed since he last played than had before he first broke into the majors.

The clapping ceased, and an eerie silence fell over the stadium as the pitcher took his stretch. Luke planted his foot near the back of the box and tucked his head behind his left shoulder. *Woooshhhh.* The pitch sailed by for ball one.

The pitcher fired the next one over the outside corner. He gave a rip. *Whack.* He sliced it into the blue boxes beyond the first base dugout. The pebble had been cast upon the pond. Soft rhythmic ripples spread forth throughout Luke's body. He felt his concentration return. *Need to get around on it sooner.*

A knee-high fast ball bore down on the plate, and Luke jumped on it, lining it to center. An eighth of an inch higher on the bat, he figured, and he would have had himself an extra base hit and the Reds a run. Instead, the center fielder snapped his mitt shut around the ball.

Cincinnati went down without fanfare in the next two frames. Meanwhile, St. Louis built a 2-0 lead.

In the home third, Luke went underground to the batting cage. His swing just didn't feel right. It wouldn't until he produced. Besides, he realized, the practice would help relieve his nervous energy.

Leading off the fourth, Logan Wells singled to center. Once again Luke's entrance stirred the fans, but the Cards' pitcher showed him no such respect; he challenged him with fast balls. Luke fell behind, a ball and two strikes. He guessed another fast ball and was right. *Thwack*—a drive into the power alley in right. Luke broke from the gate. Only a fine play by the center fielder held Wells at third, while the Stinger cruised into second.

Luke stood tall on the bag, hands on hips. He breathed deeply, more to relax himself than to catch his wind. He felt back where he belonged. The crowd awarded him a foot-stomping, standing ovation while the organist saluted with a dusty old tune. Luke felt somewhat embarrassed as he recalled the words to a '60s hit by Darlene and the Dreamers:

> He's humble and he's shy—
> He's the apple of my eye.
> I know I'm not alone
> in thinking he's so neat.
> All the girls flock his way
> 'cause he's really, really sweet.
> He's the one I love.

Not usually one for details, Luke placed the song at a point in his career. *He's the One I Love. 1962. We won 98 games but ended up finishing behind the Dodgers and Giants.*

Reynolds stepped in the box. With the new batter came a new tune. A series of staccato notes rang out, "Dun dun dun dah, dun dun

dun dah, dun dun dun dah dah!" The crowd kept pace with a rhythmic clapping. The excitement reverberated all the way down to the stadium footings.

Reynold's walk loaded the bases for Randy Kitchell. Luke glanced back to the bag, then broke as Randy drilled the first pitch to right. Wells scored easily, and Luke slid home ahead of the throw, notching the game at 2-2.

From there the game moved along with both pitchers in control. Luke flew out harmlessly to start the sixth. Then, in the top of the seventh, the visitors collected a pair of runs and sent Sweeney to the showers. Mark Shaw came in to retire the side. By then, the damage had been done.

In the eighth, Steve Cannon pinch-hit and boomed a double. He stayed put as Estabe and Wells struck out, leaving the team's hopes in Luke's hands.

The first three pitches weren't even close. Luke stared at the third base coach for a sign. With the green light on, he pulled a pitch deep but foul. The pitcher took it as a warning shot and promptly delivered ball four.

Reynolds followed with his own free pass. That brought up lefty Kitchell and a fresh arm from the Cards' bullpen. *Come on, Randy,* Luke thought, inching his way off second. *Keep that head down and front foot closed.*

Randy kept his head down, alright. He lifted the next pitch over the fence for a grand slam! Reds 6, Cards 4. The stadium erupted like a fanatical Mideast crowd at a state funeral. A round of fireworks exploded over the Ohio, out beyond center field.

There had been no such spectacles following homers at Crosley, although, if a player was lucky enough to hit the Sieber Clothing billboard in left, he won a free suit. Luke had filled out his wardrobe by knocking five such shots during his first career.

Kyle Worley shut the Cardinals down in the ninth, preserving the victory and sending the partisans home with electricity pulsing through their veins. As the crush of fans zigzagged down the exit ramps, feet floating above the pavement, shouts of "Go Reds" and "The Stinger's back" rang out. Noah credited Luke with having put the city in a time warp.

Seated barefoot on a stool, Luke faced questions from a media throng. He couldn't help think back to days in the fifties when there might not be a single reporter in the locker room.

Luke vainly tried to redirect his interviewers across the floor to the day's real hero, Kitchell. Fair was fair; he didn't want, nor did he deserve, adulation. Forget the fact that he had become a grandfather just a week before. A double and a walk were "okay." All in a day's work.

Eventually, Randy received his share of questioners.

That freed Luke to file a report in his Wallace-Adams notepad, just as he had for each game of his previous eighteen seasons. The habit began with his very first game. That came in 1955, when, a month into the season, the Reds traded outfielder Jim Greengrass, creating an opening for the rookie from Youngstown.

As the two stragglers emerged into the players' waiting room, they were greeted by Megan and Bret. "You were great out there Dad," Megan said, planting a kiss on his cheek.

Luke appreciated the show of affection from his apple-cheeked daughter, but he let her compliment float by. He turned toward his teammate. "Kitch, come on over. Some people I'd like you to meet. Megan, Bret, this here's Randy Kitchell. He's the guy who did the real damage."

"Fine piece of hitting. You really carried the team today," Bret complimented with a knowing voice, ballplayer to ballplayer.

"Thanks," Randy shrugged. "But if your dad hadn't set the table, I wouldn't of had the chance."

Teammates kiddingly referred to the good-looking twenty-six-year-old as "teen idol." But underneath his lean, six-foot frame, there existed a rock-solid body with catlike reflexes that Luke recognized made for a potential lethal advantage over pitchers. Yet, far be it for Randy to brag about his talents. And that was something Luke admired. Perhaps because of it he had developed a fondness for the first baseman. "How 'bout joining us for dinner?"

"Thanks, but I'm pretty beat. I'll take a raincheck, though," the broad-faced athlete said.

"Come on, we'll make it an early evening," Megan encouraged.

"You sure?" Luke asked. "We're just going over to the Montgomery Inn for some ribs."

"You discovered my weakness—ribs," Randy replied, swinging his jacket over his shoulder. "Let's do it."

After the meal, Luke drove off alone to the Homestead. Megan returned to her condo near Dayton while Bret headed back to UC for classes and a game of his own the next day.

As Luke's Vette wound through Southern Ohio's back roads, an empty feeling swept over him. He didn't have to wait until he arrived home to understand the cause. Gone was the woman who used to welcome him home with a smile that said win or lose, I love you. Luke had been so absorbed in making the team that he had been able to keep his sorrow at bay. Yet, in some ironic twist, this time of celebration brought to mind his greatest sadness. Everything seemed so insignificant compared to her passing. Fortunately, when he arrived home it was nearly 10 p.m. He would soon bury such thoughts in sleep.

As he pulled into the driveway, he saw a figure dance in the headlights, wiggling back and forth like some topless showgirl spotlighted on stage. Only this was a dance of joy, not lust. It was Rusty.

Hanging his keys on the pantry hook, Luke spoke to his friend. "I wish I could take you with me, Rusty. But they don't allow dogs in the park where I play." At least not since the days when Mrs. Schott let her Saint Bernard roam the field and chase the players.

Luke knelt and petted the dog's spotted coat. "You're gonna have to get used to it. I expect to be traveling into the fall." The dog rested his head on Luke's knee. For Rusty, time was irrelevant. He took things hour by hour, day by day. Luke realized the strategy was a good one for himself.

The only difference in game two was the size of the crowd— about half as large as the opener. The Reds won again, this time by a measure of four-zip. Scott Brouse combined with reliever Worley to throw a stingy six-hit shutout. Taylor and Kitchell knocked in a run apiece, while Reynolds doubled in the final two.

Luke collected a walk in five trips. His swing felt good; he was just missing. That didn't bother him, so long as the team kept winning and he kept making contact—he had yet to strike out. He knew the hits eventually would fall.

Inside the dressing room, Luke passed the winning pitcher. "Hey, Prairie Dog, you done good."

"Thanks. You inspired me," bubbled the 5'8" hurler clad in undershorts and a grey Oklahoma State T-shirt.

Brouse was called "Prairie Dog" because of his Oklahoma roots and the way he liked to wear his bushy hair with a tail in the back. But it was the wicked slider rather than his haircut that Scott became known for around the league. As a teen, the pint-sized Sooner had strengthened his body wrestling and roping calves on the junior rodeo circuit. He developed a habit of occupying his time between events by knocking down bottles with rocks from thirty yards. A local coach suggested he give pitching a try. Scott found the game provided outdoor competition without all the bruises of the rodeo.

The final game of the homestand was an evening affair. The home first began with Estabe legging out an infield nubber. Wells followed by smashing a single, setting the table for Luke. He took one, two practice swings, then slowly rotated the bat into position, like the sweep hand of a clock moving counterclockwise toward the number "2". He sighted down as the first pitch zoomed plateward, then fired on all cylinders. Rippling muscles inside toughened flesh uncoiled in synchronized rhythm, powerful but never forced, proof that the human body could be as much a machine as flesh and blood. *Contact.*

Luke didn't need to follow the ball's path any more than the fans who studied his swing or saw the ball's initial trajectory. He sprinted toward first, then, raising his head, slowed as he confirmed that the orb's path would take it well beyond the wall in left. He trotted around the bases, chin tucked in, as the night sky exploded.

Rounding third, Luke felt a chill that almost brought tears to his eyes. As one who lived by keeping his emotions in check, it was highly unusual. But he didn't need a statistician to remind him when he had hit his last home run: September 3, 1972.

Later, a member of the grounds crew brought Luke the baseball. He declined Noah's offer to send it to Cooperstown, saying he wanted it himself. He had his own plans for it.

Luke went on to collect a walk and a double before Corrigan took him out in the seventh to a standing ovation. By then the Reds were ahead 8-1 and well on their way to a sweep of last season's pennant winner. True, the Cards had lost their top hitter and a starting pitcher to free agency, but they were still a good test.

Up on the yellow press box level, columnist Stan Moore drummed his pen on the Formica tabletop as he watched Luke leave the field. The crowd's roar penetrated the floor-to-ceiling window panels that enclosed the media room.

"What do you say, Stan? Ready to admit he's for real?" writer Guy Lester needled the *Star-Gazette* columnist. The two were among twenty-some writers seated in the press box.

Stan shook his head. Okay, so Luke wasn't just a publicity stunt by Vandermark. Still, something wasn't right. "What I want to know is how he does it."

Another reporter joined the conversation. "Me, too. I could use some of whatever he has."

Stan wasn't interested for himself. No, he was interested in the story.

In the background, the PA announcer introduced the Cards' pitching change. A jingle followed promoting a local brewery, while a cartoon figure danced to the music on the screen in center.

"You know as well as I do, people his age just don't do the type of things he's doing," Stan snarled, underscoring the words "don't do."

"I'll say. It hurts me just to carry my own luggage. And he's got eight years on me!" Guy said.

A press box announcement gave the summary stats on both Hanlon and the departed St. Louis hurler. Stan spoke under his breath. "I don't know how he's doing it, but I intend to find out." He refused to get taken up in the excitement of Luke's accomplishments. For him, there was a bigger story waiting to be written.

Guy Lester held a different viewpoint. He remembered Luke from his earlier playing days and relished "what" he did, without concern for the "how." And like most reporters, he appreciated the fact that Luke's return was good for selling papers. That Sunday, after two more Reds victories, Guy captured his thoughts in his column.

Cincinnati—The December Rose

"God gave us memories,
so that we might have roses in December."

The words belong to James Barrie, the English writer who helped us dream about flight and eternal youth. They describe the power of our imagination to recollect things that once were for which we now long. Luke Hanlon is changing all that.

This aged wonder, who in an earlier time enjoyed a Hall of Fame career, is back with his team, performing magic at Riverfront. His career is once again in full bloom, despite the fact that he is playing in what, for most mortals, might be viewed as the December of their lives. For he **is** the December Rose.

Yes, we all have fond memories of No. 27 from his playing days in the '50s and '60s. But yesterday I witnessed this December Rose leading the Reds to their fifth straight win with a three-run rocket shot in the sixth, transforming a 4-2 deficit into victory.

He's back as if he never left; with the same tug on his shirt as he steps to the plate; with the familiar arm extension as he takes his cuts; with the "aw shucks" face-down-trot after each home run; and with the effortless stride chasing balls in the outfield, followed by a graceful leg kick as he tosses them in from center, like some Greek god who knew he needn't showboat to prove his worth.

No one knows how he does it, nor do we really care. The fact is he is here, lightening our hearts, lifting our spirits and those of his teammates, on what seems to be a rejuvenated club. His youthful exuberance is contagious, as the rest of the Reds have found out.

There are no thorns surrounding this rose. Luke Hanlon is sincerity, sportsmanship and teamwork rolled into one. After last night's victory, Luke refused to admit that he might be something special. "I may be older than the rest of the guys here, but that's where the difference ends. I don't see myself as anything special 'cause I'm not."

He knows nothing about complaining and cares even less about the money issues that have threatened the game he loves. In fact, reports are that he signed for a per-game rate that might make a .210 hitting reserve outfielder feel cheated.

For those who cherish the game of baseball, and count this writer among them, we only can thank God for giving us the December Rose. He's not some figment of our imagination, but a real-life hero.

24
Snapshots of a Winner

A morning breeze spun tiny white blossoms across the grass and tombstones at Cherry Hill cemetery, north of Millville. The sun reflected off a polished headstone, washing out the etched name of Katherine Graham Hanlon. Luke stood in front, arms folded, head hung in thought, eyes fixed on the chiseled roses entwined atop the Georgian grey tablet.

He shaped his thoughts into conversational sentences and spoke as if his wife were standing before him. *Kate, I know how much you like black-eyed Susans. Picked 'em this morning from your garden. Hope they brighten your day...small thanks for all the times you brightened mine. I'm sure you know how much it hurts not having you here...love you, Kitten.*

Moments later, Luke retreated for the lonely ride to the ballpark. Left behind were the black-spotted flowers. Nested on top was a bruised National League baseball that only days before had sailed more than 400 feet, tearing through record books along the way.

Sunday afternoon, Luke and the Reds made quick work of the

Cubs, the Central Division's odds-on favorite. The victory wrapped up a perfect homestand. The players boarded their evening charter to begin a nine-game roadtrip, minus Luke. He had asked Mike if he could join the team after taking care of some personal business.

The following morning Luke was the first patient to enter the Caulfield Science Center clinic. Ready to greet him was the gushing, middle-aged receptionist, Margaret. "Oh, Luke. I, er, mean Mr. Hanlon, good morning."

"Morning. Luke's fine."

"It's so wonderful to see you playing again. And you can't imagine how much my nephew loves your autograph—the one you did last time. Remember—Lindsey?" While Margaret's head bobbed about, her eyes remained fixed on Luke. "He keeps it taped to his headboard."

"Glad he likes it." *Hopefully now I've covered all of your relatives,* Luke mused.

Luke had found running into Margaret the most painful part of his clinic visits. Not that he minded giving out autographs; it was just the hero worship that she slobbered on him. *Somehow, the way she acts seems so demeaning,* he thought. But if it made her happy, then he would honor her requests. The only ones he refused were the promoters, the wheeler-dealers who enticed him with offers of big bucks at memorabilia shows. *No, one shouldn't hang a price tag on such things.* Luke viewed autographs as his way of thanking the fans for their support.

Dr. Dornhoffer leaned over the Dutch door and beckoned to Luke. He escorted the celebrated patient down the hall to his world of discovery.

Luke lay on the examining table while Doc ran a battery of tests, from whacks on his joints to an EKG. He finished up by shooting a spring-loaded, hollowed-out needle into Luke's gluteus maximus to obtain a tissue biopsy. "You may feel a little pinch, but this'll only take a second." Luke barely had time to think about that night's game when Doc announced it was all done.

"You selling my cells to some collector?" Luke asked.

"I imagine they might bring a fair price," Doc chuckled. "But no, this allows us to look at a cross section of your cells. That way we can be sure there's no unusual activity. Just precautionary."

Luke rolled over and sat upright, the protective paper crackling underneath. "How's everything else?"

"All looks to be quite normal." Doc pursed his lips as he checked his notes. "Or perhaps I should say abnormally good for someone your age. We should have results of the blood tests in a day or two."

As Doc administered another shot of *ena-1*, Luke answered his baseball questions. He admitted he was still feeling his way around the "younger guys."

"Should I order my playoff tickets?" Doc grinned.

"They'll be on me. But let's not rush things. I only said we'll be in the race."

Doc shifted the subject. "How's it feel to be a celebrity again— many fans chasing after you?"

"It hasn't been too bad. Except, of course, for Miss Sociable downstairs."

"Who?" Doc scrunched his forehead.

"Your receptionist."

"Oh, you mean Margaret?"

Luke nodded.

"Come to think of it, I should have you come up the back way. That way you won't have to worry about being seen or bothered by anyone."

"I don't know that it's necessary."

"There's a physician's entrance around the side of the building. I'll get you a resident pass."

"Just so long as no one asks me to practice medicine," Luke grinned.

"Oh, I imagine you would have made a wonderful doctor. But then, think of the ballplayer we would have lost."

Luke flew to Atlanta with time to spare before the game against

the Braves. From the moment he deplaned, he felt the interest surrounding him. The taxi driver sang his praises, his headlines cried out
from newspaper racks, and autograph-seekers pounced on him at the
hotel. He signed for ten minutes before checking in and taking a nap
prior to the game.

On the hill for the Reds that evening was second-year fireballer
Chad Lattimore, also known as "Fast Chad." The moniker reflected
the pitcher's penchant for chasing women and driving cars at speeds
even his 98-mile-an-hour heater could not top. Chad first had come
to Luke's attention the previous spring, by way of his fintailed 1956
Chevy Impala. The rookie had driven it to training camp from his
home in Waco, Texas. The fact that it was still in excellent shape told
Luke here was a guy to whom cars meant more than transportation.
The pitcher since had upgraded to a Ferrari.

That night, Chad sped through the Braves line-up, notching ten
strikeouts and a 3-0 shutout victory. Luke walked and singled and
came around to score both times. Afterwards, Scott Brouse approached
him at his locker. "I'd never know your wheels had much mileage on
them judging by the way you motor around the bases."

"I just try to stay a step ahead of you young guys, that's all." Luke
smiled as he toweled off.

"A bunch of us were getting together to celebrate Chad's first
shutout and were wondering if you'd like to come along."

"Thanks, but I'll pass."

"You sure? Go get some food and hit the floor for a little line
dancing—you know, you're not the only cowboy among us."

Luke shook his head as Ducky arrived and picked up the conversation. "C'mon, we've got ten going at last count— you don't want to
miss out on a good time."

"Don't worry about me. Besides, I'm sorta tired. Getting rest is
one of my secrets for staying ahead of you youngsters."

"Maybe next time," Scott said, motioning for Ducky to move
along.

As the players left, Luke realized it was more a matter of feeling uncomfortable around the players than feeling tired. In a way, he felt bad turning them down. Yet, as he approached his second month on the team, he found himself spending much of his free time near Mike and coach Zender. He was closer to both in age and mindset. Whereas he and Mike loved to talk sports of any kind, the players' topics of conversation ran the gamut from pending bills in Washington to their promotional deals.

The next night, Luke found out why they called Atlanta's Olympic Stadium the "launching pad-II." While the dimensions were bigger than those of the retired Fulton Stadium, balls shot out like sparks off a fire of green logs. Randy collected another homer, but the Braves roughed up Clint Twiddy for four of their own en route to victory.

In Wednesday's rubber game, it was the Red's turn to play home run derby. Luke crushed his third of the season, helping the visitors build a 5-0 lead. Reynolds, who earlier connected on a three-run blast of his own, stepped to the plate. The first pitch came in with a message written all over it near his chin, forcing him to the dirt.

Luke watched from the dugout, as Reynolds glowered at the pitcher. The towering athlete answered back, rocketing the next one down the left field corner, just foul. But the hurler got in the last word, delivering one square in his back. Luke wasn't exactly sure how it happened; the events all ran together. Two steps down the line, Treat cut to his left, his arms outstretched, his hands beckoning for the pitcher. Luke vaulted from the dugout and joined the fracas in support of his teammate.

He arrived to find Reynolds and the pitcher entwined on the ground like two pretzels. He grabbed a Brave ready to land a punch on Kurkowski. In a scene reminiscent of Prairie Dog's cow roping days, Brouse climbed atop the hurler and pinned his arms behind his back, freeing Reynolds. When the play cleared, both pitcher and batter were ejected.

Cincinnati went on to win the game. Afterwards, Reynolds made a point of seeing Luke. "Thanks, pop. I heard you were one of the first out there to help."

Luke, a towel wrapped around his neck, smiled. "You're too important to have your brains beat in. Besides, it was probably my homer that got you in trouble."

"Nah. My shot in the first did that." Treat's grin showcased his pearly whites. "Yours just added a little salt to the wound."

Treat started walking when Luke spoke. "I expect I won't be needing to run out there too often." The comment drew a thoughtful silence.

Treat turned. "You saying I overreacted?"

"You gotta determine that for yourself." To him, charging the mound was petty and risky. "It's just sometimes not worth a wrestling injury."

"C'mon, Luke!" Treat cried out. "He could've really hurt me."

"You seem to have pretty quick reflexes and a hard head."

"I don't know whether to take that as a compliment or not," Treat offered, his voice softening. "I suppose you'll tell me they never threw at you?"

Like a mine cave-in that begins with a rumble down deep, then erupts into a roar, Luke broke into laughter. "Throw at players? Some of those SOBs like Drysdale thought they owned the plate." Luke referred to the late Dodger sidewheeler, Don Drysdale. He recalled Don saying that a hitter could have the inside corner or the outside corner, but he couldn't have both. "Why, he got so mad once he plunked Blasingame, Pinson and Robinson before being ejected."

"And you're gonna tell me no one went after him?" Reynolds asked, incredulous.

Luke shook his head no. "It was all part of the game, Treat. We just dug in and tried to hit the next pitch as hard as we could—hopefully back through the box. Oh, our pitchers sometimes returned the favor. To be honest, there was none of this warning crap by the umps. We just felt it was something we should take care of within the game. Wrestling? Now that's a whole different sport."

Treat nodded. He smiled and said, "I guess it was a different game back then."

Luke smiled and patted him on the back before heading for the showers. *Not a different game, just different players, Treat.*

The Reds rolled into Houston with an 8-1 record. Not bad for a team forecast to finish fourth, Luke thought. There they made it two out of three. Luke collected four hits in ten official at bats, raising his average to a lofty .384.

The Reds' record also impacted the gate. Noah Hall paraded the locker room after Sunday's win, exclaiming that ticket sales back home were hotter than the favorite local chili. The Reds moved on to face the inept Colorado Rockies.

Playing in Denver proved a rewarding experience for Luke. Aside from the warm reception from the baseball-starved fans, there was the pleasure of hitting a ball at 5,000 feet. He launched two towering blasts on successive evenings at Coors Stadium. But the real story was Estabe. Luke witnessed Corrigan's assessment coming true. Raphael, or the "Whippet" as the lean speedster came to be known, played flawless defense. Given free access by Taylor to the gap between short and third, he displayed a remarkable ability to gun out runners from deep in the hole. Luke already had seen him rob opponents of a half dozen hits, saving several runs.

With his improved fielding, the shortstop's confidence rose and with it his batting average. "I never feel comfortable with the A's," he told reporters in broken English. "Mr. Corrigan, he told me the job was mine in the spring. That made me feel good. And I like playing alongside Dean. We a team."

The Whippet reached base eleven out of thirteen times in Denver—twice on errant throws as he raced to beat out slow bouncers. With him serving as the table setter for Luke, Treat and Randy, the Reds swept to three easy victories to close out the roadtrip.

A spring storm, sweeping out the northwest, shadowed Cincinnati's flight home. Luke sat between the window and manager Corrigan, who had dozed off before refreshments were served.

As the plane rocked along, Luke gazed outside at the surreal landscape. Bolts of lightning lit up massive, anvil-like clouds. Up ahead, an ominous grey mass, a tidal wave of ice crystals, inched closer. Luke thought how thankful he was for the 727 jet. Despite the weather, it was a relatively smooth ride. The 1,000-foot altitude drops and the stunt-like rolls that rocked the four-engine Electra prop-planes and DC-3s he had traveled in were things of his past. He recalled the time a lightning bolt had sheared off the stabilizer on the way to St. Louis. Even he had grabbed an air sickness bag. *Yes, there are some advantages to playing ball in the '90s.*

◆   ◆   ◆   ◆

Back on terra firma, Luke found two large U. S. mail sacks camped out next to his locker at Riverfront. His stool had been replaced by a rocker with an etched inscription, "Grandpa Hanlon." On its seat was a pack of adult diapers.

Luke turned to see several teammates, all smiles. He picked up the box of diapers, studied it and said, "Hey, these aren't even my size!" The comment broke up the room.

When things quieted down, Reynolds spoke. "I know some players who could use that rocker a lot more than you do."

"Tell you what, why don't we make this one of those 'player of the game awards'?" Luke suggested. "I'll lend it to the guy who plays like he's looking for a rest."

"Gee, us pitchers only get to compete for it every four days," Clint said, feigning disappointment.

"Don't worry, Clint, I imagine you'll be getting plenty of opportunity to sit in it." More laughter ensued. All knew Clint's work ethic left much to be desired.

Sitting down, Luke realized the rocker represented a welcome mat more than a resting place for someone who cared little about rest. And while he didn't come out and say it, he appreciated his teammates' sign of support.

Luke rocked forward and snapped the clasp on the first mail sack, opening it wide enough to grab a handful of letters. Was this another practical joke? A thumb through told him they were indeed legit.

"There are two more sacks waiting for you downstairs." The carefully articulated words signaled the arrival of Noah Hall.

"Well if it isn't Noah 'T' Hall," Miles Bailey greeted. His pronunciation sounded more like "know-it-all." Luke had heard other ballplayers adding the middle initial, as well.

The pudgy PR director bore a striking resemblance to a troll. He wore his brown hair combed back to a short ducktail atop his bespeckled, cherubic face. And while he knew how to eat, he also knew how to dress. This day he wore a randomly patterned, neon tie that reflected his personality more than his navy blazer. Under his left arm, he carried his trademark clipboard, complete with his daily paper file.

Luke used a positive approach while pointing to the mail sacks. "See what your press releases have done, Noah."

"Your actions speak louder than my words," Noah replied, adjusting his round wire-rims. "If you wouldn't mind holding off on your reading for a minute...."

"Sure, what d'you have?"

"Some dates for our next roadtrip. 'Good Morning America' and the 'Today Show' would like to see you when we're in New York playing the Mets on the 27th." Noah leafed through his notes. "And KABC's 'Morning Show' gave us a choice of dates for our West Coast trip."

"Hey, not so fast," Luke exclaimed, raising his hand. "I'd just as soon limit my appearances to the field."

"But Luke, people want to see you." Noah kicked a mailbag. "You've captured the heart of the fans, and the shows realize that."

"You mean they would like to take advantage of that, huh?" Luke had found out long ago that one gained as much privacy as one commanded. He was willing to fight for his.

"Sort of. But it'll be good press for you and the Reds—bring in extra fans."

"Winning ball games will put fans in the seats just as fast."

Just then, Scott Brouse wandered by and cranked his hand as if filming with an old movie camera. Noah ignored the phantom filming and scratched his neck. "The media are going to get you one way or the other. It's either the talk shows or interviews at the ballpark."

"That's fine. I have no problem givin' interviews around the Stadium. I'm just not lookin' to become some TV entertainer." Luke had all the stage experience he wanted early on in his career with a series of forgettable commercials endorsing a now defunct product, Bravo aftershave. He still winced whenever he thought back to the ads.

One such black-and-white spot featured him reaching into the bat rack and, instead of a bat, had him grabbing the product. He proceeded to slap on a generous amount in front of teammates wearing smiles reminiscent of teens who had just stuck a mouse inside someone's glove. It next cut to Luke in the batter's box, tapping the plate with his weapon. He looked into the camera and in a halting delivery, said, "I never leave *home* without using *Bravo* aftershave. Don't you." Luke then knocked the ball skyward and raced toward first base while the crowd cheered "Bravo!"

"But Luke, baseball is entertainment," Noah said.

"Maybe for you it is. For me, it's still a game. And right now it's time I let my bat and glove do the talkin'." Luke's tone grew conciliatory. He liked the young PR rep a lot more than his field of work. "I'm sure you understand."

Prairie Dog picked up the conversation. "I think the man's saying he doesn't want to be interviewed, 'No-it.'"

"It's okay Scott. He's just doing his job," Luke said.

Noah did his best imitation of a free safety backpedaling on third and long. "Okay. Okay. I'll put the shows on hold for now."

Luke shook hands to show there was no animosity. He had educated Noah about his priorities.

25
A Trip Back in Time

The Reds' juggernaut gathered speed as the team toured the National League Cities. Like an F-4 spreading napalm over 'Nam, their flame throwers—Sweeney, Lattimore and Worley—mowed down hitters, while the Hanlon-Reynolds-Kitchell combo blasted pitchers. Two out of three in New York. A sweep in Pittsburgh. Back home for a showdown with Los Angeles, whom they bested in three out of four before splitting with the Giants. As mid-May rolled around, the Reds commanded baseball's best record, at 25-6.

Luke figured heavily in both defensive and offensive categories. He dashed, he dove, he reached and robbed opponents of hits. At the plate, he exhibited a power display that amazed even those who wanted to believe anything was possible. For the December Rose, it seemed anything was. He collected seven homers before pitchers caught onto the fact that they couldn't throw fastballs by the senior citizen. An assortment of off-speeds, sliders and curves lowered his average to a mere mortal .357.

Luke was thrilled to be part of a winner. Even more, he loved being back in the game. Back in the competition, back with a group of guys whom he respected, even though he still wasn't particularly close to most.

Friday night, the Reds took the field at home against Montreal. Unfortunately, Prairie Dog's slider sailed instead of tailed, and the Expos sent him to an early shower after having collected six runs.

Wheatly put the Reds on the board in the bottom of the fifth with a two-run blast. Two outs later, Estabe beat out an infield grounder and Wells walked, bringing up Luke. Recognizing the hurler was one who liked to get ahead of hitters, Luke jumped on his first pitch. It hooked down the line for a double, which drove in both runners, cutting the deficit to 6-4.

The game moved along into sixth, seventh and eighth, when with two out, the Reds loaded the bases for Luke. The Expos sent for their star reliever. The "Abominable Snowman," as he was known—in part for the iceballs he threw— wore three days' facial growth over a permanent snarl. He paid little heed to the exuberant fans and began with a fastball to Luke. "Strike one!" cried the ump.

Luke cocked his bat. He tried forgetting the fact that an extra base hit would put the Reds ahead and thought instead of putting good wood on the ball. *Thwack!* A liner foul. The sinister reliever seemed to grow angrier at the contact made by the Stinger. With one to waste, he surprised Luke with a wicked slider on the outside of the plate—all he could do was flail at it like a child swatting a fly. "Striiiike three!" The hurler mimicked the animal he was named for and stormed off the mound.

Luke's plate appearance represented Cincinnati's last hurrah. While he had gone 2-4 with a pair of RBI's, he focused on his missed opportunity with the bases loaded.

Well after the game, after reporters had retreated to peck away at their computers, Luke sat quietly in his rocker and logged his day's performance. Wheatly stopped by and announced in his Bostonian accent, "Tough game, huh, Luke."

"Yeah. You sure put some good wood on the ball."

"I'd trade it for a win."

Luke forced a smile. "I like that attitude."

Sean started off, then stopped as he eyed the notepad. "You keeping some type of diary?"

"You might call it that," Luke said, flipping the cover closed.

"Are you gonna write a book on the season?" the Officer asked, tucking his T-shirt inside his blue jeans.

"A book?" Luke sniffed a laugh. "No, I'm no writer, Sean. I just keep track of what I do out there so I can avoid the same mistakes next time." Luke realized that there was no such thing as perfection in baseball. Why, in more than a hundred years of play, the highest single season batting average was Hugh Duffy's .438. That meant the best anyone had ever done was to make an out *just* 56 percent of the time. With such odds against him, he turned to his Wallace-Adams logbooks to find an edge.

Luke tracked a variety of factors: pitches that he hit as well as those he made out on—even noting those he ripped foul or got fooled on that didn't cost him at bat; which fields his hits went to and whether they were liners or skippers. He noted balls he caught and those he missed, including any that fell in for legitimate hits. And whom he stole on and in what situations.

"Sounds like a good idea. Did you always do this, you know, when you played before?" Sean asked with childlike curiosity.

"Yeah. Got all the books at home." Luke pictured the eighteen years of handscribed note-taking stacked on his den shelf.

"And you think you still need to do it?"

Luke nodded. "I'm far from perfect, Sean."

◆　　◆　　◆　　◆

The Reds righted themselves the following afternoon with a 3-1 victory, thanks to a Kitchell homer. Afterwards, as Luke ambled along the barren service road that encircled the stadium, he heard his name called. "Wait up, Luke."

He turned to see Fast Chad chugging after him. "What d'you say there, Chad?"

"I noticed this gorgeous '63 'Vette in the parking garage this morning. Gus tells me it's yours."

"That's right."

"I'm a car enthusiast myself," Chad admitted, throwing his windbreader over his right shoulder.

"So I've heard."

"Could I take a look at it?"

"Sure."

"I've seen you driving that yellow one, but didn't know you had another."

"I don't like taking this one out at night or in bad weather."

Luke led Chad to a space at the far end of the players' parking where he had stowed his prized possession. From its elongated nose to the four circular tail lights beneath a backswept tail, the silver car sparkled. Chad rattled off some of the automobile's unique features as he circled it. "Hidden headlights, creased belt-line....It's a beauty. And you sure take good care of it."

"Thanks," Luke said, beaming. Unlocking the door, he reached inside and popped the hood release.

Chad ducked his head under the front-sloping cowl and looked around as if studying a treasure map. "Unreal. 327 cubic inch V-8; 360 horse."

"In its prime it could go from 0 to 60 in 5.5 seconds," Luke explained with a matter-of-fact delivery.

"That's faster than today's Lotus and Porsche 911!"

Luke said nothing but smiled.

"This is where Bill Mitchell first made his mark on the design of Corvettes, isn't it?" After a nod from Luke he continued. "Caused quite a stir with that split window in back."

"Yeah, the engineer Duntov hated it. If it had been up to him, it would have never existed. But Mitchell won out."

"I ran into a guy in Texas who cut his out with a hacksaw."

Luke just shook his head.

The twosome exchanged stories about cars for the next ten minutes. The conversation helped Luke to see Chad in a new light. He found more common ground with him talking about his car than he had playing ball. Chad tended to hang around the other pitchers and bachelors. Luke saw a big difference between being a bachelor and a widower. Yes, the youngster was more than just a swinger. He could be sincere as well as fun-loving, the type of guy Luke would have enjoyed keeping company with when he broke in during the '50s.

"If you ever go to get rid of it, put me at the top of your list."

"No chance," Luke grinned. "Want t'go for a ride?"

"Sure."

Luke reached into his jeans, pulled out the keys and tossed them to the surprised pitcher.

"Thanks!" Chad exclaimed. He hopped to the driver's side and slid behind the wheel while Luke took an unaccustomed seat next to him. Chad fired up the engine and carefully rolled out of the parking space.

◆   ◆   ◆   ◆

That evening, Megan Hanlon had baseball on her mind as she sat down for dinner. The site was a favorite of hers, the Golden Lamb Restaurant. Her companion was too, Randy Kitchell.

While there was a full house at the 19th century landmark, the establishment provided the couple ample privacy. The celebrities that today's diners were most apt to talk about had names like Twain, Dickens, Clay and Harrison, a few of the prominent figures who once frequented the Lebanon, Ohio, hostelry. Situated halfway between Cincinnati and her home, Megan had suggested the place when Randy invited her out. Although she was six years older, this math teacher wasn't one to let such numbers get in her way.

"How's it you settled in Bellbrook?" Randy asked. In the background the din of footsteps and chair legs scraping against wooden planks sounded.

"My ex's office was located just up the road in Dayton. A neighbor told me about a teaching position here. Everyone was so nice at the school that I decided to stay on even after Andy and I split."

Megan attributed the breakup of her earlier relationship to immaturity on her part. She had met and married a college classmate who was an excellent athlete in his own right: co-captain of the tennis team; participant in iron-man triathlons. She now realized that the qualities her dad possessed, and which she wished for in a husband, involved more than being a great athlete. It involved having a man care about her as much as she cared about him.

A waitress in a blue gingham dress and matching headpiece brought their appetizers and a pause in their conversation. Afterwards, the topic shifted to Randy's bio. Luke's offspring was aware from previous conversations that Randy had moved around as an "Air Force Brat."

"You sure I won't bore you? It's a real travel log."

"Not at all. As much as Dad traveled with the team, he wasn't much for going places in the off-season. So I enjoy hearing about it from others."

Megan spooned her soup as Randy commenced with the tale of eight cities that constituted his father's military career. It included overseas stops in Heidelberg, Germany, and Orleans, France. The world tour ended in Jacksonville, Florida, where his dad settled down as a flight instructor at Cecil Field.

"How'd you ever get to play baseball?"

"Most bases have teams. The first thing I did when I arrived on a new one was to sign up for sports. It was a good way to make new friends."

"I bet you had no trouble the way you play."

"Oh, there were good players everywhere we went. In fact, when we moved to Jacksonville, the high school there was competing for the state championship. I was sorta fortunate in that respect."

"Did you win it?"

"No. Came in third. But we sure attracted the scouts. I impressed them enough to pick up several scholarship offers."

Randy sipped his drink, then asked, "So tell me, what was it like growing up having such a famous dad?"

"I thought it was the neatest thing having someone whom so many looked up to." Megan said, opening her eyes as wide as one could with such tiny slits.

"I'm sure they did." Randy nodded, gazing off as if picturing Luke in action. "Although he certainly doesn't let on about his ability."

"Dad? No way." Megan's voice vibrated with laughter. "And he made sure we didn't, either. He knew how to cut us down if we got too full of ourselves."

"It's hard to believe he can go about his business without getting caught up in all the excitement. I mean, it's not every sixty-year-old who does what he's doing."

"Dad's always been too interested in the game to get caught up in his press clippings."

"Luke, er, your dad, made me laugh in today's game. He stole second against a pretty fair-armed catcher, Roberto Fontana. Seeing him steal really shook up Montreal's star reliever, a guy they call the 'Abominable Snowman.'"Randy paused and shook his head before continuing. "He ended up throwing the next one completely over Fontana and the umpire."

"And you knocked him in with a homer," Megan reminded. "I caught the game on TV."

"There again that stolen base helped. After the wild pitch, the guy grooved a fastball to me. I mean it was right down the middle. I just swung easy, and, well, it jumped out of the park."

Randy's expression was as modest as his words. In that respect, he reminded Megan of her father.

"Mind telling me how your dad does it?"

"Does what?"

"You know. Play ball at his age."

Megan looked down at her baked potato as she dug into it with her fork. She wanted to avoid a white lie. *No way to start off a relationship.* "Just a matter of hard work."

"I've heard that one, too!" Randy saw that Megan wasn't amused. "Sorry. Forget I asked."

"That's all right." Megan laced her fingers, forming a bridge for her chin. "What have the players been saying?"

"There's been talk about him getting some type of wonder treatment. Like they use in growing those tomatoes that don't rot."

"It's a subject he doesn't really talk about, and I, ah, respect his privacy," Megan replied with a firm voice.

"That's fine. Say, do you think your dad could bring Mr. Twain back to read to us after dinner?"

"Very funny," Megan said. Truth was, she realized it wouldn't be any more unusual to see the noted writer from Hannibal, Missouri, stroll down the century-old staircase than it was for most fans to see her dad back playing baseball in the '90s.

"So what do you think your dad would think of us dating?"

"Why don't you ask him, not me?" Megan smiled.

It was after 11:00 by the time Randy pulled into the driveway of Megan's condominium. He kissed her good-night on the front porch and passed on her invitation for a nightcap.

"I better not. We've got a game tomorrow afternoon and it's a long ride back to town."

"Good point," she said, gently tapping his chin. "I have plenty of reasons to see that nothing interferes with the team's chances."

26
Chinks in the Armor

By mid-June the Reds led the Cubs by four games. Cincinnatians were ecstatic. A fourth-place finisher a year before, the team was now a legitimate contender. With the climb in temperatures, more fans came. But the latest arrivals were different. They came on the arms of children and grandchildren. They rested on canes and walkers. Some even rode in chairs with wheels. They came with stooped shoulders and limps that testified to their age—with grey hair and white hair and no hair. They came to see, for they already believed. They came with spectacles, to see the spectacle. These were witnesses to Luke's earlier career. Many had first heard about him on their Crosley radios or seen him on their 7-inch Dumont TVs.

Attendance also soared on the road. As much as the Reds provided tough competition, National League owners welcomed a visit by the River City ballclub. It might mean a loss or two, but it would surely mean a win at the box office. And at a time of seeing red on the balance sheets, many owners hungered to see the Reds on the field.

Sports Illustrated, *USA Today* and *Newsweek* all carried cover stories on the ageless wonder. Even the most jaded writers found themselves caught up in the euphoria. That is, all but Stan Moore. For Stan, calm seas meant a boring ride. He sought the teeth of the storm, no matter how small or obscure. In his view, one could only write so much about winning players or teams. That didn't take real talent.

"Take me off my regular assignments for a couple of weeks. If I don't turn up something by their next homestand, then I'll forget about it," Stan Moore pleaded, leaning forward and gripping the edge of his editor's desk.

His shirt-sleeves were rolled up, his collar unbuttoned and his tie loosely knotted.

"And just what d'you think you're gonna find?" grizzled sports journalist Gerry Franklin snorted.

"The real story behind Hanlon."

Franklin swiveled his chair around and drilled a pencil into the electric sharpener on his credenza. He shouted above the whir, "And what is it that I've been reading about for the past ten weeks? Seems to me the *Enquirer* and *Post* have run some pretty good feature stories, while you've been searching for this needle to burst his balloon."

"Damn it, Gerry, their stories are trash—calling him Peter Pan and Jack LaLanne! I mean, get real. He's in his mid-sixties. There's more to it than what he's doing on the field."

"You've been beating that story for three months now. You haven't come up with so much as an ass hair."

"That's why I need the time to do some investigating." Stan needed some free time. The month of May was "lost" covering the Indy 500. Now the thoroughbred racing season was in full gear at RiverDowns. Those responsibilities, coupled with his baseball duties, left little time for digging into the Hanlon story. Digging. *After all*, Stan thought, *wasn't that was what he was being paid to do?* The *Star-Gazette* had built its reputation on provocative headlines. What shock radio was to the airwaves, the *Star-Gazette* was to the print media. Stan was not about to disappoint his readers.

Gerry riveted his eyes on Stan and lowered his voice. "Let's say you find out that the guy's taking some magic potion. So what? It's like selling cars. Most people don't care how many times the pistons go up and down, or whether it's the crankshaft or the driveshaft that starts the engine. What they really want to know is how it performs; does it have enough room; does it react well when it goes over the bumps? It's the same with Hanlon. All they care about is what he's doing to help the Reds win. Understand?"

Stan bit his cheek while letting the message die out. "And tell me people wouldn't be interested if I found out he had stumbled onto some fountain of youth?"

"Bingo." Gerry pointed his index finger at Stan. "Now you've got a storyline. But you're going to have to fit it into your schedule."

"Shiiit, Gerry.... "

"Listen Stan. You're a damn good columnist. You sell papers. If I take you off it for a few weeks to trail some theory, I'd be trading off a bird in the hand."

Stan's eyes drew a bead on the half dozen framed banner headlines hanging to the left of Gerry's metal bookcase. His would hang above them all. "Okay, okay. It'll take me longer, but I'll find out. I just hope we don't get pre-empted by another paper or, worse, some TV station."

Gerry bobbed his head several times, then clicked his tongue against the roof of his mouth. "Tell you what. You show me the first bit of hard evidence, and I'll give you all the time you want."

It was not what Stan wanted, but he realized it was the best he was going to get. "I'll be back, Gerry. You can count on it."

◆　　　◆　　　◆　　　◆

At Riverfront that evening, another media representative intercepted Luke as he headed toward the batting cage. "Luke, do you have a moment?"

The mellifluous voice arrested his walk. He turned to see a stylish lady in all-American attire: a white blouse and blue poplin slacks, topped by a brass-buttoned, red blazer. Her auburn hair swept from left to right and ended in a ponytail entwined in a floral-print scarf. The media pass hanging from her pocket was her only tie to the world of beat reporters.

"I'm Molly Baker. I host a local TV variety show in town."

Luke planted his bat and rested on it without speaking.

"I know you're busy, so I'll just take a minute," she said, stepping forward. Luke experienced some discomfort with the proximity she chose.

"Have you seen the show?"

Luke shook his head "no." *Cincinnati's answer to Oprah,* he thought without saying. He had no idea what the show was about. What little TV he watched was in the evening.

"I guess you could describe it as informational entertainment. Our guests include singers, politicians...people from the arts and athletes like yourself. I was hoping I might persuade you to be one of our guests."

"Sorry. I only give interviews around the ballpark."

He placed the bat on his shoulder and began walking away when she spoke again. "Mr. Hall mentioned that. But we don't do traditional interviews; it's a variety show as much as anything."

"Don't matter. I'll be happy to answer any questions you might have right here. But as for making the media circuit, that's gonna have to wait until after the season." If she were still interested, he'd hook up with her show after it was all over, after the Reds, hopefully, went to the World Series. But for now rules were rules.

"Mind telling me why?"

"I don't like distractions."

"What about on one of your off days?"

"You mean when I don't get any hits?" He flashed a grin. "Sorry, but I've got a farm to run."

Molly shifted her tack. "Your story is more than just about playing baseball. There are a lot of senior citizens— many of whom watch the show—who I'm sure would love to hear what it's like to play again at your age. Why, I'd like to know more about it!"

Luke felt bad in a way about turning her down. She seemed genuine. And there was something engaging about her. From the corner of his eye, he saw Reynolds exit the batting cage. "I gotta get going." Luke disappeared into the cage as Molly clenched her teeth, emitted a growl and slapped her hands to her sides.

◆   ◆   ◆   ◆

While sweeping the Pirates, Cincinnati developed the first chinks in its armor. Kevin Sweeney's shoulder misery returned. An MRI of his rotator cuff proved negative, but he ended up on the 15-day disabled list. Next, Estabe went down with a pulled groin muscle while chasing a Texas league blooper. Luke comforted Corrigan when it was disclosed that the Whippet would be out for up to three weeks. "You can't expect to go a full season with injuries. We'll survive."

"I know, but they couldn't have picked a worse time. The West Coast trip will be a tough one."

Mike was particularly troubled by the team's lack of infield depth. Still, Cincinnati continued to win, taking three out of four that weekend. And the Reds got the infield help they were looking for, or at least they thought. Vandermark swung a deal for a utility gloveman, Steve Froehlich. The owner had grown tired of waiting for DiCenso to deal him a starter, so he grabbed what was available. Steve lacked Estabe's glove and range, but possessed a steady arm and decent stick. He looked good in the homestand's finale, collecting an RBI triple while playing flawlessly.

San Diego greeted the Reds with doubt. Luke read one report claiming that it was only a matter of time before the "aged wonder would begin to fade, and when he does, so will the Reds."

In the opener, Froehlich's two errors opened the gates to four unearned runs. Steve tried to redeem himself with a homer and double, but it was not enough. San Diego won, 4-2.

Saturday, Chad Lattimore awoke with a stiff neck. He complained it came from the air conditioner in his hotel room. But Luke heard reports of how the free spirit had been seen doing somersaults into the Pacific surf the day before. Clint Twiddy moved up in the rotation, but the party boy didn't have it. The Padres cruised to an easy win.

Sunday, Luke took matters into his own hands, knocking a three-run shot in the fourth. With Parker on his game, the Reds saw victory in sight. And while Froehlich donated a pair of runs with a booted ball, the Reds still entered the ninth ahead 4-2.

A walk and an infield hit—that Luke figured Estabe would have turned into a force play—brought out Corrigan, who brought on Worley. Luke had found Kyle a pleasant, hard-working individual, although a bit aloof. He found him as cocksure of himself as he was fast.

Kyle struck out the first two hitters as quickly as one could say "million-dollar pitcher." With two down, Luke backed up to guard against the extra base hit, but the fences kept him from where he needed to go. The batter drilled one beyond the wall and into a vibrating mass of colors.

Worley was philosophical in defeat. "He just beat me on my best pitch, a fastball," he explained, towering over the writers huddled around his locker. "If I had it to do over, I'd throw the same pitch— oh, perhaps I'd get it down a bit."

In the getaway game, Froehlich proved that the old adage "haste makes waste" was as applicable in baseball trades as in other lines of work. His fifth miscue in eight games proved costly in another Cincinnati defeat.

The Reds moved on to San Francisco, where their fortunes were as cool as the bay area weather. The Giants sailed to victory in the first two games. Lattimore, his neck sufficiently recovered, sought to salvage game three. He struck out ten while scattering but three hits through seven innings. With the Reds protecting a 2-0 lead in the eighth, Fast Chad walked the leadoff hitter. Corrigan immediately called for reliever Mark Shaw. Chad was not pleased and hurled his glove against the dugout as he crossed the first base line. Luke knew the losses had made Mike uncharacteristically quick to react.

Shaw completed his warm-ups and left the mound to rub up the ball. Using a backbreaking curve, he had compiled a .121 ERA in relief. But as stock watcher Logan Wells could have advised, "Past performance is no guarantee of future results." Shaw gave up a single, then hung a curve that rattled amidst the seats in left, extending the Reds' losing streak.

While undressing, Luke heard the silence of the locker room broken by a crash from his manager's office. He later learned that Mike had replayed the home run blast, using his lamplight as a tee ball.

Stan Moore rekindled the manager's Irish temper, asking him why he hadn't brought in Worley instead of Shaw. Mike barked back with a question of his own. "D'you ever think you should have gotten yourself a real job instead of just watching what others do?" Luke knew there was no love lost between the two.

As the Cincinnatians limped aboard their charter flight to LA, they found themselves behind in the standings for the first time all season. Luke took his seat next to Mike and listened as he explained, "I know it's not going to make Peter look good, but I'm about ready to set Froehlich down."

Luke tried to lift his spirit. "What's it Brosnam used to say? 'The guy's hands are so bad that his glove is embarrassed.'"

"If it weren't so true, it'd be funny," Mike sighed.

"What about using Wells at short?"

"I've thought about it. But his arm's not that strong."

"Does it matter if a guy's got an arm but can't come up with the ball?" Luke offered, tilting his seat back to sleep.

Friday was rock night at Chavez Ravine. The Dodgers had invited Lois Love to sing the anthem and attract the teens. Lois was known as much for her trademark tattoos as the quality of her voice. Tiny hearts marked both cheeks, Cupid danced around her navel, flowers grew out of her breasts, and names of past lovers decorated her derriere—at least that's what those in the know reported.

Corrigan used the opportunity to bring levity to his ballclub. He had Noah Hall arrange for Ms. Love to stop by the clubhouse and draw the starting line-up out of a hat. Shortly after batting practice, Lois wiggled into the clubhouse wearing a silver, sequined bikini. Luke looked on from his locker stool as his teammates goggled over her tattoos and athletic torso.

"Are those all real?" Kurkowski sputtered, pointing to the designs on her stomach.

"Hey Ducky, why don't you rub them and see if they come off?" Clint suggested to the delight of all. It was the first sign of life Luke had heard since the losses began.

Twiddy and Bailey rushed forward and helped lift Lois onto a tabletop. She nearly burst from her outfit as she bent to step up. From there, the vocalist literally drew the line-up from a hat. She called each name as written, "Ducky Kurkowski...Randy Kitchell...Neal Parker...Logan Wells...." Luke had to wait for eight names to be called before he heard his. "...and the Stinger. Oooh, I like the sound of that." As she searched the room, Luke's teammates pointed in his direction, chanting "Luke-Luke-Luke." Lois hopped off her perch and strutted to where he was sitting. Luke blushed as she closed in on him. She leaned over and planted an exaggerated kiss on his cheek. The players howled.

Corrigan followed Lois with a brief speech. He reminded the players that Lois was successful because she was relaxed and had fun with her job. "Keep that in mind when you're out there tonight."

Mike's strategy paid dividends. Kurkowski, batting leadoff, surprised everyone by reaching base in three out of four trips. Kitchell set things in motion with a two-run homer during a three-run first. And Luke capped it all with a bases clearing double. Neal Parker cruised to a 6-2 victory.

Afterwards, Lois belted out songs for the teens in attendance while, inside, Ducky held court. "Hey guys, don't you think I should lead off every game?"

Clint shot back, "You had nothing to do with it. It was all Lois."

We should have her stop by more often."

Luke offered no comments. He was just relieved that the losing streak had ended. The next day, however, Luke thought perhaps they should have listened to Clint and invited the female rock star back. The Reds fell 3-1, their seventh road loss.

In the hotel lobby that night, Luke encountered another attractive lady. Weary from defeat, his eyes met the stare of a girl standing near the bank of elevators. She was attired in slit-shorts and a navy T-shirt with "Fun Club" printed in blocks letters across her bosom. It might well have read, "For Good Times Call Me," for that was the expression she wore on her face. But it was not her outfit that grabbed Luke's attention. *The eyes*, he thought. Probing, penetrating, engulfed in lavender shadowing, they were inviting yet sinful. She spoke with an air of seduction. "Hi Luke. Would you sign this for me?"

Luke accepted her pen and inked his name. He couldn't resist one more glance at her face. Boarding the elevator, he heard her mutter something. He wasn't sure exactly, but it sounded like, "Want a drink?" Whatever, he ignored it. Not his type, even in his younger days. Yet, he experienced a twinge inside. It reminded him he still had a passion, a hunger, a longing for something missing in his life. It was more than a matter of youthful hormones renewed by Doc's magical treatment. No, even for a senior citizen, the void created by Kate's passing was catching up with him.

In the wrap-up to the road trip, Corrigan heeded Luke's advice and shuffled his infield. He brought in Cecil Gomez, a steady back-up second baseman. That pushed Wells to short and shoved Froehlich to the bench. Mike had decided he'd rather take on Peter than tolerate another miscue from Froehlich.

The temperature and bats were hot that Sunday. The teams exchanged leads four times over seven innings, with the Reds breaking on top, 9-7, behind Kitchell's triple—his first extra base hit in a week. Worley came on to retire the Dodgers in the home half, thanks to a great play by the newest Reds shortstop, Wells.

In the eighth, a slow grounder was hit between the mound and first. Randy fielded it cleanly, but when he tried tossing it to Worley, the pitcher was nowhere to be seen; he stood frozen near the mound. The next batter walked, putting the tying runs on base.

Corrigan jogged out for a conference. Luke thought how a win, while only improving the team's West Coast record to 2-8, would allow them to return to Cincinnati on a positive note. He paced near the warning track, bending to collect taco trays and beer cups dropped from the stands.

Kyle notched two quick strikes on the next batter, jamming him on bunt attempts. He then tried wasting one low, but the hitter transformed the sinker into a dying quail to right. Gomez backpedalled. Wheatly charged. From Luke's vantage point, it appeared an easier play for the Officer. But like two schoolgirls dancing, neither could make up her mind who was to lead. Luke grimaced as the ball fell in, driving in one and placing runners at second and third. A sacrifice fly and a suicide squeeze play put the Dodgers in front 10-9.

Never one to despair, Luke felt a flicker of hope in the ninth. He followed Wells' walk with one of his own. The pitcher had clearly lost the plate. As Reynolds clawed his spikes in the clay, Luke thought, *have patience*. But Treat, as overanxious for a hit as the team was for a win, reached for the very first pitch, a sinker near his shoetops. The ball skipped to the second baseman, who flipped to the shortstop, who pivoted to first for a game-ending double play.

The Reds' jet, once soaring above the clouds, was in a free fall, spinning out of control. They now trailed the Cubs by two. Luke knew there was time to right the craft. For one thing, the ballclub was winging its way to the friendly confines of Riverfront Stadium. But he also knew it was time to get healthy, for meeting them at the airport were the red-hot, Western Division-leading Padres.

27
The Reunion

Cautious optimism peppered the Reds' locker room before the opener of their homestand. Mike had given his troops a day off to mellow out. And in case the home field advantage was not enough, several players reverted to good luck charms. Kurkowski donned a hole-filled T-shirt he'd worn in the minors. "I wore it while we won eleven in a row in Triple A." The tee hugged the squat catcher's girth, which had grown with the losses.

Then there was first base coach Eddie Zender, who suggested players stick chewing gum beneath the bill of their caps for good luck, much to Gus Stoltz's chagrin. And starter Neal Parker insisted that his friend, Jock Sparmarti, be the one to warm him up.

Luke's amulet was his bat. He gave it a workout with an extended stay in the batting cage. He remained silent about all the player rituals, figuring if they helped their confidences, he was all for them.

Earl Masterson took the mound that night for the Padres. His shutout a fortnight before had triggered the Reds' downward slide. Dean Taylor asked what better way to turn things around than by beating the one who had started it all.

"Hey Preacher," Bailey called, hunched over tightening his laces. "Is that like the Bible says, 'an eye for an eye'?"

"Guess you could look at it that way." Taylor smiled.

Despite all their charms and incantations, Masterson bested the Reds, 3-0. The locals made him look like the reincarnation of Cy Young. Luke knew that even he had taken pitches he should have swung at while flailing at others out of the strike zone. A reporter who wrote that the Reds were tighter than a necktie on a 98-degree day knew what he was talking about.

At home that evening, Luke shared a beer with Bret, who had caught the game on TV. "You'd think as long as I've been around I'd have an answer to these streaks. But if there is one, I can't find it. We're dead-ass, that's all." Just as winning was contagious, Luke knew losing begot losses. Perched sidesaddle on the back porch rail, he stared into the night. "Mike's tried talking to the players...he's shaken up the line-up...."

"And everyone's trying to do it themselves?"

"Including me," Luke confessed.

Bret kicked back in the porch swing. "You need Doc Dornhoffer to cook you all up some amnesia medicine. That way everyone can forget about the losses and go back to playing 'em one game at a time."

Luke knew there was truth in what his son had said.

The next night the Reds fell again, 5-4. The winning run crossed the plate when the usually reliable Reynolds overthrew the cutoff man *and* the catcher. Twelve losses in thirteen games. Luke had gone hitless in the last two and offered to sit out the next one. Mike said if he used that criterion, he'd have to set down the entire squad.

Luke thought how he hadn't come out of retirement to finish second. So he decided to act. Exiting the stadium, he grabbed hold of Treat. "I was thinking of having a closed door meeting tomorrow. You know, with just the players. Would you like to help?"

"Sure. I'm willing to try anything. Have you talked to Mike about it?"

"Uh huh." Luke wrapped his arm around his teammate as they left for the reserved parking area underneath the stands. The black ballplayer towered over Luke by nearly half a foot.

With an occasional auto ignition exploding in the background, Luke and Treat plotted the meeting.

The following day, Noah closed off the clubhouse complex to the media. A hand-lettered sign greeted the players at the door:

TEAM MEETING AT 5:30

IN TRAINER'S ROOM

Luke stood before his teammates in front of a sign lying on the floor which read, 'LOSING STREAK.' Never one for speeches, he kept his brief. "Guys, Treat and I got together last night, and well, we talked about what it would take to get us back on track. Now, we don't have the answers, but we thought maybe if we all kicked it around we might come up with some."

Treat picked up his cue. "Luke mentioned something which got me thinking. He reminded me how no *one* of us can break the slump. I think I've been trying to do just that."

"You're not alone, Treat," Fast Chad, that night's scheduled pitcher, chimed in. "Last time out I was determined to throw a shutout. And what'd I do? Gave up seven runs."

Other players bared their souls with tales of where they had come up short. Then Taylor pointed out that while confession was good, there comes a point where one needs to decide what to do to avoid the mistakes of the past. Randy suggested focusing on the fundamentals: advancing the runner, throwing to the base, hitting the cutoff man, backing up the play and thinking contact rather than trying to pull everything.

After forty-five minutes, sensing the mood of the meeting had grown a bit too solemn, Luke sneaked out of the room. Moments later he returned, his shoulders slumped from wheeling a barrow slopping over with dirt. "I got some fill-dirt from my farm. Who'd like to help me bury this here losing streak?" With that, Luke extracted one of three shovels sticking out of the pile and began tossing soil on the sign referring to their skid. The players rushed to the wheelbarrow and, amid the sounds of a jovial work crew, fought to grab the shovels.

It didn't take long for the contents to be emptied, leaving a knee-deep pile of dirt, crumbs scattered about, in the middle of the locker room. Gus Stoltz stood in the corner, shaking his head and smiling.

Luke found the measure of the meeting's worth on the field. Leading off the first, Taylor legged out an infield hit. Wells singled. Luke bunted both runners over and reached himself as he had caught the infielders napping. By the time the inning ended, six Reds had crossed the plate, including three on Kitchell's 11th round tripper.

The onslaught lasted throughout the game. Reynolds and Gomez swiped two bases apiece. Kitchell delivered four hits, and Ducky added a homer. Chad turned in a complete game in a 9-2 shellacking of the first-place Padres.

Afterwards, with the dirt and 'losing' sign cleared from the locker room, Luke downplayed the meeting's significance to reporters. "We were due to have a game like this. This team is too good to continue the way we had been playing."

The wrap-up game matched Scott Brouse against knuckler and Reds-killer Hal Brewster. Estabe fanned the Reds' glowing embers by returning a day ahead of schedule.

Prairie Dog escaped a shaky first, giving up a pair of runs. It could have been a lot worse, as the bases were full when Wheatly dove to snare the third out.

The Reds flailed at Brewster's knuckler during their first three frames. In the dugout, Luke admitted to Randy, "He's got his bug working tonight, Kitch."

"That's for sure. I swung right through two of them," Randy confessed. "Next time I'm gonna time it instead of attack it."

"Good thinking. He can be had."

Raphael collected the Reds' first hit, beating out a high chopper, despite having his hamstring swaddled in a spool of tape. One out later, Luke ripped a double down the line. After Reynolds drew an intentional walk, Kitchell singled to tie the score. Taylor's perfectly executed suicide squeeze put the Reds ahead 3-2. Luke added it up; five players had figured in the scoring. Team ball was back.

Unfortunately, Brouse began hanging his slider again, and San Diego reclaimed the lead, 4-3. The game moved into the ninth, with the Reds seemingly ready to start a new losing streak. Two outs later, Luke came to the plate with Estabe on first. Five pitches later he accepted a walk. The Padre pitcher showed he was not about to let a sexagenarian beat him.

Up stepped the other half of the closed-door-meeting committee, Treat Reynolds. Luke watched as the athlete's athlete took two practice cuts alongside the plate. If talent was based on physique, he figured Treat would have been an .800 hitter.

Luke paced off the bag, checking Estabe, who had a good lead at second. The count went full. Luke broke on the payoff pitch. Two strides onto the carpet, he heard the sound, the sound of backfire in the night, of a song in the meadow, of good wood on a ball. Rounding second, he located the orb heading over the left field wall.

Luke touched home and waited with his gathering teammates for Reynolds to arrive. They heaped themselves atop the center fielder as he crossed the plate. The skein was indeed over.

The Reds reeled off five in a row and leapfrogged back into first. Luke recognized that their slump had allowed the rest of the Central Division to catch up. As June came to a close, the team was in a footrace that would likely last well beyond the dog days of summer. And following the long season, there would be a long post season—if the Reds were so lucky. A five-game playoff, followed by a best of seven, followed by the Series. A triathlon. Sure, it gave more teams an opportunity to get into the playoffs, but Luke viewed it as another example of money dictating the course of major league baseball. To him, baseball now bore a closer resemblance to a major corporation: a family business swallowed up by a multi-divisional organization. More than anything, he thought, the new structure robbed the game of its tradition, a tradition where the regular season was a battle to the end, not just a jockeying for position to land one of several playoff spots.

Visiting Mike at his home in Northern Kentucky, Luke explained his feelings. "I never thought baseball would stoop to the level of hockey or basketball. It was always much stronger than those sports."

"Baseball has faced some tough times, Luke. This way more cities are caught up in the races. That spells ticket sales, not to mention TV revenue from the extra round of playoffs."

"Damn it, that's the whole problem, Mike. Too much focus on the dollars," Luke said, glancing at Mike's furnishings that attested to the manager's modest lifestyle. "Why, these layers of playoffs are as agonizing as stripping coats of paint off some old dresser—I don't know too many folks who enjoy doing that."

"You're too much of a traditionalist," Mike needled.

◆　　◆　　◆　　◆

Monday was an off day. Ahead loomed a showdown against the second-place Cubs. While the Windy City rolled out the headlines for Cincinnati, across town the White Sox were wrapping up a series against the Yankees.

Ty Hartmann adjusted his navy stirrups over his socks inside the visitors' dressing room at White Sox Park. "Hey Ty, you've got visitors," a teammate shouted.

The Yankee slugger, barechested save two gold chains dangling from his vein-popping neck, stepped to the waiting room. "What have we got here? Somebody call up a couple of minor leaguers?"

"Hey Ty, good to see you," beamed Bailey, shaking his hand.

Reynolds did likewise.

Miles' phone call setting up the visit had buoyed Ty's spirits. Not that he needed it. Hartmann and the Yankees were running away with things in the American League's Eastern Division, nine games ahead of the Orioles. The Bronx Bombers had tallied seventeen victories in their last twenty ball games.

As for Ty, he was a silicon chip, amassing numbers by the nanosecond. During the victory spree, he compiled a .427 average, clocking 9-homers while driving in 38 runs. The opportunity to share those stats as much as renew acquaintanceships filled him with anticipation for the day's visit. Sure he was proud, maybe a bit cocky. But hell, in his view, he had a right to be.

The reunited outfielders entered the players' lounge. There they sipped Evian and relaxed in vibromaster chairs across from a 52-inch high-definition television.

"I imagine you're liking it a lot better this year, huh?" Reynolds asked.

"You got that right," Ty said.

"You sure are having yourself one hell of a season," Miles added. The Reds' right fielder could not claim the same, seeing how he now split outfield duties with Sean Wheatly.

"We've got ourselves a great ballclub. It's made it easy for me to do the things I wanna do."

Treat cut in. "How's the Big Apple—you finally getting used to it?"

"Sure." Ty drew out the word to demonstrate the ease with which he was dealing with it. "That's behind me now. Everybody's been real good to me, even the press."

"It wasn't that way last year, huh?" Miles clarified.

"No, when you're strugglin', the New York media can make it awful tough on you." Ty boasted about what he had dealt with the prior year. "They can make you feel like you're tied down in a rat-infested sewer with cheese sprinkled all over your body."

Miles burst into laughter. Treat, who just smiled, spoke. "Ever think you'd still like to be with us?"

"No way." Ty wanted to make it clear that it had all worked out in the end for him. He noticed Miles sitting forward with an admiring look. "I mean, I think about you guys and the good days we had. But the Reds? Nah. I'm surrounded by great players, got a good salary, and the team's solidly in first place. What else could a guy want?"

"How 'bout the owner?" Bailey inquired. "Is he leaving you guys alone?"

"That thing is blown way out of proportion. He's really a good guy. Last year when I was injured and struggling, he was real supportive." Ty then thought of the owner's barbs in the spring. About the time he had taken Ty to the track and shown him his horses. The owner had casually mentioned, "Ty, these guys can cost as much as ballplayers. And like players, it often takes time for them to start paying back. But sooner or later, they either put up or you ship 'em off to the glue factory."

Voices emanated from the adjacent locker room as the lounge door flew open. Two players wandered in wearing pin-striped uniforms. They grabbed soft drinks from the refrigerator and left. The pair acted as if Ty and his friends weren't there.

"Say Ty, see where you've been replaced by a senior citizen?" Miles bubbled.

"Who, Hanlon?"

"Right."

"What's the story with him anyway? Is he for real?"

"He's as real as his numbers," Reynolds replied, rolling up a magazine and swatting his hand. "Batting over .330, with 17 homers."

"Not bad. But then he has a ways to go to catch me." Thoughts of his major league leading 24 homers came to Ty's mind.

"Don't forget, he's got almost 400 career round trippers," Reynolds countered.

Ty smirked. He had enjoyed a friendly rivalry with Treat while with the Reds, a rivalry in which he usually found himself coming out on top. "Yeah, but that was back when they played with the lively ball, and without a fresh arm comin' out of the bullpen every night."

"I'd take those numbers in any era," Treat said.

Ty flashed a haughty smile as he played with the cross hanging from his chain. It was the one given him by Slim Wilkins. *Slim had never talked about Hanlon, not even once. The guy couldn't have been that great.*

"Maybe you'll get a chance to see him in the Series—if you guys hang in there," Bailey needled.

"We'll be there," Ty replied, stretching his arms behind his head. He reached down and rubbed his hairy chest. "The question is, can you guys get there?"

"Take at look at who's leading our Division," Treat shot back.

"I don't know, the Cubs look awfully tough. But good luck. Maybe we could place a little side wager if it all works out."

"I'm not sure the commissioner would like to hear you say that," Treat smiled.

Ty sensed a growing distance from the guys with whom he used to roam the outfield. Just then an older gentleman, a Yankee coach, leaned in the doorway. "Hey Ty, aren't you taking batting practice ?"

"For Christ—tell them to hold the cage. I'll be out in a minute." Ty stood and addressed his visitors. "As you can see, they depend on me. Enjoy the game."

With Ty ripping practice pitches into boastful orbits, Reynolds and Bailey settled into their box seats. They watched the Yankees route the White Sox, 7-1. Ty collected an RBI double, his 25th homer and a sacrifice fly, totaling 5 ribbies on the night. As if that wasn't enough, he gunned down a Sox ballplayer going from first to third on a single.

Jogging to the dugout in the seventh, Ty searched for his former teammates in the seats he had left for them. They were gone. *I guess they've seen enough for one night. Well, maybe I'll see them in the Series— if they're lucky.*

◆   ◆   ◆   ◆

The Reds split their games with the Cubs at Wrigley before sweeping the Florida Marlins and wrestling their first two from the Phillies. Their hitting was once again solid, and so was their pitching. Except for Clint Twiddy. His 4-6 mark stood as the lone losing record among the starters. He had lost his last three decisions, including the critical match-up in Chicago. He was scheduled to pitch the concluding road game the next afternoon.

That night, Luke sat in the Marriott Hotel's lounge. He glanced at his watch—1:20 am. He shook and folded his newspaper, then swirled the ice in his glass. A dark-haired waitress half-genuflected at a nearby table as she wiped it clean. She shot him a smile and mouthed "one minute." Luke waved off another beverage, although with what he was drinking, he didn't have to worry about becoming intoxicated.

He used the time to reflect back on the championship season of '61. It was at a hotel in Los Angeles. He and seven teammates arrived minutes after curfew. There, waiting in the lobby, was skipper Fred Hutchinson. Luke smiled and thought how Hutch, a carouser himself, was likely mad that he hadn't been invited along. When the tardy players returned, the "Bear" chewed them out and fined each $100. Luke believed it had helped turn things around for the team. He hoped to do the same with a certain individual that night.

His attention was drawn to the revolving door, which spun Clint Twiddy into the lobby. Under Clint's million-dollar arm, he cuddled a party-worn bleached blond, her breasts flopping beneath the V-neck of a cream-colored dress.

Corrigan had given Luke an earful about the perennial underachiever. He explained, "When Clint puts his mind to it he can split a (wooden) clothespin from a hundred feet." However, the six-footer didn't relate well to rules, deadlines or practices. He enjoyed breaking curfew as much as breaking the plate.

Clint himself had confided to friends how he might bust his ass only to suffer some arm injury or, worse, to have some .200 hitter flail an "excuse me" pop-up over an infielder's head for a game-winning hit—so why worry. Clint's philosophy: Do the best you can, but smell the roses as well as the beer and perfume along life's way.

Luke stood, glass in hand, and offered a smile as Clint approached with his date.

"Hi, pops. You didn't have to wait up for us," Clint greeted with an irreverent tone.

Luke ignored the slight and wrapped his arm around Clint. "I figured if I waited up long enough, you'd come along. Thought perhaps you'd be up for another evening of ménàge a trois."

Clint's mouth fell open in a priceless expression. His ladyfriend smiled at Luke. The pitcher regained his composure. "Cheri, this here's the famous Luke Hanlon."

"Pleased to meet you, Mr. Hanlon," she giggled.

"Good to see you there, buddy," Luke said, tugging on Clint's shoulder.

The pitcher pulled himself loose. For one of the few times, he appeared speechless. Of course, Luke could tell he was operating on less than a full set of batteries. "Uh, thanks, but Cheri and I would like to just spend some quiet time together."

"Aw Clint, you don't want to leave your friend down here by himself," Cheri remarked.

"How about it, Clint? Don't be shy now," Luke said.

Clint braced his arm against Luke's shoulder. "I think you need to cool down a bit. Remember, three's a crowd."

"Hey, if you'd rather it just be you and me again, I'm sure Cheri would understand." Luke realized the hoax was going a bit far, but what the hell, Clint needed to be shocked back to his senses. Twenty-four men depended on him. "What d'you say?"

Clint rolled his eyes. His escort, reminiscent of some biblical high priest facing a leper, took a step back and stammered, "Listen, if, you two guys have something else in mind, I'll, I'll just call it an evening."

The pitcher started to talk, but Luke grabbed hold of his arm. Cheri failed to notice. With a quick upward twist, he wrapped it around Clint's back. Compared to the calves Luke wrestled, this limb belonged to a puppy. "That's all right, sister. Thanks anyway." Luke handed her a $10 bill. "Here Cheri, get yourself a cab."

The groupie left without a word. Luke, his left hand still locked on Clint's arm, shoved the party boy into an open elevator.

Clint rubbed his elbow. Luke had made sure not to grab his pitching arm. "Are you crazy? You just ruined a great evening."

"Better an evening for you than a season for the team." Luke waited for the doors to close before scolding. "If you want to be part of this ballclub, you'll do your partying in the off-season. And you better sober up fast—I'm expecting you to hold the Phillies to two runs or less tomorrow."

"And if I don't?"

Luke's voice deepened. Any trace of humor was gone. "If you think it was embarrassing what I said in front of your little friend, then think about getting your ass kicked around the locker by someone old enough to be your father."

The door opened on the 16th floor. Clint exited in silence.

Luke's words packed a wallop. Or so it seemed. Thanks to Clint's pitching, the Reds defeated the Phillies the next day, 4-1.

28
The Fourth Estate

"You sure it was his car?" Stan Moore probed.

"There're not too many split wing 'Vettes tooling around Clifton. Hell, I've got a friend who's a Corvette nut. Says they made less than 22,000 for the whole *country*." A smile crept into the expression of Andy Jackovich, the Cincinnati *Star-Gazette's* Living Section writer.

"And you say he pulled out of this Caulfield Center garage?" Stan repeated, jiggling his right leg. He sensed the break he was looking for, the seam in the wall where he could insert his probe and pry open his story.

"Right. He had on a hat and shades, but I'm sure it was him, all right."

"Thanks, Andy. I owe you one." Stan jabbed his cohort in the chest.

"That's what you said last time." Andy seemed none too shy about reminding him.

"Just think, when I finally get around to it, I'll be buying you drinks all night," Stan grinned. He clicked on his answering machine and skipped from the pressroom.

Outside, Stan became engulfed in sweat. The temperature, humidity and investigation had all climbed to peak levels. There were ninety minutes to kill before his planned 12:45 p.m. stop. Experience had taught him the best time to catch doctors was near the end of the lunch hour.

Stan hopped in his dented Corolla for the 10-minute ride to UC. Along the way he placed a call from his car phone. A contact described the man in charge at the Caulfield Science Center, Dr. Adrian Dornhoffer, as "a consummate professional who shuns the media like his secretary avoids laboratory rats."

Stan took a side trip to Abbie's New York Style Deli. Any story, no matter how mundane, Stan figured, was worth a trip to Clifton if just to eat at Abbie's. And Stan usually got a free drink or potato salad from Abbie thanks to having put in a good word about the place in his column.

"Let's keep the line moving. Who's next?" shouted the gruff-voiced proprietor, Abbie Sennet. "Hey Stan, is the ink still running?"

"Sure is. The usual, Abbie," the columnist replied, standing shoulder to shoulder with drooling diners.

"One corny caraway with a pile of spuds," Abbie barked. "When are you gonna write something good about our Reds?"

Stan knew Abbie was a big Reds fan. "Hey, didn't you see my column on Estabe last week?"

"Must've missed it." Abbie refocused on his customers. "Who's next? Move along. What'll you have?"

"I'll send it to you."

"Don't bother. Just write another one."

"If the story's there, I'll write it. Good to see you, Abbie."

"Let's keep the line moving. What'll you have?"

Stan retreated, plate in hand, to a small corner table. There he ate and crystallized thoughts for his upcoming interview on a napkin. The sugar-coated story Abbie wanted would have to wait.

Stan pushed open the Caulfield Clinic door, armed with a strategy in mind. The patient chairs were empty. He approached the counter and eyed the brown swirl of hair, rooted in grey, atop a woman's head.

Her face was buried in some national tabloid. A Styrofoam container with a plastic fork and salad remnants sat off to her side. Stan tapped on the glass. An air of perfume, heavy on scent, low on price, flowed forth as she slid open the panel. Stan flashed his press credentials and sized up the lady.

"Moore, Moore?" Margaret struggled to place the name.

"I write a column, 'Moore on Sports.'"

"Oh, sure. I've seen it, ah, lots of times." Her voice drew deep as if to impress. "I admit I don't spend much time with the sports section, but ah, yours is one piece I find worth reading."

"That's very kind of you, Mrs., er, Kennsington."

"Please—Margaret." Stan watched as she stealthily folded her newspaper and slid it under the counter. "I imagine you meet hundreds of interesting ballplayers in your work."

Not one to disappoint where it might be to his benefit, Stan indulged her. "Right. I've been fortunate to work around many of the greats from right here in Cincinnati. Larkin, Rio... Munoz, Esiason... and now Reynolds and Hanlon." He watched her eyes grow bigger with each name.

"Fascinating!"

Margaret provided the fawning subject he sought. "Some are. The others, well, let's just say the others would just as soon be getting a flu shot as talking to the press."

"You'd think with all they earn they'd be more cooperative." Margaret shook her head and puffed her lips.

Especially with those of us working for what amounts to their meal money, Stan thought. "Oh, I guess they become so busy they forget we're only trying to get information for the fans. But I don't let it bother me."

"You know, one of my sons is interested in the media— television. He's fifteen." Margaret spoke as if searching for her words. "My oldest has a great voice, but he never showed much interest. Became an accountant, though, and a good one. Has his CPA."

"How about you? Working here you must meet some pretty interesting scientists."

"Oh yes."

The door opened and a woman entered, temporarily interrupting the conversation. Stan drew back while the female signed the clipboard.

Margaret raised up and examined the freshly inked name. "If you'll just have a seat, someone will be right with you." While she announced the patient on her phone, Stan surveyed the waiting room. He took note of a fly resting upside-down on a domed ceiling fixture. *A fly ball.* He smiled, proud of his own cleverness.

"So how can I help you, Mr. Moore?"

Stan swung around. "Oh, sorry. I didn't want to interrupt your work."

"No problem. Actually we're not that busy this time of year, what with school out."

Stan leaned into the opening and spoke as if revealing some ballplayer's secret lover. "I'm doing some research of my own. It's background for an article on sports medicine. I was hoping to speak to some of the experts here. You know, about studies in which athletes have been or might still be involved."

"Is there someone you had in mind—a doctor you wanted to see?"

"Let me start with you. Have you ever met any of the athletes they bring in here?"

Margaret paused to think. "One you just mentioned. Luke Hanlon. I've seen him a few times. Beyond that, I really can't say."

"Without their uniforms on, most are hard to pick out of a crowd." Stan laughed along with Margaret. He visualized spiking a ball in the end zone. *Yes, Hanlon's been here!* "Well, you've seen a great one in Luke." Stan figured he'd impress Margaret by using Hanlon's first name.

She hunched her shoulders and eyed the waiting subject before responding in a hushed voice, "If I wasn't married, I could make a play for him." They chuckled once more.

Just then a nurse entered the side door. She led the patient inside.

Soon two more subjects signed in. Stan figured he'd be there all after-noon if he let Margaret control the conversation. "Tell you what, to save the doctors' time, perhaps you could tell me something about the study Luke was involved in."

"I really don't know—they're all very hush-hush. Most of the time, he would see Nurse Metzger. I believe it was some drug Dr. Einhardt was working on."

"Is he in?"

"She—Emily Einhardt."

"Sorry, I shouldn't have assumed."

Margaret waved off the miscue. "A lot of people make that mis-take. She's out this week, but she'll be back on Monday."

"I was really hoping to speak with someone today—at least get a start on the story." Stan furrowed his brow to show disappointment. "You know, always a deadline."

"Let's see. Dr. Dornhoffer might help, but he's out of town the next few days as well."

Stan had no interest in speaking with Dr. Dornhoffer. He'd just stonewall the investigation. Then too, Dr. Einhardt might not be the best source, either. "Would you happen to have a listing of the scien-tists here—in case I have trouble reaching Dr. Einhardt?"

"I'm really not at liberty to, ah, give that out."

"What? Don't I look trustworthy? I'll let you in on a little secret; the ballplayers share a lot of confidential information with me that the readers never get to see."

"Really?" Margaret stared at him and smiled. "Just a minute." She pulled a tack from beneath the window and rose, carrying a piece of paper. Stan heard the "click-click" of a copier, then Margaret re-turned. "Here's a complete listing of those involved in the clinic. The scientists are those with two numbers after their name, one for them and another for their secretary."

"Thank you so much. I hope the people here appreciate how wonderful you are." She laughed again. But Stan figured the joke was on her.

Satisfied with his visit to the science center, Stan shifted his attention to that afternoon's ball game. The Reds played hosts to the third-place Cardinals. They won again, widening their lead back to four games.

The following morning, the players returned to Riverfront for another day game. Arrival time was scheduled for 11 a.m., but Randy straggled in at a quarter past the hour. The other players took note. Luke heard the catcalls, first from Fast Chad. "Hey, *Teen Idol*, what's the matter, party too hearty last night?"

"I hope you got a-*head* on the pitch last night—whoever she was," Miles Bailey teased.

"Shove it, Miles," Randy said icily. "Those might be the kind of women you date, but not me."

"Touchy touchy," Miles retorted.

"Just because you've got all the looks doesn't mean you have to get all the girls, Randy," Treat offered, attempting to put a positive spin on the situation.

Randy's eyes met Luke's, and he immediately looked away. Meanwhile, Miles egged Randy on. "What's the matter, couldn't you find your way past first base?"

Randy made a sudden move for Miles, his fist raised. Corrigan, who had been playing observer, tackled the first baseman from behind while Treat and the Officer wrestled Bailey, with all three slamming against the lockers.

"Easy, Randy, they're only having a little fun," Corrigan counseled. "This clubhouse is too small for feuds."

Miles stared at Randy, and he stared back. Mike slowly released his grip on Randy and waited for the standoff to end. Neither said anything, so he spoke. "If you two want to be part of the team, then you better end this right here. Now shake hands."

Miles twisted his mouth as if trying to speak through glued lips. Finally, the words emerged. "Sorry. I guess I went too far."

Randy nodded, without saying whether he was acknowledging

the apology or agreeing Bailey had gone too far. He held out his hand and shook with Miles.

Mike good-naturedly offered a parting observation. "This will give you something to think about next time you entertain oversleeping, Randy. And Miles, take it from a runt like me, I'd pick on someone your own size next time."

Luke could see that Randy was feeling a bit embarrassed. He waited until most of the players had gone on the field, then made it a point to walk passed Randy. "I hope this gal is worthy of someone like you."

Randy looked up, evidently not sure what to make of the comment. "Uh, yeah. No, she is. I guarantee you that."

Luke smiled and left. He knew more than he was saying.

If nothing else, the fight loosened everyone up. A host of players made believe they were afraid to get too close to Miles and Randy prior to taking the field. And Estabe cracked everyone up by waving a white flag as he returned to the bench in the bottom of the second. The contest itself turned into a laugher for the Reds, 16-3.

Heavy rains delayed the next night's game. Inside the locker room, players tossed money in a pot as they studied their poker hands. Others huddled around an ESPN game broadcast. Neal Parker and Mark Shaw formed a human seesaw, lying feet-to-feet with their legs entwined, rocking back and forth doing sit-ups and tossing a medicine ball in between.

The Stinger relaxed by his rocker. Earlier in his career, he had often joined in card games, usually bridge with Joey Jay, Bob Purkey and Jim Brosnam. He wasn't in the mood for that now. The relationships were not as close and the conversations were about a different era. Instead, he busied himself filling out a crossword. *A three-letter word for a New Zealand parrot?*

"I could never do any good at those things," Ducky admitted. "I guess I'm not smart enough."

"It's not a matter of great intelligence, Ducky. If it were, I wouldn't be doing them," Luke replied. "It's like anything; practice makes perfect."

"How long did it take for you to get good at it?"

"I don't recall. Too long ago." What Luke did recall was how it was a common practice with many of his teammates during those early years. And now, he continued to view it as a better way to pass time than lying around listening to some rap artist in a headset, or sitting in the players room staring at the tube. "Most guys did them before TV became popular. Then again, we had more time to kill, traveling and such."

Ducky scratched his stomach and nodded. "Maybe sometime you can help me do one."

As the catcher retreated, Luke refocused on his paper. *"Kea."* Yeah, *it fits across with "kettle."*

After the rains stopped, the Cards roughed up Brouse in a game as sloppy as the conditions, 7-4. Thanks to the weather, the contest ended in the wee hours of the morning. Corrigan showed compassion, giving his oarsmen a rest on Thursday's open date. Luke used his free time to help Derrick with chores.

While playing ball, Luke focused his every thought on the game. But at the Homestead, his mind ran free. He reflected on how much Doc's treatment had transformed him. Whereas he once viewed aging as part of life's natural progression, providing changes that renewed the spirit, he had to admit he relished his return to a youthful state.

With the afternoon sun burning holes through his ambition, Luke drove off to Roy's Tack and Saddlery. Situated halfway to town, Roy's offered everything an equestrian's heart desired. Luke found it an easy place to lose himself, whether there to check out the latest in horse equipment, select a gift from the clothes racks when Kate was alive, grab a jar of Propverts boot creme or simply pick out a Western-themed greeting card for one of his children.

Luke brushed his hand across a wool twill saddle pad. Country music played in the background, and a smell of leather permeated from the webwork of halters and harnesses hanging behind him.

"Is this where you take your glove to be laced up?"

Luke turned toward the speaker, a slender lady standing about five foot-six. She wore a pair of stonewashed walking shorts and a ribbed crew tee. She cocked her head and beamed a smile. He tried to place her. *Not one of Roy's salesladies.*

"Hi. Molly Baker."

"Uh, right." *Sure, the TV show hostess.* "What brings you in here?"

Molly held up a horse's halter, her thumbs inside each ring, and spread it apart. A frayed leather strap dangled on one side. "I need to pick up one of these."

"Looks to me like you're adding to your wardrobe," Luke said, eyeing the beige britches tucked under her arm.

"Oh, that too," she laughed. "How about yourself?"

"Checking out the saddle pads." Luke flipped the folded blanket he'd been inspecting.

"That's a nice one," Molly said, reaching for the corner and examining it. "Navajo. The double weave absorbs real well. It'll be great in this hot weather."

"Are you a saleslady or something?"

"I've been around horses for a quite a while," Molly said before pausing. "I know, you probably have this picture of me spending all my time around the TV station. But I enjoy letting my hair down when I leave the show."

And that she had. He liked the way she looked with her hair no longer bound in a ponytail. Of course, with her features he figured it didn't really matter how she wore it. "How long you been riding?"

"Over ten years," Molly said as she continued flipping through the blankets. "What color's your horse?"

"Chestnut-bay," Luke said.

"Oooo, that's pretty. This one might go well with it," she suggested, picking up another saddle pad.

"He's not too picky about colors."

His comment elicited another smile from the TV hostess. "And how's life with the team?"

"Great. We're in first." Luke knew it sounded trite, but he found it difficult to think up anything else to say. "I think I'll get this one. Listen, ah, it was nice seeing you again."

He started walking away, but Molly called him back. "Could interest you in going riding?"

Luke paused. Her suggestion had caught him by surprise. "Does this have anything to do with the show?"

"I resent that!" Molly exclaimed, placing her hands on her hips. "I thought I agreed last time to drop the subject until after the season."

"You're right. Sorry." He realized he had prejudged her, using the same yardstick he had for many in the media. "I'd be glad to. Give me a call sometime."

"What about this weekend?"

"I, ah, I'm pretty busy, what with games both days." Luke thought for a moment before continuing. "Tell you what, we're off next Wednesday, after the All-Star game. I'll be flying back early; could make it in the afternoon."

"Great. We get done with taping around twelve-thirty. You just need to give me a little time to plant a tape recorder under my saddle," Molly replied with a wink.

It was Luke's turn to smile. "I guess I deserved that."

"Figure around two?"

"That'd be fine." Luke gave Molly directions. He offered her use of Kate's horse—it received all too infrequent workouts from Megan now—but Molly said she'd bring her own.

Walking to the checkout, Luke realized he had surprised himself by accepting her invitation. A drape hid his motivation; even he couldn't see behind it. Perhaps like a policeman racing toward a crime scene with lights spiraling, the excitement of confronting a member of the fourth estate one-on-one stimulated him. Then there was the curiosity factor, a hunger to find out what made this lady tick. Then again, it might have been as simple as having an attractive member of the opposite sex with whom to race horses across open fields.

29
Never Underestimate
Your Opponent

The next few days leading up to the All-Star game flew by for Luke. He hit two more homers, which helped the team wrap up another successful homestand. Some saw his weekend power display as his way of thanking the fans for making him the leading vote-getter. But if truth be known, he felt embarrassed by the honor. He knew there were better players around the league. He knew, too, that fans were won over by his rejuvenation, which he figured gave him an unfair advantage in the voting.

Unlike the general elections, where pollsters measure the apathy level by voter turnout, that year's All-Star vote total was a positive endorsement for both Luke and the game—with balloting up some 12 percent over the previous high.

Three teammates joined Luke on the National League squad. Reynolds, enjoying his finest season, made his second appearance, his first as a starter. Kitchell was named a back-up first baseman. And then there was shortstop surprise, Raphael Estabe. Besides his steady glove, the Whippet's selection traced to his .352 average with runners on base, nearly eighty-weighty points higher than his total average. Added to that, the pride of the Dominican Republic had swiped twenty-nine bases.

Some thought that the K-Man, with his 10-3 record and league-leading 137 strike-outs, deserved an invite. However, expansion left All-Star managers fewer discretionary spots by the time a player was selected from each club.

Monday morning, Luke stopped by Randy's condominium downtown to give him a lift to the airport. It was the first time the young man had asked to share a ride, and Luke suspected there was more to it than the convenience of car pooling. His suspicions proved correct before they had crossed into Northern Kentucky where the airport was situated.

"I take it you, ah, know Megan and I have been dating," Randy queried with a hesitant smile.

"Yeah. I sort of gathered that," Luke replied, one hand on the wheel, the other griping the stick shift.

"I gotta say this is sort of awkward for me." Randy ran his thumb and index finger along the leather door pocket. "I mean, I'm not exactly used to asking permission to date people's daughters."

"Oh, c'mon, after all the girls you've been around?"

"No, no. What I mean is, I don't date that much to begin with. And it's been a long time since I've visited a girl's parents...."

"Come to think of it, I couldn't tell you the last time I've had a boy come calling at the house," Luke deadpanned.

"I want to let you know that I think a lot of Megan and, well, I know I got real fired up last week when Miles said those things. And it's nothing like what he said."

"I figured as much. At least I was hoping it wasn't." While he talked, Luke kept the car in the middle lane well within the speed limit for a change. He peppered his words with glances at Randy and the stream of vehicles zipping by his window. "Megan and I are pretty close. She's told me how nice you've been to her. She thinks the world of you, and that's all that matters to me, so you needn't say more."

"I know, but with you being my teammate and my friend, I want to let you know you don't have to worry about me taking advantage of her."

"So what you're saying is that if her father wasn't your teammate, you'd treat her differently?"

"No." Randy smiled, finally catching on to Luke's act.

"Hey, I'm opinionated enough that if I had a problem, you'd have heard about it by now."

Randy nodded before bringing up one of the warm-up events to the All-Star game. "Are you going to take part in the home run hitting contest?"

"They've asked me to. I've never done anything like that before, so it might be fun. I know I can handle a hitting machine..." Luke ended in mid-sentence as he felt a sudden tug on his wheel and heard the thud-thud-thud of his left front tire. He took his foot off the gas and put on his flashers while an eighteen wheeler behind him let out a horn blast. "Oh, the same to you, fella," Luke mumbled. He saw an opening in the right lane and coasted into it. The vibration got stronger and the noise louder. A hundred yards down the road, he pulled well onto the shoulder, where a cloud of dust enveloped his car. A check of the clock told him they had fifty minutes to flight time. "How fast are you at changing tires?"

"Fast enough that I'm not going to miss my first trip to an All-Star game."

Luke and Randy did make their flight heading to Pittsburgh, but just barely. There, Three Rivers Stadium was set to host the annual gathering of baseball's notables.

It had become a last minute fill-in when word came that the planned site, a ballpark under construction, would not be ready in time. Questions arose when the new park opened in May for play. The press speculated that the last-minute switch to the banks of the

Monongahela and Allegheny rivers was testimony to the negotiating powers of Nick DiCenso. His trump card: threatening to move out of the Steel City.

The pre-game All-Star pageantry had evolved to Olympic proportions. Bands representing the twenty-eight team-cities paraded on field, entertaining attendees and television viewers alike. Next up, performers sang and danced while the dedicated baseball enthusiasts grew restless.

Watching from the dugout, Luke thought how baseball had spared no expense with the pre-game festivities. *But then,* he thought, *it's consistent with the philosophy the owners have been demonstrating with free agency.*

The field was cleared and the stadium darkened for the final, and most dramatic, segment of the program. Satellites transmitted laser holograms from each country where baseball hoped to expand internationally. First up, a neon-like image of the Japanese prime minister wiggled near the pitchers mound while his broken English greeting was broadcast from the land of the rising sun.

All was not without glitches. The French premier was transmitted in split image. His head floated a foot above his torso, creating an eerie image. But the fans found nothing scary about it. Their muffled laughter soon grew to a sidesplitting outburst.

During the incident, Luke was befriended by Doug Lankley, a journeyman minor leaguer from his playing days, who now managed the Houston Astros. "Next thing you know, they'll be beaming players up to the broadcast booth for commentary between innings."

"Just so long as they don't beam up half our bodies," Luke observed, motioning to the Ichabod Crane-like figure on the field.

"How'd we ever manage without all these special effects, huh?" Lankley asked, shaking his head.

"The game was the showpiece," Luke replied, seated sideways on the dugout steps.

"Of course, let us not forget we got an audience out there that was raised on MTV, video games and *People* magazine," Lankley observed. "If ya threw out the electronic scoreboards, give-aways and dayglo uniforms, I'm not sure it would satisfy their thirst for entertainment."

"We don't give the game enough credit," Luke complained. He knew others would disagree, but there was no dissuading him of his beliefs. "I mean, people still think DiMaggio was something special, and what is it they remember most? What his uniform looked like, or how he swung the bat and glided after flies?"

As Luke endured the prolonged wait, his appearance began to weigh on his mind. He wondered how many saw him as another of the side show acts. *Come see the lovely lady with the beard that flows to her feet, or stop by and see the two-headed man, and tonight we have something really special, a grandfather playing major league baseball!*

Usually, he cared little about what others thought. At the root of his concern was a desire to avoid doing anything to detract from the game. Then there was the question of why him? Images of players now retired flashed before his eyes. As far as he was concerned, they deserved to be there every bit as much as he. Perhaps more. There, crouching over the plate with a bat pointed skyward, decked out in the red and white Cardinal uniform, was Stash—Stan Musial—scattering the ball to all fields. Representing the American Leaguers was Mickey Mantle, with his coal miner's biceps, attacking pitches from the right side of the plate, then the left. And in the outfield, Willie Mays, so fleet of foot, loped after the ball for one of his trademark basket catches. On the mound the lean Brooklynite, Sandy Koufax, reached back, his arm contorted behind his shoulder, his face seeming to register the strain of g-forces, as he fired lightning bolts past the next hitter.

"Ladies and Gentleman, leading off, playing second base, from the Boston Red Sox...." the announcement brought Luke back to the present. Across the diamond, members of the junior circuit trotted out along the third base line. It soon became his turn. A thunderous roar chilled him as he entered the field and slapped hands with his National League compatriots. He bowed his head and grinned, just as he had when selected for his first All-Star Game in 1956—the year Cincinnati fans literally stuffed the ballot box, electing him and seven teammates to the squad.

"I imagine this is old hat for you," catcher Ben Seabright of the Pirates remarked, taking his place alongside Luke.

"These games were, er, are always special," Luke stammered. He could hardly wait for the contest to begin. And his second place finish in the home run derby told him his hitting stroke was in shape.

Luke's first plate appearance fell short of his aspirations as he chopped an easy grounder to short. In the second, Ty Hartmann got it going for the American Leaguers, blasting a leadoff home run. His teammates added three more tallies before a new pitcher retired the side.

The game stood that way until the fourth, when Luke came to bat with a man on first. The first pitch came in tight, forcing him to jump back. His stare begot a smile, and the pitcher smiled back. There was admiration on both sides.

With the runner breaking, Luke drilled one into the opposite field corner. When the dust settled, the Nationals had men on second and third with none out. Both men eventually scored, cutting the deficit in half.

In the fifth, Ty answered back, banging one against the wall, which Reynolds tracked down. Treat relayed to short as Ty chugged around second and slid safely into third. It was then that Luke recognized Ty had it all: power, speed and grace—at least in running. If only he spent less time on his off the field activities, Luke thought.

Luke shaded the next batter in close, guarding against a shallow single. Moments later, the ball came toward him—a medium fly. Figuring Ty would be tagging up, Luke backpedaled, putting himself in position to charge the play. He grabbed the ball on the run and wound to throw as Ty raced plateward. His throw sailed toward the first baseline where it skipped off the Astroturf and into catcher Seabright's glove. Ben dove toward the runner, his arms stretched overhead like a swimmer starting his backstroke, and applied the tag with glove and free hand sandwiched around the ball. The umpire dramatized an out sign and barked the call. Ty leaped up, pirouetted and slapped his hands to his sides in obvious disagreement.

You probably didn't figure anyone could throw you out, let alone someone my age, Ty. Well, never underestimate your opponent, Luke smiled to himself.

The putout enabled the Nationals to tie the score when they pushed across three in the sixth. Luke figured prominently in the scoring, drilling a two-run shot into the yellow seats. The crowd awarded him a standing ovation. And when he approached third, the Angels' third baseman tipped his hat. Luke's teammates urged him to take a bow, but he wanted none of it. Curtain calls were for actors and actresses.

In the seventh, Ty doubled into the left field corner. Luke tracked it down and threw a frozen rope toward third. If Ty had any thoughts of taking an extra base, Luke's play in the fifth took care of that. But a clean single drove him in with the lead run, 6-5.

The score stood that way until the eighth, when, with a runner on first, Kitchell pinch-hit for the pitcher. Luke, having been lifted from the game, watched from inside the players lounge alongside teammate Reynolds.

"This guy throws darts, but he likes to pitch it high," Treat observed.

"Randy's a good high ball hitter," Luke added, his eyes transfixed on the television set. With a one-one count, Randy proved both observations correct. He smashed a letter-high fastball deep over the right field wall, giving the Nationals their first lead, 7-6. Luke was elated for Megan's boyfriend.

The game ended with the National Leaguers on top. Ty managed a single in the ninth, completing the "cycle" (single-double-triple-homer). In a close vote, he was named the most valuable player, despite having been part of a losing cause. But it was Luke who drew the most attention in the interview room. There, players were led in two at a time, one from each league. Luke found himself paired with

Hartmann.

"Luke, how different did it feel to play in this All-Star game compared to, say, your last one?"

"Oh, I didn't see much difference. They're all special. And as I recall, we won that one by a run, as well." His recollection was correct. The Nationals had bested the Americans 5-4 in extra innings at Cincinnati's Riverfront Stadium. It was 1970, the stadium's inaugural year and his last in an All-Star contest.

"How long you planning to play?" The hackneyed question came from an out-of-town reporter.

Luke ran his hand through his hair. "I'm just thinking about getting through this season right now." *Hopefully, through late October.*

"Ty, were you surprised at being thrown out by Luke?"

Ty's face tightened, then relaxed as he looked over at Hanlon. "How can you be surprised at anything a guy does who makes the All-Star game at his age?"

"Did you think you had the throw beat?"

"Sure. I, ah, felt my toe touch the surface of the plate before I felt the tag. But the ump made the call, and I gotta live with that."

Luke came to recognize Ty for what he was. He could have all the money he wanted, and Luke would feel no animosity toward him. He was someone to be pitied. He spoke more with bravado than confidence. *What was it Dad had said about mistakes?* A man who couldn't admit them, could never claim victory.

A reporter called out, "What d'you guys think of the chances of playing each other in the Series?"

Luke again deferred to Ty. The raven-haired center fielder scratched his head. "I plan to be there, and if the Reds can make it, well, I'd be glad to go up against my old mates."

"How about you, Luke?"

"That's a long way down the road. But I'd welcome it. I figure I owe the Yankees one." Luke smiled as he played with a match cover. The New Yorkers had crushed Luke's Reds in the '61 Series, four games to one. He answered two more queries before excusing himself.

Ty followed close behind, but answered more questions at his locker. More like held court. The year before he disliked the media's attempts to dissect his every move. Not now. No need to be defensive about falling short of expectations. He was having a banner season, his team was in first, and he no longer felt ashamed of his performance, certainly not on this night.

When asked again about the tag at the plate, he stuck to his story, blaming the ump. As for the loss, he took it in stride. After all, this was an exhibition game. His sights were set on winning the World Series.

Ty dressed and joined the American League's post-game party. Beneath balloons and bunting, he mingled with fellow players, owners and their companions. There he ran into Jamie Tiel, a teammate from his days with the Arizona Sun Devils, now a Detroit Tiger. The players were soon set upon by an older couple, George and Nan Yardley, Detroit's general manager and his frosted-haired wife.

"Nice job of pitching there, Jamie," the GM offered about the hurler's scoreless frame.

"Thanks."

George turned to Ty. "And you had yourself a whale of a game, son."

Ty smiled, although it burned him to be called "son." He opened his mouth to speak, but the GM's wife beat him to it. "Yes, that was remarkable. Someone said that was a first, hitting for the cycle in an All-Star game. Wasn't it, dear?"

"I believe so," George replied.

Ty soaked up the compliments. With his spirit floating above the mundane, the conversation turned to a very pregnant lady standing nearby, next to another member of the Tigers.

Nan expressed surprise. "I didn't know he was married."

George laughed, "He isn't."

The comments got Ty thinking of his own illegitimate child. While the finances were settled, it gave him a disquieted feeling. He soon made a move for the bar. Jamie followed. After tossing down a brew, Ty's thoughts turned to reliving the old times. "Hey Jamie, how'd you like to go upstairs and burn some gold? I've got some great stuff." Ty and Jamie had shared joints back during college. Ty had grown to have a renewed appreciation for the illegal substance this year. *Great high*, he thought, *yet no hangover.*

"I haven't touched that stuff since I left State. Besides, why chance getting busted?" Jamie asked.

"Hey, nobody's gonna bother you about smoking a joint. Besides, so long as you're with me, you've got nothing to worry about." Ty felt that he could dictate the rules, especially then. "This is my lucky night."

Jamie wasn't buying, and Ty returned to his room alone. There was a message to call home. He looked at his watch. Nearly one-thirty. He'd call in the morning. His mom might be up, but then so might Tony. He didn't want to deal with him right now. Why spoil a great evening by introducing his past?

He lay on his bed and turned on the TV. So confident earlier in the night, he now felt crestfallen. This time he knew the cause. Family memories stalked him. Memories of a hot summer's evening with nary a breeze through the open windows. Of his father jerking his belt out of his pant loops, flailing at him and his brother for sneaking inside to see him fighting with Mom. Fortunately, the alcohol impaired Dad's aim. Then there were the police, called to the scene by neighbors who had heard Dad threatening to kill his mother.

And now Tony was following in Dad's footsteps, drinking nearly everything he earned. *At least I know where to draw the line,* Ty thought. And to make matters worse, Tony had moved back home, in the beautiful house Ty had bought for his mom.

Ty went to his suitcase, where he pulled out a red, white and blue tin bearing the official major league baseball logo, and labeled "Baseball Glove Conditioner." He popped it open and removed a hand-rolled joint. The smoke carried him even further away from his family than Pittsburgh.

30

It's How You Act

"Harry, Stan Moore here."

"Hey Stan, what's happening?" The words came over the phone in a high-pitched voice.

"How's the next head of the FDA?" Stan asked twenty-nine-year-old Harry Hadley. A year before, Hadley had taken a promotional transfer from the FDA's Cincinnati Division office to become an investigator at its headquarters, just outside the Washington Beltway.

"Great. You should get a job here. I'm sure the *Washington Post* could use a writer with your talent, although there's no baseball team to cover. On the other hand, there are women crawling out of the alleyways. You don't need to be a politician to make it here. The only shortage is money—at least for me it is."

While Harry rambled, Stan looked across his disheveled living room to a TV set. CNN was broadcasting a film of the president apparently shouting at a news reporter. Stan wished he could hear what he was saying, but the volume was off. He turned his attention back to Harry. "I take it the raise they gave doesn't go far."

"Are you kidding? My rent's doubled, and my apartment's half the size of what I had. I've got a basement in one of those old townhouses. All I can see are a few ankles and shoes walking by outside."

"When you get off the phone, go grab one. But, sure to reach for a shaved one," Stan chuckled. He knew that watching ankles or legs or whatever was as close as Harry got to most women. His gifts lay not in appearances but in intelligence. The chubby bachelor was balding and bespeckled with a bookish look. Stan had befriended Harry in a Cincinnati nightspot three years earlier. He was a loner, which made him a perfect candidate for the type of help Stan wanted. Harry had assisted him with inside information once before. The story involved an experimental optical implant under development designed to improve night vision, especially for athletes.

"What brings you to call?" Harry asked.

"I need some medical information for a story I'm working on. I was hoping you could help me again."

"What kind of information?"

Stan recounted what little he knew about the study initiated at the Caulfield Science Center. He wanted to know the exact nature of the protocol, the drug's mechanism of action and Luke Hanlon's involvement.

"Sorry, Stan. Those files are all confidential," the investigator explained, his voice pitch rising.

"C'mon, Harry, that didn't stop you last time."

"All I gave was an opinion about the Administration's likely action. It was as much a guess as anything."

"A pretty informed guess, I'd say." Stan creaked his neck while he poured himself a light beer. "You did some asking around, right?"

"Well, er, yes. But nothing like opening confidential files or getting names of patients. Have you tried speaking with the clinicians?"

"Yeah, it's a dead end. The head guy is this German general, Dr. Dornhoffer. He's thrown a blanket over his staff tighter than a bikini on a pregnant hippo."

Harry laughed, before commenting, "I heard about Dornhoffer during my days in Cincinnati. He had a solid reputation from what I recall."

Stan's voice firmed. "Listen, if what I've heard is true, he's breaking the law."

"Really? Where'd you hear that?"

"You're not my only source, Harry. But I have to protect them just as I'll protect you when you tell me what I need to know."

"It could cost me my job. Hell, it's also against the law."

"All you're going to do is tell me a little more about something I already know a lot about. Besides, I'll make it worth your risk." The pause at the other end told him that Harry was nibbling. Stan had developed a knack for pinpointing people's weaknesses. It came in handy when he needed to probe for information. For some that weakness was sex; for others alcohol; and for many it was money. Then there were the less obvious weaknesses, like the passion Stan figured Luke Hanlon had for baseball. Harry's weakness involved money, but only tangentially. From conversations over a few beers, Stan had learned what really pleased him was outfoxing the stock market. And anything that helped him excel at it would play on that weakness.

"You recall Benjamin Kane?"

"Sure. The guy who built United Medical Discoveries from nothing to thirty zillion."

"Exactly. Well, he's leaving to take a job with another startup health care venture."

"You're kidding?"

"Uh-uh. It'll spike the stock as soon as it's announced. You get me what I want and I'll provide the name of the firm. But don't wait too long. The word will probably be out within a week—ten days at the most."

"How d'you hear about it?"

"My garbageman told me," Stan said with touch of levity.

"Your what?"

"Well, not actually mine," Stan explained. "I pay a guy who collects garbage out where the Reds' president, Vandermark, lives. He screens his garbage. Whenever he finds something interesting, he calls me. Turns out Kane lives on the same street. This dumpster-hound calls me the night before last and asks what I make of a letter which contains an employment package for Kane. Seems my man has gotten hooked on reading other people's mail."

"Have you seen the letter?"

"Of course!"

"And it's more than an offer?" Harry clarified.

"Yes. It's all about finalizing terms. Trust me, Harry. I'll bet the stock doubles within a week. Just look what Sculley did for Spectrum Technology—the damn thing tripled. And Sculley was nothing more than a marketing guy. Kane really understands the technology. He's got a Ph.D."

"He's a kingdom-maker, all right," Harry added.

"So you'll do it then?"

"I'll try. But you've got to write your story in a way that it can never be traced back to me."

"No problem," Stan reassured. After saying good-bye, he picked up the TV control and raised the volume. *CNN Headline Sports* had just come on. The announcer reported that the Reds and Yankees were the odds-on favorites to meet in the Series as the All-Star break came to a close. *Yes, but there may be a few surprises in store for Cincinnati,* Stan thought.

◆　　◆　　◆　　◆

The following afternoon at the Homestead, Molly Baker swung open her jeep door and stepped into the mid-afternoon temperature inversion. Her eyes widened as a volley of barks approached from the barn. The dog's alarm was followed by Luke, already tall in his saddle, his visage underexposed against the late afternoon sun. He wore jeans and a plum-colored Western shirt with silver-pearl snaps.

"You certainly didn't waste any time getting ready," Molly greeted.

"Afternoon, Molly," Luke said, tipping his leather cowboy hat. His mount was a gleaming reddish stallion marked with white socks.

"Have any trouble finding the place?"

"No. Great directions... It'll just take a minute to get Laureli ready," she said, moving to the rear of her ten foot barn on wheels.

While dating was something he hadn't done in years, Luke felt relaxed in his home environment. With a looping flip of the reins, he tied his horse to a white-iron hitching post. Nearby, four flowerless clay pots ascended the wooden steps leading to the porch. Dried geraniums were all that remained of last year's flowers.

Molly moved to the back of her silver-striped trailer, lifted the latch and laid down the ramp door. Luke retrieved her saddle while she led out her horse. She motioned with her arms for the leather seat, but could only stand and watch as he slung it with ease onto her chocolate mare. "Thanks."

She cinched the seat and donned her velvet riding helmet. "Lead the way."

"Click-click," he urged his horse. "Let's go, Boy."

"Is that all you call him, Boy?"

"His full name is Diamond Boy," he explained with an easy delivery.

"That's fitting."

"It's not what you think. He was named for the diamond on his forehead." Luke motioned toward the jagged star between the horse's eyes and relayed the story of when he and Megan had first checked out the yearling. "He was already named. I liked what I saw and probably would have bought him anyway. But you know how daughters are. She insisted the name proved he was meant for me."

"Do you believe in destiny?"

"I believe we make our own destinies," Luke answered.

"Looks like you've got quite a bit of land around here."

"Little over 300 acres." His voice was reserved yet proud. "We can take a trail out to the west. There's a high point that'll give you a pretty good view of the whole countryside."

The couple rode side by side at a leisurely pace toward the open fields that served as a retreat for the major league ballplayer. All around lay broad sweeps of rolling pastureland, neatly broken up by craggy rocks and groves of trees. To their left several Angus cattle grazed, black as peppercorns tossed on a rumpled green sweater. A soothing breeze brought an earthy scent.

Molly turned her eyes back to Luke. "Do you ride a lot?"

"Not as often as I like. With playin' ball I haven't been doing much of it." He left out the part about the loss of his companion with whom he enjoyed the trails. That had kept him off Diamond Boy more than baseball. Luke figured if Molly had done her homework, she knew about it anyway. Again he turned the conversation back to her. "How long have you been riding?"

"Back when I started working, I dated a guy who did it. I found it a great release from the pressures of television. Matter of fact, the first thing I saved up to buy was a horse of my own."

The riders reached a spot where the path swayed back and forth down a gentle slope. "Up for a race?"

"Sure, I like competition, too." She winked.

"See where the fence cuts across the field?" Luke motioned to the west, some 400 yards away. "I'll race you down there."

Molly didn't answer, but shifted from a canter to a full gallop. Luke waited, then raised his knees, sending Diamond Boy in pursuit of Laureli, who, by then, was four lengths ahead. The barrel-chested stallion hit full stride, eating up the distance yards at time, its hooves pounding, pounding... pounding the dirt trail, pairs of spindle-like hind and fore legs rhythmically working together. With each stride, the head lurched forward to an uneven cadence. Field grass and boulders passed in a blur. Molly turned to see him gaining. Faster and faster he came. Soon Diamond Boy was dead even. Glistening droplets clung to his coat. Pounding, pounding. The ground leveled off, and the dark chocolate tail of Diamond Boy waved good-bye.

Nearing the fenceline, Luke eased up, and Molly finished just two lengths behind. As they slowed to a trot, she congratulated him on his win. He said something about just racing against someone being his reward.

"I read where you once said that you enjoyed riding as much as running the basepaths."

"Did your research, huh?" Luke teased.

"There's been so much written about you..."

"Still looking for a story?"

Molly's head tilted like a dog hearing a sonic whistle. "No! I told you, I came here 'cause I wanted to ride with you."

"Sorry. It's just a little unusual..."

"What, that somebody from the media would want to get together without asking you fifty questions?" Molly feigned a pout.

"You got it."

Molly's speech slowed, "So what do I need to do to convince you otherwise?"

"You've just done it."

They soon came to a trough beneath the shade of a dozen oaks. Dismounting, Luke labored to raise and lower the arm of the rusted water pump, then filled two cups he had brought from his saddle bag.

Molly removed her riding helmet and shook her hair loose. She smoothed her turquoise polo shirt into her tan riding pants. A pack of mints, a treat for her horse, bulged in a side pocket. "Thanks," she said, accepting the cup. "That's pretty convenient. Who put the well in?"

"I did." Luke said, before drinking. The water iced his throat. A hint of iron flavored the drink.

"Ahh, that's refreshing."

"I used to bring the kids up here a lot—got tired of carting water along. Even had thoughts of building a house over there."

"And leave that one down below?"

"Kate, er, both of us wanted to give it to the kids. Doesn't much matter now." A detached look swept across his face.

"I'm sorry about your wife. I understand she was very special."

"Thanks. We had a lot of great times together. And I'm thankful for that." He returned to his soft, proud voice. "C'mon, let's take a look around." The couple strolled into the sunny grassland.

"How far does your property extend?"

Luke pointed toward the distant fencing that served as the western boundary, then to the choppy waves of trees that ran along Hogan's Creek to the south.

"I see why you like it up here. It's so removed from everything," she mused.

He sensed Molly also enjoyed bonding with nature. "It used to be even better."

"How d'you mean?"

"They've built it up down there—beyond the trees." Luke said, pointing. "At night it glows like some spaceship's just landed."

"I'd still take it."

"Where d'you live?"

"I have a condo in Mount Adams."

"No wonder you like it out here."

"I get away a lot on weekends."

Luke sat on the hillside, leaning on his elbows with his legs stretched out and crossed. He noticed Molly studying his face. "What're you looking at?"

"You." While lined with age, it was apparent that Luke's skin had the soft shine only young men are supposed to have. "You have such beautiful blue eyes."

"I guess." Luke grew uncomfortable with the flattery and shifted the topic. "Is Molly Baker your real name?"

"Baker is, but, ah, Molly isn't. I chose it when I started in television." Setting her cup aside, she grabbed a blade of field grass and twirled it between her fingers. "I had an aunt Molly I adored when I was growing up. So I sorta borrowed it from her," she explained with wide-eyed pride.

"What's your real one?"

"Mickey."

"Mickey?" he repeated.

"Now, you'll probably think this is a story created by some PR agent, but my dad just loved Mickey Mantle."

Luke laughed freely while Molly playfully shoved his knee. "Cut it out."

"Sorry," he said, still smiling.

"He chose it thinking they were going to have a son."

"Did you resent it?"

"I wouldn't say that. It was just… people looked at me as a tomboy growing up—and I was. When I broke into broadcasting, well, that was not the image I wanted to convey."

Luke half shook his head. "It's how you act that determines that."

"In everyday life that's true. But in television most viewers don't have the opportunity to really get to know you. They see things in two dimensions. Besides, breaking in is tough enough without having to convince a news producer you're something other than what he perceives you to be."

Molly had gone directly from college into covering news for a small station in Kentucky. Her combination of looks and personality made her a hit with viewers. As much as some reporters were abrasive, insensitive and leading, she was rated as engaging, respectful and balanced. Viewer research supplied all the support a Cincinnati producer needed to select her to fill an empty co-anchor slot for the evening news shows. That was two months before her twenty-sixth birthday.

She explained how seven years and some 3,000 shows later, she had taken a two-year leave of absence. She returned to host her current variety show, "Midday With Molly."

"What made you leave?"

"I was married at the time, and we were having trouble conceiving. I thought a rest might help. But it didn't work out."

"And the marriage?"

"That didn't work, either."

"Sorry." Luke dropped the subject as quickly as if he had turned over a rock covered with mealy worms.

Combing the grass, Molly found a pebble and rotated it between her thumb and forefinger. "We got divorced five years ago. He's out in

California now."

Luke stared ahead. "It's okay if you'd rather not talk about it."

"It doesn't really bother me. At least not like it did. Many thought the divorce had a lot to do with my career... In some ways you could say it did." She dipped her fingers inside her cup and retrieved a gnat before taking a sip.

"How d'ya mean?"

"I had held off trying until I was thirty-one. We tried for a year, but it didn't work."

"Try hormones?"

"No, turned out I had something called endometriosis." Molly's description was like taking a sentence out of a short story. Missing were the emotional details in which she and her husband subjected themselves to a variety of tests. Damaged fallopian tubes was the diagnosis. Too much of her uterine lining had grown around her tubes over too many years of waiting. "Oh, they did surgery to remove the blockage."

"And?"

"I did get pregnant several months later. What I didn't understand was how easily the tubes could become blocked again. We lost the baby." She shook it off and continued. "I got pregnant three more times. The last while I was on leave from the station. But each one ended the same way."

Molly recounted how there were eight surgeries in all during a four-year period as she raced against her biological clock. Her longing for motherhood took precedence over any physical suffering. She paused and blinked rapidly. "I even joked with my gynecologist that he ought to install a zipper across my stomach to make operating easier."

Luke sensed that for some reason, Molly felt compelled to tell her side of the story. So he let her continue, serving as an attentive listener.

"About six months after my last attempt, Steve announced he wanted a divorce. After all I'd been through, I didn't have enough fight left to resist. It was about that time I heard from my former news producer. He told me he had this idea in mind for an afternoon variety show. I jumped at the chance. Four great years later, here I am."

Luke started to place his arm across Molly's shoulders, then stopped. By now she was busy wiping away tears trickling down her cheeks. He handed her his bandana. She mixed laughter with tears. "It's sorta silly of me to cry. I mean, it's been so long."

"I'm sure it was very hard on you. Must've taken a lot of courage to keep on trying." Luke placed his hand on her right shoulder.

"I don't know. Perhaps it was, well... instinctive. I wanted to be a mother more than anything else," she said, placing her hand atop his. "You know, whoever said athletes were insensitive certainly never met you."

Luke smiled. As much as he wasn't looking to get involved with someone, he found her very disarming. And he could certainly relate to the losses she had suffered. After some lighter conversation, he asked, "You hungry?"

"Sure. Where d'you want to go?"

"If you don't mind taking a chance on my cooking, I've got a couple of steaks we could throw on the grill."

"Sounds delicious." Her bubbly talk show voice had returned.

Luke treated Molly to a meal cut from the hindquarter of his choice cattle. Molly chipped in, slicing tomatoes and boiling corn, the two remaining vegetables still growing in Kate's kitchen garden. It was nearly ten by the time Molly cleared the coffee cups. "I'm going to have to get on the road."

Molly hung her riding clothes in the jeep, then led Laureli from the corral to the trailer. A high-pitched sound of scraping metal sounded as she cranked the latch shut.

Luke, his hands tucked inside his denim pockets, stood alongside the car door waiting for his ladyfriend to hop in. Instead, Molly stopped, ostensibly to admire the clear nighttime sky. The moon was in its first quarter, and the heavens were awash with the Milky Way's shadowy brilliance. Molly locked her eyes on his. "Thanks so much." She reached out and grabbed his hands, which seemed drawn from his pockets. "It's been a long time since I've enjoyed myself so much."

"It's been a pleasure for me, too." Luke studied her face. As far as he was concerned, the Wild West didn't produce many better looking ladies. Brown eyes to shoot for, a complexion needing no war paint, skin as soft as petticoats and lips that would make a canteen wish it were alive.

"And thanks for trusting me," Molly said.

"About what?"

"About this not being a setup for an interview."

"Oh, that." He laughed off her comment. "Some people make it easy to trust."

Molly threw her arms around him, and he returned the squeeze, almost lifting her off the ground. Parting, she kissed his lips. He tasted the dew on rose petals. It had been nearly a year since he had experienced anything but a platonic relationship. He fought to block out thoughts of Kate.

"You sure you don't mind fraternizing with the media?" Molly whispered, her arms draped around his neck.

Luke didn't answer. Instead, he drew her close and returned a kiss of his own, this time deeper and longer. He massaged her clamshell-like shoulder blades and felt her heart pound against his chest. In the background, the crickets' current ran strong and steady, but it was the female of the human species whose sound he heard, the sound of soft purring.

Molly came up for air. "I'd like to see you again."

"Uh, okay."

She climbed inside her car and slid the window down. "Have a great game tomorrow."

"Thanks, I'll try getting a hit for you."

With his team in first, his successful trip to the All-Star game and now his date with Molly, life seemed wonderful for Luke. Almost too wonderful.

31
The Terrible Fax

Daylight Thursday brought to mind concerns for Luke that seemed light years away the night before. Whom was he kidding, dating a woman more than a quarter of a century his junior? There would come a time when he would no longer receive the bi-weekly injections and then what? She might like to adopt kids. It wouldn't be fair to tie someone so energetic down with someone closer to seventy than to answers. And then there was Kate. Sure, she would want him to pursue a relationship. But that was how she was. Always caring, always giving. How could he ever pull himself away to live with another?

Luke did keep his promise and delivered a hit for Molly that afternoon. In fact, he delivered three, as the Reds bested the Pirates, 5-1. But that ended his involvement with Molly. He avoided calling her and focused his attention on baseball. There was a lengthy road trip coming up and if he held out till then, well, perhaps it would all fade away.

The Reds lost two out of three that weekend to the Mets allowing the Cubs to close to within four games. They also lost Taylor with a groin pull. Luke wore the collar for all three contests. Thoughts of Molly shadowed him, especially around the Homestead: in the stable that housed Diamond Boy, along the trails they rode, in the kitchen where she helped cook up dinner and in the driveway where they kissed.

Monday, Luke made his regular morning visit to Dr. Dornhoffer before boarding the team's charter. Respectful of Doc's wisdom, he confided in him about his involvement with Molly. Doc suggested he forget about his misgivings and trust his feelings. "Think if the situation were reversed. If *you* were looking down from the heavens, what would you want Kate to do?"

The Reds arrived in Montreal to begin the season's longest road trip. Luke knew it would be a difficult one. Opponents included the teams fighting for first in the hotly contested Eastern Division, the Mets and Atlanta. Meanwhile, Chicago would be feasting on the Marlins—last in their division—along with the Phillies and Rockies.

Before leaving for the ballpark, Luke heeded Doc's advice and phoned Molly. He struggled to explain his delay in calling. "I got sort of busy with the games and finishing up some things around the farm before the trip."

"You must work pretty late into the night," Molly teased.

"Truth is, dating isn't something that I'm used to. I, ah—"

"I understand. No need to explain. I'm just happy to hear from you."

They talked for half an hour until Luke broke it off. "I've got to get ready. The bus leaves in twenty minutes."

"Listen, how about I treat you to dinner next time?"

"Okay. Megan keeps telling me I have to get used to this 'equality of the sexes' thing."

"Ha-ha," Molly answered with a sarcastic tone.

"I'll call you from the road. We can firm things up then."

Had Luke realized how much talking with Molly would lift his spirits, he would have placed the call sooner. That night, he led his team out of the box, knocking one over the wall with Wells aboard. Later, he threw out an Expo runner to smother a rally. And his two-out, seventh-inning single kept things going for Reynolds, who homered, locking up a 5-2 win, posted by Twiddy.

"Fine piece of pitching there, Clint," Luke said afterwards, passing the party boy in the locker room.

Clint, his T-shirt dripping with sweat, said nothing. His eyes drifted away. Luke continued on without saying any more. He knew a gap had been created that night in the hotel, but Clint would have to work his way out of it. He wasn't going to do it all for him.

The Reds won three out of the next five against Montreal and Atlanta. Treat Reynolds did much of the damage as he extended his hitting streak to 19 games. In the wrap-up with the Braves, he crossed the plate four times following a pair of two baggers, a single and a walk. His two stolen bases were icing on the cake.

Luke wondered whether this might be Treat's farewell tour with the Reds. It was no secret that he was in the final year of his contract, and a pivotal one at that. It marked his sixth year in the bigs, a milestone that triggered visions of dollar signs in the minds of agents and athletes.

Stories had been written conjecturing how much Treat might command. To his credit, the center fielder had kept his mouth shut about salary, claiming that the only things that mattered now were the games on the field. He told reporters that he and his agent would deal with it after the season. But did that mean Treat had already decided to leave? More than one writer had reported that the boy from Los Angeles planned to return to his hometown and don the Dodger blue.

Luke refrained from speaking with Treat about staying with the team. So long as he kept his mind on the game, he wouldn't. Perhaps later in the season. Then again, he might say nothing, for he didn't feel it was his place to interfere in a man's money matters. The one thing he did do was to urge Corrigan to sign the All-Star.

"I've been bugging Peter to ink him," Mike explained. "I know he'd like to. But it's not easy. Treat's agent is Jack Austin."

"The one Hartmann uses?" Luke asked.

"You got it. You can imagine what it's like with the two of them in a room. Sort of like asking the IRA and the British to agree on who's going to run Ireland," Mike sighed.

While the Reds bested Atlanta, the Cubs reeled off their eighth in a row. So as Cincinnati moved on to face first-place New York, they clung to a half-game lead.

The ballclub arrived at the Grand Hyatt in the wee hours of the morning. Luke knew he'd have to wait until the next evening to call Molly. It had been three days since his last call. Riding the elevator with Mike, Luke felt a hand on his shoulder. "How about joining me for breakfast?"

"What's the occasion?" Luke asked, thinking how he'd have to break with his routine of room service.

"I thought we could talk strategy."

The Mets led their division, and Luke knew they were not to be taken lightly. "Time?"

"I'll let you sleep in. Say 8:30?"

"You're lucky I'm used to milking cows."

With a double *ping,* the elevator doors parted the next morning. Luke trailed behind two attaché-carrying women in suits, one of whom had a tissue stuck to her shoe. He began to say something, when the women were greeted by their associates.

While he felt as comfortable in jeans on the road as on the farm, Luke wore khaki slacks and an open-collared dress shirt for his breakfast meeting. He turned to his left and passed a sequoia-sized support column. It was then that he detected movement. It came from the vicinity of the lounge to his right. A reporter charged with a microphone held high, a beacon leading his way. A cameraman followed, pulling a cloak off his videocam. Luke wheeled around to see more journalists decending on him like a mass of red ants. Up ahead, one knocked over a woman descending the marble steps. Luke helped her to her feet.

Now what do they want? Sure, he was swinging a hot bat, a .319

batting average with 25 round trippers, including two in the just completed Montreal series. But there must have been a bushelful of stories more important than his. After all, this was New York where stories were as plentiful as the yellow cabs. With hands on hips, he stood and faced his pursuers.

"Luke, what d'you have to say about Stan Moore's column?" a reporter shouted.

"Exactly what kind of drugs are you taking?" The TV reporter thrust his mike in Luke's face. His partner zoomed a mobile cam in close.

"Whoa, guys. I don't know what you're talking about," Luke said, although he had an idea. His skin tingled.

"Today's *Cincinnati Star Gazette* column by Stan Moore," another answered.

"Haven't see it."

"He claims you're taking an illegal drug."

A woman with a recorder strapped to her hip explained, "Says that's where you've been getting all your strength. Is it true?"

Luke's head swirled, and a chill shuddered his spine. "Like I said, I haven't seen it. I'd, ah, have to read it first."

"Here." Someone handed him a faxed copy of the column.

Moore on Sports—Cincinnati, August 1

HANLON TAKING ILLEGAL DRUG
Reds Slugger Miscast As Hero?

The most popular question in Cincinnati baseball circles since whether Pete Rose bet on baseball has been answered. For those of you who have been wondering how Luke Hanlon can compete after six decades on earth, read on.

Hanlon has been receiving an illegal drug since January. The drug is a genetic compound known, interestingly enough, as The Enabler. Hanlon was placed on the unapproved substance in direct violation of a decision by the Food and Drug Administration. Just late last year, the FDA demanded that it be withdrawn from any further testing in humans following a number of unexpected side effects.

This is not some form of steroids—it's much more powerful than that. We're talking about genetic engineering, altering the very essence of life. Aside from the ethical questions of dabbling somewhere between God and the devil, one must ask the question—who is responsible for the statistics Hanlon has compiled this year? Is it him or is it this wonder drug?...

Luke read no further. While the facts were stretched, his little secret was out. He drew a deep breath and tried rubbing away the tension from his neck. Someone had cold-cocked him, and he was still reeling. "All I can tell you is I'm not taking any illegal drugs. Beyond that I can't comment."

"But you admit you are taking some type of medication."

Before Luke could speak, two hotel security guards stormed into the melee. "Gentlemen, ladies, please, there are no cameras allowed here," one cried out. "Julio, call Ritchie."

The second guard, holding a walkie-talkie, spread his arms and pushed the reporters back. "We must ask that you respect our guests' privacy. Now please, you're going to have to leave."

The press paid him little heed and continued to fire away. "What do you think the commissioner's office will have to say about this?"

A third Hyatt employee appeared and shouted. "How the hell did they get in here?"

Luke used the distraction to slip up the steps to the Crystal Fountain Restaurant. There, he saw Mike seated at a window table, throwing his head back and waving, oblivious to what had just transpired. Luke lumbered along, the fax paper still clutched in his hand. Left behind was his appetite.

"Morning, pardner."

Luke forced a smile without answering. Droplets of sweat bubbled from his temples. He wore a dazed expression.

"What's the matter?" Mike asked, his voice dropping an octave.

Luke shook his head and stared off into the forked branches of the ficus tree in the reflective planter behind Mike. Trees... the farm... the Homestead. That's where he should have stayed. This was not some Ray Milland movie. Hollywood hadn't scripted his story. Life had. He should have known there was no guarantee that this university-based scientific discovery would have a happy ending.

"Luke... you all right?"

He looked back at Mike. "I'm going to need some time off."

"Sure. What's it, the family?"

A coffee-carrying waitress offered to fill Luke's cup, but he waved her off. His expression read like a "Do Not Disturb" sign. He handed Mike the quartered paper.

Mike unfolded it and flipped it right side up. He tilted his eyebrows as he read.

Luke gazed out the window at cabs and buses locked bumper to bumper across the street. A sanitation truck, short of space needed to make its turn, was wedged against a mailbox, blocking the Lexington Avenue intersection. A crowd of pedestrians moved en masse around it. In the background he heard the pitter-patter of rain. But it wasn't coming from outside. It was the sound of the restaurant's water fountain. *An artificial recreation of life,* Luke thought. *That's what I've become.*

"Is any of this true?" Mike asked.

"Some is, some isn't," Luke said.

"You're gonna need some help."

"I got myself into this; I'm the one who's gonna have to figure a way out."

"I want to help," Mike implored, leaning forward.

"Afraid there's not much you can do." Luke figured there wasn't much anyone could really do. The story would be sensationalized on the front pages. Major league baseball wouldn't look the other way, not even for someone as "beloved" as he. In the age of heightened sensitivity to drugs and athletics, he anticipated the consequences. It was time to retire his Wallace-Adams notepad. How could he have been so blind not to have foreseen all this?

"You can start by telling me your side of it."

Luke introduced Mike to the main players in his fairy tale: Dr. Dornhoffer, the Enabler and his own competitive instincts. Corrigan's nods and utterances provided a measure of support.

Luke checked his watch. He figured Doc would be at his lab by now. "I'd like a few minutes tonight to talk to the guys." Luke wanted to be sure his teammates heard his side of the story.

"Consider it done. I'll close the clubhouse to the media."

Luke rose from the table. "If you don't mind, I'll pass on breakfast. There're some calls I need to make."

Mike leaned forward and clutched the discredited hero's forearm. He looked Luke straight in the eye and smiled. "We're in this together." Luke knew he could count on Mike. From then on he couldn't count on much else.

Out in Ohio, Dr. Dornhoffer steered his late model sedan into his reserved space in the medical center garage. His fingers clutched the key, ready to silence the engine, when news headlines from the car radio stayed his hand.

"...two men killed in an attempted robbery in Finneytown, the governor opens the Ohio State Fair today, and a report that Cincinnati baseball player Luke Hanlon has been using illegal drugs. These and the rest of the stories making headlines, just ahead..."

Doc listened to the detailed report, then leaned back to assemble his thoughts. The complexities of the situation were a challenge even for his mind. He always knew the potential existed for the information about Luke's treatment to be disclosed. Yet, he was amazed by the way the story had been portrayed. *This is as slanted as it gets.*

Stan Moore was mentioned by name in the story. *Moore, Moore,* Doc thought. *Yes, that's the name several scientists mentioned as having received calls from in recent weeks. But they all claimed to have given him no information. Where, then, was the leak?* He turned his thoughts to dealing with things as they were. The past was prologue. He'd have ample time to tell his side of the story now.

Doc didn't have to wait long. A horde of journalists mobbed him outside the Science Center. Adrian blew puffs of smoke as he addressed their questions. "Sorry, but we do not give out information on any patients or studies."

"So you admit Hanlon is being treated under your care?"

"Those are your words, not mine, sir," Adrian replied, squinting through the sun and smoke. He was not easily rattled. Whether it be University board members, board students or FDA examiners, he followed his own internal clock. *He* would determine when, where and what information to release.

Doc again displayed his quiet confidence when Luke phoned. "No need to be apologetic. It was my decision as much as yours."

"You seem to be forgetting my visit last December," Luke replied solemnly. "I asked for the treatment. Said I'd accept all risks."

"What you don't realize, Luke, is how many requests I do turn down." Doc's voice retained its cheery confidence. He added with a chuckle, "Now some of them would get me in *real* trouble."

"Glad you can still laugh about it. But believe me, based upon what I've seen, the media are going to have a field day with this. I'm concerned what that may mean for you and the University."

"Oh, a few reporters already stopped by for a little chat this morning. It went just fine. I gave them a dose of double talk."

"Any word from the medical people?"

"You mean the FDA?" Doc asked.

"Yeah."

"No, they don't react as fast as the media. Should be no problem; I've dealt with them on a lot of sticky issues over the years." Doc had heard from the University's Medical Review board. He had an appointment to see them in a hastily convened session the following morning. There was no need to involve Luke. Not yet.

"Well, when you do, I want to be there."

"I imagine they'll be interested in speaking with you," Doc acknowledged, referring to the FDA.

"Doc."

"Yes?"

"How serious is this—I mean, for you?" Luke asked.

"It's nothing I can't handle. After all, people know me well enough. I've worked hard to earn my reputation as a maverick. This will only reinforce it."

Megan Hanlon had been enjoying a light summer schedule, teaching remedial math in the mornings at Incarnation Elementary School. By noontime she was either relaxing poolside or swinging her tennis racquet.

This day she arrived at school just before 7:30 a.m. and checked her mail slot. There, taped to the front, she found a message slip calling her to the principal's office.

She entered the office wearing a polite smile.

"Have a seat, Megan," Sister Mary Paula instructed in a subdued tone.

Megan sat down and adjusted the folds of her knee-length dress. While she found the principal fair and impartial, she never liked the seat opposite her.

"Are you aware of the article in today's paper regarding your father?" Sister asked, clasping her hands in a prayerful pose.

"No." Megan said, shaking her head. She leaned forward, straining for a glimpse of the paper the nun held in her hands. "What's it say?"

"I thought you probably hadn't." Sister handed her the newspaper.

There on the front page, above a photograph of her dad in action during happier times, a banner headline cried out, HANLON TAKING ILLEGAL DRUG. Megan fumbled with the paper before opening it to the second page, where she scanned the story. She shook her head as she read. Her Irish temper rose to a boil, her complexion matching the stripes in her pink dress.

She hadn't quite finished when she heard Sister's patient voice. "If you would like to take the day off, I'll understand."

"This is ludicrous!" Megan shrieked before quieting herself with her hand. "It's a bunch of lies."

"I've never been a fan of that paper myself," Sister comforted. "Someone brought me the article."

A clock on the credenza chimed for the quarter hour. Megan realized she'd have to make a decision quickly as to whether a substitute would be needed. It was a decision she had already made. She headed home to call Dad.

"Sorry, there's still no answer on that line," the Grand Hyatt's operator greeted Megan on her third try. "Would you like to leave a message?"

Eventually, Megan got a message through to Randy, who relayed it to Luke. It was afternoon by the time father and daughter spoke. "It's just some reporter for a desperate paper trying to grab a headline," Luke said, fighting off a headache. He downplayed the seriousness of the situation, which he had only recently come to understand himself. "To my knowledge there's nothing *illegal* about it." That was the question likely to be discussed the next day. Baseball Commissioner Lyle Vossler had called an impromptu meeting at his Park Avenue office.

"Doesn't the fact that it was used in a clinical study mean anything?"

"I would think so." Luke sensed Megan hanging on his every word.

"Then why do they make it sound like you were taking heroin? Even the radio stations are talking it up."

"There'll probably be a lot of crazy things written and said before this thing blows over."

"Oh Dad, I can't imagine anyone questioning your integrity," Megan sighed.

"Don't worry, I've got me plenty of supporters. How're you doing? Anybody say anything at school?"

"Only Sister Paula—I took the day off after she showed me, ah, you know, the article."

Luke's heart sank at the thought that Megan felt compelled to leave school. "Keep your chin up. You know how it is when controversial issues surface."

"I know." Megan mimicked words that Luke had used on more than one occasion. "Like a pack of Springers cornering a fox, none of them wants to back off."

"How's that boyfriend of yours?"

"Randy?"

"Who else?" Luke said.

"I adore him almost as much as you."

Luke thought how his daughter's blossoming relationship with his teammate gave credence to his lingering belief that, in some way, he was meant to have been with the Reds that season.

An hour before gametime, Luke stepped to the front of the visitor's locker room at Shea Stadium. He knew others would control his fate in the coming weeks, but he was determined that it not stop him from doing the right thing now.

Mike had little trouble getting everyone to quiet down. For each of them gathered there—coaches, ballplayers, the trainer and equipment manager—the tabloid article had cut through the emotions of the pennant race. The ugly side of life had erupted out of the baseball diamond like some mucous dripping, bumpy-headed cinema monster. Luke sought to bury the creature and put the playing field back in place, at least for them.

"By now you've all heard about the stories that I've been taking some sort of illegal drug. What's true is I, ah, have been receiving supervised medical treatment with a new drug. Experimental, yes; illegal, no. But the more important issue is what it all means to you and the team as a whole. I never envisioned this causing anyone harm— I realize now how badly I miscalculated. To the extent I've, ah, become a distraction or have brought shame to you and the Reds, I deeply regret it. I don't expect to be pardoned, but I do hope you'll accept my apology."

Luke paused and scanned their ashen faces before returning to his penciled outline. "Ah, tomorrow morning, Mike and I have a meeting with the commissioner. I'm sure he'll be keeping you posted. All I can tell you is no matter what happens, don't let it get in the way of your drive for the pennant. Nothing would make me feel worse than if my problem distracted you from winning one game."

Luke attempted to return to his locker but found himself surrounded by the players, expressing their full support. Several patted his back. He welcomed their encouraging words, but it didn't relieve what he saw as a serious mistake in judgment on his part.

None of the Reds felt like playing ball. The weather saw to it that they didn't have to. What started as a soothing patter of raindrops turned into a gushing outburst streaming from the heavens. It was as if nature were shedding tears for the accused.

The players took turns checking out the conditions, sloshing into the watery dugout and watching puddles grow on the tarp. Some caught sight of an occasional T-shirt clad fan racing onto the field and slip-sliding across the protective covering. Overhead, the downpour provided a discordant drumbeat on the dugout roof.

An hour after "gametime," two inches of rain had fallen. The umpires shut down the landing approach by Flushing Bay. As far as Luke was concerned, the day had been a total washout, and so might the rest of his season.

32
What Dreams Are Made Of

Events surrounding the Enabler unwound faster than a coverless baseball on a wet sandlot. By the time dawn broke in New York, one couldn't turn on a TV newscast or pass a street corner kiosk without seeing pictures of Luke.

Noah Hall kept busy fending off media requests. Reporters from the three networks, plus ESPN and CNN, had milled about outside the Reds' locker room during the rainout. Fox and TBS called to schedule interviews, while Lifetime's Healthline show proposed an entire episode featuring Luke and Dr. Dornhoffer. In the morning, sleepy-faced reporters descended on the sidewalks surrounding the Grand Hyatt. This time the hotel's security guards kept them at bay.

Up on the thirty-third floor, Luke met with Corrigan, Vandermark and team attorney, Stephen Davidoff, in the owner's suite. They nibbled at a tray of fruit and pastries while the red-haired lawyer described the participants they'd be meeting at the commissioner's office. "Alan Carter is the deputy commissioner. He can be one tough cookie."

"You don't have to tell me," Peter added. "He used to be with one of the West Coast teams. Got real involved in that unsuccessful fight against the Satellite network. The guy's a womanizer and drunkard. I still don't understand how he got a majority vote."

"Maybe they thought he could relate to some of the players," Mike suggested, prompting a frown from Luke. "Hey, I drank as a player."

Stephen played it straight. "I guess they figured they'd put somebody in who wasn't shy about dealing with the commissioner. And I've heard if there's dirt to be found, Carter knows about it. Guess it takes one to know one."

Davidoff picked at his front tooth and continued. "Peter brings up a good point. Carter really has limited loyalty to the commissioner. He's the owners' representative."

Luke recalled hearing how the owners had reconfigured the commissioner's office. The deputy commissioner was now selected by them instead of the commissioner, and he served as an ex-officio member of the owners' executive committee. The rationale was to "keep communications open between the commissioner's office and the owners." It was also a means of keeping the commissioner in tow.

Davidoff next characterized the commissioner, Lyle Vossler. "He's rather personable, although it seems he can never get enough information. His favorite line is, 'Help me get more comfortable.' He'll likely lean on Carter to do the questioning."

Stephen recounted a story from an Ownership Committee meeting. A team executive had brought in a blanket and thrown it on the table, saying, "Here, we can send this to Lyle. Tell him to hold onto it when he reads our proposal. Maybe it will make him *more comfortable* with the decision."

"Then there's Dr. John Grissom. He's baseball's drug adviser. Has absolutely no bedside manner."

Shortly after 9:30 a.m., the quartet sneaked out the hotel's side door. The day was as hot as the story that enveloped them. Heat waves were visible above the blacktop, and puffs of steam belched through sidewalk grates. Corrigan stepped into the gutter and waved as five—

six—seven taxis passed. Finally, one swerved across three lanes of traffic and pulled curbside. The entourage ducked inside, just ahead of the paparazzi who caught sight of their getaway. An unshaven driver in rumpled army fatigues snapped the fare lever and sped off.

Conversation inside the cab was light. Vandermark spoke with Davidoff while Luke, wrapped in guilt, reflected on recent events.

The taxi zigzagged through nine blocks of traffic on its way to the commissioner's Park Avenue chambers. Seventeen floors up, the quartet entered the cherrywood-paneled offices of major league baseball. Above the receptionist, an electronic scoreboard flashed results of the prior day's games.

The group exchanged greetings with Commissioner Vossler inside his conference room. Lyle cut a professorial appearance at well over six feet, balding with a long nose and a hesitant smile opening onto a set of capped teeth. The contrast with Deputy Carter was evident. The former team attorney had beady eyes and a square jaw that underscored his clenched-tooth smile. Luke detected alcohol on his breath.

The participants took their seats around the well-waxed, oval table. Attorney Davidoff sat to Luke's left, with Corrigan and Vandermark, respectively, to his right. Their backs faced the windows.

Lyle situated himself directly opposite Luke, flanked by Carter and Grissom. A stenographer, outfitted in a poorly pressed short-sleeved shirt and ill-fitting tie, passed out legal pads and pencils. He took a seat at the far end of the room, next to an American flag.

On the table, an insulated coffee pitcher rested alongside eight inverted, gold-trimmed mugs decorated with the sport's silhouette logo. Mike, his top shirt button open, his tie loosened, poured coffee for everyone. Luke let his eyes roam the room, settling on the nine oil paintings of the previous commissioners: Kenesaw Mountain Landis, "Happy" Chandler, Ford Frick, General William Eckert, Bowie Kuhn, Peter Ueberroth, A. Bartlett Giamatti, Francis "Fay" Vincent and Vossler's immediate predecessor.

Kenesaw's stern stare caught his attention. The white-haired federal judge had also hailed from Millville, Ohio. *Would he show a neighbor mercy? Hardly,* Luke thought. The staunch prohibitionist would've banned him for life, just as he had the eight members of the Black Sox. "Luke Hanlon, you say you took this unapproved drug, the 'Enabler'? Baseball has no place for drug users. Henceforth and forever, you are to be banned from the playing field. I am also instructing Baseball's Hall of Fame to remove your plaque and all references to your ever having been a member."

Luke shuddered to think of the possibility. He realized, too, that in all his years, he had never set foot inside the commissioner's office. He felt a reverence, as much for the office as the individual in charge. This was the fountainhead of baseball. Here resided the power to shape the actions, initiate the changes and uphold the rules of the game.

Rules of the game. Had he indeed violated the rules of the game he held so dear? *Damn, what did I get myself into? A hearing, lawyers, testimony, judgments. How did it end up like this? If only I could wake up and find it's all a bad dream.*

The commissioner's preamble told him it wasn't. "First, ah, let me say, Luke, we in the commissioner's office have the utmost respect for what you have meant to baseball, your commitment to the game, your sense of fairness and your accomplishments on the field. Having said that, there are certain guiding principles that we need to abide by for baseball to continue as it has for more than a century. The intent of this hearing is to make sure that there has been no compromise of those principles."

Luke nodded as he massaged his mug. The commissioner continued, splicing his words with smiles, "I hope that we can have an open discussion of the facts surrounding your return to baseball, including any medical treatments or drugs that may have played a part in your return."

Commissioner Vossler's voice retained a certain high-pitched twang developed while growing up in Endicott, New York. Were he talking on the phone, one might have a hard time telling if it were a man or a woman on the other end. It was certainly an incongruous tone for the broad-shouldered, Brooks Brothers executive.

Lyle began with a series of rudimentary questions covering Luke's earlier career and his twenty-five-plus year hiatus from the game. Deputy Carter listened intently, voicing scattered comments. Vandermark held his pencil in his fist, flicking at the eraser, as if trying to ignite a flame, while Corrigan revealed his artistic talents with a cartoon rendering of Mr. Baseball, which he shared with Luke. Only Davidoff used his writing instrument for its intended purpose.

The bat handles on the wall clock pointed to 10:50 before Lyle spoke to the matter at hand. "Luke, perhaps you could tell us, in your own words, how you came upon this treatment referred to in Mr. Moore's column."

"The Enabler?"

"Yes."

Luke recounted his shoulder injury and the encounter with Doc, all leading up to his enrollment in Dr. Einhardt's clinical study. His voice was calm but flat. He wanted to be as open as possible. He had no desire to hold anything back. Only in that way, he thought, would people be able to judge what he had done and why he had done it.

Deputy Carter joined in the questioning. "Why, after it was decided to shut down clinical testing, did you seek to resume treatment?"

"I just wanted to play baseball."

"Could you elaborate?" Carter asked, squelching a burp.

"While I, uh, was taking it, I got to hitting and throwing some with my son..." Luke's voice trailed off. He found himself dancing around mention of his wife's passing. The last thing he was about to do was bring her into the discussion.

Mike cut in, "His son's a pitcher for the University of Cincinnati."

"I see," Lyle acknowledged. "Go on."

"I got to wondering if I might just be able to play again. You know, on a major league level. It really hit me during those practice sessions how much I missed playing."

"And so you contacted this friend of yours, Dr. Dornhoffer?"

Deputy Carter asked.

"Yes. But it was totally my decision."

"Luke would prefer to keep Dr. Dornhoffer out of the matter," Mike added.

"I don't see how we can help but bring him in," Alan said. "I mean, he was the one who administered the drug."

Luke scrunched his mouth in displeasure. Davidoff spoke on his behalf. "I think the doctor's importance relates to the fact that it was a medically supervised treatment. This was by no means some drug Luke had bought off the street."

"Yes." Lyle bobbed his head slowly. "What I'd like to hear, Luke, is your understanding of what this enhancer drug does."

"The Enabler," Davidoff clarified. "It was called the Enabler."

"Right. In your own words, Luke, what exactly does it do?"

"As I understand it, it helped my body grow like it did when I was in my teens—it sure got rid of all my creaks and aches." Luke did not intend to be humorous, but Lyle chuckled at his comment.

"I have here a copy of certain information that was transmitted to me by Dr. Dornhoffer." Davidoff waved a sheet of paper from which he proceeded to read. The abstract described a "natural process" by which *ena-1* allowed for cellular reproduction in all body tissues. It detailed how Doc had administered Luke bi-weekly treatments for three months under a carefully controlled, approved clinical protocol. It concluded by explaining that Doc had arrived at an "informed decision with the subject" and resumed treatment over the most recent eight months. When finished, Davidoff passed out copies.

"Luke, is there anything you'd like to add?" Lyle asked.

"No. That pretty much sums it up."

"So it enabled you to gain certain capabilities you otherwise wouldn't have," Deputy Carter added.

"At my age, right. But I didn't see any harm in that. Seemed no different to me than putting some fertilizer in the ground to make the crops grow. You know, like adding back nitrogen that's been depleted." Luke's explanation drew smiles from Mike and Peter.

"Although one could make the same argument with steroids, no?" Carter countered. "I mean, they're chemicals produced inside the body, too. Isn't that true, Dr. Grissom?"

"Right." The physician broke his silence. "Although steroids actually exert a stimulating effect on cellular activity. From what Doctor Dornhoffer reports, this drug doesn't actually cause tissue growth; it only eliminates the suppressive action of other genes. Of course, that's so much theory at this point."

Luke shoved aside his mug and folded his hands. Using some of the prepping Doc had provided him with, he responded. "As I understand it, steroids grow muscles. In my case, I had to work out to get back in shape. The drug didn't do anything by itself to improve my performance."

"Good point, Luke," Peter cheered.

Carter softened his tone, "Let me go back for a moment. We have a treatment here that supposedly alters the genetic makeup of one's body. And it had been withdrawn from clinical testing. We know that much, right? Did it ever occur to you, Luke, that in taking it you might be in violation of baseball's drug policy, let alone the law?"

Commissioner Vossler raised his neatly trimmed eyebrows while Vandermark registered a look of concern.

"No. Never did."

The Reds attorney spoke next. "I think it's important to keep in mind that this was a drug Luke had been treated with for three months in a controlled clinical study, a study approved by the FDA."

"Yeah, but Stephen, even LSD was tested on patients at one point," Carter said.

"I object to these comparisons. LSD, steroids!" Davidoff blurted out, while Peter nibbled on a knuckle. "It suggests that the Enabler is in the same class of drugs. And that couldn't be further from the truth."

"I have to side with Stephen on that point, Alan," the commissioner said, shifting side to side in his high-back chair. "While I don't necessarily condone the usage of unapproved drugs, we must be careful about lumping them with things that are clearly illegal."

"I just want to make sure we understand where the parallels and differences lie between this Enabler and other types of drugs, that's all. If I implied more than that, I apologize," Carter said.

"I'd like to remind the counselor that the American judicial system was founded on the belief that a man is innocent until proven guilty." Davidoff smiled sarcastically. "Perhaps we should view this drug on the same basis."

"What I'd like to know, Luke, is why you never notified Peter or anyone else connected with the team that you were taking this treatment?" Lyle asked.

"I didn't see any reason. To me it was a personal matter."

"Didn't your agent explain the rules regarding such notification?"

"Luke doesn't have an agent," Peter explained. Lyle's whimsical look indicated that fact was worth a point for Luke. "I accept responsibility for not explaining the policy to him. I'm sure the rule wasn't in effect when he played before."

The meeting ran for another fifty minutes without any substantive new information being brought to light. As discussions drew to a close, it was Peter who sought answers. "Lyle, how do you see the situation? Have we satisfied your concerns?"

Lyle ran his finger around the rim of his mug. It was as smooth and rounded as the information he desired prior to making any decision. "You'll have to be patient, Peter. This is a unique situation. I need to get a bit more comfortable with the information before reaching a decision."

"Please keep a focus on the fact that this was a medically supervised treatment, with a drug the FDA had previously judged worthy of usage in humans."

"I'll keep that in mind, Peter," Commissioner Vossler acknowledged, standing. "I want to thank you all for coming, especially on such short notice. Luke, I may need to speak with you before you leave town. I'd appreciate your keeping your plans flexible in case that becomes necessary."

The Reds defense team exited through the narrow hallways. They accepted greetings from the staff along the way without stopping.

Luke was relieved that the hearing was over, although he knew that the worst was perhaps yet to come. The thought that Commissioner Vossler, would be making a ruling regarding his playing career unnerved him. He held out faint hope that somehow the commissioner would find in his favor. But what if he did? Surely he would ban him from using the drug. How could he play without the treatments? Still, it would at least clear his family name. That was most important. Important for Megan, Bret, David and Sheila. And even for little Tracy and Sean.

The foursome crowded into another cab for a short ride to Pietro's, a secluded Eastside dining spot. Attorney Davidoff recalled the fine Italian restaurant from his days practicing law. The prices served to screen out the commonfolk—the cost of the house chopped salad rivaled that of a seat at Yankee Stadium.

The help took their arrival in stride. Distinguished lunchtime guests were common. Mayor Andrew Gillespie himself presided over a gathering just three tables away. Before Luke could order, the politician marched to his table and flashed an endearing smile. "Welcome to New York, Luke. I've been following your performance this season—remarkable!"

"Thanks, your honor," Luke answered, rising and shaking the mayor's hand like ten thousand before him. Gillespie seemed smaller than his pictures, with a grainy, uneven complexion.

"Please, just Andrew." The mayor topped off the handshake with his free hand and shook vigorously, as if mixing a cocktail. "If I can do my job half as well when I get to be your age, I may still be in office."

"It might be better if you just retired."

Corrigan's belly laugh made Luke realize his words hadn't come out the way he wanted. His meeting with baseball's leadership had scrambled his usually steady mind.

The mayor ignored the *faux pas* and greeted Luke's tablemates. His honor had something meaningful to say to each of them. *We could have used him at the hearing,* Luke thought. The charismatic mayor parted with a wish. "All the best in your dealings with the commissioner."

"Thanks, er, Mr. Mayor." Luke protected the fact that the hearing had already taken place. He proceeded to bury his head in the oversized menu.

As he had done so many times, Corrigan sought to bring some levity to the somber gathering. "Doesn't the mayor realize we don't vote here?"

"His wishes were sincere," Davidoff replied. "He was a pretty fair ballplayer back in college."

"Really?" Mike asked.

"Yeah, played for Columbia."

Luke caught fragments of conversation murmured between the owner and lawyer. He sensed Peter was saving his debriefing until he and Davidoff were in private. Stephen reminded everyone that if things didn't work out, they could always appeal to the Players Association. Luke could file a grievance immediately following any action by the commissioner which affected his playing status. An arbitrator would then rule on the appeal. "We'd have an answer in three or four days."

"Save the arbitrator. I'm really not interested," Luke muttered between bites.

"Let's hope we don't need that option," Peter said.

Davidoff shifted his eyes back and forth, indicating skepticism.

At the hotel, Luke returned a call from Dr. Dornhoffer. Doc advised that the FDA wanted to hold a meeting in Washington a week from Thursday. The timing would allow the agency's director of compliance to attend the session. Doc tried to downplay the fact that his involvement was rather unusual.

That night, on the press box level at Shea Stadium, Vandermark watched his team work out. Seated next to him were Noah Hall and the team's director of player personnel, both slopping down their lapfuls of food and drink. Suddenly, attorney Davidoff charged into the suite.

"Peter, we need to talk." The attorney glanced at the others. "In private."

Peter motioned with his head toward the glass-enclosed room behind them. He and Davidoff went inside and shut the door. "It's about Luke, isn't it?"

"Indirectly. Our friend, Ty Hartmann...he was taken in this afternoon—cocaine possession."

The mid-summer tan disappeared from the owner's complexion. "You've got to be kidding. What the—where'd you hear that?"

"A contact at the Players Relations office just tipped me off," Davidoff answered, tightening his lips.

Peter shook his head in disbelief. He turned to the picture window and exhaled his disgust. "Damn. This isn't gonna make it any easier for us."

"Yes, but keep in mind in Ty's case they're dealing with an illegal drug. With Luke, the treatment was simply experimental," the attorney rationalized.

"C'mon, Stephen. No need to soft-pedal it to me. This will just focus more attention on where they draw the line between drugs that are acceptable and those that aren't."

"In the morning I'll put a call into Carter. You know, make sure he doesn't lose sight of the distinction."

Peter grabbed a handful of cashews off the bar and popped them in his mouth, with several falling onto the floor. He remained focused on the field. Davidoff stood in silence, arms folded. Peter finally caught sight of Luke shagging a fly ball. He felt bad for his left fielder. Winning seemed somehow less important. He thought how Ty must have had the same attitude. "Amazing. Here's a guy who's got all the money you could want, playing for a first-place team, and he risks it all for what?"

"They say he's had problems before with alcohol and pot."

Peter spoke between chomps on the nuts. "And here I thought we had put our problems with Hartmann behind us. Where'd this all happen?"

"Some dogs sniffed him out at LAX." The attorney relayed the events that had taken place at the Los Angeles airport. "Customs agents had their K-9 unit on duty to check some luggage coming in from South America. They were patrolling the terminal when the dogs accosted Hartmann."

"Where was the team?"

"He had stayed behind to visit with some friends— the Yanks had an off day. Anyway, the dogs kept sniffing at his duffel bag. One cop recognized him and even got him to sign an autograph. Apparently, they were ready to release him—they said they figured it was just his smelly gym clothes the dogs were after. But he seemed rather nervous, so they opened things up. Found four ounces stuffed inside one of his gloves. Can you imagine, hiding coke in his glove?"

"Sounds like he's bought himself more problems than even *his* money can handle."

"Don't be so sure. First violation. With a little luck and a good lawyer, he'll get off with probation."

"What about baseball?" Peter threw down some more cashews.

"Depends if he goes for treatment. He can strike a deal there, too."

Peter grabbed two sodas from the cooler and handed one to Davidoff. As he drank, he thought about Ty Hartmann. A thorn in Cincinnati's side for more than a year, the multi-millionaire continued to plague his former teammates. The only consolation was that Ty would knock Luke off the front pages. Yes, the Yankees, who for years had relished the ability to steal headlines—especially when their team was not in the limelight—once again would find themselves taking over the lead story.

The cloud-covered sky held off the rain that night, but the Reds couldn't hold off the Mets. They lost 3-1, wasting a fine pitching performance by Fast Chad. It was clear the team's thoughts were on more than the game. The Reds tallied but six hits against a subpar pitcher, and the winning runs were unearned. As for Luke, Corrigan pulled him in the seventh after he went down swinging for the second time. The wilting rose dressed quickly and watched the final out on TV. He left the stadium, moments before the press descended upon the clubhouse.

Early the next morning, the commissioner called Vandermark to clarify whether Luke had made any attempt to notify the team of what he had been taking. Peter admitted he hadn't, but reminded Lyle there was no intent to deceive. He explained that Luke had given his word to Dr. Dornhoffer to keep the drug—a drug he thought perfectly within the law—a secret.

At 3:10 p.m. Eastern Standard Time, as the team was about to leave for the stadium, Peter received a hand-delivered envelope from Major League Baseball. Inside he found a letter from the commissioner, which read, in part:

> After taking into consideration all of the facts surrounding Luke Hanlon's use of the experimental drug ena-1, I regret to inform that I have decided to suspend him from baseball for the remainder of the season. While Mr. Hanlon's play has always been exemplary, the fact that his performance was aided by treatment with an unapproved drug is counter to the spirit of baseball's drug policy.
>
> Should Mr. Hanlon remain drug-free and wish to be reinstated at the beginning of next season, I would be happy to consider that request.
>
> Sincerely,
>
> Lyle M. Vossler

Peter slumped on the edge of his bed.

After pulling himself together, he conferred with attorney Davidoff, then enlisted his manager to help break the news to Luke. They reminded him they could fight it with the aid of the Players

Association. "Think about it, Luke. It's your decision, but you deserve better than to have your season end this way. Stephen thinks we have at least a 50-50 chance of winning in arbitration."

Luke again declined Peter's offer. He had already decided to abide by whatever the commissioner ruled. The game was bigger than any individual, including himself. He wanted to put it behind himself as quickly as possible. "Thanks, Peter, but this is the end of the line. I guess I should have realized it's just what dreams are made of."

It had been a great half season. The wins, the losses, the hits, the outs, all so insignificant now. Or were they? No, he really would miss it all and the people he had met. As much as he had complained privately about all the changes, he had grown to love being back at it. Yes, it pained him to have it end up like this. It pained him not to be able to see it through to the end.

33
Backlash

"It's called an 'open plea,'" attorney Vic Morreti advised Ty Hartmann.

"You're telling me to agree to the charges without any guarantee of a deal?" Ty asked, scrunching his eyes.

The navy-suited lawyer clasped his hands on the conference table across from the seated ballplayer. His gold, lion-headed cufflinks shined against his white shirt. "You can guarantee yourself of staying out of jail. Just some community service."

"Yeah, and while I'm at it, I get suspended from baseball." Ty knew that if he pleaded guilty to cocaine possession, his season would be over. Kiss the post-season good-bye. Forget the fact that the Yankees were eight games in front.

Los Angeles attorney Wes Fischer joined the discussion. "If you lose the case, Ty, I'm afraid you'll end up doing at least twelve months, maybe more." His even-toned voice contrasted with Vic's flair for the dramatic. Morreti had arranged for Wes to serve as Ty's attorney of record while in California.

"I thought they only sent repeat offenders to jail," Ty commented, turning his head to the side in disgust.

Vic motioned to the other attorney. "Tell him about the judge."

"I checked with the DA's office. My sources tell me Superior Court Judge Judith Torrence will be handling your case. She likes nothing better than to clamp down on celebrity drug abusers."

"I'm not a drug *abuser*," Ty said, slamming his hand on the table. "I just happened to try the stuff once and got caught."

"Doesn't matter," Fischer said.

"You heard of Stone Saunders?" Vic interjected.

"The movie star?" Ty recalled Stone as the latest in a series of actors to play James Bond.

"You got it. Anyway, he was picked up on the highway with a bag of the stuff hidden in his console. His record was as clean as this table. But he fought it and lost. Judge Torrence sent him to the county jail for—what was it, eighteen months?" Vic looked back at Wes, who nodded.

Ty realized he was at a crossroads. Plead guilty to cocaine possession or risk going to jail. The open plea meant he'd have to own up with baseball and agree to undergo rehabilitation. *Rehab.* Ty thought the word was meant for serious drug users. Not him. After all, he wasn't an addict, not even an alcoholic. His dad, well now there was one. But he'd never fallen down or passed out, at least not *outside* his home. Certainly never on the street.

As unattractive as rehab was, the alternative, jail, was even less so. Sure, he could claim someone had stuffed his glove with the coke, but who'd believe him? And if they didn't, he'd end up in the slammer. *No way. Not that. Nothing was worth that, not even baseball.*

"How long is this rehab supposed to take?"

"Normally six weeks," Vic said, mopping his sweaty brow.

"Six weeks, huh," Ty mumbled, rolling a pencil between his palm and legal pad.

"Keep in mind you're only twenty-eight," Vic reminded. "You've got the rest of your life ahead of you. Play your cards right, and you'll have many more great seasons."

"Besides," Vic Morreti reassured, "as long as you're in rehab, you'll still be eligible to collect your baseball salary."

Ty nodded. A silly mistake, that's all. The plea bargain was the easiest way out.

"So then, you'll enter the open plea?" Fischer clarified.

"From what you've told me, I don't have a choice."

◆　　◆　　◆　　◆

Delta Flight 963 screeched to a halt in Cincinnati, just after eight in the evening. Luke Hanlon stepped out amid the deplanning passengers. He had wasted no time in leaving New York following the commissioner's ruling.

His peaked cap and sunglasses were not enough to hide his identity from the handful of reporters stationed outside the security gates. The suspended player made quick work of their questions with one-word answers. As he approached the carpeted staircase, a girl and two boys closed in on him. One in a Bengals T-shirt called out, "Hey Luke, we're behind you all the way."

Luke nodded.

"The commissioner doesn't know what he's talking about," the tallest and most athletic of the trio added.

Luke signed autographs for each before descending the stairs. A skycap and several more travelers passed along their wishes. After a troublesome stay in New York, they made for a warm homecoming. Homecoming. The Homestead. Luke sparked to the idea. A place to recharge his batteries. A refuge where he could replenish his spirit, which had been worn down by the media circus surrounding the Moore article, not to mention the commissioner's ruling.

What thoughts Luke had about himself and Vossler's ruling gave way to concern for Dr. Dornhoffer. In just eight days, he and Doc would travel to the FDA's offices in Maryland. Luke was determined to do everything in his power to see to it that *he* was the only one receiving any kind of suspension.

He recalled a news story from the early '90s, about a respected department head at the University of Minneapolis being forced to resign. He, too, had used an unapproved drug. *Something like AGL or ALG*, Luke recalled. The name didn't matter. What mattered was that the drug had been a true lifesaver—not simply an elective therapy for some old ballplayer looking for one more shot. It was a drug designed for use in preventing organs from being rejected by recipients. Kate had brought the story to Luke's attention. It struck them both as odd, seeing how it had been successfully used during his mother-in-law's heart transplant. The story had gotten lost in the recesses of his mind, until now. If only he had made the connection before, when he considered asking Doc to treat him with *ena-1*.

Bret and Rusty greeted Luke at home. His son listened as his dad recounted the commissioner's hearing.

"I almost forgot. Molly called," Bret advised. "She said to tell you she was real sorry about how things worked out. Said she'd like you to call her."

Luke retired without returning her call. He figured he'd have plenty of time to reach her tomorrow or the next day or the day after that. Instead, Molly called again in the morning. Luke made a veiled attempt to convince her he was doing just fine.

"I find it all so unbelievable," Molly exclaimed. "As a reporter, I have to say it doesn't sound like they're being very objective."

"Well, it wasn't exactly a jury trial," Luke said.

"You'd think they'd be glad to hear about the drug's success. What about an appeal?"

"The commissioner's the highest court," Luke replied, leaving out arbitration.

"Well, it doesn't change how I feel about you." Molly's voice transmitted a smile through the wires. "How about I treat you to dinner Saturday?"

"I'm not sure I'd be the best company right now."

"Excuse me? Just a minute ago you said you were doing great.

Remember, I still owe you a meal."

"I guess," Luke grunted. Then he realized he had plans already. "Oh sorry, I can't. David is bringing his family down from Chicago."

"What about during the week?"

"I've got a hearing with the FDA coming up." It was only a day trip. Still, Luke knew he couldn't give Molly his undivided attention with the meeting on his mind.

"Why do I get the impression you're avoiding me?"

"Maybe I am."

"You promised to let me treat you to dinner."

"I did, didn't I."

"If you don't come along willingly, I might be forced to ride over with my six guns and take you hostage," Molly advised with good humor.

Visions of his cheery riding companion came into view. Throughout his recent difficulties, and perhaps because of them, he had continued to think about the TV hostess. About the things they shared in common—their enjoyment of the outdoors; their hunger to escape life's frenetic pace; her sincerity; and her softness and warmth. Luke also harbored a desire to share his innermost thoughts with someone. And so, as much as he sought privacy, he knew he couldn't hold her off forever. "What d'ya have in mind?"

"I'm not the greatest cook, so how about I buy you dinner?"

"I'm, ah, trying to keep a low profile..."

"Don't worry. I know places where privacy isn't a problem."

Luke accepted her offer. Friday at seven. The hearing would be over. He'd do the driving. Molly would do the buying.

◆   ◆   ◆   ◆

Commissioner Vossler's ruling ignited a backlash of protest. The path of complaint spread quickly throughout the towns and cities of America, growing to resemble the shatter marks on a windshield surrounding a shotgun blast, a blast centered in Cincinnati. Here was a sports protest they could wrap their minds around.

Luke's supporters lit up the switchboards at local TV and radio stations. Letters, many of them crafted in shaky pen strokes betraying the authors' ages, jammed the media's fax machines.

In New York, the commissioner and reporters now had Hartmann's usage of an incontestably illegal drug on their minds. Yet Luke dominated the calls to their offices with fans expressing outrage at the suspension of their aged idol.

Two days after his ruling, Commissioner Vossler was hit with another headache. Mrs. Adele Drewes, a wealthy Cincinnati widow, launched a national campaign in support of Luke. Adele placed an advertisement in *Modern Maturity*, the mouthpiece of the American Association of Retired Persons. It urged all members to boycott baseball games until such time as the commissioner reinstated Luke and his treatment. It read, "The commissioner's ruling is a direct affront against all senior citizens... Here is an individual who has subjected himself to testing a potential medical breakthrough... a treatment offering hope for the millions of us who have experienced the ills of aging..."

Few were taking Adele's protest lightly, not with the magazine's 36 million readers. It certainly raised concern with several team executives who were already sorry to see Luke—a popular draw all season—depart the diamond.

Then there was Ohio Congressman Charles Niederman, along with Representative Melissa Seibert of Florida, who aligned themselves on Luke's side. They called for congressional hearings into the FDA's Clinical Hold on testing *ena-1*, as well as on the authority of Baseball to suspend a ballplayer.

Only the "Divine Naturalists," a religious fundamentalist group, could be counted on the commissioner's side. They urged a permanent ban on testing the treatment, claiming its use amounted to playing with the very foundation of human life: "Aging is part of the natural process for all living creatures... If God had wanted us to stay young forever, to never suffer the decline in our bodies known as senescence,

He would have so equipped us."

As the new week broke, the Reds returned home looking for a renewal of their own. The team had finished their road trip by losing four out of five. "Chicago's Express" had roared to a four-game lead. Corrigan tried to get the team to accept the fact that Luke was gone. The number "27" each player had written in black magic marker on his shirt-sleeve told him it would be easier said than done.

That night, Chad Lattimore whistled to Miles Bailey, dressing two lockers away. He tossed his head in the direction of Stan Moore now entering the room. "Hsssssss. Say Miles, you got any of those snares you use for roping snakes? I think we got one crawling 'round in here."

"Well, if it isn't that guy from the *Cincinnati Star-Gazer*," Bailey greeted, buttoning his uniform, his eyes riveted on Stan.

Stan ignored the slight. "Hi guys."

The players turned away. Stan continued past the gauntlet of players. One by one they turned to face their locker bays. He stopped to speak with Kurkowski at the far end of the room. *Ducky would no sooner miss an opportunity to talk than to eat,* Stan thought.

"Hi Ducky. How's the arm feel?"

The backstop shook his head in disgust. His gut protruded more than it ever had that season.

"Oh, come on. I can understand you guys being upset, but I wasn't the one giving Hanlon the treatments." Stan turned back to Ducky. "Okay, you're angry with me; so let's talk about it."

Ducky grabbed his glove and brushed by the reporter. He headed toward the trainer's room. Stan stood there slackjawed.

Stan had found himself at the center of controversy often enough that it usually didn't faze him. There wasn't a day that went by without one or more angry letters about his controversial column. He fed on the correspondence like a Pavlovian dog, for an increase in mail signaled an increase in readership, which eventually led to an increase in pay.

Reversing his field, Stan headed toward the manager's quarters, where the silent treatment continued. "Mike, let's be adults about this. All I did was report the facts."

"Yeah? And who ever told you he was being treated with some illegal drug?" The Reds manager once again went face to face with the columnist.

Stan tottered back. He recalled Harry Hadley's statement that under no circumstances was the drug to be used while it was on Clinical Hold. "The FDA had banned it."

"Oh, really? That's not what I heard. If anyone's a criminal, I think it's you," Mike bellowed.

The thought suddenly occurred to Stan that, in making his little deal with Hadley, he, too, had overstepped the government's rules. *But that was in pursuit of the truth,* he thought.

The manager said nothing further; nor did Kitchell, nor Estabe, nor Sweeney, nor Worley, nor Wells, nor Reynolds, nor any member of the clubhouse staff. Riding the elevator to the fifth-floor press box, Stan's silent treatment persisted like a bout of indigestion. The button-pushing operator stared ahead. The Reds' vice president of baseball operations, Jesse Washington, shot Stan a harsh glance before exiting for his office. Only Guy Lester spoke as the two signed in the press box registry. "Looks like you bought yourself a bit of trouble, Stan."

"They'll get over it. Give them a day or two. They always do."

"You sure? I've had it happen with a player now and then. But never an entire *team.*"

Guy's words sizzled on Stan. *How dare this group of overpaid athletes—grown boys who can't see past their own egos—take their frustrations out on me?*

As was the custom with major league clubs, the Reds provided free food within ready reach of reporters during games. The buffet table at Riverfront was set up in a room adjoining the press box. Besides complimentary beverages, the menu ran the gamut from cold cuts and chips to lasagna and salads. That night, the Reds served up a reporter's dream: sirloin-tipped shish kebobs. For Stan there would be none. A security guard barred his entrance. Vandermark's orders. He left in the seventh with the Reds comfortably ahead, complaining of boredom.

Stan next appealed his case to the people of Cincinnati. Radio station WWIN, anxious to host anyone connected with the hot story, invited Stan on the show. After two days of silent treatment, he welcomed an opportunity to talk with the public.

All seven lines flickered on the console phone. Host Ken Kraft adjusted his headset and thumbed an OK to Stan. The journalist nodded and scooted his chair toward the engineer's window, triggering a squeal from its rollers. Stan jumped in his seat. Ken offered a reassuring smile. A moment later his producer announced the name, location and topic—as if there were any doubt—of the first caller.

Ken: Anthony, you've got a question for Mr. Moore?

Caller: Yeah, I was wondering if Stan could tell me if he always pisses in his coffee before drinking it...

Langley slammed the emergency red cutoff switch. The station went dead for several seconds. When it powered back up, the host spoke.

Ken: Sorry 'bout that, folks. Next time I'll try to be quicker on the button. While we're waiting, Stan, let me ask a question. It's no secret that the Reds players are a bit miffed with you. Have you ever thought about holding something back because of player reactions?

Stan: (A brief laugh) No. I'm paid to get a story. I figure they'll get over stuff eventually.

Ken: And if they don't?

Stan: If they have a problem, I'd just as soon have them come and talk with me about it. Usually we can work things out.

Ken: Okay, let's try line four...Bob from White Oak. Welcome to WWIN, home of the winners. I hope you have a question that won't get us thrown off the air.

Caller: Yeah. But I understand how the last caller felt.

Ken: Okay Bob, what's your question?

Caller: Stan?

Stan: I'm here.

Caller: Do you feel sorry at all about your story now that Hanlon has been suspended?

Stan: Let me ask you, Bob, would you pose that to a reporter who writes about a politician with his hand in the till who, say, ends up in jail?"

Ken: Whoa, now, just a minute, Stan. Surely you don't mean to imply that Luke is a criminal.

Stan: Well, er, not exactly.

Caller: But that's what you just said.

Stan: Not quite. I was, ah, just making the analogy to explain that as a writer I can't be spending my time worrying about the impact a particular story may have. I just try to draw out the facts.

Caller: (In a raised voice) Since when do you deal in facts? It looks to me like there's a lot of editorializing in your articles.

Stan: Well, sometimes I do that, too. After all, that's the role of a columnist.

Ken: Thanks, Bob....Okay, let's move on to Betty from Fort Thomas.

Caller: Hi Ken. I want to ask Mr. Moore what makes him think he has a right to dig into a player's private life—I mean, to go beyond reporting what happens on the field?

Stan: It's all part of my job.

Caller: Is it?

Stan: Betty, ballplayers enjoy a status far beyond the average worker. As far as I'm concerned, once they buy into the rewards that go with their celebrity status, they open themselves up to public scrutiny. They must deal with the consequences.

Caller: So what's wrong if they profit from their public positions? Don't you do that too? Don't you profit from the stories you write about them?

Stan: I'm paid to search out stories, if that's what you mean. But there's no comparison with what these guys make.

Stan answered calls for the next hour. Defended himself would be more accurate. While Kraft's show usually picked up callers on both sides of an issue, the evening's participants ran fifteen to one in favor of Luke.

Long after the show ended, the Reds fell to Atlanta, 3-2. Without Luke, the Reds had been held to less than three runs in six of seven games.

34
Medical Findings

The white Towncar sped off from Washington's National Airport. Its destination: the Food and Drug Administration's headquarters in Rockville, Maryland. Inside, Luke drummed his fingers on a raised knee. Joining him for the ride and day's hearing were Dr. Dornhoffer and Dr. Emily Einhardt.

Luke half listened as Emily commented about the benefits of traveling with a major league ballplayer. Doc translated, explaining how they often boarded a crowded Metroliner from the airport to a subway stop across the street from the FDA.

Doc, his arm braced against the supple leather seat, shifted his shoulder back and forth. His eyes met Luke's. "So how have you been feeling?"

"Not bad. But try asking after this thing's over with."

Normally accepting of most situations, Luke longed for control over the day's activities. He felt responsible for the hearing facing his adviser. He had seen the letter addressed to Dr. Dornhoffer, and read the words that the physician was being "called for cause." He refused to accept Doc's assessment that a simple discussion of the facts would "probably set the matter to rest."

"Come now, Luke, you certainly have nothing to be concerned about. You're there to serve as what we call *amicus curiae.*"

Luke flashed a perplexed look.

"It means 'friend of the court,' one who's there to lend testimony," Dr. Einhardt explained.

"Thank you, Emily. Yes, they'll be interested in meeting you as much as hearing your testimony."

"And you?"

"You needn't worry about me. What's the worst that could happen—they send me into early retirement?" With that, Doc slid his hand further into the seat-back. "What the devil?" he asked, pulling out a pair of white lace panties.

"I wonder who last rode in this car?" Emily quipped.

"D'you suppose it was one of our congressmen?" Doc asked, smiling.

The comment evoked laughter from all, including Luke. He found it a welcome break in the tension that had engulfed him throughout the morning.

The Lincoln rolled to a stop in front of the nineteen-story office building at 5600 Fishers Lane. The four-wing structure that housed the main offices of the FDA sat curbside on a well-traveled road in the suburban Maryland community.

Overcast skies greeted them as they stepped onto the sidewalk. Luke surveyed the nondescript grey brick building. It reminded him a bit of an old ballpark. Periodic cracks connected the '40s styled steel windows, which were in need of washing and, in several cases, replacement.

Up on the twelfth floor, a young black secretary led the trio down a faded yellow hallway that smelled like old popcorn. They arrived at a hearing room used by the Center for Biological Evaluation and Research (CBER). Drs. Dornhoffer and Einhardt carried with them three 2-inch binders—the maximum size set by the FDA. The first two contained information on the drug itself. The third was filled with Luke's laboratory test results, which he had volunteered to release.

Dr. Milton Lashkey, the chief medical officer and reviewer in charge of *ena-1*, welcomed the visitors. Lashkey, who stood more than six feet, had bulky shoulders and a pillowy chest. His hair hung down in sheepdog-like bangs, nearly touching the top of his glasses.

Dr. Dornhoffer introduced Emily and Luke to Dr. Edward Thermopolous, division director of CBER, and Dudley Chapman, general counsel for the FDA. Doc had told Luke that he had known Dr. Thermopolous since the director's days as a young scientist with the National Institute of Health (NIH).

They were joined by several FDA staffers, with too many names and titles for Luke to remember. Doc had told him that, as a rule, they could expect the FDA to have at least as many attendees as they. This day, they completely outflanked their guests. There was Dr. Nathan Rudovsky, supervisor of pharmacology; William Brennan, consumer safety officer; Dr. Aradhna Khairi, biomedical statistician in charge of epidemiology; Dr. Alicia Hayes, scientist from biopharmaceuticals; and Dr. Henry Eisenstaedt, regional director of the FDA's Mid-Atlantic regional office in Cincinnati.

Also in attendance was Dr. Ahi Nishida of the NIH's Recombinant DNA Advisory Committee, otherwise known as "RACK." RACK was charged with reviewing any federally funded study involving biological drug testing. Since much of the Caulfield Center's work had been funded by grants from RACK, it came as no surprise to Doc that the NIH would want to have a say at the hearing and in any decision the FDA handed down.

The government representatives aligned themselves on one side of the scarred conference table, a relic from World War II. Behind them, dusty orange drapes darkened a set of windows. Doc grabbed a seat between Luke and Emily.

Two FDA-ers, there as observers, squeezed into grade-school desks at the far end of the elongated room. They were introduced simply as Ms. Desalvo and Mr. Hadley. Yes, Harry had requested permission to sit in on the hearing, citing the fact that he was familiar with the Caulfield Center from his days at the Cincinnati office.

For the better part of an hour, Luke listened as the FDA scientists, following a tightly crafted agenda, fired questions at his companions. Dr. Einhardt explained to Dr. Rudovsky why they had missed the broad implications of *ena-1* in the earlier clinical testing. "The animal models we used failed to demonstrate the changes we've seen in humans. And, of course, with the younger patient populations in the Phase I clinical, the Enabler protein was still very much present. It wasn't until we expanded both the duration and the demographic groups that we came to understand the gene's full activity."

Regional Director Eisenstaedt offered his support for the university scientists, citing that his office's inspection of the labs had uncovered no falsification of records. "And the protocol followed was consistent with that outlined in the original NDA."

"Protocol?" Lashkey asked. "How can you call it a protocol when it wasn't even a study?"

Luke was unaccustomed to the mood of the hearing. As much as reporters could ask tough questions, for the most part their queries were innocuous and their tone informal. Here, the questions seemed designed to keep the invitees on the defensive. He would later describe the hearing as if there were two teams battling for first place, knotted at one-one in the ninth. Through it all, he observed Dr. Dornhoffer maintaining his confident and friendly demeanor. He rode a magic carpet several feet above the burning inquiries. Luke understood what his late wife had meant when she referred to Doc as "maze bright"; he knew exactly where to turn before most ever saw what was coming.

Medical officer Lashkey picked up the questioning.

"Dr. Dornhoffer, didn't you think of the legality of resuming treatments after the drug had been placed on Clinical Hold?"

"I thought about what was in the best interest of the patient. I concluded that it was within a reasonable measure of safety to resume the course of therapy."

"What interest?"

Luke's eyes were met by Doc's. After a pause, the ballplayer nodded, and Doc continued, "The patient had recently lost his wife." The words hung heavy on the audience, especially for Luke.

Dr. Hayes from Biopharmaceuticals interjected, "Why didn't you request treatment under a hardship clause?"

Doc adjusted his plaid bow-tie before answering. "There was really no hardship. Not for a man who, considering all his years, was in excellent health. What are the odds that you would have granted permission?"

"That's not the issue." A cynical smile crept across Lashkey's face. "The point is, that would have been the only correct course of action."

"And what does 'correct' mean?" Doc shot back. He planted his elbows on the table and rubbed his palms together. "I believe Webster defines it as conforming with fact or logic. You might argue that the FDA procedures hold the facts. But I held the logic; as his personal physician I felt it was in the patient's best interest to resume treatment."

Casey Stengel couldn't have answered it any better, thought Luke.

At the end of the room, Harry Hadley coughed, clearing what must have been a lump in his throat.

"Are you saying that the patient had nothing else to live for?" Dr. Hayes, the only woman besides Emily at the hearing, asked.

"Clearly not. But I did view it as giving him a fuller life without *artificial* drugs or stimulants. And after all, isn't that one of the reasons we're here on earth?"

"You're assuming there were no risks. With its mechanism of action, there's the possibility of unregulated cell growth and oncongenesis. Is that not true?" Lashkey asked, honing in on the drug's potential to cause cancerous tumors.

Doc rubbed his earlobe, then replied, "One can never know for sure. But we had seen where the gene hadn't been permanently inserted into the patient's genetic material."

Emily, her binder opened, her eyes moving between the document inside and Dr. Lashkey, blurted out, "Under Section III of the pre-clinical testing, you'll find the results of the contact inhibition studies. They were all negative." Luke knew nothing of the studies, which involved injecting the genetic protein into mice skin cells as a check for uncontrolled cell growth.

Doc turned to the reviewer. "We also checked patients involved in the earlier clinicals for possible reduction in their cytotoxic t-cells."

"And?"

"In all but one case, there had been no change in the quantity of cancer-fighting cells." Doc paused to drink some water. "The exception involved a woman who developed breast cancer. However, further investigation showed a significant family history of the disease."

"And you decided to throw her case out?" Dr. Rudovsky interrupted, stroking his goatee.

"I considered it within the context of all the evidence we had gathered," Doc explained. "Only then did I make the judgment that it was most likely unrelated to her treatment with the Enabler. In all, we had accumulated twenty-eight months of very positive medical histories. They included those who had participated in the early clinicals. The subjects had a remarkably better health profile than the general population." Doc slid a stapled document across to the supervisor of pharmacology. "A full summary is contained in that report."

Doc waited while the pharmacologist skimmed the paper. "I should point out that if Mr. Hanlon hadn't been part of the original clinical study, I wouldn't have administered the Enabler drug to him during the Clinical Hold. You see, if there was to be any long-term damage, it was just as probable that it would have been triggered by his initial course of therapy."

Dr. Lashkey caught Luke while his thoughts were drifting. "Mr. Hanlon, how much did you understand about the drug's potential ramifications?"

"You mean, like side effects?"

"Exactly," Lashkey smiled pompously.

Luke, having anxiously awaited the chance to defend his friend and medical adviser, seized the opportunity, "Doc was real clear about that. At first he refused to let me back on it. As you were talking there, I, ah, recalled him telling me how it might lead to some form of cancer."

"How long after you requested permission did he give you the okay? A day? Two?"

"I don't recall exactly... maybe a week. He said he needed to talk it over with some of his scientists. And even then, he didn't start until after laying out those things you mentioned—ah, side effects."

Lashkey gave a series of slow, steady nods before speaking again. "And you decided to go ahead anyway?"

"Uh huh."

"Didn't you take his warnings seriously?"

"Sure. Knowing Doc like I do, I knew he wasn't just making it all up. But I figured what was meant to be would be," Luke shrugged. "You know, like me getting involved in the study in the first place. Besides, when you get to be my age, you tend t'stop worrying about what's going to get you."

Dr. Lashkey gazed in the direction of the senior representative, CBER Division Director Dr. Thermopolous. The Greek native with the ebony glasses and matching curly hair puffed out his lower lip. Thermopolous picked up on the questioning. "Mr. Hanlon, could you describe for us, in your own words, the medical checkups you received? I'm talking about during your second round of treatments."

"Doc was a real stickler when it came to follow-up. He wouldn't let me out of his office without hooking me up to a heart monitor or taking some blood." Luke paused to think. He heard his heart pounding. "And, ah, every other visit he did some sort of tissue biopsy. Then there was the usual stuff like checking my blood pressure."

Dr. Thermopolous scratched some notes. "Anything else?"

"One thing that bothered me at first was how he made me come in exactly every two weeks. I had sorta hoped we could work around my road trips, but he insisted on every other Monday. Sometimes I had to take commercial flights to catch up with the team."

During the next ten minutes, Dr. Thermopolous and Dr. Nishida asked Luke more questions, some of which he could not answer. His answers communicated the bond that existed with Doc.

Dr. Hayes turned toward Emily. "Dr. Einhardt, earlier, Dr. Dornhoffer mentioned that this drug has a different mechanism of action than human growth factors. Do you agree with that statement?"

"Yes."

"Could you explain?"

"The *ena* gene doesn't actually initiate cell growth; that is triggered by other messengers inside the DNA. Rather, I like to think of it as returning the body to a steady state, the condition the cells are found in when one is in his or her early twenties. It doesn't add to a person's height or increase one's strength beyond what it was in one's prime years. If Mr. Hanlon could, say, run the 40-yard dash in 4.2 seconds during his twenties, then that's the best he could have done while under treatment."

"That's still theory, is it not?" Dr. Hayes asked, looking over her Ben Franklin glasses.

"In part. But we have some very definitive laboratory evidence to support it."

"I assume you've brought that evidence?"

"Yes." For the next fifteen minutes, Emily held her audience captive explaining her theory of aging. She described the role she saw for the *Enabler* protein in gene expression and suppression, as depicted on two-dimensional gel graphs. Like rookies watching a savvy coach expound on hitting, Luke sensed most were buying what she had to say.

Dr. Nishida tapped his pen and, speaking in an Asian accent, asked, "Dr. Dornhoffer, did you ever consider the social implications of the drug?"

"In what context?"

"Well, if we were to actually extend the life span of individuals, there would be a significant impact, say, on population control. As it is, developed countries haven't even begun to adapt to the large numbers of people entering their retirement years."

"Judging by Mr. Hanlon, individuals wouldn't need to quit working." Doc winked at Luke. "One thing we'd have to do, though, is get rid of those who insist that people must step down from their jobs just because they hit sixty or sixty-five."

The discussion of "social impact" extended the meeting beyond the allotted two and a half hours. Dr. Thermopolous cut in. "This is all very interesting, but it's beyond the scope of this meeting." The division director shuffled his papers against the table and scanned his notes. All fixed their eyes on him.

Luke sensed a wrap-up coming. His ears were ringing. He knew not what to expect. That was the most frightening part. Would the director render a decision right there? If so, would Doc have his medical license suspended or revoked? Would the Caulfield Science Center lose responsibility for any future testing of the drug, as Emily had conjectured during the car ride? The baseball hearing and subsequent ruling seemed light years away. He could deal with that. He was not sure how he would deal with sanctions against Doc.

"Well, then, what have we found here?" Thermopolous paused to survey the spellbound faces. "We have heard evidence that there has been no falsification of records nor any intent to deceive. And the doctor in question, as well as his entire department have an admirable record." The director glanced at Dr. Dornhoffer. "Yet, it is clear, Dr. Dornhoffer, that you have practiced outside of the protocol, with a drug under Clinical Hold. That is something we cannot endorse, whether it be with a hundred patients or just one."

Doc maintained a placid expression while slowly rubbing his ear.

"As we consider whether any disciplinary actions are warranted, we will, of course, take the materials you've brought under advisement. I hope to get back to you with a decision within the next two weeks. In the meantime, I assume we have your assurances that such violations will not be repeated."

"You have my word," Doc said, folding his hands on the table. "I continue to believe that I acted in the best interest of the patient. At the same time, I have great respect for the FDA and its division director."

Counsel Chapman added, "Understand that any further usage of this drug would likely result in the matter being turned over to the Justice Department."

"I understand," Doc leaned back and spoke as if instructing a child throwing a tantrum. "There's no need for threats."

At the hearing's end, a few members of the regulatory agency exchanged good-byes with the *defendants*. Harry Hadley, for one, made no attempt to shake hands with anyone. Instead, he slithered out behind those lingering to talk with Doc and Luke.

By the time the Ohioans emerged from the FDA, the skies had cleared. Yet, it was still partly cloudy as far as Luke was concerned. He'd have to wait as long as two weeks before knowing what fate awaited his trusted friend. Doc professed to being optimistic, saying the hearing had gone "about as he had expected."

◆　　　◆　　　◆　　　◆

The following evening, Luke kept his promise and met Molly in Mount Adams. She directed him to the Celestial Restaurant, located nearby. There they were seated at a secluded table tucked between knotty pine panels, next to the atrium window, which provided an aerial view of Cincinnati. It was a city quite different from the one painted in Luke's mind when he retired in '72.

The metropolis, once known as "Porkopolis," had undergone a twenty-five year building renaissance. From the neoclassical twin towers of Procter & Gamble to the red lighted letters climbing out of the landmark Central Trust tower, the downtown shimmered with lights and glass. And, off to the left, separated from the skyscrapers by a span of highways, sat the arena where Luke had displayed his own renaissance.

Luke gazed at the stadium, lost in thought.

"How'd the hearing go?" Molly asked, swirling her beverage. Luke updated her on the FDA meeting. Missing was the proud, confident voice that had guided her around his farm.

"Here's hoping they show more wisdom about this thing than Vossler did."

"I made the mistake, not him."

"Now don't be so noble. You chose to partake in pre-market usage of a new drug," she said with a measured delivery. "It's done all the time. There is nothing *illegal* about the drug itself."

"How's your show going?"

"Funny you should ask. We just signed a deal with stations in Indianapolis, Louisville and Lexington. They're going to carry us starting in January."

"Hey, that's great. Congratulations!" Luke clinked his glass against hers and released his pent-up smile.

"Thanks." Molly brushed back a loop of her neatly coifed hair. The brilliance of the day's sun was apparent on her nose, cheeks and shoulders, which were laid bare in a navy halter dress.

"It's beyond me how anyone could walk away from someone as talented and pretty as you." Not given to making compliments, Luke surprised himself with the remark.

"Why, thank you." Molly folded her arms and tried rubbing away the goose bumps. "Actually, I never really thought of myself as beautiful."

"That's like me saying I never thought of myself as a hitter."

"No, really. My eyes are two different sizes, and I, ah, have this here bump in my nose. I mean it's tiny, but still." She ran her index finger over the flaw.

True, Luke could see what she had "complained" about, how her left eye indeed seemed somewhat larger. But as in the sport of baseball, beauty was to be found in all the natural irregularities. And Luke found the sum total of Molly's irresistible. "I wouldn't change a thing."

"Don't worry," Molly laughed. "I've learned to accept myself as I am. In my business, you either do that, or the critics and producers will channel-zap your mind."

"Do what?"

"Channel-zap. You know, like with a remote control," she replied, holding her hand out and pretending to click away.

"Oh right—I don't watch too much TV."

A waiter in a pleated white shirt and black bow tie came to take their orders. Afterwards, Molly turned the conversation back to Luke. "Have you given any more thought to appealing the commissioner's decision?"

Luke shook his head.

"From what I read, they give you better than an even chance."

"In a way I don't mind that it's over." Luke's cognitive dissonance was hard at work. "Oh, it was great fun while it lasted. But I belong on the farm."

"But Luke, the Reds need you, baseball needs you." Molly implored, clutching her fork.

"Easy there. You're not on TV now," Luke countered. He smiled as if he had just trumped Molly's ace.

Molly pulled her water glass back in a mock wind-up, "Oh shut up."

"As for the guys, they should know a team doesn't live and die by one ballplayer. If they don't, it's time they learn."

A truce ensued while the waiter served their entrees. Luke shifted his gaze outside. With a game in action at Riverfront, the Stadium glowed like a branding iron. He had tried to avoid thinking of the Reds' plight. Yet, it was hard not to. They were no longer "the team he once played on years before." He knew the manager and each of the players quite well. Leading the Division for most of the season, they were now in danger of missing the playoffs. He had read that much on his return flight from Washington. They had fallen five games behind the Cubs, and San Diego had moved ahead of them in the Wild Card race.

"Why don't you at least try the appeal?" Molly asked.

"There are enough lawsuits without me adding to them."

"You're so stubborn at times."

"Perhaps if I was born at some other time I'd feel different, but I wasn't and I don't—call me out of date, if you like."

"No, I don't think you are out of date, or out of touch. You're sure different, though—" Molly reached across and placed her hand atop Luke's. He tensed, then relaxed. It felt warm. It felt good.

After dinner, Luke treated Molly to a ride in his '73 Corvette. The temperature was mild, and he had left the top at home. Molly shook her head playfully as her hair flew back. She directed Luke inside Eden Park, around Mirror Lake and toward the memorial groves. There they strolled, hand in hand, propelled by a summer breeze down the presidents' walk, where they caught glimpses of the half moon and shadowy clouds sailing by.

"I never knew this place existed," Luke admitted, stopping by a red oak dedicated to President Tyler.

"And you thought Mount Adams was all buildings. This whole area used to be vineyards," Molly said, spreading her arm out.

"Judging by this tree, that was a long time ago."

"Many are more than a hundred years old. They planted a large number back on the first Arbor Day in 1882."

"What were you, a history major?" Luke grinned.

"No, I just keep up on things that interest me. Come here." Molly led Luke by the elbow through the umbrella of trees and down a slope to the right. Soon they came to Heroes Grove. There, Molly offered to plant a tree for Luke.

"Plant as many as you like; just don't name any for me."

"That's okay. Some people I know don't need a plaque to prove they're a hero." Molly folded her arms and leaned against the stone monument to the heroes of 1776. "Besides, you already have a hero's name."

"Huh?"

"Hanlon. Don't you know what it means?"

Luke shook his head side-to-side. "Suppose you tell me."

"It's Irish for 'great warrior' or 'hero.' Now tell me no one told you that?" Molly asked, surprised.

"If my dad knew, he wasn't the type to say. He believed actions determined what you were. And I'd have to agree with that. Names don't mean much. Names are just that."

As they strolled up the hill, Luke suddenly stopped. "What the..." his voice trailed off as he shuffled his foot in the grass.

"Oh, I should have warned you," Molly chortled. "People walk their dogs here!"

"Now you tell me." But Luke could only smile. For some reason, her teasing didn't bother him. The only other adult female whom he could say the same about had been Kate.

Luke joined Molly on a bench. There they shared a quiet moment together. Everything seemed to fit...protective trees... intimacy of nighttime's darkness...arms entwined...bodies embracing...kisses as passionate as the setting was romantic. If there was any doubt about how Molly felt toward him, it was erased that night. The heights Luke experienced at 128 Hill Street were far more exhilarating than anything the Celestial afforded.

A week earlier, Luke had severed his ties with baseball. Now he had severed his earthly ties with Kate. For the first time since the story broke, he was able to put his banishment completely out of his mind, for one tender moment.

35
Moving On

While awaiting the FDA's ruling, Luke buried himself in chores around the farm. The few crops he raised—wheat, oats and alfalfa—weren't due for harvesting for another three or four weeks. So he pruned dead branches, scraped and repainted fencing—anything to make the time pass. Luke's contacts with the outside world centered around family and Molly. He entertained the TV hostess once again at the Homestead, although thundershowers cut into their plans for a ride. They exchanged good-byes after dinner—he couldn't bring himself to have her stay the night at his home, Kate's home.

As for baseball, Luke avoided it altogether. Mike, Treat and Randy all called, but he declined their invitations to visit the team. Excuses came easy. Remedies for his hurt at being banished did not. Still, he knew the Reds were also suffering. They struggled to play .500 ball. With Labor Day fast approaching, they needed to turn things around soon, or their season would be over as well.

Luke returned from the fields and encountered Bret, seated in one of two Timberlake rockers on the back porch. "You've got some real supporters out there, Pop," his son said. He folded back the newspaper. "Says here, 'The Reds have been averaging over 3,400 fewer fans since Luke Hanlon's banishment compared to the previous home dates.'"

"You sure it's not just a coincidence?" Luke shrugged. "I mean, the team has fallen out of first." It was hard for him to imagine, let alone admit to, such an outpouring of support for himself.

"No, listen. 'Adele Drewes has apparently found a goodly number of sympathetic supporters in her protest of Hanlon's suspension. Attendance is down in the heartland cities of Pittsburgh, Milwaukee, St. Louis and Cleveland... the retirees in Florida appear to be especially irked by his departure. The Marlins' attendance is off over 4,000 a game.'"

Luke pulled the second rocker close to the railing and propped up his legs. Rusty curled against his chair. "Baseball is in real trouble if my suspension can take fans away that easily."

"You underestimate yourself, Dad."

"Does it say who this lady is?"

"No, but I saw her on *ABC's Nightline*. She seemed pleasant enough. I'm sure she's sincere in wanting you back. Said she plans to run another ad in this week's *USA Today*."

Luke shook his head and stared out at the corral. The last thing he wanted was to have fans stay away from games. And to think he might somehow be responsible.

Luke lay awake that night. He reflected on the Reds' problems on the field and his impact at the gate, at Riverfront as well as around the league. He faulted himself for making the comeback.

As his thoughts turned to dreams, he couldn't shake the subject of baseball. He saw himself driving downtown toward Riverfront with a proclamation in hand signed by millions of seniors, granting him permission to suit up for that night's contest. He pulled into his parking space beneath the cement pilings and jogged toward the players entrance. But instead of the roadway that encircled the stadium, Luke found a flooded moat with shark fins visible amid six-foot waves. He exited and dashed up the ramps to the plaza level. More water stood in his way! Luke could see the field lights through the entrance gates, but there was no way to get over the churning seas. Several fans and ticket takers beckoned him from the other side. He listened as the announcer introduced the starting line-ups, "...batting third, Number 27, Luke Hanlon..." In desperation, Luke dove into the seas and swam. The waters proved to be too rough, and he began to sink. For one of the few times in his life, Luke experienced panic. He was drowning! It was then that he awoke, drenched, not with the high seas, but with sweat.

That Thursday, Luke, accompanied by Bret, left for Chicago and a long Labor Day weekend. Playing ball had limited his visits to David and Sheila to a pair of road trips. Luke relished the opportunity to see his new grandson—not to mention granddaughter. He realized that their young miracle might help him forget about his own that had existed for half a season.

An hour outside the Windy City, Luke scanned the channels for weather. He had promised to take Tracy to the zoo Friday morning, assuming it was clear. But the news came first. The broadcaster reported, "The Food and Drug Administration announced today that it will work to expedite resumption of studies of a genetic compound known as the Enabler, believed to hold a key to unlocking the aging process..."

"Hey, that's great—" Bret began.

"Shush." Luke held up his hand.

"In a related action, the University of Cincinnati announced that Molecular Biology Department Chairman Dr. Adrian Dornhoffer, who oversaw testing of the drug, has announced his decision to step down."

Bret and Luke made eye contact, but neither spoke. The words unnerved Luke. Doc didn't walk away from anything; there was more to it than that.

Upon their arrival in Chicago, Sheila recognized all was not well with Luke. She asked whether he would like to lie down. He retreated to the back bedroom, where he placed a long distance call to Doc.

Luke got right to the point. "They forced you to step down, didn't they?"

"It was my decision, Luke."

"And I suppose you'll tell me the fact that it gets dark during an eclipse is purely coincidental."

"You're right, Luke; I'm...I'm not being straight with you. I guess you could say I negotiated a settlement. Sometimes we can help others by joining in, and sometimes we can help by moving on. In my case, I removed an obstacle from the University by moving on. It's no big deal. Besides, there weren't a lot of mountains left for me to climb."

Luke didn't know what to say. What he knew was that Doc had worked all his life to get to the top of his profession, and now he was being forced to step aside. "What about your friend Thermopolous? Couldn't he help?"

"He did what he could. Actually, he negotiated the deal. Others inside the agency wanted to bury me *and* the University."

"I can't tell you how sorry I am."

"There's no reason to be sorry, Luke," Doc comforted, sounding chipper as ever.

"If it hadn't been for me—"

"Now Luke, I will not allow you to play the martyr. You wouldn't want me to pass off responsibility for something I did, would you? You've already paid a price for your actions. Let me pay for mine."

Luke searched for the right thing to say. "What will you do now?"

"Pat and I are looking forward to a nice long vacation. It's been some time since I've taken any time off. Maybe this is a blessing in disguise."

Luke wished he could believe Doc.

◆   ◆   ◆   ◆

Inside the *Cincinnati Star Gazette* offices, Gerry Franklin and Stan Moore discussed other matters involving the FDA. Stan sat on the edge of his seat. Gerry had called him back from the Reds' road trip. The editor said he needed to talk about some pending, big news story. Stan itched to hear what he needed to do and get on with it.

"Stan, you never said who your sources were for that story about Hanlon."

Stan froze for a second while Harry Hadley's face flashed before him. "No. Why's it matter?"

"The source isn't so important. It's how you got the information."

"Persistence," Stan smiled with a touch of sarcasm. "I did a lot of digging around the Caulfield Science Center. You know how it goes; you ask enough people the right questions, and sooner or later you get the answers."

Gerry raised his folded hands and glanced at a piece of paper lying underneath. "You know a Harry Hadley?"

"Uh, yeah," Stan acknowledged. He suddenly found himself the interviewee, and he didn't like the feeling. He shifted back in his chair and pulsated his right leg. "He works at the FDA. I thought you wanted to talk about some news story?"

"Mr. Hadley's been spilling his guts," Gerry snarled, rubbing the grey stubble on his chin. "Says you bribed him in exchange for a look at the confidential clinical file on that Enabler drug,"

"Hadley has a pretty good imagination. All he did was confirm what I had already found from my sources," Stan lied, his voice firming. "But I never bribed him or anyone else."

"And what did you offer him for this information?"

"I offered him confidentiality, just like I give to all my sources. I guess those same rules don't apply where Mr. Hadley works." Stan twisted the end of his moustache and tried stealing a glance at the paper on his editor's desk.

"Let me get right to the point, Stan. Hadley says you gave him insider information on Ben Kane becoming the new chairman at SciLifeCo. He bought 15,000 shares right before the announcement, and the Securities and Exchange Commission picked it up. He's now in hot water with both the SEC and FDA, and he's ready to take you down with him."

"Who're you going to believe, Gerry? I mean, look at this guy—he disclosed confidential information, made insider trades—what kind of credibility does he have?"

"Offhand, I'd have to agree with you," Gerry said with some disappointment. "But the SEC has a tape in hand he gave them in which someone—who he says is you—relayed the insider info."

Stan slammed his fist into the arm of his chair and shouted, "That's inadmissible evidence if it was done without my consent." He realized what he had said. It was too late. He gritted his teeth and sucked in the air. "Okay, okay. I passed along some info I had heard about. But it wasn't insider information. It was just something I had picked up on the street." Stan thought back to his friend with Refuse Management.

Gerry shook his head and registered a look of disgust as if his own son had been caught selling drugs. He brushed back several strands of grey hair dangling on his forehead. "In other words, you bribed him with it."

"I made a trade."

"It's unethical and probably illegal, Stan. But I'll let others decide your guilt or innocence—"

"I appreciate your support, Gerry," Stan interrupted, his voice softening.

Gerry turned to the side and pressed his intercom button. "Phyllis, send up the two gentlemen from the Securities and Exchange Commission." He turned back to Stan, who by now was standing. "These guys are investigators from Washington. As you might expect, they want to speak with you. Be thankful I talked them into letting me discuss it with you first."

"Aw Gerry, this is crazy. It's being blown way out of proportion." Stan paced back and forth, swinging his hands wildly. "So I made a little deal for some information. So what? Rules were made to be broken."

"Not if it means breaking the law, Stan." By now Gerry had backed up and was seated against the edge of his credenza. "And until the matter is resolved, I'm going to have to suspend you from the paper."

"What?" Stan exclaimed in disbelief. His platform had just been yanked out from under him, and only time would tell whether the noose hanging overhead would be tightening around his neck.

"Stan, we're in the business of covering scandals, not creating them."

With that, the door opened, and two blue suits entered. They asked Stan to accompany them to the Federal Building across town. Just in case he refused, they handed him a subpoena. Stan hung his head and walked out of the room.

36
An Island Shelter

Ninety-eight bumper-to-bumper miles from New York City lay Shelter Island, an unevenly shaped vacation jewel floating between two exploded knife blades that made up Long Island's eastern end. To the south sat the wealthy playground of the Hamptons; to the north lay grids of farmland and abundant horse pastures.

Friday, a forty-car ferry carried Lyle Vossler and his wife, Elizabeth, from the one-time whaling town of Greenport to that tranquil island across the bay. Driving off the North Ferry, the Vosslers passed tiny Victorian houses that, for many New Yorkers served as way stations along life's hectic journey. Theirs was a comfortable seaside mansion that overlooked the fishing and recreational waters of Gardner's Bay.

Lyle welcomed the holiday weekend. It was an opportunity to clear his mind from the pressures of baseball's top job, pressures that had increased as league attendance decreased in protest over Luke's suspension. A number of owners had called on Lyle to reverse his decision.

Saturday, he awoke to the chirping of blue jays and mocking-birds. After brewing a pot of coffee, he entered his study and positioned himself at his weighty walnut desk, a desk once owned by a whaling captain. That same blubberhunter had built the weathered cedar mansion during the 1880s.

Lyle gazed out the window. A trail of sailboats drifted toward Orient Point. He was to feel none of the bay's salt spray that day. Most of his morning hours were spent on the phone. He retrieved a fax sent from his New York office, then turned to answer the phone.

"Lyle, Duke Tutweiller here."

Lyle recognized the voice of the outspoken Cleveland owner. He knew him to be a shrewd businessman. In just a few short years, Duke had earned respect around the league, turning the also-ran Indians into a winning club. He was as tough in dealing with the commissioner as in negotiating the trades that had brought his team respectability. And as head of the Executive Council, he would lead the selection of the next commissioner—when the time came.

"I read through your plan for celebrating baseball in the Year 2000—well done. I particularly liked your vignette idea. That should bring in some nice revenue." Lyle had borrowed the concept from his television days. A production company would edit footage from baseball's archives. Two-minute clips would be sold to sponsors to be aired during ballgames throughout the year. Income would be divided among the ballclubs.

"I did have a few thoughts on it—I'll share them with you at the quarterly meeting."

"Fine. What else is on your mind?" Lyle asked as if he didn't have his suspicions.

"I was interested in your reaction to the FDA's ruling, you know, regarding the drug Hanlon was being treated with?"

Lyle thought how Duke had used care in choosing his words; "treated with" conveyed a different message than "taking."

"I'm still digesting the information." Lyle glanced at the fax. The FDA's ruling had given him reason to reassess the matter.

"I've talked with several owners. They're all hoping you'll review the situation."

Vossler's voice firmed. "I'm doing that, Duke. But that doesn't mean I'm going to change anything."

"Vandermark tells me the Players Association is going ahead with an appeal, with or without Luke's okay."

"That's their prerogative."

"But Lyle, the FDA's statement was very positive. Nothing about enhancing performance."

"There's more to it than what the drug does, Duke. I'm still not comfortable with a player taking medications that haven't been approved."

"Come on Lyle, he was supervised by a physician the entire time. Listen, there are a lot of teams out there losing revenue over this thing. Before you continue dancing on the head of some ethical pin, you need to consider what it means to the fans."

"The fans? That's your concern, the fans?" Lyle bristled.

"Well, yes. They're casting their votes with their ticket purchases, or lack thereof."

Lyle knew what the falloff in attendance meant. On average, each fan spent $34 for a ticket, souvenirs, parking and refreshments. But to him that was an *economic* rather than *fan* issue the owners were talking about. *I'm the one thinking about the fans' interests.* He grew angry with the implied threats. "I told you, Duke, I'm studying the issue."

"Any idea when you'll have a decision?"

"No." What Lyle did know was that he would make it himself. He had leaned heavily on the advice of the owner-selected deputy commissioner in reaching his original decision. Perhaps he had listened too much. And now those same owners were after him to reinstate Luke. There was only one way he could find peace within: make sure this decision was his.

Lyle got help with his knitting throughout the day. Calls came from other owners, the head of the Players Association and the media. He placed a call of his own to his parish priest.

Prior to becoming commissioner, Lyle had been the chief financial officer for one of the TV networks. The closest he came to sports management was serving as president of his Long Island country club, where he befriended Nathaniel Bolden, the Mets' owner. What Lyle didn't know about baseball—and he admitted he hadn't attended a game in three years at the time—the owners figured they could take care of themselves.

Lyle's network TV ties had proven to be of little value. Making matters worse, he chose to be more involved in day-to-day issues than the owners had expected or wanted. A situation arose early on when Lyle got wind that the Orioles' new owner, a proprietor of a microbrewery, printed a hologram on his team's tickets showing a fan chugging his company's beer. Lyle ordered him to scrap all four million ducats, stating that the ad "was not in the best interest of baseball."

The $120,000 printing costs were hidden in suds sales, but the lost promotion opportunity was not. Lyle soon found himself *persona non grata* around Camdem Yards. Still, he had planted a stake in the ground signaling his intentions to do more than just line up network packages.

After studying the full text of the FDA's decision in the Pink Sheets—the agency's official communication document—Lyle phoned baseball's medical adviser, Dr. Mark Grissom. "Did you see the FDA's decision?"

"No, I'm still waiting for a copy to be sent over."

Lyle scanned the fax. "It says here that they 'recognize *ena-1* as a significant potential breakthrough... (with) possibilities as a treatment for the long-term deleterious affects of aging.'"

"That's rather aggressive for the FDA. I think they ought to stick to safety and efficacy, and leave out the editorializing," Dr. Grissom offered.

"Do you view it in any different light now?" During the handling of the Hanlon matter, Lyle had become well aware of Dr. Grissom's view regarding drugs that altered the body's "normal growth patterns."

"I remain opposed to using genetic therapy for the enhancement of human performance. What this boils down to is whether one views aging as a disease state or an inevitable part of life. In the latter case, the drug is simply altering the natural course of life. There is no clear answer. But that's not uncommon in the world of medicine."

Or in the world of baseball, Lyle reflected. While handling finances for the TV network, Lyle had been able to reduce most decisions to black and white. There were few gray areas such as could be seen in the matter of Luke Hanlon, areas that made him "uncomfortable." The result had been an impeccable record of achievement.

Lyle found that his new job marked the first time that the goals of the position and those of the people paying his salary were different. Team owners wanted that which would turn their ballclubs into winners, or at least make them more money. League presidents wanted what was in the best interest of their leagues. The Players Association wanted what was in the best interest of the players. He was charged with protecting the best interest of the game, which wasn't always in sync with the other three.

After an early Sunday mass, Lyle poured over the extensive medical and legal information in his Hanlon file. He wrote lengthy lists of pros and cons. He even drafted letters in favor and opposed to reinstating Luke.

At the request of his wife, Lyle took a break to walk outside with her in the mid-afternoon. They headed down their sloping front lawn toward the water's edge. A rush of seaside air helped clear his head. He watched a fishing vessel, a day's work in its hull, maneuver around the channel markers. His eyes fell to the ground where the jagged shoreline sank, then rose. A lone black mussel floated free of the grasses that were awash in the changing tide, one moment visible, the next swamped under water. Up and down, in and out. He saw himself caught in the tide. Was it coming in or going out? He had to decide— would he stay with his decision, perchance to drift further away from the owners' and, in this case, the fans' wishes? Or jump overboard? He heard the cries calling for him to jump.

"What'ya thinking?" Liz asked.

"About how baseball got so complicated."

"Is it?"

"Certainly seems that way."

"Oh, you've just been thinking too much about Hanlon." She slapped his chest for emphasis.

"You're probably right." Lyle smiled at his companion. He drew her close to his side.

"What are your plans for tomorrow?" she asked.

Tomorrow. Labor Day. Lyle knew the date well. It had become a rather unpopular holiday for the commissioner's office. A decade earlier, Commissioner Giamatti had died while on Labor Day recess, after grappling with the suspension of Pete Rose. Then there was 'Mournful Monday,' the Labor Day on which Fay Vincent resigned following an owners' mutiny.

Lyle's eyes ran down his grey planked dock, which mapped a path to freedom. There, tied to a piling, his 42-foot Hatteras bobbed on the waters. "I think it's going to be a great day to go fishing."

"Now that's the best decision you've made all weekend."

◆   ◆   ◆   ◆

Two days later, Luke soaped up his '73 Corvette, scrubbing away the bugs and tar that had built up during his holiday trip to Chicago. As he squeezed his sponge into the vehicle's sugar scoop side vent, Megan called from the house, "Dad, Mr. Vandermark's on the phone."

Luke dried his reddened hands on his shirt. A trail of water followed him into the kitchen. "Yeah, Peter, what can I do for you?"

"Hello, Luke. Are you sitting down?"

"Why?"

"The commissioner's lifted your suspension!" Silence greeted the owner's enthusiastic announcement. "Luke, you still there?"

"Uh, yeah." He slowly wiped his free hand on his shirt.

"After reviewing the FDA's report, he's concluded that there's no reason to keep you from playing."

The announcement had come just shy of a month after his ouster, but to Luke it seemed more like a year. And mention of the FDA brought to mind Doc's banishment. He half listened as Peter read from Vossler's letter:

> ...My view on the usage of performance-enhancing drugs has not changed. However, new information has come to light that indicates the treatment administered to Luke Hanlon is of therapeutic value.
>
> Admittedly, Mr. Hanlon exercised poor judgment in failing to notify his team and the league of his treatment per Major League Baseball's guidelines. I am confident that such non-compliance was purely unintentional. Therefore, I will consider his four-week suspension sufficient punishment for that infraction.
>
> As of noon today, I am advising the Reds' officials that Mr. Hanlon is free to rejoin the team.

"That simple, huh?" Luke said. "One minute, I'm kicked out of baseball, and the next, I'm free to go back."

"It wasn't as simple as it sounds." Peter paused, then continued when Luke again said nothing. "Regardless of his reasoning, Luke, we want you back."

"And what if I say it doesn't much matter to me anymore?" Luke turned and saw Megan standing in the doorway. He didn't know how long she had been there. He forced a smile.

"I can understand your feeling a bit hurt," Peter said.

"A bit? This whole thing has been hell for my family, not to mention Dr. Dornhoffer!" Luke cried, then stopped. He realized the commissioner wasn't to blame. "I'm sorry, Peter. It was my fault."

"Don't apologize. I'm the one who's being insensitive. Listen, I've got more good news. Remember Stan Moore?"

"How could I forget?"

"Well, you won't have to worry about any more articles from him if you come back. He's been arrested."

"What?"

"Yep. Charged with bribery and passing along insider information."

"You're kidding?"

"Seems that's how he got the details on the study you were involved with."

"So what d'you say? Will you come on back?"

"No. And even if I wanted to, I'm not sure I could still play." Luke heard the screen door slam shut.

"C'mon, you could hit with a cane. Listen, we've still got a shot at winning this thing—at least get the wild card spot. To do it we're going to need every bit of help possible, and that includes you."

"You forget I've been off the drug for a month. I can already feel the effects."

"Already?"

"Right now, it's just morning stiffness—"

"We could sure use you, even if it means playing part time or pinch-hitting. Tell you what, you come back and I'll kick in the pay for the games you missed."

"It's not the money, Peter. Never was."

"I know. I know. But I want to be fair. I never thought you'd done anything wrong in the first place."

"Maybe they should have made you the commissioner," Luke replied good-naturedly. The news about the lifting of his suspension coupled with the report that Stan Moore had obtained the information illegally relieved some of his pain. But there was still his angst over Doc's resignation.

"No thanks. I wouldn't want that job for all the money in baseball. Listen, the team's in Houston until Thursday. If you like, I could arrange for someone to work with you today and tomorrow at the stadium."

"Sorry, Peter, but the answer's no."

Peter refused to accept Luke's answer as final. He said he'd give him a day to think it over. "Keep in mind we've got five games to make up and less than a month left."

Walking back to his car, Luke found his path blocked by Megan, her hands in the front pockets of her jeans.

"Sorry for listening in," she said, coyly fanning her elbows. "Did I pick up something about them allowing you to play again?"

"Yeah, if you weren't so big, I'd put you over my knee."

"Oh, Dad." Megan waved him off and smiled with anticipation. "What are you going to do?"

"What do you think? Stay here."

"And what will that prove?" she scolded, folding her arms. "That you can pretend you don't need baseball, while your teammates and fans wonder what might have been?" Luke stared off as she spoke. "And you—won't you always wonder what would have happened had you gone back?"

"No. Once I make a decision, I don't look back."

"I'm glad you can be so stoical. Here's hoping everyone on the team is, too." Megan frowned.

"Come here, you." Luke wrapped an arm around her and forced a smile. "I wish it were a simple matter. Tell you what, I'll think about it. And I want you to think about getting back home," he advised, knowing she needed to get up early the next day for the opening of a new school year.

"I know it's hard, Dad. I just want you to make the right decision."

Luke had resigned himself to accept this retirement as final. The thought never crossed his mind that he'd be reinstated, let back in the game he loved.

37
A Feeling In The Air

Luke did a double take of the empty Reds dressing quarters. He checked the time. *A quarter past four.* With no one there to distract him, he dressed quickly.

Grabbing his glove from his duffel bag, he stood and reflected, *Where the hell is everyone?* He peeked in the trainer's room, the equipment room, and the players' lounge. Nothing. Back in the locker room, he scratched his head before donning his hat.

Luke had come for the evening's game, but his teammates were no-shows. In front of him was Corrigan's office, opened and darkened. *Mike always arrives before everyone else.* And not even Gus Stoltz, the clubhouse man, was to be found. Luke felt like pinching himself.

He traversed the tunnel to the dugout. Outside, the field was empty, save the batting cage. He scanned the stadium. High above the red seats, seven or eight doves flapped amid the light stanchions. Even the scoreboard was blank.

"Hi Luke. Glad to see you're back."

He spun around and saw an out of shape security guard, a walkie-talkie clutched in his hand. Luke had seen him before, but his name escaped him. "Hi, uh, where're the rest of the guys?"

"I dunno. Are they supposed to be here?"

"They better be—there's a game tonight. At least I thought there was. *What's happening? I checked the schedule. I think. Mike said to be here suited up by 4:30, I'm sure.*

"You might check upstairs. I imagine Mr. Vandermark could tell you."

"Thanks."

"Oh, and the phone in the trainer's room is broken. Try the one in the weight room."

Luke retraced his steps down the cement corridor. Somehow he must've gotten the information wrong. It wasn't a businessman's special, was it? He stopped by the weight room. A poster board inscribed in black magic marker hung on the door: "ABSOLUTELY NO LIFTING 2 hours prior to gametime. (Signed) Mike Corrigan."

Luke grabbed the steel handle and gave a turn.

Whoosh! Whoosh! Luke jerked to his right, then left, almost getting whiplashed in the process. Four spring-loaded plastic snakes flew past his face.

"Surprise!" "Sure took you long enough!" "Welcome back!" Thirty-some ballplayers, coaches and staff shouted their greetings. The pranksters were crammed between and on top of exercise equipment. They were all there: Treat, Fast Chad, the Officer, the Preacher, Prairie Dog, Mike Corrigan and Randy Kitchell. The Whippet was perched atop the Nautilus; Wells stood frozen in stop-action on the Versa-Climber; Worley sat on one of four Lifecycles, knees drawn up, his size thirteen feet resting on the handlebars; and Gus Stoltz balanced his stocky frame on the weight bench.

It was a warm welcome for a rapidly aging star. Luke feigned a cough to reclaim his voice. "I was beginning to think I'd lost it. You all did a pretty good job of fooling me. I, ah, am not sure I'm worth all the fuss. But thanks anyway."

"Now don't give us that humble shit, Luke. We only did it because we're expecting big things from you." Corrigan smiled and extended his hand.

Luke passed on the shake and gave him a hug instead. "Thanks, Mike. I'll do what I can." Luke whispered. He looked around. He sensed the players were waiting on his next word. "Okay guys, let's go catch those damn Cubs!"

A cheer rang out.

It was what had brought Luke back—he thought of helping his teammates compete for top honors. He had contemplated staying away. After all, he no longer had the wonder drug to ward off old age—his hourglass had but a few grains left up top, and he knew it. And he still felt guilt over Dr. Dornhoffer's forced retirement. But Doc's words had struck a chord: *Sometimes we can help others by joining in, and sometimes we can help by moving on.* He recognized he could be of most help by joining his teammates in their fight for the pennant.

Luke realized, too, that despite all the pretentiousness and self-ishness that had become prevalent in the sport, despite autograph sales and symmetrical stadiums, the camaraderie he had once enjoyed was still to be found, at least around the locker room at Riverfront. That mattered as much as anything. It was what made for winning teams and what, in his view, gave the Reds hope, however small, of regaining first. And so with encouragement from Megan and Molly, he was back.

Counting Thursday's game, the Reds had twenty-two chances to catch the Cubs, now five and a half games ahead. While that made for slim odds, fate was in their hands; the teams still had six head-to-head contests.

That night, more than 42,000 fans greeted Luke's return. His comebacks were becoming so common that Treat Reynolds christened him "yo-yo" man.

Luke acknowledged that he felt rusty and sat out the start. Midway through the game, he gave Mike the thumbs-up should the situation arise. It did in the eighth. With the Reds nursing a 4-3 lead against Philadelphia, Kurkowski singled Wheatly to third, bringing up Taylor with the pitcher up next. When no one filled the on-deck circle, hundreds, then thousands picked up the chant, "Luke, Luke, Luke…"

The cry turned thunderous as Number 27 emerged and powdered his bat with rosin. He slipped the weighted donut down the smooth ash and twirled it high overhead, then pulled it across his shoulders like taffy.

Taylor's strikeout gave way to a standing ovation. At first, Luke wished for it to stop. Finally, he resigned himself to the adulation and exchanged friendly banter with the home plate ump. The Philly catcher wished him well, but Luke simply nodded—for him there was no fraternizing with the other team during play, under any circumstances.

With Wheatly dancing down the line, Luke lifted a pitch toward right. The outfielder backpedaled back to the warning track. He made the catch, but the Officer skipped home with an insurance run. Luke suppressed a smile as he returned to the dugout. There his mates joined the crowd in standing to greet him. Worley came on and earned the save, sending Cincinnati and Luke home with a big "W."

Corrigan eased Luke into the line-up over the weekend, pinch-hitting him again on Friday and playing him five innings Saturday. Two more victories gave the fans added incentive to come and cheer on Sunday. By gametime, the packed house was a rockin'.

When Luke came to bat in the fourth, the bases were empty and so was the scoreboard. Looking for his first hit since returning, Luke rifled one into the gap. The ball skipped all the way to the wall. Rounding second, he decided to hold up, sensing he had lost a step over recent weeks.

Treat followed with a liner up the middle. Again, Luke pulled up at third. A one-bounce throw from the center fielder to home supported his decision. Things weren't quite the same this time around, although moments later Luke did score on Kitchell's sac fly.

In the seventh, Luke had no trouble circling the bases. He capped a five-run outburst with an opposite field homer that brought the Reds from behind, 7-5, a lead they held.

By Thursday's open date, the Reds had reeled off six in a row and closed to within three and a half of Chicago. Buoyed by the victories, Luke joined Molly and Megan for dinner at Randy Kitchell's Adams Place condo. The building was the latest of Cincinnati's waterfront developments. From the expansive lobby, paneled in African sapeli, to the twin copper roofs, now green with acid-induced patina, nothing had been spared.

"This is fabulous, Randy," Molly complimented. His ninth-floor terrace gave them a clear view of the Ohio River where it hooked around the foothills of Kentucky. "You could use a place here, Luke. Say for night games?"

"Nah. Nice view. But I like the one I've got at home just fine." He looked skyward to where a multi-million dollar penthouse sat atop the tower. Randy's was among the more modest dwellings. "Now I know why you work so hard, Randy—you need the money."

"Luke!" Molly shot him a queer look.

"Actually, I bought it as an investment. It's appreciated quite a bit," Randy explained, unflappable as usual.

Megan stepped through the sliding door and onto the balcony, carrying a tray of drinks. Randy helped her pass out the bubbling beverage before taking one himself. He raised his glass toward Luke. "I'd like to propose a toast. To Luke Hanlon, for one of his finest accomplishments... giving the world his daughter, Megan."

Luke lifted his eyes from the ground and joined in elevating his glass. He suppressed a knowing smile.

"I also want to toast Megan, whom, with Luke's permission, I'd like to make my wife."

Molly squealed and threw her arms around Megan. The blushing bride-to-be stepped to her father for a congratulatory hug and kiss.

"Love you, babe," Luke said. Megan had confided in him about the engagement, but he let it be a surprise for Molly. He wrapped his arm around Randy. "I couldn't have chosen a better son-in-law if I got to hand-pick him." And he meant it. He had never felt that way with Megan's first selection.

"I was going to wait till after the season to announce it..." Randy said.

"Why wait? You don't want to give the lady a chance to change her mind," Luke grinned.

Ever since Megan's marriage broke up, Luke had longed for her to meet someone like Randy. The divorce had put Luke's most protected offspring on her own for the first time. While in many ways he knew that was good, he also knew how much she wanted a family. And who better for her to spend the rest of her life with than the man who stood next to him? An individual who would put Megan first, just as he had always put his team first.

Over the weekend that followed, the Reds hustled and clawed their way to victories in three out of four over Houston. They flew off for their final road trip with high hopes; next up were the cellar-dwelling Rockies.

Denver's starting nine bore little resemblance to the early season line-up. With last place safely locked up, they had peppered their squad with minor leaguers. That created problems for the Reds, who were as unfamiliar with Denver's pitchers as Sweeney and company were with the Rockies' hitters. The combination spelled defeat in the opener. A Cubs victory put the deficit back to 4 1/2.

Wednesday night the Reds played with one eye glued to the scoreboard. Tight faces turned to smiles when Chicago's defeat was posted in the middle innings. But they lost, 5-3. A golden opportunity wasted. Time was running out. Just ten games remained.

Fast Chad choked off the losing streak by pitching the Reds to victory in the getaway game. From there it was on to Chicago.

A packed crowd filled Wrigley for the Friday afternoon showdown. Luke savored the surroundings. The ivy walls, natural turf and sun-soaked bleachers provided the perfect setting for a division battle. Kevin Sweeney accepted it as gut-check time, hurling his second consecutive shutout—an achievement that was to merit his selection as "Buckley Rent-A-Car's" National League Player of the Week. Treat Reynolds was the hitting star, accounting for three RBIs with a double and homer.

Cincinnati made it three in a row Saturday, slicing the lead to 2 1/2 games entering Sunday's finale. While no Red would say it, each knew how valuable a sweep would be. Neal Parker matched goose eggs with the Cubs' pitcher through six. In the seventh, the Reds mounted a threat with the first two reaching safely, bringing Luke up to bat. He felt tired, but he refused to take himself out of the game. Not at this critical juncture. Monday was an off day. He could rest all he wanted then.

Luke shook off the fatigue and fouled a pair back before slapping one to short that was turned into a routine double play. When Mike offered to sit him down, he grudgingly agreed. He hung around the dugout, wearing a path to the water cooler as the game moved into extra innings. He grabbed a bat and spun it between his palms while he sat and watched the Reds advance runners into scoring position in the tenth, twelfth and fourteenth. Each was left on board.

Chicago didn't get a runner to second until their home half of the fourteenth. A single brought him home and the Cubs a victory.

The defeat sent the Reds packing 3 1/2 games back with just six left. Thoughts of what might have been interrupted Luke's sleep throughout the hour plane ride home. He didn't need someone to explain the situation. Unless the Cubs lost against the stumbling Giants, Cincinnati would have to win all of its remaining contests, including three against Chicago, just to tie for the title. To make matters worse, news came that San Diego had locked up the wild card spot. Either the Reds would have to win the Division outright, or they could forget post-season play. That was the way Luke wanted it anyway.

Back home, the Reds exacted revenge against the Rockies. They routed the visitors on consecutive nights. Luke rejoined the offense with a pair of doubles and a homer. Four games left. Three games out.

Perhaps looking ahead to their weekend series, the Reds dug themselves a hole in the wrap-up game with Denver. Entering the ninth they trailed 5-2. A loss would be devastating. Luke, who had been given the evening off, conceded nothing. He picked up a sense of destiny in the air, a feeling that somehow the Reds were going to come from behind. He told Corrigan about it. Then he told Kitchell and Reynolds and Estabe. Soon the entire team was talking about it. They were going to do it. Come from behind, just as they had on twenty-two occasions that season.

Luke had recognized it as a sensation that certain teams in certain years come to experience. Even the Rockies must have sensed it, as four of them, including their manager, huddled on the mound following a walk to Reynolds. Several Reds put balls under their hats for good luck. No sooner had the Cubs skipper reached the dugout steps than Kitchell laced one to left: first and second with none out. Wells ripped a pitch to right: 5-3. Kurkowski singled in another: 5-4 with the tying run advancing to second. Luke's premonition was looking good.

While the Rockies changed arms, Corrigan sent Thumper Thompson in to run for the Duck. Bailey went down swinging for the second out, but the faithful erupted as Dean Taylor stepped to the plate. Actually, the cry was for Luke, who entered the on-deck circle.

Two on, two out, and two in. Luke said a prayer that Dean would somehow get on. He wanted that one shot. He knew as well as everyone in the crowd that another run and the Reds would draw even. But one more out, and the Reds' season would be over—unless the Cubs blew their 4-2 lead in the eighth.

Luke never got to hit. Taylor drilled one straight away. The Rockies center fielder raced back, stretching in vain as the ball ricocheted off the "404" foot marker. Bailey raced home to tie while Thompson motored toward third. The shortstop grabbed the relay, turned and pegged a throw plateward. Luke crouched and signaled Thompson to slide. The catcher pulled the ball in and blocked the plate. Runner and backstop met in a cloud of dust. "Safe!" barked the ump. The

Reds had pulled it out.

Afterwards, the Preacher shared credit for his gamer. "I imagine with Luke on-deck their pitcher wanted to make it happen with me. So I thank God and Luke for helping me get the hit."

The entire team thanked God when word came that Houston had come from behind to beat the Cubs. The Reds were within two with three to play, all against Chicago. Of course, it also meant they had to win them all.

Leaving the batting cage prior to Friday's opener, Luke saluted the fans behind home. There, amidst players' families and friends, sat Bret and Derrick alongside Megan and Molly—Luke hadn't given her much attention of late, such was his focus on the game. Two rows back were the retirees, Doc and Pat Dornhoffer. And, perhaps most pleasing to Luke, next to them were David, Sheila, Tracy and baby Sean.

The start of the game was delayed while the Hamilton County Senior Citizens presented Luke with a plaque. Doing the honoring was a white-haired, dignified lady in a red pantsuit, Mrs. Adele Drewes. While initially concerned that her campaign in his behalf might damage baseball's following, Luke came to appreciate what she had done. After all, she had spoken for the fans.

"So nice to meet you, Luke," Adele said in a soft-spoken voice, which surprised him, given her national protest. Standing there, Luke felt his stomach tighten and realized he had forgotten his notes. *Oh well, a simple thank-you will do.*

Adele approached the mike. "In behalf of the seniors of Hamilton County, Ohio, and baseball fans everywhere, I want to thank you, Luke Hanlon, for helping us see that dreams can come true."

Luke accepted the plaque, gave his two-word *speech* and stepped back. With that, the flashcubes fired away. Neither seemed to care about the publicity shots, but instead exchanged looks of admiration.

Luke leaned down and spoke into Adele's ear. "Without your support I'm not sure I'd be here today. Thanks." They hugged momentarily before Adele turned to walk away. Luke called after her. He reached into his glove and handed her a baseball. Adele's eyes widened as she saw his autograph inscribed on the rawhide. She clutched the ball close to her chest and left the field, with Luke at her side.

From that moment on, Luke focused his every thought to the task at hand—winning. In the first, Estabe struck out, bringing up Wells. Number 27 knelt in the on-deck circle. He angled his body forward and pressed his weight against a bat as he studied the southpaw's every move. He thought about the 1964 pennant race, about the knee surgery that kept him out the final month of the season. Back then there was another critical, season-ending three-game series. The Reds had come home nursing a one-game lead. But Luke could only watch from the press box, his leg in a cast, as the Phillies swept his teammates. This was payback time. The opponents and players were different, and he wanted the outcome to be as well.

Wells blooped a single. More than 55,000 fans urged Luke on as he got set in the batter's box. He studied the wind-up, and watched the ball rush plateward. Strike one. He stepped out and checked for signs. Back in the box, he glared out at the pitcher and watched a fastball barrel home. He saw it all and got it all—a drive that rose high into the green seats in left, some four hundred and fifty feet away. He felt twenty-one again as he jogged around the diamond.

The blast set the tone for the evening's play. Reynolds and Kurkowski added homers of their own, and Prairie Dog continued his mastery over hitters. Luke added a single and a double before stepping down in the seventh, forgoing a chance to hit for the cycle. It was as close to a "laugher" as the Reds were apt to see, winning 7-1. The Cubs' lead was down to one game, and the Reds were believers.

Afterwards, reporters interviewed Luke in the whirlpool. His legs ached as if struck by some Asian flu. As he had found years before, advancing age took its biggest toll on his wheels. But this was no time for babying oneself. Another do-or-die game loomed just fifteen hours away.

Saturday's match evolved into a pitcher's duel, with Sweeney turning in the star performance for the home team. Goose eggs lined the scoreboard for seven innings. Luke struggled to grab hold of the opposing pitcher's wicked slider, and so did his mates. Fans munched nervously on their salsa-covered nachos and mustard-topped dogs. A concerned quiet settled on the stadium. A Reds loss would be fatal.

After retiring sixteen in a row, the K-man walked the leadoff batter in the eighth. Two outs later, a scratch single created the first serious threat. Corrigan huddled with his battery mates. Down along the right field line, Worley threw fast and furiously. "Try to fist him," Mike instructed. He patted Kevin's backside and left the mound.

Next up was the Cubs' clean-up batter, who fouled off several of the inside fastballs called for by Corrigan. The runners moved off first and second. Sweeney wiped a pint of sweat from his brow, then delivered a hanging curve. The ball exploded off the bat, out toward left center. "A tweener," people called it.

Luke sprinted left. He saw Reynolds was too far away to get it. He thought about cutting it off and holding the Cubs to a run. But no, with two outs the runners were going. Both would score. Faster and faster Luke ran. Oh, how his legs ached, but still he kept on running. As he got closer, the ball began a sharp descent. Luke left his feet, his body stretched out, his left arm extended. Inches from the Astroturf, contact was made. Smack, it hit the webbing. Smack, he hit the carpeted pavement.

Luke rolled twice before coming to rest with a scoop of vanilla ice cream protruding from his glove. Reynolds curled around to congratulate him. The fans roared while the twosome jogged in tandem from the warning track. Luke heard him say something like "nice catch, old man." He couldn't be sure, muffled as it was by the uproar. Corrigan, already halfway to first when Luke stopped his imitation of a tumbleweed, waited to greet him.

Luke didn't feel the sting of the impact with the ground until he was seated on the bench. He ignored the ache in his shoulder and ribs.

More eggs went up on the board through eleven innings. It went without saying what Luke's catch had meant. In the twelfth, Kitchell singled to give the Reds a leadoff runner for only the second time all game. Bailey stepped out of the box and studied the hand and body movements of coach Zender before laying down a perfect sacrifice, advancing the runner to second.

Luke grabbed the Preacher, who was exiting the dugout for the on-deck circle. "Watch Ramerez when he takes the sign. If he moves the glove toward his right knee, it's a fastball."

"How do you know?"

"Trust me, he does it every time," Luke winked.

Taylor was no doubting Thomas when it came to Luke's ability to pick up the finer points of the game. He watched a curve cut the plate for a strike, then watched the pitcher take the sign. He saw the movement of the glove the way Luke had described. Dean was ready for it—a waist-high fastball. He swung. It zipped passed the pitcher's knee. The shortstop, roving to his left, dove behind second, but the ball had picked up speed with a bounce on the turf and darted into center. Kitchell rounded third, nearly taking out Zender, and raced home with the winning run.

Hopping, whooping, hair-rustling players celebrated all the way off the field and down the tunnel to the locker room. Booming blasts of color, reduced to blackened splats against the afternoon sky, exploded above center field. Fans danced by their seats while rock music played in the background. No one wanted to leave. For the first time since Luke's banishment, the Reds found themselves back in a tie for first.

The spirited end to Saturday's game carried over into the Reds' dressing room for the regular season finale. Luke dressed in silent concentration while his teammates socialized. That is, until Corrigan reminded them, "The past 161 games mean nothing if we don't win today. Let's not forget, guys—hard work got us here, and it's hard work that's gonna win it for us today."

The Cubs showed they, too, were serious about winning, scoring twice in the very first inning. They added a third tally before Twiddy settled down. In the past, Clint had handled Chicago as well as any ballclub, so a disgusted Corrigan stuck with his starter. But one more big hit and the only thing Twiddy would be throwing, Luke knew, would be chairs inside the clubhouse.

Cub hurler Steve Bonaventure burned through the Reds' line-up with ten strikeouts in six innings. He looked unstoppable, as did the Cubs with their three-run lead. In the stands, dejected fans searched for scapegoats, lamenting the four-week suspension the commissioner had imposed on Luke.

The seventh-inning stretch and singing of "Take Me Out To The Ballgame" breathed some life into the Cincinnatians. With the third baseman playing in tight, the Whippet slapped one in the hole for the Reds' second hit. Wells walked. The cheer gained momentum. The Reds had their first legitimate rally with Luke swinging on-deck. The situation prompted a convention on the mound. The one-time Cincinnati Stinger thought that if the Cubs realized how he felt, they wouldn't be half as concerned. He had already struck out and rapped a weak ground out. His shoulder throbbed from his encounter with the turf the day before.

Luke took the first pitch for a ball. A "charge" call came from the scoreboard, and the crowd clapped and stomped along. Luke was oblivious to all sounds, including the prop plane buzzing overhead with the phone number for another pizza delivery service. All he heard was his heartbeat and his mind telling him to *bear down.*

The next pitch came smoking to the plate, and Luke gave a rip. Not even close—strike one. He backed out of the box, as much to take a practice swing as to think. He made his decision then and there. With the runners edging off first and second, Bonaventure stretched and threw. A curveball. Luke turned toward the pitcher, laid his bat out and dropped a bunt down the first base side of the diamond.

Raphael and Logan raced toward third and second, respectively, while Luke sped past the slow roller, now curving toward the line. It was not a question of whether he'd beat the throw, but whether it would stay fair. The first baseman, catcher and pitcher surrounded the baseball and followed it toward first, resembling children taking a new dog for its first walk, urging it to turn right. The ball was now on top of the chalk, turning, turning slowly—now half on it—slower still, just another turn or two...

Oh, it was close. So close in fact that a dash more sidespin from Luke's bat, a tremor in the stadium footings from a passing powerboat on the Ohio or a bit of kinetic energy unleashed by the wrath of Father Time over what Luke had done to old age, and the ball would have surely ended up foul. Instead, it came to a stop, balanced precariously half on and half off the foul line, twenty feet shy of where Luke was now standing. It was a base hit of immense proportions saved by events that did not transpire.

In the stands, a hailstorm of popcorn flew out of spinning boxes. Cups of beer were knocked over, but no one seemed to care. The loyalists had their first reason for excitement that afternoon.

Luke stood on the bag, clasped his hands on his helmet and sighed. He felt a congratulatory slap on the back from coach Zender. His bunt had taken the Cubs by surprise, but he knew as he stood there that it represented his best on a night when he did not feel as such.

Bonaventure let some of the steam out of the partisans by inducing Reynolds to pop up. That brought up lefty Kitchell to face the right-hander. Luke checked the position of the first baseman and inched a lead at first. He wanted to make sure to break up any double play that would end the inning, and perhaps the season. A fastball sailed in for a strike. Luke glanced at the runners wandering off second and third. With good speed on the bases, he figured both should score on a single; he hoped to make it to third where he could score on a fly. A pitch was fouled back. Luke again took his lead and tried mental telepathy with Randy.

Luke's future son-in-law jumped on the next pitch and rocketed a clean single to right. Estabe scored easily, and Wells followed close behind. Luke made an aggressive start toward third, but seeing the throw cut off, he returned to second.

The deficit had been reduced to 3-2. *Let's tie it up,* Luke thought as Wheatly stepped to the plate. Time was called while the Cubs brought on a fresh arm. The Reds had succeeded in chasing Bonaventure, something that had seemed nearly impossible an inning earlier.

The Officer delivered a pistol shot down the left field line. Luke dashed across the plate while the ball spun around in the corner. Randy, fast on his heels, scored the lead run, while Wheatly chugged into second.

By the time the inning ended, Sean, too, had come around for a 5-3 lead. One sensed that the Cubbies viewed the loss as a foregone conclusion. The uprising had so demoralized them that they failed to muster another threat. Corrigan brought on Worley, who preserved the win.

The final out came, fittingly enough, on a fly to Luke. While there was nothing unique about the play, it served as a poignant reminder of how much he had hurt Chicago throughout the weekend: with his bat, with his glove and with his mind.

Inside the locker room, Luke exchanged congratulations with players and coaches. He spoke while they shouted, smiled while they roared and strolled while they danced. But just the same, it felt good. Oh, did it feel good. Sure, much work was left to be done for the ultimate championship: two rounds of playoffs and then the World Series. But no one could ever take this achievement away from him or his teammates. His only concern now was how much his body had left for the post-season.

38

Yesterdays and Tomorrow

"Is that how you recharge your batteries?"

"Smart ass," Luke replied, watching his manager finger wires hooked to a transmitter on his shoulder.

"How's it feel?"

"Better than yesterday." But yesterday Luke could barely raise his arm. He was paying the price for making the game-saving catch against the Cubs. The team physician had diagnosed it as a "mild separation of the acromioclavicular ligament, an AC sprain." He prescribed rest. The playoffs allowed for no such indulgences. So Luke asked for and received this electrical stimulation designed to reduce the inflammation. The year had made him more accepting of modern medicine.

"Well, take it easy. No need to rush it. There's two more series after this one," Mike said, thinking optimistically ahead to the second round of playoffs.

"I'm not doing this just so I can go back to farming," Luke said, repositioning the wires on his arm.

"Gotcha. But I'm starting Bailey in left for the first two. If you feel like pinch-hitting, okay."

Playing without Luke, the Reds split their road games against the

Western Division winners, the Giants. They returned home to Riverfront, where Luke struggled to play four innings. Still, they bested the Giants, 5-0. Reynolds and Wheatly clubbed back-to-back homers, while Lattimore struck out nine. Reporters observed how the Reds continued to be inspired by their injured teammate's effort.

In game four Luke finally collected a hit and scored. Meanwhile, Sweeney had his fastball darting and dancing for a full nine. His second playoff victory gave the Reds the series, three games to one.

The post-game celebration was subdued compared to the season-ending clincher. Luke explained to Molly that the game's outcome would have been significant only if they had lost. After all, they had already won the Division and the next milestone, the pennant, was still a playoff away. Only then would they earn a ticket to the World Series. To do that they would have to defeat the Mets.

Luke wished for his shoulder to heal. He also wished for an extension of his fountain of youth. Each day he felt more and more as if he were swinging and running through water. To remedy the situation, he gave in and borrowed one of Dean Taylor's 32 ounce bats. He also got himself fitted with a new pair of glasses. While his sight was still better than before the Enabler, the ball had appeared a bit fuzzy of late.

The Reds' jet banked left on its approach to LaGuardia Airport. "There it is." Randy Kitchell thumbed the window. "This time tomorrow we'll be fighting it out down there."

Directly below the gyroscoping craft, Luke saw Shea Stadium. He nodded. "I'm looking forward to it."

"You know, I've never even attended a playoff or Series game," Randy reported.

"I expect you'll have a field-eye view of both soon," Luke said, making a prediction that was contrary to what most writers had forecast. Their opponents, the Mets, had swept by the Padres, outscoring them 22-4.

A scenic cruiser took the Cincinnatians on the final leg of their journey to Manhattan. Luke stepped into the exhaust-filled air and stared ahead at the Hyatt. The hotel had put on extra security for the playoffs, and because of what had happened during the Reds' last visit. Noah handed Luke several favorable press clippings to ease his mind.

In the privacy of his room, Luke digested the newspaper columns. He was surprised at the warm reception. The writers talked about what he had meant to the game, rather than how he had been *enabled* to play this last year. Flipping the pages, he found an article on Ty Hartmann. It reported on his release from a rehabilitation clinic only days before. For Ty there would be no post-season. The press release said the team and Ty looked forward to his return in the spring. So far the Yankees were doing just fine without him, having defeated the Rangers in their opening series.

Luke was impressed with Ty's printed apology to his teammates and fans. It sounded much different from his tone at the All-Star game. Perhaps Ty had learned something during his seven-week stint in rehab. Or was it just a facade? The interview ended with Hartmann boasting he'd be back the next spring to "lead the Yankees to a repeat championship." Luke preferred to give the young man the benefit of the doubt.

In the opener at Shea, the Reds fell to the Mets 4-2. Game two ended with similar results. Slugger Durk Ferraro homered in each game and drove in six runs. When not hitting, Ferraro was often seen cradling a cellular phone inside the dugout. His cavalier attitude incensed the Cincinnatians, who headed home down two.

Scott Brouse got the nod over Twiddy in game 3. Corrigan knew there was no margin for error. Prairie Dog threw strikes past the visitors in the first. Then the Whippet set the table, legging out an infield hit in the home half. Logan followed with a walk, bringing Luke to the plate.

Luke entered the batter's box, dug a toehold and felt the excitement. The atmosphere told him the playoffs were more than just a refueling stop on the way to the World Series. Fan banners and patriotic bunting flapped in the October breezes, while the crowd's cheers seemed to take on a different tone. Lest he forget what it meant to win, there were the championship flags. Pinned to the right field wall was the '61 pennant, his first and most cherished.

Luke fidgeted with his bat handle and let a ball sail by for a strike. He stepped out for a practice cut, then returned in time to jump on the next pitch for a slap single to left. The move to a lighter bat had finally paid dividends. Estabe and Wells scampered across the plate, clapping their hands as they did. The man behind the scoreboard got so excited that he accidentally set off the fireworks reserved for homers. The crowd loved it, roaring even louder. The Reds tallied three more that inning, en route to an 8-2 pasting of the Mets.

The Reds' bats sizzled all weekend while Brouse, Sweeney and Twiddy, backed by Worley's flawless relief, baffled Ferraro and company. The Mets managed but three runs during their lost weekend in Ohio. It was their time to turn tail and leave town after having been swept. But the pre-series favorites were conceding nothing.

Molly and Megan accompanied Luke to New York for game six. The midweek schedule necessitated their taking off from work. "I only expect to stay for a day," Molly said.

"I wish you wouldn't say that," Luke countered. To him, baseball was very much like life. He took nothing for granted. He knew that now more than ever.

"If it goes seven, Megan and I will just have to spend more time shopping," Molly laughed.

The Mets proved the reality of Luke's fears, jumping out to an early 2-0 lead. The partisan crowd taunted the Cincinnatians with red handkerchiefs printed with a slashed-through black-circle.

Reynolds made the fans see red in the seventh. He took the Mets pitcher high and deep into the bullpen with Luke and Logan on board, giving Cincinnati a 4-3 lead. Worley, loosening up at the time, caught the ball. He jogged in to pitch the ninth and nodded confidently on the mound when his eight warm-ups were done.

Two strikeouts later, Durk Ferraro strutted to the batter's box and rotated his shoulders as if preparing to lift weights. "Strike one," bellowed the ump. Ferraro took two practice cuts and dug in deeper, more determined. He turned on the next one and drove it deep to right. Luke stiffened, then saw it hook into the seats just ten feet foul. A relieved Worely stepped off the back of the mound, tasted his fingers and rubbed up the ball. The reliever shook off a sign and with a lanky leg kick fired away. Ferraro swung, his body spinning into a pretzel twist as the ball smacked into Kurkowski's mitt, punctuating the pennant victory.

Afterwards, Luke beamed as he passed among his friends inside the locker room, shaking hands and exchanging congratulations. With his hair mussed like a field of Bluestem grass, he sat and patiently answered reporters' questions.

Luke did not want to celebrate so much as savor. He saw the victory from the balanced perspective one finds at the outer edge of a baseball career. As a young player, he had relished his first pennant with a sense of youthful invincibility. He thought back to the celebration downtown in '61. He could almost feel the thousands of fans rocking the team bus. He listened; he heard Jerry Lynch's war whoop as the bus teetered on one side. Then came the voice of the team's announcer, the late Waite Hoyt, warbling a vaudeville tune on Cincinnati's Fountain Square.

At the time Luke figured there'd be several more pennants around the corner. Instead, he had to wait nine years before returning to the fall classic. This time he knew it would be his last. So he sought to preserve the action as snapshots in his mind: of Bailey dunking Kurkowski with a bucket of ice; of Worley, his chest foamed with champagne, standing on a makeshift platform accepting the MVP award for saving three of the victories; and of Brouse, Reynolds and Thompson carrying a fully-clothed Corrigan to the showers, the skipper's arms flailing away.

Luke warmed with delight for Mike. His friend had ridden the minor league rails for nineteen years before reaching the top: Peoria, Cedar Rapids, Lynchburg, Billings, Chattanooga and Indianapolis.

Reporter Vic Gagliardi extended Luke a handshake. "Congratulations, Luke. How's this one feel?"

"Hard to put into words, Vic." He paused to think. "All I can say is, it was worth coming back for."

"How'd you compare it to your other pennant winners?"

Luke rubbed his chin and thought about the Reds of '61, '70 and '72. He thought about his teammates, especially those whose eyes were now closed—Coleman, Hoak, Hoyt, Kluszewski, Merrit, Post, Ruiz, Temple and, of course, Hutchinson. This one was for them, them and a lady named Kate. "I don't know if you can compare. Each one's a little different. Each has its own special meaning."

"What will you remember most about this one?"

Luke dropped a ball from hand to hand. "How great it still feels to win—at any age. Guess it shows it's a timeless game."

Long after the celebration, after the ride to the airport and while resting on the flight home, Luke thought again about his World Series experiences. They reminded him that more work needed to be done. For each had fallen short. He longed for a championship ring. Yes, the World Series. The words sparkled like visions of Christmas for a child. Luke knew he was not alone in failing to win one—there were numerous greats who also fell short—Ernie Banks, Ted Williams, Billy Williams, Jim Bunning, Carl Yazstremski and Gaylord Perry. But unlike each of them, he had another chance.

◆　　◆　　◆　　◆

After a practice at the stadium, Luke joined Mike and several teammates in watching the concluding game of the American League Championship. When it was over, Gus Stoltz packed swimsuits and suntan lotion for a trip out west. The Angels had defeated the Yankees, minus Ty, to earn their first pennant.

The Angels were a brash group of youngsters, with a payroll ten years out of date by most measures. Most of the athletes were unknowns around the National League, and that was a concern to

Corrigan. On the other hand, he knew his team was hot: winners of 24 out of 31, a .774 percentage since Luke had returned, all under the pressure of a pennant race.

Along the ride to their Anaheim hotel, Luke noticed signs for Disneyland. He thought how it was fitting that the Series take place a mere mile or two from the theme park. Frontierland, Fantasyland, Tomorrowland. After all, hadn't he visited each during the season?

Anaheim Stadium itself was a three-tiered ballpark rising out of acres of concrete and set against the backdrop of the San Gabriel Mountains. Luke surveyed its grass field. With his tired leg, he knew the natural turf would be a blessing.

In game one, both teams were still searching for a run, when Estabe walked in the seventh. He side-hopped to a lead and promptly swiped second. Moments later, he stole third before Wells struck out. Luke came to bat weary, but as determined as ever. He fouled one off along first, sending fans and their beverages scattering. He reminded himself all he needed was a deep fly. But he, too, struck out.

Reynolds swatted at the first pitch and looked like another strikeout candidate. Estabe danced off third in an apparent attempt to force a balk. The Angels' pitcher ignored the bait and threw plateward. The Whippet accelerated down the line. No one expected it, not with the cleanup batter at the plate. Raphael went airborne ten feet from home, his arms extended, his left hand drawing a bead on the base. Inside the dugout, Luke leaned forward, hoping to lend body English as the ball and player arrived together. "Safe!" came the call. The Reds players mobbed the diminutive Dominican.

Next inning, Estabe performed more wizardry in the field. With two on and none out, he leaped high and grabbed a liner, then flipped to second to double-up the runner. Worely snuffed out the Angels' rally in the ninth, preserving the 1-0 victory for K-man. Afterwards, Luke thanked the Reds shortstop for getting the Series off to such a successful, exciting start.

In game two Luke had himself dropped to fifth in the order and played but four innings. His legs needed a rest, and so did his shoulder. The Angels spoiled a fine pitching performance by Fast Chad, earning a 3-1 win. Corrigan was nonetheless pleased to fly home even up. He felt confident that his hitters would find their groove at Riverfront and he'd have Sweeney and Lattimore back for games four and five.

Monday, Luke joined the team for a light workout before returning home for a quiet evening with Molly.

After dinner, she knelt alongside him and kneaded her fingers into his sore shoulder. "I missed you this weekend."

Luke, folded atop an oversized pillow, smiled but said nothing. A crackling fire warmed his shirtless body.

"I was surprised you didn't call," Molly said.

"Sorry. It seemed whenever we weren't sleeping or eating, we were at the ballpark."

Molly sat back against the couch. Luke turned to see her running her fingers along her drawn up legs. "Luke, I love you dearly, but if it's going to be all one-sided, maybe we should go our separate ways. I can't—"

"Hey, hey, what's the matter?" He rose and slid his arm around her shoulders. Just as quickly she threw it off. Rusty, sensing all was not well, slinked across the room.

"I don't know... it's just... it seems I'm usually the one doing the calling. Either that or you invite me along to some affair. I can't handle being just a companion."

"You shouldn't take it personally. Understand it's been a long time since I dated." Luke realized that deep down he loved Molly. Five games remained; then he could give her the time and consideration she deserved. Kate had understood his priorities. Of course, she had grown up with his career. Then, too, perhaps his ties to Kate held him back as much as baseball. He recognized the need to move on, for yesterday's victories, yesterday's lives, yesterday's loves could not bring him fulfillment tomorrow. He wrapped his arm around her again. This time she didn't fight it.

"You sure you want to?" Molly looked up and wiped away a tear.

"Want to what?"

"Date!" Molly softly elbowed his side.

"Only if it's you." The age difference didn't matter to him anymore, and he knew now that it didn't to her, either. They enjoyed one another, and that was what mattered most. "Bear with me one more week."

"And I suppose things will be different then?"

"Look, give me some credit. Six months ago you don't think you'd have found a lady reporter in my family room, do you?"

A smile crept back into Molly's face. "I don't think I'd have found a reporter, period." They kissed.

Molly resumed her massage. It now resembled more of a caress, her hands moving in slow, wide circles.

Two loud pops came from an unseasoned log. The evening's 30-degree temperatures made the fire inviting but baseball not. It was late October. And if the Series went the distance, the seventh game would be played on Halloween—assuming there were no rains or snowouts. "You'd better wear long johns tomorrow night," she suggested.

"Oh, the dugouts are heated. Once the game begins, I won't even think about it."

"They really ought to schedule these games in the afternoon."

"They used to. But then again the Series used to be over by now. We can thank your friends in television for the time change, and even the extra playoffs." He felt Molly's reply, her thumb pressed deep, just below his shoulder blade. "Ugh!" Luke muffled a grunt.

"Hey listen, they need prime time ratings to pay you guys the big salaries."

"Don't look at me. They could air the games at two in the morning and still afford me." With a swift roll, he wrestled her to the pillow.

All Molly could do was laugh and plead her case. "I guess it's time I was getting on home."

Luke propped himself against the pillow. "You wanna stay over?"

"And break your training?"

"I don't have to be at the stadium until three. Besides, I might need another massage in the morning."

Cincinnati's home opener had the look and feel of a football game. Fans bundled themselves in sweatshirts and blankets. Temperatures plummeted to the freezing mark at gametime. The Angels didn't seem to mind; they roughed up Prairie Dog for five in the third.

Wheatly's two-run shot sparked a Reds comeback. They knotted it in the seventh, with Luke doubling in two. But California pushed a pair across to grab the lead once again in the eighth, 7-5. They threatened to break the game wide open in the ninth. The bases were loaded with two out. A regular Lil' Abner stepped to the plate and ripped one down the line. Randy, who had been playing off the bag, dove and snared the fast-moving jumping bean that had double written all over it. His flip to Kyle extinguished the threat.

Randy's play buoyed the Reds' spirits as they came to bat in the ninth. Luke led off. He looked for a pitch he could steer the opposite way and surprised even himself by pulling a fastball for a single. Wheatly doubled him to third, putting the tying runs in scoring position. After a pitching change, Taylor walked, bringing up Kurkowski with the bases full.

Delirium spread among the fans, and Luke grew optimistic. *Anything but a grounder*, he thought—the plodding backstop was an easy double-play man.

Luke edged down the line. Ducky wiggled his large frame into a set position and unleashed a wicked cut. The resulting drive allayed any fears Luke had about a double play—the ball sailed well over the fence. A grand slam and a come-from-behind 9-7 win. Cincinnati took the Series lead, two games to one.

Luke was drained but heartened by the seesaw battle. Even his aches felt good—souvenirs from a hard fought victory.

Like a novice fighter who doesn't know when to quit, the Angels came right back at them on Wednesday. Luke recognized trouble when the K-man walked three in the first. All scored as California eased to a 6-1 victory. Corrigan lifted Sweeney in the third so he'd have him ready for game six or seven out west.

Game five had special meaning for Luke. It went beyond the need to win to take a Series lead back out to Anaheim, for it marked his final home appearance in this, the most emotional year of his career. He wished in some small way to thank the fans for their support through it all.

In the fourth, he approached the plate to the rhythmic clapping of a full house. It seemed ages ago that he had stood in the same batters box for the season opener, chilled by the fans' welcome. The ending felt the same. He stretched and took several adhesion-pulling practice cuts while the pitcher rubbed up the ball. There was no pain, just passion. After studying two pitches, Luke locked on a chest-high fastball rotating toward the outer edge of the plate. He went with it, knocking it over the right field fence and into the green seats—a heat-seeking missile, drawn to the warmth of his supporters.

Crossing home, Luke did a double take of Lyle Vossler seated alongside the dugout. Normally impartial in such contests, the commissioner had joined those around him in applauding, although he remained seated.

Led by Luke's shot, Cincinnati went on to win, 4-0. Thus, the Reds took off for California with a championship in sight. Molly, Bret and Megan all followed on a commercial jet.

For game six Corrigan debated going with Brouse on three days' rest or bringing on Twiddy. Clint had pitched only two innings of relief since his victory in the League Championship, thirteen days earlier. Mike preferred the right-handed Twiddy over the southpaw.

Clint pitched well through six before losing the drop on his curve. Corrigan pulled him, but not before four Angels had crossed the plate.

Luke consoled Mike after the manager had dealt with reporters second-guessing his choice of pitchers. "In some ways it seems only right that it should all come down to a seventh game." A fitting end to a hotly contested Series. And while he very much wanted the win, Luke was torn by a desire to see the season continue.

A rollicking crowd swarmed into Anaheim Stadium for the finale. In the locker rooms and on the field, ballplayers acted like children. Kurkowski asked Noah Hall to get him a baseball signed by both teams as a remembrance of all who participated. Wheatly offered to wager a case of beer with a fellow Bostonian on the Angels, until the friend reminded him that any form of betting was illegal. Corrigan asked Luke how he felt. "Like I'm fifteen, back playin' for the Youngstown Parks Department championship."

TV scheduling placed the deciding game after NFL football. That meant prime time on the East Coast but four o'clock California time. It created an advantage for the pitchers, who threw out of the sun and into the shadows for the first five frames. But when the shade crept across the mound in the home half, the Angels reached the K-man for two runs. In the sixth, the Reds answered back. Randy doubled. Treat, Luke and Ducky all followed with hits in building a 3-2 lead. The game moved along into the bottom of the sixth, seventh and eighth without further scoring.

In the top of the ninth, Luke came to bat. Anticipating it would be his final plate appearance, the fans gave the stunned player a standing ovation. Luke mustered all his energy in blooping a base hit. Standing on the bag, he accepted congratulations from the Angels' first baseman, who remarked, "I'll be glad when you go back into retirement."

Luke just smiled. Out of the corner of his eye, he saw Mike raise his hands, palms up, in a questioning gesture. He returned a quick wave signaling his intent to stay in the game. He ended up stranded as Wheatly and Taylor popped out, sending the contest into the hoped-for final frame. Three more outs and Luke would earn his coveted Series ring. But he wasn't measuring his finger yet.

The Angels picked up a runner, putting the tying man on base. The hit brought out Corrigan, who brought on Worely. The managerial wheels churned as the Angels put on the sacrifice. It failed. One out, a runner still at first. Worley aced the next batter. Out number two.

Nine men on the field, five in the bullpen and a score on the bench stood, their hearts twitching double time, rooting for Worley to get the final out. Meanwhile, 65,000 spectators clamored for a hit. Luke watched as the Angels' stocky backup catcher readied himself to pinch-hit. He twirled a pair of bats in the on-deck circle, then selected his weapon and strode to the plate.

Worley quickly moved ahead in the count, one ball and two strikes. From Luke's vantage point, Kyle appeared to be in some type of trance.

The batsman stepped out, hitched his pants and took a practice cut. He returned and worked the count full, fouling off five pitches in the process. The Reds' relief ace stretched, paused at the belt and fired plateward. The hitter connected, sending the ball out toward Luke. He took two steps back, looked up and watched it soar high overhead.

Unlike most other sports where a clock ends the game, baseball ends on a play. And as Luke would attest, sometimes that play alters the outcome. This one did.

Manager Corrigan closed the locker room for fifteen minutes after the loss. He kept his message brief, thanking each for his efforts and reminding them what a great season it had been. He ended with a prediction: they'd be back in next year's fall classic. Only Kurkowski's sobs could be heard above the silence that followed.

When the press was let in, Luke was still in uniform, scribing a final entry into his Wallace-Adams notebook. He put it aside as members of the media gathered around. A TV newscaster spoke. "Luke, I know it was tough losing this way. But could you share with us some of your thoughts?"

Luke gazed in the distance, as if searching for an answer across the room. Several reporters shifted to the balls of their feet. "Losing a big game always hurts..." He paused, then continued in a slow, reverent voice. "But you know, it was one heck of a series."

39
Reflections

Ten days later, outside his barn, Luke leaned inside his raised tractor hood. He nudged his glasses with the back of his index finger and eyed Dr. Dornhoffer's car pulling into the driveway. Luke walked toward him, wiping his greasy hands on a towel along the way. "What d'you say, Doc?" Luke cried out. "You're just in time to give me a hand."

"You don't want me messing with your engine," Doc assured him, approaching with his pipe in hand. "What seems to be the problem?"

"Just tuning it up before the rough weather."

"And what do you call this?" Doc rolled his jacket collar around his neck. The day's wind-chill factor had dipped into the twenties.

"Good to see you," Luke said, shaking Doc's hand and grabbing his arm for emphasis. "How're you doing?"

"Fine. Fine. I came to tell you we're moving."

"What?" Luke said it more as an exclamation than a question.

"Pat and I have decided we've had enough of this cold. We're heading to warmer climes."

"You're gonna go lie in the sun?"

Doc smiled and slowly shook his head no. "I've taken a position with a small biotech firm."

"Where? What'll you do?" Luke asked excitedly, relieved to think that Doc's career hadn't ended after all.

"It's in Charlotte. They're making me an executive vice president of research—can you imagine, me a corporate VP?" Doc chuckled as he lit his pipe. "It's a small firm, but they're into some exciting things; they focus exclusively on developing anti-viral agents. I'll be overseeing the selection and development of a variety of such drugs."

"I'll miss you."

"You won't get rid of me that easily. The job involves quite a bit of travel. I'll be stopping back here to check on you." Doc smiled. "That's another great feature of the job—the company's established investment partnerships with nine universities in the U.S. and overseas. I'll be visiting them regularly, and I get to take Pat along whenever I want. So she'll finally see the world while I get to go back to work."

"Do the folks at the FDA know about it?" Luke asked, dancing on eggshells.

"No problem there. Dr. Thermopolous has been very kind. The only limit he put on my work was that I not act in the capacity of a clinician. In my new role, I'll be letting others do the testing." Doc paused to puff on his pipe. "And how about you? How's life after baseball?"

"Oh, I think about it a lot." And he had, each day since the long, quiet flight back from California. But there was no remorse. Rather, the joy over his experiences of the past year had only begun to sink in. Several times in recent days, he had experienced an indescribable high, seemingly as energizing as the Enabler itself. To think, he had had the opportunity to play ball again. "I can't tell you how thankful I am for you making it all possible, not to mention putting your career at risk."

"Things worked out for the best," Doc said.

Luke nodded. His final season had worked out well in the end. Forget the bumps along the way; in some ways they had made it all the more worthwhile. True, Luke would never have a World Series ring, but that was only one measure of a player's worth, and in the total scheme of things, he viewed it as one he could certainly live without. There were other more important things he had learned to live without, starting with Kate.

Luke stared at the empty corral and thought about being on the field, name your ballpark. He thought about the changes he had witnessed in the game, some good, some not so good. He had come away with a greater appreciation for the pressures of playing in the modern-day, media-dominated sports world. And he thought about the players he had gotten to know, the friendships he would cherish. Friends like Treat who had called the day before to announce his signing of a three-year contract renewal with the Reds, rather than having tested the waters of free agency.

Doc diagnosed his thoughts. "Experiencing some withdrawals?"

"Nah, just pleasant memories." Withdrawals, if any, would come in the spring. Corrigan had left the door open for his return to the coaching lines, although Luke felt he had made all the contributions he could to the team and the game. As for now, he turned his attention to Molly. He pursued her with the same zest that he had for baseball.

Just then, a ponytailed female emerged from the barn. "Hello, Molly," Doc called out. "Don't tell me Luke has you cleaning the stables?"

"Hardly. He's been kind enough to allow me to store Laureli here. I was just brushing her down when I heard your voice."

Yes, Luke had sold Kate's mare, creating a place for Molly to store hers. He realized Kate would always be there in spirit, but the time had passed for hanging onto her earthly belongings. How was it Doc had put it: *There are times for moving on.* Luke spoke. "Rather than stand here freezing, let's go inside. Molly made a wonderful apple strudel." The threesome stepped toward the house with Luke in the middle, his arms wrapped around Doc on one side and Molly on the other.

Epilogue

In December, Luke was joined by relatives and friends, including most of his teammates. The occasion was the wedding of his daughter to Randy Kitchell.

The proud father of the bride took the march down the aisle arm-in-arm with Megan. All agreed she was as radiant in her silk-taffeta dress as her father had been in his final season in uniform.

Her first marriage annulled, Megan was to be married in Bellarmine Chapel at her alma mata, Xavier University. There, student volunteers formed an honor guard that kept the press and cameras at bay.

After handing Megan over to his teammate, Luke entered the pew alongside Molly. A few rows back, Mike Corrigan sat, fresh from inking a contract extension. Nearby were numerous Cincinnati ballplayers: Kevin Sweeney, looking forward to another shot at a championship ring; Ducky Kurkowski, ready to shed more tears, this time out of happiness; Fast Chad Lattimore, who had cruised to the church in the new sports car purchased with his losers' earnings from the Series; Kyle Worley, recipient of the Rolaids Reliefman award for his regular season performance, which softened his Series defeat; the preacher, Dean Taylor; and all the way from Los Angeles, Treat Reynolds.

The check Luke wrote for the wedding paled in comparison with the anonymous million-dollar one he made out to the Baseball Assistance Team, a fund for struggling retired ballplayers. The enjoyment he derived from playing the game provided all the reward he wanted.

Outside the church, reporters fired questions from a distance as Luke passed by with Molly. He wished the media representatives a good day and kept on moving. Overhead, a light December snow fell. A dusting settled on the bridal bouquet that Molly clutched in her hand.

After ducking inside the limousine, Molly snuggled against Luke, then pursed her lips and blew a stream of air at the flakes. Some flicked off the blushing petals as easily as they had landed; others melted under the warmth of her breath. Once again, the roses looked as healthy as when they were first picked.

Postscript

Luke Hanlon. You say you never heard of him? Close your eyes and reflect back to a different era, a time of black and white TV, of angles and pillars at the park. There, somewhere between the sunlight and shadows, he stares out from the on-deck circle. Study the intensity in his face. Watch as he swings the bat and rounds the bases, thoughts of money furthest from his mind. Scandals that might have touched him furthest from yours. Whether his name is Luke or Treat, Joe or Ted, Willie or Mickey, Duke or Stan, Jackie or Warren, it really doesn't matter.

What's that you say? Now you remember...